CW00497524

Gods of Avalon Road

Leilanie Stewart

First Published in 2019 by Blossom Spring Publishing

Gods of Avalon Road Copyright © 2019 Leilanie Stewart.

ISBN 978-1-9161735-2-1
E: admin@blossomspringpublishing.com

W: www.blossomspringpublishing.com

"To Joe, my own immortal love".

Chapter 1

The baby piglet lay on a bronze platter with an apple stuffed in its mouth. It had been roasted, but as delicious as it smelled, it suppressed Kerry's appetite to see a full animal in the middle of the large, round table with its legs and head still intact. The two front legs of the beast were stretched under its chin and the back legs were tethered behind its rump.

"Wow, this is quite the feast," said Gavin. From the look on his face, she knew their hosts had baffled him as much as she was baffled.

The dinner ware had been arranged on the table beforehand. Kerry looked at the bronze plate in front of her. She flicked a finger and thumb against it, expecting to hear the tinny ping of ceramic under a bronze glaze, but instead the dish made a deep metallic clang. Her wooden knife, fork and spoon had twisting lattice designs snaking along the handles. Hadn't she seen a similar design before? Yes, in a book of Neo-Celtic art; a 'kissing spoon' in traditional style. How romantic. Oliver Doncaster certainly was a posh, but strange guy with such an interesting choice of dinnerware. Strange-good, not strange-bad. The dinnerware wasn't the only thing about Doncaster Manor, Avalon Road: the décor was odd too. Oliver and his girlfriend, Jenna, had fashioned their house with wicker furniture and hanging wreathes. Their *Au Naturel* taste was different, quirky. Different was good. Kerry liked different. She couldn't have backpacked around the world for the past six months and *not* like the unusual.

Their host, Oliver, sat facing Gavin across the round table with their hostess, Jenna, on his left and Kerry on his right. He held what looked like a small, red satin bag with gold embroidered patterns on it in Celtic latticed style.

1

"I name this feast in honour of the new additions to our household - Kerry Teare and Gavin Bryant. May they become good friends and may their time here be fruitful," said Oliver.

Kerry noted how he had used their full names. Rather formal, was it not? Then again, she and Gavin were entering into an employer-employee relationship with Oliver and Jenna, based on business. It *should* be formal under such circumstances.

Oliver loosened a drawstring and reached into the bag. Kerry heard the jingle of money. He threw a fistful of gold coins across the middle of the table, spreading them evenly between everyone. He tipped the rest of the contents on the table and dropped the empty bag between the food dishes.

A coin rolled into Kerry's lap. She picked it up, expecting it to be chocolate money. The thin circular disc was bigger and heavier than a ten pence piece. Her jaw dropped.

"Are these real?"

Oliver smiled. "Twenty-four carat."

Kerry realised she was gawping and shut her mouth. Another eccentricity, in addition to the dinnerware; though certainly an entertaining charade before their meal. She gathered a pool of coins and handed them back to him.

Oliver shook his head. "They're for you to keep."

Now was Gavin's turn to gape. "For real? Are you sure?"

Jenna scooped a small pile into her lap. "It's part of the fun of feasting. You'll get used to it."

"Used to it?" Gavin looked incredulous. "Is this like, a salary advance or something? If it is, we don't need it."

"It isn't that," said Jenna. "It's a ritual we do on the

solstices or if there's a special occasion - like you coming today."

Kerry swept a pile of coins into her cupped hand and stacked them ready to count. Twenty-two coins for twenty-two years; a fitting early present for her birthday on the first of May.

Oliver proceeded to carve the piglet with a large, curved, bronze knife. Kerry peeled her eyes away; she'd be happy to eat the meat once it looked like ham and not pig. Instead, she turned her attention to inspecting one of her coins. It had an engraved image of a woman wearing a long tunic, roped at the waist. The woman held a small branch with fruit; maybe oranges or apples, over a cooking cauldron as big as a bathtub. Steam rose from the pot and beneath it, a small fire showed, depicted in stylised flames.

"Each of these coins must be worth a fortune," said Kerry.

"About a tenner each," said Jenna.

"Where did you get them?" said Gavin, his eyes wide.

Oliver set the biggest chunk of piglet on his own plate. "I had them minted myself. The design is my own, based on artefacts that have passed through my shop over the years."

Kerry looked at Oliver's plate. Wasn't it rude to serve yourself before your guests, and with the biggest piece of meat, no less?

"Artefacts?" Gavin raised an eyebrow. "I thought Sequana's sold furniture and antiques?"

Oliver dished the second biggest chunk of meat onto Gavin's plate. "Yes, that's true. But sometimes ancient artefacts appear that have been handed down for generations in old English families. Occasionally a great aunt Mabel dies here or there, and the treasures end up in my shop."

Kerry watched Gavin play with the coin in his hands, tossing it from palm to palm. "And your business is doing well enough to, you know, give away these as tokens?"

"Why not?" Oliver paused. "As your host, it is my duty and my honour to share with you my wealth. Please accept it as a custom."

Gavin's ears reddened. "I didn't mean to offend. It's very generous of you. It's just, well, we can't pay back your kindness."

"You already have. Both of you will be working for me. My businesses are doing so well that we need the extra hands. Gavin, your help at Sequana's will be a huge favour. And it will be a great help to Mistress C to have you on her staff, Kerry."

"Mistress C? I thought I was going to work with Jenna, doing waitressing?"

"Oh, you will. Jenna works for Mistress C too," said Oliver. "But it's a lot more than waitressing. It's a private restaurant for a start. Mistress C only lets in certain clientele. And it's full of wonderful, old paraphernalia; the most beautiful antiques collected over the centuries. The ambience is great."

Kerry lowered her gaze. Instead of the bronze plate in front of her, she saw herself served up on a silver platter. Was Mistress C some kind of *madam*? What did Oliver mean about clientele? She wasn't going to be some kind of hostess, like in those seedy bars in Thailand, China and Japan? Kerry looked at Jenna. Jenna was petite and curvy: pretty with her short, blonde, curly hair. Kerry herself was what most people thought of as attractive: tall and slim, maybe striking too with her green eyes and long, black hair. They were quite the contrasting pair of women; different

4

types that might have been poached for different tastes. Had Oliver lured her to London to do a risqué job; something borderline illegal?

Jenna seemed to have read her mind. "Oh, don't get the wrong idea. It's not like one of those jobs where you have to wear hot pants or a bunny girl outfit," Jenna said, and laughed.

Kerry paused, digesting her words. There was an edge of nervousness in Jenna's laughter. Or had it been her imagination? No matter; Kerry dismissed it. "Is Mistress C your business partner then, Oliver?" said Kerry.

Oliver set a small chunk of pork on her plate.

"Yes and no. Mistress C is the proprietor, but technically, I own it, in the sense that I bought it for her. She's looking forward to meeting you tomorrow. You'll start at nine."

How could a furniture shop and a restaurant pay for a million-something pound house and enough gold to throw around to perfect strangers? Wasn't Oliver a bit young to own so much; he couldn't have been more than thirty-five. And what sort of man was he to buy a restaurant for a woman who wasn't his lover, without there being a catch? Or maybe Mistress C *was* the catch. But that couldn't be so, since Jenna definitely appeared to be his lover. Could it be that, like her and Gavin, Mistress C was doing Oliver a favour in exchange for the generosity? Kerry watched Oliver, but his face gave nothing away. The situation was certainly strange; curious-strange, but not necessarily uncomfortable-strange.

After serving Kerry, Oliver dished a small piece of meat for Jenna. Kerry noted the procedure; Oliver first, Gavin second, Kerry third and Jenna last. Wasn't the order a bit sexist? Not to mention the fact that he had placed the importance of his girlfriend, Jenna, last of all. Kerry stared at the butchered piglet carcass. No; this was a ritual. The dedication of the feast, the coins - the order of serving had to have significance too. Oliver and Jenna were pagans, weren't they? In pagan culture, food was probably served to the master of the house first. Oliver sure was one intriguing guy.

Kerry's appetite returned now that the meat no longer resembled a piglet, but rather a delicious slice of roast pork. She spread some apple sauce on her food. As she dished vegetables onto her plate, Kerry noticed Oliver's intense blue eyes on her face. She lifted her gaze to meet his.

"So tell me Kerry, how did you two meet?" said Oliver.

"We did the same course at Uni together," said Kerry.

"How romantic. And you two got together then, I take it?" he went on.

She exchanged grins with Gavin. "We aren't a couple," she said.

Well, except for the one time when they had shared an inebriated, above-clothes fumble in Thailand after smoking some Zero on the beach and drinking a supposedly karma-cleansing Jasmine wine. Gavin had seemed to get the wrong impression then that she fancied him. She wasn't even sure why she *didn't* fancy him: she normally liked muscular blonde men. But, he was simply Gavin, her best friend, nothing more. Kerry snapped out of her musings: Jenna was watching her, a hint of a smile on her lips.

"Isn't that nice?" said Jenna to Oliver.

Isn't that nice? What a strange thing to say. It was the second time she had felt that Jenna had read her mind. Jenna reached for Oliver's hand and interlaced her fingers with his. Momentary annoyance needled Kerry. Was this a display to show superiority that she had a sex life, while Kerry was single and celibate?

Oliver turned his head to face Gavin, but his eyes lingered on Kerry a moment longer. "I wouldn't have taken you for an Art graduate," he said to Gavin, "but I'm glad you are - your expertise will help at Sequana's, no doubt."

Gavin frowned. "Art? Huh? Kerry and I did History at Leeds."

"I assumed you studied Art, Kerry, since you did all those paintings in your dad's café," said Oliver.

"Thanks, I'm flattered. That must mean I'm good, if you thought my work was graduate level." Kerry flicked her hair back off her shoulder. "I studied Celtic Art and warfare in some of my Ancient History modules, but I didn't major in Art. The work in my dad's café is more of a hobby."

"I never saw you working there. I would have remembered you if I had seen you. It's strange I never saw you, because I was up there a lot." Oliver gazed at her with a puzzled expression. "In any case, I remembered your work," he said.

Kerry reached across and prodded Gavin's hand with her wooden fork. "See? I told you so."

Gavin winked at her before turning to Oliver. "Kerry thinks the reason you hired us is because you like her paintings."

"Gavin! Sheesh," Kerry rolled her eyes. Gormless Gavin; now Oliver would think her conceited.

"Actually, it's half true. I got to know your dad when I was in Leeds on a commission - it turns out my own father went to school with yours, although as you can tell, I'm a decade older than you, at least. I'm originally from up North myself - my family have lived in Doncaster for centuries. Some of my contacts suggested your dad's café as a good place to discuss a business proposal - they recommended it for the aesthetics."

Oliver paused, his gaze roving Kerry. She felt her face grow hot. By aesthetics did he mean her, or her artwork?

Oliver went on. "Anyway, I got talking with your dad and he told me how he'd bought the café but that the investment was turning out to be a tough one. I gave him a bit of a helping hand and we kept in contact."

"So I'm here to repay the favour?" said Kerry.

"Not at all. The other way round in fact - I needed the workers and your dad suggested you. He said you'd been waitressing for him, and the customers were all really taken by you."

A fresh heat-wave assaulted Kerry's face; she was sure she looked beetroot. Was Oliver joking? Didn't seem so; his expression was sincere.

"I thought it would be a double bonus, seeing as you were the artist behind the intriguing Celtic paintings I'd bought in the café too," Oliver added.

"Well, I'm certainly flattered - and grateful. I've always wanted to live in London," said Kerry. She turned her gaze to her food to avoid Oliver's piercing blue eyes. He sure knew how to give a compliment. From her peripheral vision, she could feel Jenna watching her; she knew why, and she couldn't really blame her. Even though it wasn't Kerry's fault Oliver flirted with her, it still felt awkward to be taking all of Jenna's boyfriend's attention.

Time to excuse herself, perhaps. "Erm, I think I'll just go and get myself a drink," said Kerry.

"That reminds me." Jenna jumped up. "I totally forgot the apple cider."

"I can get it for you, if you like," said Kerry.

"You can get it and I'll grab the tankards."

Perfect. Alone together in the kitchen would be a good time to smooth out any possible misunderstandings woman-to-woman, especially if they were not only going to be flat mates, but colleagues at the Herne's Hunt restaurant. Got to make it clear that Oliver's flirtatious exchange was one-sided and harmless; nothing more intended.

She followed Jenna into the kitchen. "Are you from up North too, Jenna?"

"No. I'm from Glastonbury. I moved to London last November."

"With Oliver?"

"No, alone. I met him through a mutual friend. It worked out great since I was looking for a place to stay and of course, Oliver doesn't advertise his rooms. You have to be in the right circles to know these things."

"Isn't it nice how fate sometimes brings people together?" Good, subtle, but a compliment, nonetheless. "You two are lucky to have met one another."

Jenna grinned. "Oliver and I have a symbiotic thing going."

What the hell did *that* mean: *symbiotic thing going*? What was a 'thing'? Friends with benefits? Flat mates who used each other? How could it be that Jenna was able to be both blunt and subtle at the same time? Maybe she shouldn't have been so subtle with Jenna herself; it had simply been an opportunity for her hostess to give a cryptic answer.

Jenna handed a wooden bucket of apple cider to Kerry. Kerry saw apple leaves from the home brewed drink floating on top.

"Men and women need each other in this world," said Jenna. "You and I-" She picked up two wooden

9

tankards and held them by their bronze handles. "Gavin and Oliver-" She picked up two more tankards, "Are people made of flesh capable of creating more flesh."

Jenna moved closer to Kerry and pressed her large chest against Kerry's arms, which were wrapped around the cider bucket. Was the gesture to emphasise the whole 'flesh creating flesh' comment? Kerry took a step backwards; no, the gesture had been to intimidate her, probably because Oliver had flirted with her.

Kerry, uncomfortable, turned around to lead the way back to the dining room. No: she was wrong again. This wasn't woman-to-woman bonding. Jenna was coming on to her.

Gavin could see the toilet on the far side of the dining room. As he opened the door, incense wafted over him from a stick burning on the window ledge. In such a confined space, it was choking. Would Oliver and Jenna be offended if he stubbed it out?

He banged his head on the low ceiling and winced. Seemed it sloped to fit the shape of the front porch stairs above. How many rooms did Oliver's house have? So much space for all manner of secret goings on; like witchcraft. Oliver and Jenna's love of pagan décor hadn't gone unnoticed. Pungent herbs hung in bunches from the ceilings of the rooms he had been in so far and neo-Celtic artwork.

What would Kerry think about it? Doubt her dad could have known about Oliver and Jenna's lifestyle; otherwise he mightn't have recommended the jobs.

As he pissed, a familiar painting on the wall above the toilet caught Gavin's attention. Interlacing Celtic-inspired scroll patterns showing a male and female form coming together in a kiss: Kerry's painting. What would she think when she found out her precious artwork hung in Oliver's bog? *Nuts*, should he tell her? Guess he should; though he'd wait until she'd had lots to drink over dinner to soften the blow. What did that mean anyway; that Oliver liked her work enough to hang it in his house, or that he thought it was crap - literally - by hanging it in the bog?

Why would somebody choose to live a Neo-pagan lifestyle? Had Jenna imposed her unorthodox lifestyle onto Oliver, or had he been into it of his own accord? Could be that Oliver had brought it with him from Doncaster. Or maybe it had been an idiosyncrasy spawned from life in the Big Smoke. Who knew? Could be Oliver and Jenna had both got each other mixed up in it. That was all fine and well, provided they kept him and Kerry out of it.

Wait a minute; Doncaster. Oliver Doncaster. Could it be he was part of an old aristocratic family? That would make sense; a million pound house couldn't be paid for by a modest restaurant and furniture business, but centuries of old money would explain it.

When Gavin came out of the loo, Jenna, Oliver and Kerry were already tucking into dessert. A steaming bough of apples protruded from a large, bronze, cooking cauldron, which sat in the middle of the table. Why had they cooked them? What a weird dessert; another pagan thing?

Gavin plucked an apple off the stem and put it in his bronze bowl. He poured custard from a bronze jug on top and looked at the strange dessert for a moment before slicing it with his spoon. The apple flesh slid off the core with hardly any touch. Gavin spooned it into his mouth and pushed it around with his tongue. Surprisingly good.

But weird. He washed the unusual dessert down with a tankard of homemade cider. It had a tart taste, but not bad. He had been so preoccupied with the strange dessert and strong cider that it took him a moment to notice that Kerry had swapped seats with him while he had been at the loo. She ate her dessert with tiny, careful bites, almost as if she was sampling rather than savouring. Gavin smiled; he knew how she felt. The whole meal had been weird: the piglet, the gold coins, the boiled fruit, the bronze plates, the wooden cutlery and the home brewed cider.

Gavin gulped down his last mouthful of cider and wiped his mouth. No sooner than he had set down his tankard, Jenna reached across with a large ladle-full of cider. As she bent over to fill his tankard, her low-cut black top gave an eyeful of her ample chest. Gavin felt his cheeks burn.

After spending all evening in Oliver and Jenna's company, how could he only now be noticing how sexy she was?

Wait a minute: sexy? Not only was Jenna his boss' girlfriend, but she wasn't his type. Kerry was more what he liked; though she'd made it clear he wasn't her thing.

Jenna watched Gavin as she sat back down. "How do you like my dessert?"

"Great," he said. "What do you reckon, Kerry?"

"Lovely." She gave him an apprehensive sidelong look. Gavin suppressed a smile.

"The dessert's a new culinary experience for most people," said Jenna. "They aren't used to having ripe, juicy apples melt in their mouths like that."

She leaned forward, perching her chest on the table. Gavin spluttered on a mouthful of custard. "Yup, that's something, I'll bet?"

Out of the corner of his eye, he saw Kerry's body shake with silent giggles. "Yes, Jenna, very well cooked," Kerry said. "What would you say, Gavin? Succulent?"

Gavin looked at Kerry. Her impish behaviour

meant only one thing: she was tipsy.

"I'm glad you both like it so much." Jenna pressed her chest forward, making her cleavage swell. Gavin couldn't help staring. Not his fault; she was doing it on purpose. What was the *deal* with her? Was she Oliver's girlfriend or not?

More to the point, what was with *himself*? It had to be the cider, making him lusty as it was making Kerry giggly.

"And I'm pleased you think my apples are succulent, Kerry," said Jenna.

Jenna reached for Kerry's hand and squeezed it. Kerry's large, green eyes widened.

"You're welcome," said Kerry. She snatched her hand away and put it under the table.

Gavin almost dropped his spoon. The tone of Jenna's voice, the look on her face; she had just come onto Kerry, and Kerry knew it.

Got to snap out of it. Gavin took a big swig of cider; what was *wrong* with him? He was getting hot and bothered like a horny schoolboy, letting his imagination run wild.

"Have some more cider, Kerry." Jenna ladled a generous amount into her tankard.

Over the top of his tankard, Gavin could see Jenna's playful smile at Kerry.

Was Jenna deliberately trying to get them both drunk? But why? They were already loosened up; the conversation had been flowing all evening.

Oliver was watching the two women with as much interest as Gavin; the boss' eyes were glassy from cider and half shut from his contented smile. So that was the score, was it? Oliver wanted both Kerry and his own girlfriend? Greedy sod. Gavin wasn't sure what he thought of him.

13

On the surface of it, he seemed nice. But there was an untrustworthiness about him; something in his tall, thin, pale demeanour, with those ice-cold eyes that his smile didn't quite reach, and slick black hair, like an actor from a thirties vampire movie.

Still, Gavin had to admit his own hypocrisy; a fleeting thought of Jenna making a move on Kerry across the table had crossed his *own* thoughts. He had wiped it out with another swig of cider before realising he was intoxicating himself with the very thing that was poisoning his brain. He was a rugby player, an athlete, not a drinker; never mind a high-alcohol, home brewed drinker. *Nuts,* what an evening!

Gotta divert his attention from amorous thoughts to the dinner conversation instead. Oliver was talking to Kerry.

"But one thing, Kerry, that I find peculiar is how such a gifted artist as yourself has never found the time to do a self-portrait," Oliver rambled on. "I thought that's what all artists do? And considering what a stunning beauty you are, well, all I can say is, I'm very surprised."

"Really?" Kerry tossed her hair in a haughty way, but Gavin saw a hint of a smile. "That's not true. I'm not beautiful."

"Oh, but you are," said Jenna. "You have a wild Celtic look with your raven hair and emerald eyes."

Kerry straightened her back. "Uh, thanks Jenna."

"If you were to do a self-portrait, I would certainly buy it to decorate Sequana's," said Oliver.

Kerry leaned forward on her elbows, her sleepy gaze at Oliver full of lust. So she was feeling the effects of the cider too? Gavin pushed his empty dessert bowl away and rubbed the slumber from his own eyes. Better stay cool. If Oliver and Jenna had *designs* on Kerry, or himself, or both, he needed to stay sober so that they wouldn't accidently get into a dipping-the-pen-in-the-office-ink situation with the boss and a colleague. If Oliver and Jenna were *swingers*, that was fine, so long as they kept their lifestyle to themselves. Past Christmas party mistakes had seen the end of Gavin ever making a similar mistake again; not to mention *almost* ruining his friendship with Kerry because of drunken fooling around.

Jenna made goggle-eyes at Kerry and Kerry made goggle-eyes at Oliver. Oliver returned Kerry's, making Jenna turn to Gavin. He could see the edge of a black, lacy bra appearing, as Jenna swept the shoulder of her dress aside. Gavin stared. How long had it been? A year? Not since before graduation. It could be all too easy, but he would regret it; Jenna would regret it. He'd be doing them both a favour.

She was the boss' girlfriend. He had to think of anything but her lovely breasts jutting towards him, her small waist, her round ass, her shapely legs…

No, it was wrong.

It was his cue to go to bed.

"Have some more cider, Gavin, it's a celebration," said Jenna, slurring her words.

"That's alright, I think I've had enough."

"Maybe it's for the best. My homemade wine is always stronger than the supermarket brands."

"Yeah, I don't want to end up legless before my first day on the job tomorrow," said Gavin.

"I could help you upstairs to bed, if you like," said Jenna.

Such temptation. What temptation. Apples and Eve and snakes and he wasn't even religious.

"It's fine, I can manage. Well, cheers for the feast. I'll be off to bed then," said Gavin. "Kerry, you coming?"

15

Leave Oliver and Jenna to their pagan debauchery amongst themselves.

Kerry got unsteadily to her feet. "Yes, thanks for a lovely dinner. I think I'll head on up to bed myself."

"Our pleasure," said Oliver.

"Glad you're both satisfied," Jenna added.

"Let's have one more final toast," said Oliver, his voice clear with sobriety, despite all the cider he had drunk. He raised his tankard. "A toast to fresh, new bodies to add to the team."

They bumped tankards. Gavin sipped the last swills from the bottom of his tankard and set it down. He staggered out of the room leading Kerry by the hand. What was with all the innuendo? Pleasure and satisfaction. The cider had certainly been an aphrodisiac. He let the booze wash away his doubts. 'Fresh bodies' seemed like an unfortunate choice of words.

Chapter 2

Gavin leaned against the bannister as he climbed the stairs, the alcohol dulling his senses. He could hear Kerry panting along behind him. The kitchen and dining room were on the basement level, and a door on the ground floor next to the main reception room must have been where Oliver and Jenna stayed. He and Kerry were staying on the first floor. Two flights of stairs were no mean feat with a belly fully of pork and cider. Whilst the cider numbed his muscles, it made his eyes more alert. He noticed wooden plaques on the walls with carved tendril motifs and twisting snake-like designs, all Celtic inspired.

"Is it just me or were things pretty weird downstairs?" he said, over his shoulder to Kerry.

"I'm glad you thought so too. That was definitely the oddest dinner I've ever been to," said Kerry.

They reached the first floor landing. Gavin's room was to the back of the house. A mistletoe wreath hung from the door. Kerry's room was to the front of the house, adorned by a wreath of nettles.

Gavin fumbled with the door handle to his room.

"You coming in for a while before bed?"

"Good idea," she slurred. "Loads to tell you. That drink was *potent*. Don't get me wrong, it was lovely, but it went right to my head."

They went into his room and flopped down on the sofa bed. "Yeah, I agree," said Gavin. "Wonder if those leaves in the cider were some weird herb, like dope or something."

Kerry pushed loose strands of hair out of her face. She pointed at the mantelpiece above the fireplace. "Those are wiccan candles."

17

Gavin looked at the thick, orange candles, the wax burned low. How had he not realised they were smoking, or noticed their heavy scent? Had they been burning the whole time, since he and Kerry had arrived that afternoon? "How do you know they're wiccan?" he said.

"Isn't it obvious? Jenna's a witch. All that talk about the solstices and rituals?" Kerry wrinkled her nose.

"Oliver must be into all that occult stuff too. They're definitely pagans, but each to their own, I say." Gavin shrugged.

"As long as they don't try to make us sacrifice animals or dance naked around the full moon," said Kerry.

"Well, when you put it that way, it doesn't sound so bad. You and Jenna can get started any time."

She gave him a playful shove. "But seriously, you won't laugh at me if I tell you this-?"

Gavin turned to face her. "Go on then - tell me," he said.

"That drink kind of made me feel...." Kerry closed her eyes, her face reddening. "OK, I'm going to just say it - turned on. Did it make you feel, you know, randy too?"

He nodded. "I had to restrain myself at one point."

Kerry looked relieved. "I'm so glad to hear you say that. And is it just me, or were Oliver and Jenna both flirting with me?"

"Yeah - I thought they were both going to jump you at one point."

"Oliver's easy to brush off. It's not the first time a boss has made a pass at me. If Jenna's bi though, that's her business, but I'm not into that kind of thing. If she fancies me, it's going to be awkward to work with her. And that's besides the fact that they're a couple." Kerry pulled a face.

Gavin thought of Jenna squeezing Kerry's hand; it had seemed more charade than anything. "To be honest, I don't think she does fancy you. I reckon they were acting on the horny goat weed in the drink, or whatever it was."

Kerry's face puckered. "I'm not so sure Jenna *was* doing it cause she was drunk. I didn't get a chance to tell you, but when we were alone in the kitchen, she sort of came onto me - and that's before we were drinking."

Gavin laughed. "Don't knock it till you've tried it."

He got up and walked to the window. The candle smoke was stifling, and the room was hot enough without Kerry's anecdotes adding to the heat. His window overlooked the back garden. Secret garden, more like it. The high walls were covered with greenery and two trees, a blossom tree and an apple tree, at the end of the garden obscured the remaining view from the neighbours. Secretive; a place where sordid sex parties could happen, unnoticed. Gotta get the thoughts of pagan debauchery out of his mind. He opened the window, the fresh air clearing his head.

Gavin perched against the window frame and watched Kerry stretch out across the sofa, letting her head loll. "Yeah, and what was with Oliver telling me how beautiful I am?" she slurred.

"It's true, isn't it? You are beautiful."

"Oh Gavin, don't start that." Kerry tossed her hair.

"What do you mean, *don't start that.* You know it's true and you love the attention that comes with it. You were the centre of attention with everyone tonight."

Kerry gave a pretend pout.

"But seriously, what do you think of their lifestyle? I mean, we're working for them now, and living with them. Do you think we can hack too many more pagan stunts?" he said.

She joined him at the window, and bumped her hip against his, so that he made room for her.

19

"Well, I definitely don't mind the gold coins. Or the home brewed cider made from that-"she jerked her thumb at the apple tree in the garden, "-so long as the after effects don't ever lead to me screwing the boss." Kerry laughed and hiccupped.

"You shameless woman!" he teased.

"You know I'm joking. He's not even my thing." She winked at him.

Kerry bumped his hip again. He bumped her back, and she staggered, drunkenly, against the chest of drawers in the corner, by the window. The clang of a heavy object hitting the wooden floor sounded. Kerry got down on all fours. Gavin saw her emerge with a large, cast iron knife in her hand from behind the drawers. It was a foot long and curved with a beautifully crafted wooden handle inlaid with red glass beads in Celtic design. It had been hidden on top of the drawers, under a handkerchief.

"Looks like I wasn't far wrong about the animal sacrificing," Kerry said, grinning.

Gavin took it from her and held it up to inspect. "Pretty nice artefact. It's probably from Sequana's. I'll bet those two are modern-day Druids. I could imagine them waving it about in the air while they dance round Stonehenge."

"Crazy, but probably true," said Kerry. "Jenna mentioned to me that she moved here last November from Glastonbury. Glastonbury is a big centre for Celtic mythology - you know, the Arthur legend and all that. Oh yeah, and she said she came across this house because of being in the right *circles*. We'll have to look out for pentagrams on the walls."

"Pentagrams are black magic, though - I've seen it on TV. Maybe she's a white witch instead. I'll bet that's why there's a Christmas wreath on the door - because she came in winter and the big pagan festival is-"

"Ssh!" Kerry sat upright. "Listen. Do you hear that?"

Gavin strained his ears. Bumps and bangs; Oliver groaning, then Jenna making yelping sounds.

Kerry put her finger to her lips. "They're doing it!"

"Lucky for them." Gavin sighed.

"Oliver's saying something now. Can you hear?"

Gavin walked over to the TV and grabbed the remote. "No, and I don't want to. I can't say I'm interested in them shagging."

"Oh, don't put the telly on," Kerry snatched the remote away. "Listen - it's seriously odd."

Against his wishes, Gavin fell silent to hear. Oliver's voice filtered up, muffled through the floorboards. He spoke in monotone.

"It's some kind of chant. I can't make it out. It sounds like another language - Latin or something." Kerry paused, then sniggered. "And she's barking like a dog - do you hear?"

"I don't know why you find all this amusing. It's way more information than I want to know."

Hopefully Oliver and Jenna weren't planning to shag all night; he didn't think he could stand hearing Oliver romancing her in a dead tongue, while she yelped like a chihuahua. It might amuse Kerry since it was OK for her; she didn't have to sleep in the room above it. They were a kinky couple, no doubt.

Kerry walked across to the door. "Well, that's about enough fun for tonight. I'm off to bed."

"Easy for you to say - you don't have to sleep above those two going at it like rabbits," he said.

"Goodnight, lover boy!" Kerry stuck her tongue out at him before leaving his room.

Oliver grunted in ecstasy. Jenna howled.
Gavin sighed.

Kerry opened her eyes in the blackness of her bedroom. The room was new, unfamiliar. Disoriented, it took her a few minutes to adjust to where she was; London, her first night staying at her new address in Avalon Road, Fulham. Her eyes acclimatised slowly to the dimness. It had to be some time in the early hours of the morning. A sliver of moonlight through a gap in the curtain fell as a blue rectangular shape on the wall above the door.

When she had been eight years old, Kerry had believed such rectangles of light to be ghosts. Some of the shapes had been orange, others white or grey and some had moved. They had travelled across her childhood bedroom and fallen onto her bed, making her scream. As she had got older, Kerry realised they were lights created by passing cars, or lamp-posts outside. But this shape stayed fixed in one spot, an ethereal blue glow in the room watching over her. She watched it, recalling her days of believing in spirits.

A creak in the floorboards from below alerted her to the other residents sharing the house. Oliver and Jenna were certainly strange, but she didn't feel they meant anything harmful by their pagan rituals. She had to admit, she liked the bizarre nature of the eccentric couple. Nothing out of the ordinary happened back home in Leeds. It was one of the reasons she'd been looking for work elsewhere. That and the lack of jobs.

Kerry heard the sound of running water in the darkness. Had Oliver or Jenna left a tap on? She hadn't heard a toilet flushing. Why would either of them randomly turn on a tap in the early hours?

As the sound continued unabated, Kerry wondered whether she should go and investigate in case there might be a flood. What if one of them had been sleepwalking? Or had got up to wash their hands, then had an accident and passed out?

Kerry rubbished the thought; if either of them had had an accident, she would have heard a bang from the fall. Instead, she looked at the blue rectangle on the wall and her eyelids grew heavy. The running water lulled her into a relaxed state. Trickling, gurgling, flowing; she was ready for sleep.

Flowing water. She could smell the sea. Sea air and the sound of gulls. She saw a wide river. There were reeds and islands of marsh.

Kerry stood on a jetty that extended five metres into the river. It was an archaic pier made of thick oak posts that had been sunk deep into the Thames mud. A walkway had been created by placing flat planks of wood horizontally, secured with an interlacing birch, ash and alder fence. She stood at the end of the jetty overlooking the flowing river. She could see beds of reeds below the waterline. Sitting on top of the reeds near the surface, at the foot of the jetty, Kerry could make out a golden horse about the size of her palm. She crouched and tried to reach it, but it was deeper than arm's length in the clear water. Squatting with her head leaning over the edge of the jetty, she could distinguish the details. The Golden Horse was styled in long, curved lines. Behind its hindquarters, there was a spoked circle: a wheel.

Who had lost it? It looked like it had been deliberately, almost lovingly, set there. Why had an object of such high worth been abandoned? Why was it discarded in the lonely, marshy river?

Chapter 3

Kerry walked along Avalon Road on her way to work. She smiled to herself thinking about what Gavin would say when he found out that her workplace was three minutes around the corner. Sequana's had to be a twenty minute walk along Wandsworth Bridge Road. She'd have to tell him about her dream too. It had probably been inspired by the Celtic ritual of the feast the night before.

Her favourite boutique dress swished around her knees as she walked. The colour was appropriate: green. A Celtic colour. If her boss was pagan, she'd at least make the effort to fit in.

At the end of Avalon Road, she saw the Herne's Hunt restaurant on the corner. Her first impression was of a converted Victorian pub, but as she got closer she could see stained glass windows on the upper floor adorned with saintly images, like those of a church and wooden window boxes with seraphic motifs. The flat-topped roof had colourful potted plants lining the edges. There were wooden friezes of cherubs decorating the painted green stucco of the building and gargoyle heads carved in high relief, inset with geometric lozenge shaped frames. Ornate Neo-classical statues and Roman-busts seemed incongruous with the vibrant, if very English exterior of the place. The windows of the ground floor had stained glass windows, but unlike the upper floor with its saintly images these had Celtic scroll motifs and tendril designs, some with zoomorphic forms: elongated horse faces and curving bird shapes. Kerry lingered in front of the window studying one of the horse head patterns, the abstract lines curling into tendril forms. Above it, in the top right corner was a spoked wheel.

Kerry stared, frozen. Golden Horse. Spoked

Wheel. Abandoned in a lonely river.

The latticed window frame had peeling white paint, but the Celtic stained glass window looked new. Had Mistress C replaced the old window in an attempt to rejuvenate the dilapidated restaurant? The building gave Kerry the impression of a place that had once been derelict for some time and now thrived with new life.

Kerry pushed the heavy oak front door, expecting it to be open and found it locked. Mistress C wanted her to start the shift at nine thirty. She tried to remember what Oliver had said, the details of which were hazy with alcohol-induced amnesia. The clientele was private. If it was a secret place, was there a secret code to enter? She looked at a wooden plaque mounted on the door showing two Greek-inspired male figures holding their loosely clad togas to cover their modesty, each raising a hand to display a menu board in the middle. No menu had been written for today, but Kerry saw a note scribbled in loopy handwriting instead.

"Kerry. Throw gravel at the upstairs window. I will come."

Kerry reached into one of the lower window boxes and grabbed a handful of gravel. As soon as she threw it at an upstairs window, the net curtain pulled aside and swiftly fell into place. A few minutes later the door opened about a hand's width.

"Hello?" said Kerry. She tried to push it open, but it jarred, as if on a chain. Kerry put her face to the gap and peered in.

What she saw didn't resemble a restaurant. It looked like a cluttered living room in a cottage that had been abandoned since Victorian times and was now suddenly seeing the light of day again. The faint ray of sunshine streaming in from outside highlighted a wall of dust that swirled in a disturbance of wind.

"Let her in," said a deep, female voice. The woman sounded old but had the penetrating tone of a dominant person. Kerry peered around the door as it opened. A tall stooping man held the door wide. He didn't appear to be older than about forty, yet he had the wizened physique of a man two decades older. He was pale and his skin hung in loose folds as if he had lost several stone in a short space of time or had once been well-muscled but had suffered a chronic illness. His eyes were a watery blue and he had stringy, shoulder-length brown hair and a rats-tail moustache that drooped like he did. He wore a baggy tunic that swamped his hunched frame, hanging over loose flannel trousers much too roomy for his dishevelled body. Oliver had said Mistress C only accepted an exclusive clientele; yet, the man looked like a vagrant. Kerry kept her eyes on him as she stepped inside. He stared back at her, his eyes shifty.

"Welcome, Kerry, you're right on time."

Mistress C was every bit as powerful as her voice had implied. She was an old woman of maybe sixty or seventy years, but tall and slender with a strong physique. Her waist-length hair was pencil-lead grey shot with bright silver streaks. She wore a long, blue tunic-style dress in an unfamiliar fabric. Could've been woven out of water for all Kerry knew; it certainly moved with fluidity over the older woman's toned frame. If Kerry looked anything half as beautiful by the time she was Mistress C's age, she would be happy.

"I'm Mistress C, the proprietor of this institution."

Institution? Imposing words and imposing figure; Mistress C strode towards Kerry and led her with a firm hand into the depths of the cluttered establishment. This woman was *Amazonian*. Kerry had always felt tall at five eight, but Mistress C dwarfed her. She had to be six foot, at least.

They passed through a narrow passageway full of erotic Victorian artwork. Kerry slowed to study the paintings. She had always imagined the Victorians were prudish people. Course, it was Oliver's restaurant and he wasn't shy when it came to sex.

"I see you enjoy the decor. I'm planning to keep these, although the rest will go. I always appreciate a good display of erotica," said Mistress C.

Kerry cringed. First Oliver flirting with her and now Mistress C discussing pornography. Didn't these pagans have any boundaries? She *had* to have been a pagan; such people would naturally gravitate to Oliver's 'circle', as Jenna put it.

Mistress C led her into a small kitchen. "Have you eaten breakfast?" she said.

"No. I only ever have tea in the morning," said Kerry.

"Nonsense!" Mistress C tugged at Kerry's coat and Kerry removed it. She hung it on a wooden peg by the kitchen door. "I cooked some apple oats. Take yourself a bowl."

It wasn't a question, it was an order. Kerry took the bronze bowl handed to her, a wooden spoon and a wooden tankard. If she hadn't experienced such items at the feast the previous night, she would've found it incredibly eccentric.

Mistress C stirred the contents of a huge, bronze cauldron on the stove. It was identical to the one in which Jenna had served the cooked apple dessert at last night's feast.

"Let's go through to the dining area. Bring some more utensils for Morfan," said Mistress C.

27

Morfan? A strange name for a shrivelled character. Kerry grabbed another bowl, spoon and tankard and followed Mistress C into the restaurant. The old woman carried the huge cauldron by its handles without a trace of effort. Her tunic-dress swished as she walked, and the rope-belt swung like a horse's tail. Kerry thought of the coins from the feast. There was an engraved image of a woman with long hair, wearing a long tunic roped at the waist. She held a bough of fruit over a steaming cauldron. Had Oliver modelled his coins on Mistress C? But why? Why was she so important that she had become his artist's muse?

Mistress C nodded to an oversized stuffed armchair and Kerry sat. The old woman's mannerisms were abrupt; even rude. Why didn't she take offence? If anyone else had issued such non-verbal commands, Kerry would've told them where to stick it. With Mistress C, it seemed natural to do as she bid without complaint. She was strong-willed and had a maternal persuasion.

There was a chess set on the low, round table in front of Kerry. The Queen was bent in doggy-style and the king jutted his huge erection forward, as though they would fit together if anyone cared to try. Bit too explicit for breakfast; Kerry pushed it aside with her elbow and set the bronze bowls, wooden spoons, and tankards down. Morfan shuffled over and set a bucket of juice in the middle of the table, before lowering himself into the antique armchair across from Kerry. Mistress C set the cauldron on the edge of the table and began ladling gruel into their bowls.

"I apologise for the clutter. These trinkets have been here for decades, no doubt. I'm in the process of redecorating. Jenna's been a massive hand and Morfan will help, now that he's here too. Morfan is my son. Morfan, this is Kerry. Kerry, meet Morfan."

Son? Kerry stretched her hand out to him. "Nice to meet you," she said.

He didn't take Kerry's hand. He dipped his head in a quiet bow to her. Kerry bowed back. His watery eyes never broke contact with hers as he bowed. He really *was* shifty. Either that or shy. Or both.

"Morfan arrived earlier than expected. I'll have to speak to Jenna about her role when she arrives for her shift." A shadow crossed Mistress C's face for a fleeting moment. "Never mind, I'm sure you'll fit right into the team, Kerry. When you've finished your breakfast, I'll get you started on a few tasks. Take your time."

Mistress C lifted the cauldron off the table and walked away.

The porridge didn't look appetising, but Kerry didn't want to be rude. She blew on her first spoonful and sampled it. It tasted coarser than the supermarket oats she was used to and the apple provided some sugary relief. Interesting, but not a culinary delight by any means. Kerry ate it, convincing herself that it was a nutritious treat.

Kerry and Morfan ate in silence. He shovelled his oats hungrily, holding the bowl close to his chin. When would Jenna start her shift? Mistress C seemed nice enough, but her son made Kerry uncomfortable, although she didn't know why. From time to time as he ate, he cast a secretive glance her way. Why did he not trust her? Was he odd like this with Jenna? Was Jenna even working today? Jenna had said Mistress C was flexible regarding time off. At any rate, Kerry hoped she would come by. Eating with Mistress C's strange son was quelling what little appetite she had.

As Morfan ate, Kerry noticed that he no longer seemed stooped. He sat upright, his broad shoulders no longer hunched over the bowl. The rhythmic chewing even seemed to remove the shadows from his face. Kerry looked again. No; his cheeks had *physically* become more solid, as if the food was transmogrifying straight into muscle. He became less gaunt; the hollows of his eye sockets filled out. Maybe the gruel did contain vitamins after all? Kerry munched with more vigour than before.

Morfan scooped the last of the porridge into his mouth, the bowl concealing his face as he leaned his head back, devouring every oat. When he set the bowl down, Kerry almost dropped her spoon. Morfan looked like a man twice as broad as the shrunken wretch who had answered the door, and half the age. He had Gavin's rugby-player bulk. His tunic, which had seemed so loose-fitting only twenty minutes before was now stretched across a body packed with muscle.

Was her mind playing tricks on her? Kerry looked at the contents of her own bowl. It couldn't be because she was hungover. Was there a hallucinogenic herb in her breakfast? Her imagination was not that good.

Morfan poured himself a tankard full of juice and gulped it down, the liquid streaming down his rat's-tail moustache and dripping onto his hulking body. Was he really that thirsty to abandon his table manners? Kerry tried it; it had the tart taste of home prepared apple cider. Morfan stood up, big and broad, easily six five and built like a warrior. She let her eyes travel up his body. Pity he wasn't handsome, or he would've been quite the catch. He had a flat, boxer's nose and his deep-set, pale blue eyes peered from under a heavy brow-ridge. She hated to use the word ugly, but there was no other way to describe his face.

Mistress C returned to clear the bowls. "Good. I'm glad to see that you both ate well. There's a hard day of work ahead of us."

"What time do you open for business?" said Kerry.

"We aren't yet. So far we've only entertained small, private parties. It'll be a while before we get this place in shape. The first of May is coming up and we'll be having much to celebrate and much feasting."

Kerry's heart sank. "My birthday is on the first of May. I guess I'll be working."

"We'll be closed on the first. My other son, Affie, will be arriving then and I need to be on hand to welcome him."

Kerry felt happier. It would be nice to do something fun on her birthday; maybe hit the clubs on Piccadilly Circus. Jenna and Oliver could maybe come too, if they didn't have plans. They'd been so generous, it would be rude not to invite them.

"Jenna's shift starts at midday and she'll be helping me to organise the plants upstairs. I want to hang more herbs from the ceiling in here too - fennel, sage, laurel, sandalwood, all the usual. Kerry, you can get started polishing the windows. I need there to be a lot more light for the greenery. Morfan, now that you've filled out, and about time too, you can start clearing away junk. Oliver and his new worker will be bringing me furniture from Sequana's in time for the Beltaine festival on the first of May."

Filled out, and about time too? Kerry set to polishing the windows. So she *hadn't* imagined it. Mistress C's words disturbed her. It was true; Morfan had doubled his size because of eating the gruel.

No way. What crazy thoughts.

"Kerry, can you get rid of all those ugly paintings and those ballet shoes strapped up there? I want to build an altar on that fireplace."

Kerry dropped the thoughts and walked across to clear the fireplace. She boxed up the dusty trinkets and wiped the mantelpiece with a rag. Mistress C set two black candles on either side of the fire and lit them.

The smoke was thick and the musty scent heavy. Kerry couldn't place the smell. A hint of vanilla? Bergamot? She wasn't knowledgeable about incense. All she knew was that the orange candles in Gavin's room had a lighter fragrance in comparison and that these ones made her head swim. She sneezed, almost blowing one out. What job was she supposed to be doing? She spun on the spot, one hand on her forehead, the other steadying her balance against the fireplace.

Time passed in a dizzying haze. Kerry polished all of the downstairs windows. Jenna arrived for her shift. Was it midday already? Kerry was glad to see her. Only the previous evening and Jenna's flirting had made her uncomfortable, but now she welcomed her company if it meant she didn't have to be alone with domineering Mistress C, her creepy black candles and Morfan, her bulky brawn.

"Hey Kerry. Enjoying your first day?"

Kerry forced her head up and down in a heavy-headed nod.

"Gavin and Ollie are on their way with a delivery. You'll be able to go as soon as they get unloaded. Ollie's letting Gavin off too."

"Great," said Kerry, her tongue thick.

"Where's Morfan? I'm dying to meet him."

"You don't know him? Haven't you ever worked the same shifts?"

"It's not that - he's new. There'll be a lot of changes around here. Apart from the Midwinter solstice and the summer solstice, May the first is a big time of year for us.

You'll be seeing a few more new faces around here before the week is out."

Jenna glided across the cluttered dining area into the back. Kerry resumed polishing windows. Footsteps upstairs suggested introductions were being made above. Soon, Morfan returned to haul paintings and junk outside. Mistress C and Jenna followed him downstairs; Kerry heard their voices grow louder as they made their way into the kitchen.

Mistress C spoke first. "It wasn't the right time. It was undignified."

"But you said six days before and after Beltaine," Jenna protested.

"I gave you clear instructions that you were supposed to do it on the first of May. Not before, not after, exactly on the day. You abused my trust."

"I didn't abuse." Jenna sounded desperate. "I'm sorry, I made a mistake."

"It wasn't a mistake. You left the tap running on purpose," said Mistress C.

What did that mean? Kerry paused and let her arm drop to her side, still holding the polishing rag. Why would Mistress C imply abuse of trust over a silly running tap? Hadn't there been a tap running the night before, downstairs in Oliver and Jenna's bathroom? But how would Mistress C know about that; and even if she did, why would she care? Oliver's house was his concern. Unless, maybe Jenna had also left a tap running at the Herne's Hunt and caused a flood in the kitchen. Perhaps Jenna was careless?

Kerry's mind drifted to the sounds of running water from the night before, recalling her dream. Running water and a river… Her fingers loosened and the polishing cloth dropped. It had been no dream; it had really happened. Not in the present day, but in the past. The dream was real, right there, in London. It had happened by the Thames. She had to tell Gavin.

Chapter 4

A Rolls Royce. Oliver owned a *Rolls Royce*. A fourteen foot long, black vintage beauty. Gavin got into the passenger side. A boss who could throw gold coins around at feasts like confetti, owned two businesses, drove a Royce and owned a million pound house was definitely a good one to work for - and get promoted by.

Wonder if Oliver would allow him a spin through London in it someday? What would it be like to drive a Rolls Royce? Kerry could sit in the passenger side and he'd drive them to Knightsbridge to pop into Harrods. Jolly good and all that malarkey. Gavin smirked at himself in the wing mirror. He bounced up and down on the leather seats, feeling a tremor of excitement. Would Oliver ever let him drive it, even once? Even park it? Probably not. He wouldn't, if he were Oliver. He wished he owned the car.

"Ah, I see you like The Balor."

"The Balor?" said Gavin.

"She's a vintage beauty, isn't she? She was the fastest car ever to travel on the public highway when she was made in the seventies, did you know that?"

Gavin raised an eyebrow. "What, this thing is?"

Oliver looked smug. "She can go at over two hundred miles per hour."

"I didn't know that," said Gavin.

"She's got a Spitfire engine. And a classic Rolls Royce radiator. I'm glad you can appreciate the finer things, Gavin." Oliver smiled at him, his eyes narrowing to slits. "We have an exciting day ahead. I'm expecting a huge delivery in time for Beltaine on the first of May."

Beltaine? What was that; some obscure Gaelic way of saying Mayday?

The drive to Sequana's on Wandsworth Bridge

Road took five minutes. As they arrived, Gavin saw a delivery lorry waiting on the wide pavement outside Oliver's antique and furniture shop. He couldn't read the Gaelic sign on its side. There was an interlacing lattice symbol next to it. Yet more Celtic stuff.

They parked behind, but not too close to the lorry and got out.

"You're really into all this Celtic art, huh?" said Gavin.

"I'm from an old Celtic family, so it's entirely appropriate," said Oliver glibly.

"I would have thought Doncaster an Anglo-Saxon name."

Oliver looked sheepish. "My family are old Britons. They've been in Doncaster since the first people arrived. The name is from Yorkshire, originally."

Gavin scratched his ear. "Didn't mean any offense, of course."

"None taken." So Oliver said; yet, his tone was dry.

"Course, I was under the impression that the first people in England were Homo Heidelbergensis - your people have been in Doncaster for eight hundred, thousand years?"

Oliver laughed, his eyes crinkling. "I didn't take you to be the wry sort, Gavin. I'm sure we're going to get along just fine."

"I'm sure we will. I didn't take you to be the inficete sort," said Gavin.

Oliver's false smile faltered. He didn't understand but would never admit it. Score; Balor: one, Inficete: one.

"We need to bring some things inside Sequana's, then do a run over to the Herne's Hunt. The last item is for me. After that, we'll finish early and you can have a half day. But paid full wages, of course."

"Maybe I'll take Kerry to see some sights. You could lend me Balor?" said Gavin.

"Nice try," said Oliver.

They got out to meet the delivery man.

"Alright, Ollie? Got another nice shipment for you today. These for the auction?"

"A few of the cabinets, but the rest is for personal use."

"You still kitting out that new restaurant then, I take it?"

"Nearly there. Ceridwen doesn't want a fussy interior. She wants a few panels for the walls and some oak tables and alder chairs."

Gavin lingered next to Oliver. Ceridwen? Who was that? Was that Mistress C? Unusual name but had a nice ring to it. Sounded Welsh.

"This must be your new worker. He looks like a fine, strong lad," said the delivery man.

Oliver patted Gavin's shoulder. "That he is. Gavin, I'd like you to meet Glynn."

Glynn. That was Welsh too. If Glynn and Mistress C - if that was who Oliver meant by Ceridwen - were from Wales, then that would explain the Celtic connection.

"Glynn, this is Gavin. Gavin is from back home, up North. Glynn is my regular driver. Even does cross channel trips for me when I need shipments from Gaul."

Gaul? Gavin raised an eyebrow. He kept himself from laughing before either of the men could notice.

"You have your work cut out for you, Gavin. This Ollie here is hands on with the furniture. No dollies for him," said Glynn.

"I wouldn't have any of my fine Gallic artefacts chipped by clumsy modern means - what would the artisans say?" said Oliver.

Gallic artefacts? Artisans? Modern means? Did Oliver think he was living in the Iron Age? Gavin guffawed. Dollies weren't that sophisticated; bet the Druids did use such simple mechanisms.

"I think we have a sceptic here," said Glynn. "He'll change his mind soon enough when he sees how much these objects can fetch at auction."

"More when he takes a cut of the profits himself," Oliver added.

Profits? Maybe Glynn had a point.

Glynn's eyes narrowed into slits with his wide grin. "I thought that would catch his attention. You'll make Ollie a good partner one day at Sequana's, if he lets you. You feeling ready for a workout, son? We have a heavy one in back here."

"I can handle it," said Gavin.

"Told you he could do it. He has a fine Northern temperament on him too, I wouldn't hire anyone with half his fire." Oliver winked at him. Gavin didn't mind. If there was money to be made, they could be as condescending as they liked.

Glynn opened the back doors of the lorry, revealing the contents. Gavin saw an oak cupboard, a dark coffee table that looked like it was made of twisted pieces of driftwood and behind them, a huge cauldron. It was as big as a mini. The lower portion was bronze, and the upper rim made of a silvery metal.

"Is that gilded silver?" said Gavin.

Oliver admired it, his hands on his hips. "Ah, good guess, you know your artefacts."

Gavin felt smug. "I did my honours in History, I've studied the Iron Age well."

"It's actually electrum, an alloy of silver and gold. I assume you must know electrum, if you've *studied* the time period, then?" said Oliver.

"Who mixed it?" said Gavin. Better cover his ineptitude; this guy was competitive.

"Electrum is a naturally occurring alloy and therefore very rare," said Oliver. "And by the way, this isn't an artefact. I had it made as a replica."

Gavin folded his arms. "What are we moving first?"

"The friezes and the coffee table are for the Herne's Hunt. The cauldron is for my house. Everything else can go inside."

They worked in sequence taking turns to move the items and guard the lorry. Every time Gavin stepped inside the lorry, his eyes fell on the magnificent cauldron. The bronze lower half had engravings of Celtic deities, their eyes inset with red glass giving them a fierce, maniacal look. At the very bottom below the deities were images of warriors fighting a huge battle. The upper portion made of electrum had designs of horses and birds blending into tendril and scroll motifs.

"That is one impressive piece of craftsmanship," said Gavin.

"Nothing but the best from my smiths. I'm glad you like it. It'll be the centrepiece of my Beltaine celebration."

"I didn't know you had things made specially - I thought you only dealt in antiques?" said Gavin.

"I have objects for personal use specially made. The people who made the cauldron also make my coins."

Oliver signed a delivery note and Gavin counted the items for Sequana's. Glynn closed the back of the lorry and Oliver locked the front doors of his store.

"Next stop my place, if you will, Glynn. We'll follow behind you," Oliver instructed.

Profits. What kind of profits from auction did Oliver and Glynn mean? More than he could imagine. He could imagine a great deal.

The lorry stopped in front of Oliver's house and he parked The Balor across the street.

"This one's going to be tricky to get through the front door. We'll have to get her out, then turn her onto her side," said Glynn.

The cauldron looked difficult enough to contend with, without considering its weight. For starters, the shape was awkward. The rim had a small lip to help stop sliding hands. Gavin hoped his sweaty palms from all the lifting would provide friction for a good grip; it probably weighed 200KG.

"We'll do it on three," said Glynn. "One, two - three!"

All the years of playing rugby and weight-lifting were being put to the test. Gavin could feel the strain on his lower back. It was hard to keep good form and navigate their way up the steps in front of Doncaster Manor. The thing felt as heavy as a mini, as well as being the size of one. At the top of the steps, they braced it against the wall with Glynn and Gavin supporting it, while Oliver opened the door. With Oliver in front and Glynn and Gavin behind, they rolled it on its side through to the narrow hallway.

"Where do you want it?" said Glynn.

Oliver panted. "Back garden."

They rolled it towards the stairs. Oliver and Glynn managed the cauldron from either side in front as they pushed it to the edge of the stairs leading to the lower ground floor.

They had got to be kidding.

Down the stairs, with Gavin keeping the balance

behind. Through the dining room, into the kitchen and out onto the back patio. Another flight of stairs led up to the garden. Gavin braced it with his knee to get a better grip as they tackled the last set of steps. They gently tipped the cauldron over and set it on the grass of the back garden.

"I'm glad I'm taking a little holiday after this," said Glynn. "Grainne and I are taking the girls to Devon for a week. It'll be our last family holiday before Saiorse goes off to university."

Gron-ya. Sher-sha. Such Gaelic names. Irish? But Glynn was Welsh. Oliver liked to keep his close knit circle of friends Celtic it seemed.

"Is Saoirse eighteen already?" Oliver puffed.

"Yes, time flies, doesn't it? She'll be at Kings College this autumn."

"I'll have to keep an eye on her while she's in London."

"Speaking of which, she came up with me this morning," said Glynn. "I dropped her off at the Student Union on my way."

"You'll have to send her my way," said Oliver, with a jovial smile. "I'll get her a part-time job at the Herne's Hunt."

"That you must, Chieftain." Glynn winked at Oliver. "She'd be honoured to work for our fair goddess."

Chieftain? The whole Celtic thing was going a bit far. And why did Glynn say Mistress C was 'our fair goddess'? Was she a stunner, or was it more pagan madness?

Kerry finished soon after Jenna started her shift at midday. Gavin and Oliver had dropped off a coffee table and a bookshelf and Gavin had become acquainted with Mistress C and Morfan. Gavin had been giddy as a

41

schoolboy before meeting Mistress C and deflated after. Wonder what that was all about? What had he been expecting?

"Come on, let's go." Kerry pulled on her coat as she walked out the door. She grabbed Gavin's arm and dragged him.

Gavin yanked his arm out of her grip. "Woah, what's the rush?"

"I have something to tell you," she said. Her dream, the Thames; she had to keep it fresh in her mind.

"Like what? Something good? Bad?"

"Something strange." Strange, but compelling. Reeds, a pristine river in a past time.

"*Tell* me about it." Gavin sped up alongside her. "Whatever it is, bet I can beat it on weirdness."

Kerry crossed the road away from the Herne's Hunt. "You wouldn't believe the *night* I've had," she said.

"Like?" he said, intrigued.

What a night. What a premonition. Or was it; premonitions usually showed a future event, not a vision from the past. But what if a part of the past could be there waiting, for thousands of years, to be discovered in the present? Could the artefact still be there after all that time? The thought fuelled her on through the twisting streets to the main drag of Kings Road. Soon they reached Wandsworth Bridge Road. She started to slow and caught her breath.

"You're not taking me to Sequana's, are you? I just came from there," said Gavin.

Kerry stared straight ahead. "No, a bit further. It's too weird to explain. It's by the river. I need to check out something."

"Like what?" Gavin's voice had a note of frustration in it.

42

"I'll tell you when we get there. It'll be easier to show you."

Easier to show him, supposing she could find the right location. The area wouldn't look the same at all as it did in her dream, but it wasn't what guided her. This was instinct; a sixth sense. Her feet propelled her forward as though guided by an unseen force. A shiver ran down her back. Kerry tensed. No; nothing supernatural. This was a cold April, an unusually cold winter. Still, she needed a distraction. She peeled her eyes away from the bridge ahead to glance at him. "What's this weird thing that happened to you? Hope it wasn't as strange as my day."

"Yours was mental too, huh?" Gavin took a deep breath. "Well, first of all, Oliver has a Rolls Royce that he calls The Balor."

"The Balor? Like the cyclops from Celtic mythology?" said Kerry.

"Right. And second of all, we deliver this big, like, huge cauldron to his house. And I'm talking, swallow-a-mini huge."

"What did he order such a huge cauldron for?"

"Not for sale. He said it's for Beltaine, some festival or other."

"That's funny, Mistress C said something along the same lines. She wanted to have her restaurant done up for a feast on Beltaine, which is apparently on my birthday."

"Well I don't know what sort of feast they're planning to have, or for how many people but that cauldron could cook a whole cow."

Kerry imagined a whole cow carcass bubbling away; not a pleasant thought. "I wouldn't put it past Oliver to do something like that, after the piglet we had last night."

Gavin guffawed. "You know, it's funny, of all the

places we could've ended up in London, we found ourselves in the midst of a bunch of modern-day Druids."

"Maybe it's not a laughing matter. I don't think I'm much keen on all this witchcraft business," said Kerry.

"They're not that serious. It seems more for show than anything. You don't believe in a bunch of spells and hokum, do you? I never took you for the superstitious type," he laughed.

Kerry sniffed. "Maybe I am. You wouldn't believe the crazy dream I had last night. I mean, it was so vivid, it took me a while to realise I was asleep."

Gavin stopped walking. "Wait a minute - you mean to say you're dragging me all the way down here because of a dream?"

"Oh come on." She tugged his arm. "Humour me a bit? I saw something in my dream, and I swear to you, it was so real I need to find out if it's there or not."

Gavin narrowed his eyes. "Hmm. Depends what it is."

"Alright then, if you want to know, it was a Golden Horse."

"Gold? Real gold? How much?"

Kerry pulled him along by his wrist. "Knew that would get you moving. Come on."

They reached the riverside path at Wandsworth Bridge in thirty minutes. The Thames was wide. The sea air smell and sound of gulls were familiar from Kerry's dream, but the view wasn't. The tidal river didn't have reeds or marshy banks as it had in an earlier time but instead was surrounded by industry. A towering, red crane on the opposite side lifted barges to be filled by sand, probably for transport to the Sand works on their side of the river. Huge concrete walls with iron railings raised the pedestrian walkway above the flood level of the Thames.

Kerry looked over the railing and saw the green, mossy line indicating the high tide mark. The Thames could get frighteningly deep. But for now, it was at low tide. Luck? Or fate.

"Well? Whereabouts is this Golden Horse?" said Gavin.

Kerry didn't answer. Below, the low tide exposed a stony shore. She spotted a rusted metal ladder fastened to the concrete wall by rivets. Kerry swung her leg over the wall and onto the topmost rung of the ladder.

"What are you doing? Are you mad?" Gavin's face was red as he looked down at her.

"Maybe." She descended, holding tight to the metal railing. This had to be the place. The smell was right; the feel was right. The view had completely changed, but her feet knew the way. Why did her feet know where to go, when she had never been there before?

"This is where my dream happened," she said. The words came out of her mouth with such conviction, she had to believe them.

"Kerry, stop. You aren't allowed down there, that's an access ladder for rescuing people. It's off limits to the public."

Kerry watched his face fall into shadow as she descended. "Stop being such a moan!"

Gavin looked one way, then the other and followed her.

"I can't believe I'm doing this," he said. "You're barking, do you know that? One of these days you're going to get us both killed with your crazy schemes."

"Where's your sense of adventure?" She walked towards the water's edge, where it lapped over stones and rubbish. The Thames looked murky, not like the clear calm water in her dream, the virgin river it had been in the Iron

Age.

"In my dream there was a prehistoric platform made of birch and ash branches. The dream took place in an ancient time. I was standing on the end of the jetty looking into the river."

"You're thinking of that Bronze Age bridge that was found at Vauxhall," Gavin said. "That's further along the river on the other side."

"This was different. It was a later age and it was here, right here. The feeling came to me this morning when I was doing some cleaning for Mistress C. She was burning these black candles, like the orange ones Jenna had put in your room, and at first I felt dizzy cause they were so pungent. But afterwards this memory came back to me, a memory of my dream. My feet just led me to this spot."

Gavin didn't look impressed. "So you took us down here cause you got high on some incense?"

Kerry walked further along the shore by the water's edge. The incense hadn't made her high; but Gavin wasn't far wrong. Had it opened a pathway in her mind? The Iron Age vision had really happened. It was as though she had been taken through a channel into the past. "In the dream I saw an artefact in the water, beyond the end of the jetty. It was caught in a bed of reeds. It looked like a Golden Horse, kind of made in an abstract Celtic style. There was a spoked wheel behind it. It was over there and it really happened, thousands of years ago."

The shore was littered with sea glass and broken pieces of Victorian brick. Kerry overturned a licence plate from a car and nudged aside a long piece of plastic guttering with her foot.

"This is all junk. There's probably sewage too," said Gavin. "I don't think we should go any further."

Kerry poked the toe of her pumps into the muddy

46

sand near the water's edge. She crouched down. At first, she thought it was water reflecting the sun, but the colour was too bright; a deep, rich yellow. Kerry stuck her fingers into the mud, working her hand around an object as wide and heavy as a side plate. The suction made a faint popping sound as the object pulled free. She placed it in the palm of her hand and used the Thames water to clean the remaining mud off it.

The horse was even more intricate than in her dream. She knew it was at least two thousand years old, yet it looked as new as if it had been made yesterday. A red glass stone had been inset in the horse's eye. The spokes of the wheel gave the impression of wood grain.

"Nuts," said Gavin. He squatted down beside her. "That's it, isn't it? That's the thing you saw."

"Horse and wheel." Kerry held her palm flat to display her find. "Told you."

Gavin picked it up. "This thing weighs more than a brick."

She puffed out her chest. "I knew it was real."

"You're seriously a freak, do you know that?" He looked amazed. "If your dreams can come true, then tell me, what are the winning lottery numbers for this week?"

Chapter 5

Kerry sat at the foot of her bed cross-legged with the Golden Horse on her lap. There were too many unanswered questions. Like, who abandoned it? Why couldn't she see them in her dream? The thing that bothered her most about the dream was the lack of people; a lonely river and a lonely artefact.

"It was clearly an offering to the gods," said Gavin. He paced up and down her bedroom: window to bed, window to bed. His flurry of excitement made her nervous.

"But it doesn't make sense. Nobody would offer a prestigious object without a ritual. There was no ceremony, there weren't any people."

Gavin pointed at the Golden Horse. "That thing must be over a kilo of solid gold. I'll bet it's worth a lot of money. We should get it valued. Oliver could help us. If we sell it to the right collector-"

"I'm not selling it, it's mine." Kerry traced her fingers over the golden mane and around the wheel, feeling the smoothness. "It wasn't shown to me in my dream to make money."

"What do you suppose it all means, you having a dream like that?" said Gavin.

"I don't know." Kerry cradled the Golden Horse against her chest. It was definitely Iron Age and definitely sacrificial. But the Iron Age was poorly represented in British prehistory. What were the odds of her finding a valuable Celtic artefact that even in its time represented a vast amount of wealth?

Gavin stopped pacing. "Maybe you might have another dream tonight. There could be a hoard of golden artefacts waiting under the Thames."

"This wasn't a coincidence, Gavin." Kerry stared at

the Golden Horse, willing her memory to work. "There's something else, something I can't quite put my finger on."

"Like what? Was it part of a bigger collection?" Gavin snapped his fingers together. "You know, I'll bet it was an ornamental detail from a golden chariot. If we go back tomorrow, we might find some more pieces."

"No, nothing like that. That's not what I meant. I think my dream happened after the Golden Horse was offered to the river. That's why I was alone. It was there for all those centuries in the water and I found it now for a reason."

"Exactly - to sell. Listen, Kerry, I don't want you to think I'm obsessed with money here, but the only reason that I can see for you finding it is to sell it. Think about it. We're in the right place. Oliver knows this antiques business like the back of his hand. We could sell it and go off travelling again for another half a year. We never even made it to Australia and New Zealand."

Kerry sighed. "I don't want Oliver and Jenna to know about it, OK? It's mine. I'm keeping it."

Gavin's face fell. "What are you going to do with it - wear it round your neck? Let it sit around gathering dust?"

"I didn't say I wanted to keep it indefinitely. I need time to think about why it came to me," she snapped.

"Well, just remember you invited me along to share in your discovery. That makes me part of it too." His voice was cold, offended. "I really think you should consider how much we could make from it."

"I will," said Kerry.

Gavin's voice relaxed. "Listen, I'm going to go out for a walk and pick us up some takeout, alright? Oliver and Jenna must still be at work. You have a think about what you want to do while I'm gone."

Kerry didn't look up from her Golden Horse.

49

"OK. Can you get me a chicken korma with some garlic nan? And a diet coke."

"I was thinking Chippy."

"Ham omelette then with loads of ketchup."

Gavin ruffled her hair. "Back in twenty."

He clicked the door shut behind him. Kerry lifted the Golden Horse with both hands, careful not to drop it on her bare feet. Where could she put it while she thought about what to do with it? She looked around the room. On top of the dresser.

If only she could recall more of her dream. Who had put it there? What had they looked like? Who were these people?

She propped the Golden Horse up on the dresser, then stood back to admire it. It outshone everything else in the room. Kerry sat on the end of her bed and stretched out her hands to make a circle around the artefact with her fingertips and thumbs. A sudden inspiration took her.

Her travel-art supplies were in her bag under the bed. She got out her A3 sketchpad, graphite pencils and her set of watercolours. Once she got settled, she would buy some proper canvas and oil paints, but for now, this would suffice. She balanced the sketchpad on her lap. A quick glance at the Golden Horse showed her that all the perspective lines in the room drew her eye to it; she traced them through thin air with her pencil. She touched lead to paper and began to outline the shape of the horse and the wheel in an off-centre position on the pad. Once she had sketched in the Golden Horse, she drew wavy lines to show the reeds as they had been in her dream. She dotted in the rough V-shape of the birch and ash platform, then began filling in the shape of the wooden branches with dark heavy lines. She plotted in a straight, horizontal line to show the edge of the gentle, marshy river Thames and more reeds on the other side. Using light strokes of the pencil, she gave shadow and tone to the picture and rubbed her sweaty thumb on the page for shading.

Kerry stopped and looked at her work. She hadn't drawn herself in the picture. But why would she? She was only there in a dream. She wanted to capture the real moment in antiquity; the day the Golden Horse had been offered to the river.

With her eyes closed, she imagined herself standing on the ancient jetty, nearly two thousand years ago. The image returned to her, clear as day. She flipped over to a new sheet in her sketchpad.

Her hand touched paper and moved as though guided by an unseen force. An energy took hold of her; streaming from her mind, down her arm and spouting onto the page. She could see herself standing on the jetty, but facing inland, instead of out over the marshy river. She started with details far away. In the distance four roundhouses: she dotted these onto her page with an HB pencil. The conical rooftops were made of hay, which she coloured using yellow, green and brown lines, all mixed to form a mustard colour. She showed the wooden walls by dashing horizontal interlacing dark brown lines. The roundhouses had an outer layer of wattle and daub which she coloured with khaki pencil; water would give it a nice wash later. She used a 2B pencil to imply heavy smoke rising from one of the roundhouses. These were farmsteads.

Using dashed lines in dark brown pencil, she sketched a perimeter fence of birch and ash around the settlement. The thicker posts were staked into the ground; she coloured those a lighter brown for differentiation. She drew a cow the size of her thumbnail and a couple of goats the size of her pinky nail to indicate the distance, far from the marshy, dangerous Thames.

Kerry used her HB pencil to sketch a small crowd of people gathered on the banks of the river, near the wooden platform. The men, women and children wore simple belted tunics. The women's tunic-dresses were dyed in bright colours; red, blue, green, yellow, with embroidered detail on the hems. Their darkly checked leggings, cloaks and leather boots suggested the cool climate of their ancient environment. The women wore their hair loose. All of the men wore their long hair tied at the neck. A few men wore leather caps. Some of the men wore simpler tunics and no cloaks and had short beards and moustaches. A few men wore ornate clothing, with embroidered hems and carried swords in scabbards. These noble men had cleanly shaven chins and long moustaches that hung in twisted strands on either side of their mouths.

In the foreground, Kerry sketched two men standing on the jetty, both wearing long white robes. They were Celtic priests, Druids overseeing a ceremony of great importance. Behind them, the aristocracy, warriors, farmers and artisans of society all watched from the shore.

The old, silver-haired man dominated the foreground of the picture. He wore a laurel wreath on his head and had a huge torc around his neck. It was plain, except for the elaborate horse-head terminals that rested on his collarbone. She filled in the eyes of the horse motifs with red pencil to show the inset wax and coloured the torc with both grey and yellow pencils. This implied the delicate Mercury gilding, giving a silver appearance below a thin coating of gold-plating to simulate solid gold. Kerry was happy with her interpretation of the colours, as they would have been in real life.

The young, dark-haired man stood near him, but further back towards the shore. Like the older man, he wore a laurel wreath. He had a golden torc of twisted bronze around his neck and wore a chunky armlet of cast bronze. It had enamelled roundels fixed in place with iron discs, a design to depict the sun. His simple white tunic was roped at the waist. He wore sandals showing Roman influence with leather straps that fastened around the ankle.

Only one thing was missing. Who stood at the end of the jetty, poised to offer the Golden Horse to the water? Who stood where Kerry had been in her dream, witnessing the end result of the ceremony; the lonely artefact sacrificed to the whims of the gods?

Kerry flipped over one more page and concentrated hard.

She started with his face. A well-defined jaw and high cheekbones. His blonde moustache fell to touch his neck. His blue eyes were captivating, his expression showing determination and humility in the face of the gods. He had a strong, furrowed brow. He gazed to the right of the picture. Kerry highlighted the right side of his face white to show the morning sun in the East as he stood on the jetty. He was young and handsome in his early thirties, an incredibly strong warrior in the prime of his life. Around his neck, he wore a heavy, gold torc. Unlike the Druid priest, the warrior's torc was of solid gold, not Mercury gilding. It was twisted around a core of alder. Kerry coloured it yellow to match his hair.

A golden man. He wore a ceremonial golden, two-horned helmet. It was made of cast bronze with a coating of gold. How did she know this? Kerry wracked her brain to think but couldn't. Automatic pilot, automatic thought. The engravings showed scroll motifs in high relief; Kerry felt her artistic skills pushed to the limit trying to depict the raised decoration, which she achieved with a hint of shadow from the morning sun. Bronze studs in symmetrical formation held the sheet bronze sections of the helmet together. At the base of the helmet, which rested upon the Golden Man's forehead, were symmetrical patterns produced with basket weaving texturing and detailed with leaf designs and mistletoe berries.

Kerry drew rows of yellow circles to show each golden loop of his chainmail vest. He carried a large iron sword in a sheath at his hip. The brass hilt and scabbard were inlaid with red and yellow enamel; she coloured a row of squares to show this. The front plate where the hilt met the iron sword had engraved loops in scroll motif to match his helmet.

When Kerry had finished, she held the picture at arm's length to survey the bearer of the Golden Horse, which now rested on her dresser. Who was this gorgeous, Golden Man?

She lay back on her bed, cradling her sketchpad against her chest. Her images had been incredibly detailed. Had the pictures come from her imagination, or an unknown inspiration, a more mystical source? She had a good knowledge of Celtic Art, and of Iron Age warfare, but not to draw in such detail without a subject in front of her.

Movement registered in the corner of her eye. Kerry sat bolt upright and froze.

In the twilight shadows of the room, she could make out a face. His face: The Golden Man. But there was nothing golden about the grey phantasm near her dresser, a transparent apparition that stared straight at her. He was tall and powerfully built, filling the doorframe. He wore the two-horned helmet and chain-mail vest she had drawn only moments before. His brow was creased; she couldn't tell whether in anger or deep concentration. One thing was certain though; concentration on her.

She gasped.

Without taking his eyes off her, the ghostly warrior lifted his hand and reached, slowly, towards her Golden Horse on the dresser.

Kerry screamed.

Chapter 6

"Kerry?"

Gavin dropped the takeaway food and rushed to her. Kerry lay face down on the floor. Her sketchpad and watercolours lay around her. Gavin gathered her in his arms and raised her into a sitting position. She slumped, still unconscious.

"Kerry!"

Gavin gently patted her cheek.

"Wake up."

She opened her eyes and blinked.

"Stay away!" She swiped her hands at Gavin's face. He caught her wrists to steady her.

"Calm down, Kerry. What happened?"

She pointed a shaking finger towards the door. Gavin looked behind. Nothing there.

"What is it?"

She wet her lips but didn't say anything. He helped her onto the end of the bed. Her body trembled in his arms. This was more than a fainting spell; she was terrified. Her eyes flitted from the door to the dresser and back. Gavin put his hand on her chin and turned her face towards his. "Kerry, what the hell happened?" he said.

"He- he came in here."

"He? Who?" Gavin looked from the dresser to the door and a sudden rage overcame him. "Oliver?"

Kerry shook her head. "The Golden Man. He took my Golden Horse."

"What do you mean, 'Golden Man'?" said Gavin. "You aren't making any sense. Did someone hurt you?" Adrenaline surged.

"No. I was drawing. I put the Golden Horse on top of the dresser to sketch it and then he appeared." A wild look came to her eyes.

"He? Who's he? Tell me."

"The man from my drawing."

Gavin's anger ebbed. "It's OK, Kerry, I think you fell asleep. You must've had a nightmare."

Tears rolled down her face. "It wasn't a nightmare. Look at this drawing."

She leaned over the edge of her bed and retrieved her sketchpad from the floor. Gavin looked at the drawing thrust under his nose. Since when had Kerry got so good? The detail in her picture was incredible; an excellent depiction of a Celtic warrior in golden armour.

"Did you do this?" he said.

Kerry's eyes blazed. "Of course I did. Don't you think I can draw that well?"

Gavin faltered. "I didn't mean to imply-"

"I'd barely finished drawing when I saw this ghostly form over there reach for the Golden Horse." She pointed a shaking finger towards the dresser. "Go on, look for yourself and see. You won't find it."

Gavin didn't see the Golden Horse behind the dresser or anywhere else on the floor. He looked under the bed, doing a quick sweep with his hand among her bags. Nothing there. He looked on the bedside table, in the wardrobe and above it. Nowhere.

"It's not there, is it?" she said, in a shaking voice.

There had to be a reasonable explanation. Gavin took a deep breath and exhaled. "You must have hidden it somewhere. I've heard of people doing things in their sleep that they can't remember when they wake up."

She watched him with pursed lips. "It wasn't like that. I told you, I didn't hide it in my sleep. He took it."

She looked so desperate he thought it best not to argue with her. Gavin picked up the takeaway food. "Why don't we eat? You'll feel better in a bit."

"Don't patronise me, Gavin." Kerry swept her hair out of her face. "Yesterday I thought I was dreaming, and it turned out to be real. So why not this time?"

He sat down beside her on the edge of the bed.

"OK, so supposing you did see a ghost - or whatever you want to call it. It still doesn't explain how the Golden Horse could vanish. Ghosts can't take physical objects, can they?"

"How should I know what ghosts can and can't do - I'd never seen one before this," she said.

Gavin didn't know what to say to that. Kerry opened her ham omelette and started shovelling fork-loads into her mouth. Maybe she'd be calmer after dinner and they could work out a rational explanation for the missing Golden Horse. All the commotion had given him an appetite too. He munched on a chip in one hand while he leafed through Kerry's sketches with the other.

"These are really good, especially this Druid stuff," he said. The picture of pagan life seemed so real. He cast a sideways glance at her. Apart from a few rough sketches while they were in Asia, Kerry hardly practised drawing at all. And any pictures she did took her hours. How did she manage to not only draw three incredibly detailed pictures, but within an hour of him going to get food and returning?

Gavin flicked over another page and saw her impression of the Golden Horse caught in a bed of reeds in the Thames. "You don't think these dreams and your drawings are anything to do with, well you know, witchcraft?"

Kerry stopped eating. "Maybe that's one way of putting it. But I'd prefer to call it supernatural. Witchcraft has an ugly ring to it, doesn't it?"

He closed her sketchbook. "Don't get me wrong, I

don't believe in the supernatural. I reckon there's a rational explanation for everything - including witchcraft and including all this stuff about the Golden Horse."

Her brow creased. "What are you getting at?"

Gavin walked to the door and opened it. There were no sounds from the landing. He shut the door tight and lowered his voice. "I'm saying that earlier, when we talked about getting the Golden Horse priced, maybe we weren't alone."

Kerry looked alarmed. "I know we weren't - the Golden Man followed us back from the river."

"I'm not talking about the *ghost*, Kerry, I'm talking about Oliver. I'll bet he heard us and took it-"

"I told you a ghost took it! How many times do I have to say it?"

Gavin closed his eyes. This was going to be hard. "I was about to say, after you saw that figment appear and you passed out."

"I know you don't believe me, so what are you suggesting?" She sounded hurt; he hated hearing that tone in her voice.

"It's not that - of course I believe you. Do you not think that earlier was the most mental thing I've ever seen? I mean, you dream of something that turns out to be real. If I hadn't seen it with my own eyes, I wouldn't have believed it. But facts are facts, Kerry. You have lost a valuable artefact and I'm sure a ghost didn't take it."

"But, why would Oliver or Jenna take it?"

"They're into witchcraft, aren't they? Maybe they want to use it in a ritual, who the hell knows? They're pagans and it's a pagan artefact. For all we know, they might think they own it in some way. He's an antiques dealer and she's a white witch, after all."

Kerry chewed her lip. "Oliver doesn't need it. He

has enough Celtic artefacts as it is. Unless there was some significance about it... do you think? What kind of ritual?"

"They've both been going on about some Beltaine festival or other since we met them. I'm sure they could come up with a million uses for such a thing at their pagan feasts. I wouldn't put it past Jenna to see it as some kind of pagan omen for Mayday. Didn't she herself say they celebrate the solstices and the first of May?"

"I don't think we should start pointing fingers without any proof though, Gavin. They've been good to us so far. Maybe we could ask them if they've seen it, or at the very least, tell them about what I saw. They're not likely to think I'm mad. They might even know who the Golden Man is," said Kerry.

"I don't care about that. If there's a spirit here, all I can say is they caused it. What I care about is your stolen property. What kind of people invite strangers in under the pretence of friendship, then rob them? It isn't right. I'm going to get to the bottom of this." Gavin marched to the door.

"Where are you going?" Kerry's voice was high-pitched with fear.

"To get your property back," he said.

Gavin went downstairs. He hadn't seen either Oliver or Jenna in the reception room or kitchen and hadn't heard them on his way up, but he wouldn't give up so easily. If they were out, all the better. He would sneak into their room as they had most likely done to Kerry, and he would take back the Golden Horse.

There were two doors next to the reception room, both adorned with wreaths. He tried the middle door. Bathroom. Onto the next one; their bedroom. So they *were* a couple after all. Even after their flirting with Kerry - with both of them - over dinner.

Gavin went in. A pentagram had been chalked onto the bare wooden floorboards next to the door. Two empty drinking vessels made of bronze, an hourglass full of blue sand and a big purple silk bag with a drawstring lay next to it. Could the Golden Horse be inside the bag? Nope; only a handful of pebble-sized blue stones. Lapis Luzuli? He didn't know geology that well. There were two white candles on top of the headboard. Jenna and Oliver liked to display artefacts, yet the Golden Horse was nowhere in sight.

The wall above the bed showed a Celtic frieze in a dark wood. Alder? He didn't know types of wood any better than he knew types of stones, but he remembered studying that the Druids liked oak, birch, ash, alder or dogwood for their ceremonies. Oak was pale, birch silvery, and he guessed the rest were dark. The bed sheets were the simple white linen kind. It didn't look to be the scene of the raucous sex he'd heard the previous night; he'd expected something kinky, like chains or a sex-swing, perhaps. Gavin searched the room. No Golden Horse stood out among the white, brown and green décor. There were more white candles on the bedside table and a small bookshelf adorned with a pentagram that housed occult titles: *Self initiation into the Golden Age of Aquarius by Enya Dunn; The Sacred Oak Tree by Gunoda Fordham; Candle Magic and Witchcraft in Practise by Ben M. Kendall.*

Gavin couldn't resist. Had Jenna's candles triggered Kerry's ESP? Or caused some kind of hallucination that had led Kerry to think a ghost had taken her Golden Horse, to cover for their own crime? He flicked open the book on candle magic. A couple of pages were marked:

Orange candles are to be used for creativity and

growth, for boosting self-esteem and building confidence.
Jenna had put her own pencil-written note in the margin:
To help Kerry and Gavin settle in quickly and be reproductive at work.

Gavin scoffed; she'd written 'reproductive' instead of 'productive'. Jenna had sex on the brain. He closed the book, feeling a twinge of guilt. Whether Jenna's candle magic had been real or not, she had tried to cast a spell on them for good, not evil purposes. Was it right that he should go snooping in their house? He reproached them for theft, yet here he was trespassing; committing another criminal act.

But the value of the stolen Golden Horse outweighed his guilty conscience. He tossed the book back onto the bed and went next door to search their bathroom.

Nothing.

He looked at the stairs leading to the lower ground level. Could the Golden Horse be in the dining room? Seemed like a weird place to put it, but he had to check everywhere, to be sure.

Gavin put his ear to the door and listened. He could hear footsteps and voices. His heart beat faster. He was ready for the confrontation. One way or another, he would get Kerry's Golden Horse back, or at least uncover the mystery of what had happened to it.

He knocked and waited. He heard the slap of bare feet on tiles and saw the handle turn. The door pulled back. Gavin inhaled, ready to ask his question. His mouth fell open.

A young woman stood at ease, completely naked. Her long, white-blonde hair hung around her pale, pert breasts. Her posture was relaxed, and she smiled as comfortably as if she were fully clothed. She did nothing to cover her modesty, allowing Gavin an eyeful of her nakedness.

"Hello," she said. "Are you looking for some-one?"

"Oh - sorry to interrupt," he said, struggling to stay composed.

"You must be looking for Ollie. He's in the kitchen. I'll get him."

Gavin took a step back. "It's OK. I'll talk to him later. You're obviously busy."

She gave a teasing smile. "You could come in, if you want?"

"Err, no thanks." Gavin gulped and turned.

"Suit yourself." She turned, exposing her shapely ass, and smiled at him over her shoulder.

Gavin forced his eyes away from her bare, milky form. He went back upstairs, feeling drained. Yet another mysterious woman. And where was Jenna? Was Oliver having an affair? His head spun. He tried to gather his thoughts and stay focussed on the Golden Horse. But the sight of the provocative girl kept clouding his thoughts.

Chapter 7

Kerry's head swam with thoughts of the previous evening; the ghost, the missing Golden Horse and after Gavin's fruitless search to find it, his reports of the flirtatious nude girl in the dining room. She dawdled on the Herne's Hunt rooftop long after she had potted the plants for Mistress C, trailing her fingers through the crumbly earth. The plants stank of unfamiliar pungent herbs. She looked at her watch; quarter past twelve. Jenna would have started her shift already. What should she say to her? Gavin hadn't said much about the naked girl, other than she had seemed blasé about her nudity. Kerry didn't know Jenna well enough to break the bad news.

Potential bad news. What if Oliver wasn't having an affair, what if the girl had come over for one of their pagan rituals? Besides, there were more pressing issues. Like, where was her Golden Horse? Had one of them really taken it, or had it been the ghostly man?

Kerry sat back on her haunches and stared across the rooftops, her thoughts on the ghost. Once she had gotten over her fear of the initial shock, she had been intrigued. He hadn't seemed to want to cause her harm. He wanted the Golden Horse, nothing more.

Why didn't he want her?

What on earth was she thinking? Was she seriously lusting after a ghost? Yes, she was. Last night too, as she lay on Gavin's sofa-bed, head to toe with him. Gavin was such a nice friend to put up with her and let her sleep in his room. He was her best friend; good, solid, dependable Gavin. But he was a follower, not a leader. Boyfriend material? Definitely not. She wanted an older man for a relationship, someone with more experience. Someone decisive who could lead when times got tough. Gavin couldn't get tough with anyone. Last night he had come back upstairs with no Golden Horse in his hand looking to her for what to do next, despite the fact that he had been the one to insist on retrieving it from Oliver in the first place.

Gavin was too flighty; he wasn't the type for commitment. He wanted fun, travel, adventure. She wanted those things too, with a man she could connect with in a deeper way.

She wanted someone like... the Golden Man.

Kerry lay back on the rooftop and succumbed to laughter, letting the joke escape her body; she was infatuated with a man who had lived two thousand years ago, a man who could only come to life in her paintings. He was a long dead warrior who visited her as a ghostly presence and not for any romantic liaison, but to reclaim his long lost property.

She caressed her shoulder, then arm, then midriff with her right hand; the hand that had created the image of the Golden Man. She closed her eyes, imagining he had his arms around her; that he stroked her in a loving embrace. The Golden Man was a warrior among his people. They had stood, watching him from the banks of the Thames. Even the Druids revered him. Had he died because of the Golden Horse? Had he sacrificed his priceless offering to the gods in exchange for a dangerous wish? Her hand rested in the folds of her dress, caught in the crook between her legs.

"Kerry?"

Kerry jolted upright into a seated position. Jenna stood in the rooftop doorway. She cringed; Jenna had seen her touching herself like an idiot.

"I thought you might need a hand," said Jenna.

Kerry saw a hint of a teasing smile on Jenna's face,

which she wiped clear once she'd been spotted. What did that mean? Jenna was good at double entendres; either it was innuendo hinting at a lesbian encounter, or she genuinely wanted to help pot the plants. Kerry doubted she meant the plants. Jenna might be a white witch, but what about her attempted seduction over dinner?

"I've already finished, actually." Kerry scrambled to her feet.

"I can see that. You did a good job. Why didn't you come back down?" said Jenna.

Kerry tried to give a nonchalant shrug but failed. "Oh, well you know, I was daydreaming up here. My mind drifted and I lost track of time."

"That can happen on this rooftop, I've done it myself. Don't worry, I dream about him too," said Jenna.

"Huh? Dream about who?"

Jenna looked coy. "You should know. He's been very good to us both."

Heat prickled Kerry's neck and face. "Who, Oliver? Gosh, no! I wouldn't think about your boyfriend in that way. I don't like him like that. I mean, he's a friend of my dad's."

"Oliver isn't my boyfriend, he's a means to an end," said Jenna.

Kerry paused. What on earth was she talking about? It seemed they were having two separate conversations. Was Jenna talking about Oliver, or did she know something more? Kerry couldn't help but get the feeling again that Jenna was reading her thoughts. Jenna would keep playing her enigmatic games if she didn't come up with some tactics to get the information she needed. Time for action.

"I hope Gavin and I didn't bother you too much last night - we were being a bit loud."

"I wasn't in. I'm sure Ollie didn't mind - he didn't mention it."

"Oh, so you weren't home last night?"

"No. I came to see Mistress C last night. She and I were having a great girly chat, well into the early hours, so I stayed over here. You must've noticed there are a couple of rooms on the second floor? She lives here with Morfan."

"She lives here?" Kerry recalled seeing two doors on her way to the rooftop. "But, it's too small."

"It's a temporary thing while they get settled into modern London life."

What did she mean by that?

Still, she had been pleased with the outcome of her own games; to know that two things were clear. Jenna had been out the previous night, which meant that she hadn't taken the Golden Horse, and she didn't know about the naked girl who had been with Oliver. But neither of those things shed light on the mystery of her missing artefact.

"Jenna, I've got a quick question. I had an ornament, a Golden Horse in my room and I seem to have misplaced it. You wouldn't have seen it about by any chance, would you? It's stylised with a golden wheel behind it. It's quite precious to me."

"Are you asking me if I've seen it, or are you asking me do I have it?" Jenna said.

Kerry squirmed. "Sorry, I... I didn't mean it to come across that way. It's very special to me, that's all."

"No and no. I haven't seen it and I don't have it."

"I didn't mean to be rude - of course you aren't a thief. It was wrong of me to-"

"Oliver has it," said Jenna.

"Pardon me?"

"Don't worry, you'll get it back. We didn't want to

alarm you."

"Oliver took it? I don't understand."

"I took it," said Jenna.

Kerry studied Jenna for any trace of a smile. So Gavin had been right - it wasn't the Golden Man. Was this a joke? "Why would you take it?"

"You had a dream and you went and found it, right?"

"Yes, it's mine," Kerry said. "Wait a sec, how did you know?"

"It's tainted. It's pretty simple, really. It was buried in the mud for thousands of years. Now that it has been uncovered, the ghost of the former owner has been called back from the Otherworld to reclaim it."

"How do you know all this?"

"Because it's a sign. A sign that his old way of life has been restored on earth. If it sees the light of day, so too does he," said Jenna.

"So, he's here to stay?"

"I suppose so. And since you brought the tainted object home, now you and Gavin and the house have to be cleansed."

Kerry forced herself to think straight. "Why didn't you tell me this last night? You didn't have to go into my room and take it without letting me know. Not to mention, leaving me lying passed out on the floor."

"I'm sorry about that Kerry. I heard you scream, and I dashed upstairs. I saw you unconscious, but I checked your pulse, so I had to tend to the talisman first. I saw him lingering around it - I recognised him from a dream I had a couple of nights ago. He was a shade, he couldn't touch it, but not for lack of trying. So I shielded my eyes from the talisman, gathered it in my dress, making sure my bare skin didn't touch it, and took it straight out

68

of the house to Mistress C for her advice on the matter. She's much more knowledgeable than I."

"Mistress C knows about this?" Kerry gritted her teeth. "I'd like my artefact back now, please."

"You'll get it back after the ceremony. I'm afraid it isn't very simple."

This was starting to irritate her. "What exactly isn't so simple?"

"Tomorrow is Beltaine. I've already told you how important that date is to us - I'm sure Oliver and Mistress C have done so too, so you can imagine that we already had events planned to celebrate it, but now this has happened. If dark forces from the Otherworld, Avalon, are brought into our world on a day of heightened spiritual energy, there could be serious negative repercussions," said Jenna.

"Like what?" Kerry shouted, spit flying from her mouth.

"Come downstairs, Mistress C can explain it better." Jenna reached for Kerry's hand, but Kerry pulled away.

"Is she some kind of, I don't know, grand high witch or warlock, or other?"

"You could say that. I think of her as more of a priestess," said Jenna.

Alarm bells rang, warning Kerry not to get involved in any of their witchcraft. What if they made her sacrifice a goat as part of an initiation ceremony, or worse? Gavin had said each to their own, but he had also hinted that the pagan practises might be having an effect on her, and for reasons that she couldn't explain, supernatural occurrences were happening to her, whether she liked to admit so or not. Furthermore, she couldn't deny that however reticent to join in any pagan ceremonies, a large part of her felt intrigued by the Golden Man.

"Will you participate in our ceremony? Or even just speak with Mistress C about it?" said Jenna.

Kerry walked towards the stairs. "I'll talk to her first to see what it involves. But, I have to be honest, when I think of the Golden Man, I don't feel any harm. If he's a ghost, he can't touch me, right?"

"No, he can't touch you, but some other evil forces from Avalon will try to enter through the opening between this world and the Otherworld which you have created, and we need to cleanse the talisman of all negative energy." Jenna led the way downstairs. "Mistress C can tell you more."

Kerry was alarmed. "What would this cleansing ceremony involve? Not animal sacrifice, or anything like that?"

Jenna curled her lip. "A few simple incantations and a bit of candle magic, that's all."

"And that will really be enough to cleanse my Golden Horse?"

"I'm pretty positive that, yes, it will." Jenna pressed her lips together.

"*Pretty* positive?"

Jenna's eyebrows turned upwards. "That's why I want you to talk to Mistress C."

Mistress C came out of the kitchen to meet them at the bottom of the stairs. "Did I hear someone mention me?"

"Yes. Can you explain to Kerry about the procedure for our Beltaine celebration tomorrow? *Because* of the Golden Horse."

Kerry looked from Jenna to Mistress C. Did Jenna think she hadn't seen her eyes widen as she emphasised the word 'because'. What was it Jenna wanted Mistress C to tell her; or perhaps to withhold from her?

They sat down in armchairs in the restaurant, with Jenna and Mistress C facing Kerry; she shifted her focus from one to the other, careful not to miss anything.

"Certainly, I'll tell her. I'd be pleased to," said Mistress C. "Firstly, I'll answer the questions that I can see ready on the tip of your tongue. Yes, we will borrow the Golden Horse until it is cleansed tomorrow, after which you shall have it back. And yes, you will be visited by the Golden Man again tonight."

Kerry felt as though a fish-hook pulled from the pit of her stomach. "His ghost will come to me again?"

"Not a ghost, but in your sleep. It isn't safe for the living to retain too much connection with those in the Otherworld. Tonight, I will prepare you a tea to ward him off so that he may be permitted to visit you only in your dreams," said Mistress C.

"But - but what if I don't want to ward him off," said Kerry.

Mistress C's mouth puckered. "Strange, I didn't take you for a fool. You will drink the tea and keep Avalon at bay. If the channel in Oliver's house is open to one, it will be open to worse. I forbid you to put everyone at risk."

"I can brew her the tea, if you prepare the ingredients for it," said Jenna.

"That would be best." Mistress C fixed Kerry with a maternal stare. "And make sure you drink it."

Kerry processed all the information carefully. "If I hadn't asked you about the Golden Horse, Jenna, were you going to tell me?"

"Of course. That's why I came up onto the roof. But then I found you a bit preoccupied." Jenna smirked.

Kerry cringed. She let the powerful scent of the black candles wipe away her embarrassment. The heavy perfume had a strange, twofold effect; clouding and unclouding her mind at the same time.

"Tomorrow is our celebration of Beltaine, where we cleanse impurities with fire." Mistress C's voice sounded as though projected through a long tunnel. "Your Golden Horse represents a deity - the God of the Sun. Since fire and the sun are one and the same, the token has been offered back to us from Avalon. It's a symbol, a gift, and we must use it carefully. But first, we must restore it to purity."

Kerry's head swirled. She gathered the last of her brainpower amidst the smoke to recall Gavin's words; *I wouldn't put it past Jenna to see it as some kind of pagan sign for Mayday.* He was right. They did see it as a symbol to use it for ritual.

"After the Golden Horse is cleansed tomorrow, will I not be able to see the Golden Man's ghost any more?"

"No. But you will need to take part in the ceremony no matter what. And Gavin too."

"What would happen if I didn't?"

Mistress C sat forward. "The Golden Horse was a vessel for his strength during his lifetime. Once offered to Avalon, it became a talisman for his soul. I can only predict, but I would guess one of two things might happen. The ghost you saw owns it in the Otherworld, and now you are the new owner in this world. That creates a rift; a gap, whereby spirits, good and evil can move between worlds. If your soul was to become attracted to the darkness and chose to tear free of its flesh and blood form."

"Then what would happen?" Kerry leaned forward.

"With neither talisman nor flesh, you could get lost

forever in Avalon, a mindless wandering spirit if you like, vulnerable to evil forces. It would be a fate worse than death."

"That can happen to a soul?"

Mistress C gave a solemn nod. "It would be a pitiful, non-existence, the worst fate imaginable."

Blood pounded in Kerry's ears. What would it be like to be dead? Deader than dead?

Jenna jumped up. "Let me get us some soothing tea."

"For the ceremony tomorrow, you must wear the clothing you had on when you found the Golden Horse. Gavin will need to do the same. Do you remember what you had on yesterday?" said Mistress C.

"Yes. I wore my green dress."

Jenna returned from the kitchen with the tea. "That's perfect. Green is a good colour to invoke the magic we'll need."

"Tomorrow, after the Golden Horse is cleansed and blessed, it will become a talisman for the living again - your talisman. We have to instil it with pure energy and drive out the residue of the spirit world. The gods of the spirit world will no longer control it," said Mistress C.

Kerry drained her tea in three painful gulps, feeling the liquid burn her throat. Her eyes watered. She wiped them on her sleeve. The dregs in the bottom of her cup showed a horse-shaped pattern with a spoked wheel behind. Jenna and Mistress C were right; the residue of the Otherworld was attached to her.

"When I drink the tea tonight, will it keep me safe from any harmful spirits?"

Mistress C gave a thin-lipped smile. "Try not to worry. Ghosts of the past will show in your dreams but won't be able to hurt you. And the Golden Man himself means you no harm."

Jenna pressed her lips to her own teacup, but not before Kerry had seen her envious expression.

"When did you dream of him, Jenna?" said Kerry.

"The Golden Man? The same night you did."

Kerry felt a sudden chill. "How do you know what I dreamed?"

Jenna's eyes were wide and innocent. "Because I saw you in the dream too, standing on the pier. And I also saw him. He led me away as I tried to come to you. I didn't see the Golden Horse in the river. He meant for you to find it."

Mistress C reached towards Kerry and placed her hand on top of hers. "It would do you best to stay with the living for the time being. Breathe the scent of the black candles. They banish fears. They help you to leave behind old worries and open your mind to new possibilities. We all need a little help from time to time."

Kerry took a deep breath. "I'll be honest with you both. I'm not keen on the idea of taking part in a pagan ceremony tomorrow. But it seems I have no choice. Whether or not I believe in your Otherworld isn't the issue here - I have a connection with that Golden Horse. I found it without either of your influence, so I believe that there are..." She paused to think of the right words. "Forces acting on me that I don't understand. And since you both know more about what is happening, I'll put my trust in you to keep me, and Gavin, safe."

Jenna crossed to Kerry and sat on the armrest of her chair. She placed an arm around her shoulders. "I'm glad Kerry. I promise you nothing dangerous will happen to you tomorrow and once your Golden Horse is cleansed, you will have it back. Our ways - that is to say, the lifestyle Oliver, and Mistress C, and Morfan and I lead - is more

74

about aligning us with the natural world and that includes the spirit world. It should be harmonious, but only if it's all kept in balance. Everything will be fine after our celebration, darling."

Darling? Kerry looked up at Mistress C for reassurance. "There won't be any more ghostly visitations?"

Mistress C gave a soothing smile. "No. You needn't be afraid of that."

Kerry sank back into her armchair. Despite her relief, she couldn't suppress her disappointment.

Chapter 8

Gavin had spent the morning preparing Victorian paintings for auction in the saleroom of Sequana's. After that, Oliver had made him move antique furniture into the front of the store. Lacquered chests and ebony trunks; heavy work. He stopped for a breather.

"Doing alright there, Gavin?" said Oliver.

"Sure," said Gavin, stretching his back.

"I've just finished the stock take, so how about we lock up for lunch? I could do with a good ale."

"Sounds fine by me."

"Glad to hear you say it. We have to get all the catalogue numbers ready for the bank holiday auction when we come back, so you'll be glad of the alcohol break."

"I'm gladder not to be lugging any more chests or tables into the warehouse."

Oliver gave a false laugh and slapped him on the back. "You're a fine strong lad but trust me you'll be wanting to do more manual work before the day's out."

Gavin followed him out the front and Oliver locked up. They started down the street.

"Aren't we taking the car?" said Gavin.

"We're only going a few doors," said Oliver. "The Balor is round the back anyway. Too bad you had to walk this morning - I'm sure you wanted another ride in her. I had to get an early start to do the stock take, otherwise it would've taken me days and we're closed tomorrow."

Of course; the first of May. "No worries, I enjoyed the walk this morning actually, it was a good chance to jog."

Oliver pointed out the Apollo restaurant several doors down and Gavin saw the ostentatious front as they approached. It had a beer garden on the street, enclosed by a wooden fence. There were potted trees and Neo-classical statues of gods on pedestals. Oliver took a seat at a table in front of a tall male god with a golden halo on his crown and real flaming torch in his hand. Not a bad representation of the sun god.

The waiter came to take their order. Gavin flipped to the drinks menu at the back.

"We'll have two of your finest. Briton Brew today, Mario," said Oliver.

Gavin tsked under his breath. What sort of way was that to say 'Mario'? He rolled the r to sound like an h. Oliver might have been nice to give them jobs, and generous with his money, but it didn't excuse the fact he was still a pretentious git. Not to mention an all-round sleaze: cheating on his missus and potentially a thief to top it off. Guilty until proven innocent where Kerry's valuable Golden Horse was concerned.

"I'll have a Stella instead," said Gavin.

Oliver gave a knowing nod. "You'll like this better. Best Yorkshire ale money can buy."

Gavin exhaled through his nose. "Sure. Why not?"

"I have the restaurateur deliver it specially as a favour to me," said Oliver.

"I can imagine," said Gavin. Rich people could do whatever they pleased. Oliver probably had enough dough to buy the whole restaurant too, if he wanted.

Mario returned with two wooden tankards, identical to the ones they had used at Oliver's feast. Gavin eyed Oliver's placid smile. It seemed obvious now; Oliver had supplied the statues, the utensils, probably the staff too, for all he knew. Gavin looked at the golden ale in the tankard set before him.

"Try that. Is that not the best ale you've ever

tasted?"

Gavin sipped and wiped froth from his lip on his sleeve. "Not bad."

Oliver puffed his chest out. "Maris Otter malt and a variety of traditional English hops."

"It's light though," said Gavin.

"Perfect for lunch, only four point two percent." Oliver opened his menu. "Order anything you want for lunch, it's on me. Though I highly recommend the moussaka."

Gavin perused his menu. Did that mean he was being given a choice, or that Oliver was going to order the moussaka for him? What was it with his new boss and *control*? He controlled his job, his living arrangements and whether or not he got to choose his own food.

"How's Kerry doing? Jenna said she had a fall last night," said Oliver.

Gavin searched Oliver's face. "She did. How did Jenna know?"

"She found her on the floor."

"So it was *Jenna*?"

Oliver frowned. "What was Jenna?"

Crap. "Err, I meant, did Jenna mention seeing anything in Kerry's room, a trinket, a Golden Horse about the size of my hand?"

"She did, as a matter of fact. And it's no trinket," said Oliver.

Gavin paused. "Does Jenna know where it is?"

"It's safe. I have it."

"You have it? What's going on?"

"We didn't steal it," said Oliver. "I have enough artefacts, as you must know by now, after being in my warehouse all morning. Jenna took it away because Kerry is in danger."

"In danger? From who?" Gavin's shoulders tensed. "If anyone hurts Kerry-"

"Nobody alive will hurt her. Kerry is in danger from herself."

Gavin leaned forwards. "I don't know what you mean by that."

Oliver looked serious. "Jenna saw the ghost in her room. *He* is attached to her now through the talisman. It needs to be cleansed, she needs to be cleansed - and so do you."

"I don't believe in ghosts. You know what I think? Jenna's candles made Kerry high. She hallucinated something." Gavin fell quiet. He wanted to believe that, but it didn't explain Kerry's dream and how she found the Golden Horse. Unless-

Gavin reeled. "That's it. I got it - the Golden Horse. You said so yourself - you have enough artefacts. This is some kind of game, isn't it? I'll bet the Golden Horse is one of your artefacts from Sequana's and Jenna put it by the Thames for Kerry to find. You wanted her to find it and think it's some kind of spiritual thing, cause you need her in your Beltaine festival tomorrow - for whatever reason."

Oliver laughed. "You have a vivid imagination, Gavin."

Mario returned to take their order, interrupting Gavin's thoughts. His anger ebbed; he felt foolish. What had he done? He had accused his boss of deception, without any evidence, or motivation.

"Greek salad for me, Mario. And Gavin will try the moussaka."

"Actually, I was going to order a Caesar salad."

"Nonsense." Oliver dismissed Gavin's order with a wave. "You'll need something with stodge after hauling all that furniture."

Gavin shrugged. "Whatever you say."

Mario left. Gavin stared at Oliver.

"Let me ask you something, Gavin. Have I given you any cause to think I'm playing games with you?"

Gavin shifted in his chair. "Not that I know of."

"And has Jenna been dishonest, to either you or Kerry, in any way?"

"I don't think so."

"Good. Because we haven't. So why would you think we set up a malicious trick with the talisman?"

Gavin shrugged. "Just joking. Kerry and I used to play pranks on each other at uni all the time. That's the kind of people we are."

Oliver drank his ale without taking his narrowed eyes off Gavin. "You might not believe in ghosts, Gavin, but Kerry does. Tomorrow, she will be taking part in our Beltaine cleansing ceremony. If you want to support your friend, I would suggest you take part too."

"You would suggest, like how you *suggested* I have Briton Brew ale and moussaka for lunch?"

For a second, Oliver stared at Gavin, straight-faced. Then he broke into a wide-mouthed laugh. "I like you, Gavvy. I told you I wouldn't have hired anyone with half the fire."

Gavvy? What a tit. Oliver raised his tankard. Gavin reluctantly bumped his tankard against Oliver's and they both drank.

He was off the hook, for now; Oliver seemed more relaxed, at any rate. Good; he'd bought it. There was no doubt in Gavin's mind that Oliver and Jenna were up to something. Kerry had never had any supernatural experiences before. She had never claimed to have seen a ghost. He would talk to Kerry later and see what Jenna had

80

told her. Which reminded him...

"How do you know Kerry plans to take part in your ceremony tomorrow?" said Gavin.

"Because Mistress C and Jenna will have told her why it's imperative that she does."

"*Imperative*? What sort of ceremony is it?"

"Oh, this and that. A few chants. Sacrifice and debauchery before the full moon." Oliver's tone was taunting. Gavin didn't rise to the bait.

Mario arrived with their dishes. "Are you talking witchcraft again?" said the waiter. He raised the corner of his mouth in a half-smile to Gavin. Gavin nodded to him.

"No, my friend. Only tricks," said Oliver.

Tricks? Mario must've thought the whole conversation was bull too. Regardless of whatever game Oliver was playing, Gavin needed to be there for Kerry. If she really *was* going to take part in a hokum ritual, better he was there to look out for her.

"What's my part in this celebration tomorrow?" he said.

Oliver looked impressed. "I'm glad you're making sense at last. I could've convinced you earlier by mentioning that you'll be paid double time tomorrow, since it's a bank holiday, and whilst astute, it wouldn't have been very classy of me."

Gavin ignored most of what Oliver said; the derogatory tone, the insult, the waffle - but double time? What kind of practises merited double time?

"All you have to do tomorrow is come down to the dining room wearing the clothes you had on when Kerry found *His* talisman by the Thames. The residue of the Otherworld is attached to you and the material possessions you wore. You'll have to be stripped of all negative energy. The rest of the purification ritual will be down to Jenna,

Saiorse and I."

"Saiorse? That's Glynn's daughter, isn't it?"

Saiorse. *Saiorse.* Of course; the naked girl who had given him bedroom eyes.

"She's taking part?"

"Naturally. Why do you think I was preparing her last night?" Oliver's lip twitched into a sordid smile. "Come now, you couldn't have forgotten so easily - she told me your eyes were on stalks."

Gavin clenched his fist around the handle of his tankard. "I wasn't that bad - I've seen naked girls before."

"Saiorse has an integral role to play tomorrow. She's a virgin."

Irritation changed to doubt. "You aren't going to sacrifice her, are you?"

Oliver's nostrils widened. "I wouldn't do anything that her father, Glynn, didn't approve of."

If Oliver didn't intend to sacrifice Saiorse, then what other way could a virgin be of use? Gavin pictured her seductive manner as she tried to invite him to join her. Oliver was going to *deflower* her.

"I thought Saiorse was still in high school?"

"She is. She's just turned eighteen. She saved herself for this event. A sweet maiden such as her wouldn't have kept her girlhood for long if it weren't for an important cause, believe me."

Hmm. The whole charade sounded dubious, if not illegal. "I hope Glynn isn't going to be there to see his daughter take part in... well, you know."

Oliver looked like the cat that had got the cream; smug git. "He won't. But he has put her under my protection. She's in London for the week to see Kings College. I'll be putting her in Mistress C's capable hands from tomorrow."

Tomorrow. The cleansing ceremony made sense, and the virgin deflowering, but there was still one thing left unexplained.

"What about that cauldron, Oliver? How many people are you planning to have for the Beltaine feast?"

"A small number, but enough. Beltaine is an ancient ceremony that marks the start of summer fruitfulness. There will be a celebration fit for the gods."

Cauldron. Virgins. Beltaine. Fruitfulness. Gavin gulped. "That cauldron's big enough to feed an army."

"The cauldron won't be for feasting. But trust me, you'll enjoy it nonetheless."

Gavin tried to drown his worries with ale but couldn't. If the cauldron wasn't for feasting, then what? Why would a fresh, eighteen year old Gaelic virgin come to a Beltaine festival, if not to be deflowered? And sacrificed for the feast? Prime Irish meat?

Gavin spluttered beer froth all over the table. As he reached for a napkin, he caught sight of a devious glint in Oliver's eye.

Chapter 9

Kerry flew through the low lying cloud. She swooped lower over the Tameses, her eyes scanning mile after mile of dense woodland for a place to land. Here and there were clearings with farmsteads, where roundhouses and fields with grazing cattle were enclosed within wooden fences. In the distance towards Kent, she could see a fortified settlement on top of a grassy mound; a manmade hill with a ditch forming a ring around it. The hillfort drew her eye far beyond the southern banks of the Tameses. Tales of bravery had reached the Beltaine tribes; of how the Atrebates had built it in great haste to defend themselves from the outsiders who were invading.

This wasn't the modern landscape she knew; yet she recognised it. She felt the wind whip her hair and stream through the gaps in her fingers. The sensations were too real for it to be a dream. She was travelling through time, deep in her mind, to a place she had been before and the present was blowing away, far behind her.

Below, she could see the red and gold armour of at least a hundred invaders. They called themselves Romans. It was a strange word. She had been taught about Romans and their legions and cavalry from the village Elders. The Elder ones, the ones in white robes who did magic, knew everything. Kerry had listened to their stories and learned.

But she was no longer Kerry: such a strange name, not known to her people.

She swooped down and landed on the riverbank next to a jetty. When her feet touched ground, the light, bodiless feeling of herself in flight disappeared. Her legs were tired, as if she had been running. Her chest heaved with heavy breath. She was real, alive. With all feeling intact, she crouched behind a bush to watch the Romans.

Did they mean to kill the Beltaine tribe and steal their land? Their intentions weren't clear.

As the Roman invaders marched closer, she crept onto the jetty, ready to drop into the river and hide, if need be. The Beltaine were proud of their jetty. The men had made it from birch, ash and alder and it jutted into the Tameses, supported by thick, oak posts wedged deep in the riverbed. Offerings were made to the gods there by the Elders. On rare occasions, *He* too made offerings there; the Beltaine King. He was higher than the Chieftain, higher even than the Elders. Some even said he was a god. They said he was born, by magic, from the old oak where the Elders tended their shrine. That was why he visited their lowly farmstead. When *He* came to their community, there would be much feasting.

From her crouched position on the jetty, she caught sight of her reflection in the water and gasped. Instead of her usual pale, oval face she had a round, peachy complexion. Her hair wasn't straight and black, but orange and wavy. She had blue eyes, not green. The girl looking back at her appeared no older than sixteen, not twenty-two. Kerry was gone. This was Aithne, named for the colour of her hair: fire.

Her watery reflection was unfamiliar, yet she recognised it. She hadn't seen this face for nearly two thousand years.

As her modern mind connected with ancient self, a tunnel between past and present opened. Kerry knew she was seeing a time before the Roman invasion of AD43. The Britons had not yet been subjugated to Roman command. But there were threats. She could see about eighty men marching nearer. Their colours were stark in the untamed woodland; red and silver amongst the dense green and brown. The Elders told her that the Romans called groups of around eighty to a hundred men a *centuriae*, led by a centurion. *Centuriae, centurion*; strange words from a strange land.

A *centuriae* seemed a lot of men to her, but the Elders had talked of many more: five *centuriae* made up a *cohort*, and two or more *cohorts* made up a *legion*.

Aithne thought of her own tribesmen, the Beltaine. They never formed rows or marched like the Romans did, in a centuriae. And they were led by a Chieftain, not a Centurion.

These invaders, these Romans, moved inland from the Tameses, from a place far to the Southeast in a distant land across the sea. The Elders said the Romans were foraging further and further West; closer and closer to the territory of her people, the Beltaine. What would it mean if they met?

In the midday sun, she could see the Romans well. They were unaware of her presence as they rested in a clearing. Their long javelins and curved body shields had been set aside. Even as they relaxed, they kept their heavy armour on; bronze helmets with cheek and neck guards and connecting sheets of armour covering their chests and shoulders in heavy layers. Underneath, they wore leather groin straps on top of their cloth tunics. Only their legs were bare, and their sandaled feet. Maybe this was so they could run. She was a girl, she didn't know that much about fighting, but she knew that if your legs were free, you could run fast. She also knew that the Roman soldiers hid themselves well behind their large shields.

The Chieftain had told her that Romans burned farmsteads and butchered her people. Yet these men seemed more like explorers than murderers. Aithne moved closer to watch them, creeping from bush to bush for cover. The men looked different than her people. They were shorter. She was a girl of sixteen, yet she was taller than most of them. Some of them were swarthy. All of the Beltaine People were pale skinned. The Elders said it was because they lived in the north. Maybe these men came from a place further south.

To her left, Aithne saw movement among the trees that the two Roman Sentinels on look-out didn't see. She had grown up beside the Tameses, so she was good at spotting people hiding among the woodland. Maybe that was why the Romans didn't; the Chieftain said they lived in stone towns, far across the endless blue sea. Where was the endless blue sea? At the end of the Tameses. One day she would love to see it.

The Beltaine warriors hid behind an overgrown earthen rampart which they had built, next to a trench. Trees made good cover. The men had defeated invading Romans this way before. Aithne couldn't count quickly enough, but she guessed there were more Beltaine than Romans; several hundred waiting warriors.

In a flash of sunlight among the trees, the Beltaine King appeared in his leather-panelled, two-wheeled chariot pulled by two sturdy horses. A charioteer worked the yoke as the King stood, with his spear poised, ready to hurl. Behind him, a handful of chariots carried the Chieftain and the other noblemen into battle. But why was the Beltaine King fighting in a skirmish? Aithne remembered the date; because it was his day; Beltaine. No hostile invaders were welcome on their sacred land, especially not on Beltaine.

Today, the King wore a bronze helmet shaped like an acorn, bronze chain-mail vest and a red linen tunic with an embroidered gold hem. He had brown and black trousers in a checked pattern. His chariot had a wooden platform supported by double loops of bent wood on either side, with leather panels and iron rimmed wheels.

His blonde hair, caked with lime water, hung stiffly where he had tied it at his neck with a leather thong.

The Beltaine King charged East towards the enemy. He jumped from his chariot and hurled his spear at a Roman. Blood spurted from the wounded soldier's stomach, where the spear had pierced his armour. As another Roman raced towards him from the right with his short sword, ready to jab him in the ribs, the King gracefully dodged behind him, jumped, and plunged his sword downwards through the opening at the neck of the soldier's armour. It pierced him diagonally, the sword tip poking through his body at his left hip in a fountain of blood. Without uttering a sound, his face frozen in shock, the Roman crumpled to the ground. Either the sword had punctured his lung rendering him unable to scream, or the attack had happened so fast he hadn't been able to react; Aithne didn't know which. All she knew was that the Beltaine King fought with a godlike fury.

The other noble warriors hurled their spears as they charged the Romans. Cavalry supported the chariots; the horse back riders were ready with their swords. Pulling up the rear ran shirtless warriors on foot, wielding spears and circular shields with brass bosses.

Beltaine war trumpets sounded over the fray. The Roman soldiers broke formation and scattered, their mouths frozen open in terror. One soldier pointed at the long, thin carnyxes with their horses heads and shrieked words in a language that Aithne couldn't understand.

Aithne felt proud as she stood, watching the Beltaine warriors fight the invaders. The Romans couldn't reorganise themselves ready for combat. Their heavy armour repelled many attacks, giving a few time to recover and use their short swords in close combat. The curved shields deflected the slashing blows of the frenzied

Beltaine, but the Romans didn't have time to rally. The King of the Beltaine fought with a fervour that made her heart flutter; he was brave, and bold, and handsome. His warriors fought alongside him with an alcohol-fuelled ferocity, revelling in the din of the terrifying war carnyxes.

The unprepared Romans had no choice but to run. A few of the Romans, who knew they couldn't outrun their foes, chose to stand and fight. Instead of attacking the noblemen on chariots, or the cavalry, they attacked the shirtless, unarmoured Beltaine warriors pulling up the rear. Aithne saw a Roman sword spill the intestines of a grey-haired warrior while another of the invaders used his *pugio*, a short sword, to jab a man in his groin. The man screamed and dropped to his knees. Aithne winced.

The Beltaine King dashed and jumped back on his chariot as the charioteer worked the yoke. Together with the cavalry, the chariots chased the remaining Romans before they could escape into the trees. The warriors slashed, spilling blood across the clearing. Satisfied that every last Roman had been killed, the Beltaine King gave one last look back in case of any further attacks, before his horses led him away. His Beltaine warriors followed him back to their woodland fortress. The honourable dead were draped over horse back or loaded onto chariots to be given the rites of Avalon later. Enemy corpses were dragged behind horses through the mud and brambles: a trophy for the Elders.

Wind began to blow. It assaulted Aithne, lifting her off her feet. The tempest whirled her through the air, high above the Tameses. As the wind whipped her east, her physical self became merged with her spiritual presence and she began to understand. The tunnel of time between her past as Aithne and her present as Kerry showed her more than what she had known in life: the spirit forces were showing her the larger landscape that shaped the lives of her Beltaine people and shaped the destiny of the Beltaine King himself.

She was far above the land, far from her farmstead. The Tameses shone like a wide sheet of beaten bronze in the morning sun. The mists of memory unfogged, and present knowledge, flooded Aithne's mind from Kerry's present. The modern city of London didn't exist. Ludenwic hadn't even been built yet; it would be many centuries before the Anglo-Saxons would invade. On the grassy verge next to the river below, Aithne saw a massive square settlement that she knew didn't belong to her kind. Her people lived in farmsteads that held only two or three roundhouses comprised of extended families. This gigantic settlement would have housed *all* of the Beltaine tribe, and the neighbouring Atrebates. She could see Roman people, not in red and gold as soldiers, but in simple tunics. Had the Roman soldiers driven out the Beltaine and replaced them with their own tradespeople and farmers? If the native tribes had been forced further north to seek refuge in the land of the Trinovantes, then would it be only a matter of time before her farmstead would be forced to flee their home too?

Aithne landed. As before, once she was grounded, feeling returned to her body. Her heart raced. Her mind burned. She knew where she was: The Elders had talked of this place. Plowonida. The rape of Plowonida. Here, where the Tameses was much wider, the river had once brought lush beauty to the green, grassy verge with its gently smoking roundhouses. Once. But now the straight lines of the new settlement looked nothing like the conical houses of her people. The invaders had driven out the natives, burned their roundhouses and built rectangular foundations of houses.

Aithne hid on the grassy verge as Romans busied themselves. There was no boundary fence to their settlement. Didn't these people fear reprisals from the Tameses tribes? Their settlement didn't look like any kind of temporary camp. If they weren't building a farmstead, then what? It looked like they were erecting permanent, stone buildings. Furthermore, their workmanship hinted at a construction on a much bigger scale than what she had ever seen before; they must have been building a fortress, or a town.

Anger consumed her. What gave these Romans the right to destroy the fertile fields of Plowonida and purge Tameses people of their rightful land? The invaders weren't welcome in the sacred land of the Tameses tribes; the Beltaine and the Atrebates. Aithne crept closer and hid behind a foundation wall, close enough to hear their words; one hasty act and she might be killed.

Two men talked. The words were foreign, but she understood their gestures as they pointed to the foundations scattered about. The men repeated one word many times during their talk: Londinium.

Londinium? Strange word, strange sound on her tongue. Was this to be a town; Londinium?

A commotion on the Tameses drew her eye away. A large Roman galley rowed in towards Plowonida. It had a long, slender wooden hull and thirty oarsmen lined either side with two large sails to aid their efforts in bringing it ashore. Any further inland and such a huge ship would have run itself aground. She was glad a vessel of its size would never be able to reach her people's sacred jetty.

Wouldn't the Elders stop the ship? If it landed they would bring more stone and supplies to ravage beautiful Plowonida.

Movement among the trees reminded Aithne that

she should have known better. The Tameses people, the tribes of the Beltaine and Atrebates would never let such injustice go unpunished.

Aithne looked once more to the galley. A rope ladder had been unrolled over the side. The Romans began climbing down, their long shields fastened to one arm and slung to the side as they descended.

But as the first Roman jumped off the rope ladder into the water, his screams of pain filled the air. In a panic at hearing his screams, the second descending Roman froze, causing the third to slip. The third Roman fell off the ladder and screamed as he too hit the water, not with a splash, but with a wet tearing sound and a stream of blood.

Aithne scanned the dark water to see what lay hidden underneath. When the tide ebbed, she could see a fringe of sharp, projecting stakes under the surface that the dark waves revealed as quickly as they concealed. Some of the Beltaine warriors must have erected them overnight. The two Roman soldiers had been impaled. But Aithne had seen enough to know that this wouldn't stop them.

Two Roman maniples swept in on the Beltaine, from the left and right; about a hundred men in total. The tightly-formed, highly-organised soldiers descended on the surprised Beltaine warriors and their Tameses allies, driving them out of the woods. Aithne saw the Beltaine King holding his spear high as his chariot charged forward, his blue tunic rippling in the wind.

The Romans used their curved shields to cover their unit from the front and above in a tight formation to repel the blows of the Beltaine, while their short swords wounded many of the shirtless men. The Beltaine warriors fought in a disorganised manner, each man fighting for himself and his own glory. Still, Aithne marvelled to watch them. Most of all, she marvelled to watch the Beltaine

King. He inspired them, giving them a sense of berserk courage as they roared forward into the fray.

Her Beltaine warriors had their own tactics. They fought in small groups with wide intervals in between. When they grew weary, or were wounded by the quick, thrusting jabs of the Roman short swords, they would disappear into the woods to be replaced. Unspent warriors would wait at hidden stations, on standby to support the battle-weary. But they were heavily outnumbered by the Romans. The warriors that fought bare-chested, without helmets or armour, in only their woollen breaches fell first. Aithne knew they would be given a hero's welcome in Avalon. She had heard the warrior tales around the fire before: to fight bare-chested was to fight with prestige. They had died as proud fighters defending their land.

The Beltaine King didn't fight bare-chested, but then *He* was different. His blue tunic symbolised his royal authority. It was well deserved; he was the only one who never grew weary, never needed replaced. He fought with a godlike power.

Maybe he *was* a god.

Far beyond the battle on the banks of the Tameses, Aithne saw roundhouses on fire. Plumes of black smoke rose far into the sky.

Fire. What about her farmstead? What about her family? Aithne dashed back into the trees. Panic drove her onward towards her home.

All four roundhouses of her farmstead were on fire. Aithne staggered with shock and steadied herself against a tree trunk. Behind her burning home the small, rectangular sanctuary was not aflame. The brown wattle and daub structure, facing the Midwinter sunrise, cut a glum sight against the orange inferno. The sacred oak that it was built around was also safe. Thank the Mother

Mathonwy. If the Elders were unharmed, then the gods would listen.

Aithne raced towards the sacred building. The special totem for battling warriors, a boar's skull, was intact outside. She looped around the wooden stake, careful not to bump it and bring bad luck. The two horses' skulls on either side of the doorway were still in place too. Thank the gods the Romans had either not seen, or not known the importance of the sacred sanctuary.

She dashed inside. The smell of decaying innards was overbearing. An Elder priest wearing a laurel crown stood next to the tree trunk in the middle of the sanctuary. He studied the human intestines that had been carefully draped over the branches of the oak tree shrine. Aithne covered her nose with her hand as she approached him.

"Elder One, what's going to become of our people?"

He sighed. "These are bad times for us, my girl."

"Can't we do anything to rid ourselves of these invaders once and for all?"

He lowered his head. "I'm afraid the omens are bad. Do you see the growth on this liver? The pattern of blood that has dripped onto the floor is not a good sign for the Beltaine. Go now. I must chant alone."

Aithne stared for a moment at the dangling human innards. Who was the Roman soldier they had taken them from? The bark of the old oak felt coarse under her palm as she stroked the trunk. The Golden Man, Beltaine King, had been born to the world at the foot of that very tree. It was his sacred shrine. What would become of him and her people?

Outside, smoke swirled around her. Aithne stumbled along, light-headed. How long had she been walking?

94

When the air cleared, Aithne saw a blue sky. She couldn't say how, but she felt a little bit different. The ground was a little bit further away. She felt a little bit closer to - she kept walking - to what?

To him?

To the river.

This was a special day. Everyone from all of the Tameses tribes would be there. The Elders would be there. Many battles had been fought and won for the Beltaine, but the successes were becoming few and far between.

Pain stabbed her heart; pain for her people and their future in their land. She would get her answers at the jetty. A sacred offering to Tamesisaddas would give them all their answers.

As she got near the river, Aithne saw a massive crowd gathered, comprising all members of the Tameses tribes on their side, the West side, of the river. Aithne weaved her way through the people, towards the jetty. They nodded to her as she passed and moved aside to let her through.

The noble warriors wore ceremonial dress; chain mail vests and cast bronze armour. They wore helmets engraved with curling scroll motifs, inset with red wax. Today was a day of ritual, not battle.

At the end of the jetty stood a stunning golden chariot on a platform, complete with two white horses. It looked like the one the Beltaine rode into battle, only it was gold-plated, ornamented with a boar design and elongated raised motifs, all highlighted with red coral studs. The horses were secured by a wicker fence, but it seemed unnecessary; they waited patiently as though ready for instruction on where to pull the chariot. The pole and yoke were leather, and the harnesses were decorated with gold threading. The end of the jetty had been reinforced with wider, cross-wedged slats of wood to support the weight of the chariot.

The crowd parted. Aithne turned to see *him*, the Golden Man, approaching the jetty. Today of all days, he was the pride of his people, King of the Beltaine people and the Tameses tribes. He was magnificent to behold in his full, golden armour, head and shoulders taller than every other man; she was breathless as he approached. His golden tunic covered his broad frame, below which he wore a woollen jerkin covered in gold dust. An intricate golden torc looped around his neck; twists of solid gold around a core of prestigious imported dogwood, finishing in horse-head terminals with inset red glass eyes. On his head he wore a cast bronze two-horned helmet with gold-plating, decorated with engraved loops in scroll motif. He carried a shield as long as his arm on his left side; copper alloy sheeting with inset red glass over a wooden panel, a prized antique among his tribes, already over a hundred years old. Around his waist he carried an iron sword, with cast brass hilt and scabbard inlaid with red and yellow enamel. The ornate craftsmanship and metalwork displayed the highest skill among her people.

Aithne could feel her face burn as he approached. She was wearing her best blue dress, with a yellow woollen cloak that she had hand dyed herself. Her red hair had been braided with interwoven sprigs of yellow primrose. The Golden Man passed without a glance at anyone, but as he drew level with Aithne, his eyes rested on hers. Aithne's breath caught in her chest. He looked divine. She couldn't help herself; she touched his hand.

Her Golden King remained composed, but he squeezed her hand in return. Her heart skipped a beat. He had acknowledged her with his subtle show of affection. His gaze remained fixed ahead as he strode along the jetty and climbed onto the chariot platform. He took hold of the harness with his right hand and kept his shield firmly in his left arm.

The Elder One and his apprentice approached the jetty; old, silver-haired master and young, dark-haired novice walking side by side. They wore white tunics with golden torcs and bronze armlets. Both wore gold-plated headdresses that fanned outwards from the head in radiating elongated lines to represent the rays of the sun.

The Elder One began to chant to the heavens. "Hear us today, great Dis, father of the Druids, on the birthing day of our King and God, Belenus, to give to you his sacrifice so that you may open the gates of Avalon and receive our offering. We beseech you to smite the enemy of Danu's Children and lay ruin to their stronghold of Londinium."

Belenus. The name resonated through her mind, connecting past and present: Tameses Aithne, London Kerry. She looked at the Golden King; Belenus.

Belenus. Beltaine.

The novice spoke over the river. "Mighty Tamesisaddas, accept our sacrifice for help in battle. Send the galleys of Claudius back across the sea. As the Gauls defeated the enemy in Rome four hundred years before, in our King Belenus' time, so too do we ask for the power to drive our foe from our lands again."

Belenus addressed the Sun in the East. "Mighty Arawn, father of Avalon. Receive my sacrifice on my day of delivery into this world, as I ride into battle against my foe in the East for the last time. Receive my offering so that the tribes of Tameses will always drive our enemy from our shores. Acknowledge our sacrifice today and bless our Queen in the North, Boudicca, that she may lead a successful battle against Londinium."

Belenus raised his bronze shield aloft. The crowd gasped as it reflected the rays of the sun, making a dazzling display of light; a good omen.

The novice now gave his response. "May this day of Beltaine, forevermore be celebrated by the descendants of the first people, in honour of our god and king. May our people, on whichever distant corner of our kingdom they survive, light bonfires and be fruitful from now until the end of time."

With a cry, the crowd raised their swords, spears, staves, and fists to the sky. Aithne raised her fist too and punched the air.

"To Belenus, our god and king, and to the feast of Beltaine!" the crowd shouted, with one voice.

With his shield over his left arm, Belenus raised his sword in his right hand and pointed it to the sun in the East. For a moment, the sun glinting lit him up entirely white. White flames no bigger than Aithne's index finger skittered along the sword and engulfed Belenus. The crowd gasped at the display, clearly a good omen from the gods.

The flames grew larger. As they sped down Belenus' armoured body and reached the wooden jetty, tongues of fire licked outwards. The horses neighed in terror, but their legs had been bound with leather straps. Aithne's jaw dropped. This was no trick. The gods had sent fires from the Otherworld to consume him. Belenus, the Golden Man, was offering himself as a human sacrifice. He stood proudly facing the sun, his back straight and his head erect, holding sword and shield in hand, ready to do battle with the Roman foe one last time, in spirit. He stood still as a statue while the horses, chariot and jetty burned, and the flames rose upwards around him.

Aithne couldn't peel her eyes away, frozen with the others to witness the spectacle. Why had Belenus offered himself? Because of the omens in oak sanctuary? Surely a human life wasn't worth that?

But she relaxed; her people didn't fear death. The soul couldn't die. It could only be transported to a temporary destination in the Otherworld to await new life.

The horses were frenzied, screaming and writhing as ash and smoke billowed from their glowing manes. Yet Belenus stood immovable, swamped by flames. The whole platform glowed golden and black ash cast high into the air with the billowing fire. The Druids chanted and warbled an eerie, bird-like tune, their vocal cords producing two tones at once.

The platform began to crumble. Chunks of burning wood toppled into the river. The horses plunged in first, burning fireballs quenched by the Tameses. Belenus kept his sword raised high above the flames as the chariot began to slip. In one thunderous crack, it crashed forward and Belenus pointed his sword at the sun as he was submerged. Only his golden shield remained floating, as the water bubbled where the jetty had been. The shield was pulled downstream on the drift, swept into the middle of the river, before the water drowned it. The horses were gone, the chariot was gone, and their Golden King, Belenus, was gone. The gods had accepted the sacrifice amidst the inferno. Belenus hadn't uttered one cry of pain, but his ordeal must have been agony.

The warrior who had sacrificed himself, Belenus, King of the Beltaine tribes and leader of the Tameses people, had been a man in his prime. Yet he had sacrificed himself believing that he would come back to fight for his Britons in battle another time.

Darkness and cold consumed Aithne as past flowed into present. She blinked; her eyes were open, but she could only see a thick, grey fog. Wet, damp, a fog in her mind, a space between two times. She was Kerry, back in the present, not Aithne in Hammersmith in 47 AD.

Belenus, the Golden King of the Beltaine and leader of the Tameses tribes had sacrificed himself for the gods to favour his people another day. His shield had been found; the Battersea shield, now in the British museum and his helmet had been found too, the Wandsworth horned helmet. Plowonida, where the modern City of London stood, had held the embryo settlement when he had died. He sacrificed himself for Boudicca to lead her people to sack Londinium and murder its people, but the time of the Britons was over. It would be many centuries before Londinium would fall to ruin and Britannia would be taken over by more invaders.

The Romans had invaded in 43 AD; four years before Belenus' immolation. Kerry had been Aithne then, a young woman who believed that Belenus was a god born of magic from the sacred old oak. Now, as her mind acclimatised to the present, what did she think? God or not, one thing was for sure; they shared a birthday on the first of May. Maybe Belenus had been born at the foot of the oak tree, and since oaks were worshipped as religious tokens by Druids, he had been named by his people as a god.

Kerry saw a sign: Wandsworth Bridge Road. The grey fog she had been walking through was real; an early morning mist. Her slippered feet were cold and numb. She shivered in her bathrobe.

Belenus waited in the Otherworld. The Britons knew this Otherworld as Avalon. Oliver's house was in Avalon Road. The farmstead where she connected with the ancient Britons, the same farmstead from her drawing, had stood in ancient Fulham. Her people, the Beltaine, had set fire to their own four roundhouses to distract the Romans from the real prize; the secret oak sanctuary behind. Belenus, Beltaine, oak tree shrine.

Her feet plodded on, taking her from the place of the ancient jetty back to the location of the oak tree shrine. Although it was no longer there, replaced by a young apple tree and a meadowsweet blossom tree, she knew where it had stood for centuries, two thousand years ago.

In the garden of Doncaster Manor, Avalon Road.

Chapter 10

May the first; Beltaine. Gavin rolled out of bed and stretched. He had slept a deep and dreamless sleep.

Was Kerry up yet? The clock said half eleven. He grabbed her present; a horse-shaped necklace to match her Golden Horse, then went to knock on her bedroom door.

"Gavin, is that you?"

"Who else would it be?"

Her voice sounded hoarse. She'd be really pissed off if she'd caught a cold on her birthday. She opened the door wide to let him in. Her hair was tangled, and she looked puffy-eyed.

"What happened to you? You look as if you haven't slept?" he said.

"I haven't." She yawned. "I thought you were Jenna."

"You didn't drink that tea she gave you last night, did you?" He tutted. "I told you not to."

"It didn't work anyway. She's bringing me some mead at midday to start the cleansing ritual."

He peered out on the landing before shutting her bedroom door. "Listen, I don't want to sound melodramatic or anything, but Oliver and Jenna have more than candle magic lined up for today. I'm not taking part in any crazy ceremony of theirs - and I don't think you should either."

Kerry's face sobered. "You said you would yesterday, you can't break your promise."

"Promise? Kerry, I think you were high on that tea when you agreed to take part. It's not like you to lose your common sense."

He knew he'd gone too far.

"Listen, I didn't mean to have a go at you," said

Gavin. "The idea of this pagan ritual sounds nutty to me and I think their lifestyle is having a bad influence on you, that's all. Why don't we go out and celebrate your birthday, just the two of us?"

Kerry's nostrils flared. "You don't understand. This is more than hallucinogenic tea. I went on a journey last night that I can't explain. I was this girl, you know, back in the Iron Age. The Golden Man was there. I even found out his name - Belenus. He was King of the Beltaine tribes, leader of the Tameses people. He was born, two thousand years ago today - my birthday, Gavin. Don't you see the connection? Belenus... Beltaine. I have to take part in this ritual today."

Gavin ran his hands through his hair. "This sounds really dodgy, Kerry. Don't you see, this is even more reason why you *shouldn't* take part? They've got you drugged, or something, and you think these hallucinations are real. I'm really worried. I think we should go back up North."

"It wasn't a hallucination. Look." Kerry lifted her foot. Her slippers were caked with mud. "I went back to the river last night."

"So now you're sleepwalking? You know, you've been acting weird since we first came here. I think we should let your dad know what's going on."

"Why would we do that?" She looked angry. "It's no one else's business except mine, and Belenus' and our Golden Horse."

"*Our* Golden Horse? Kerry, don't you hear how you sound? You're talking about a drawing as if he was a real person."

Kerry's face reddened. "The Golden Horse is real, so who's to say he isn't? I could tell you details from the time period that I couldn't possibly know. They even spoke a different language - Brythonic - but I understood it. I'll

103

try to remember some now to prove it."

Gavin raised his hands in a defeated gesture. "You don't have to." This was going to be tough. "All I'll say is that I'm worried. I don't think either of us should eat, or drink anything they give us today. That way, our heads will be clear when we take part in this Beltaine ritual - or whatever the hell it is."

Kerry's face brightened. "So you're saying you'll participate?"

"Yeah, I guess so. It's clearly important to you, so I'll do it." He sat on the edge of her bed. It was neatly made; she hadn't slept in it at all.

"What's the worst that could happen, right? They said it's some candle magic and chanting. It sounds harmless enough," said Kerry.

"Sure, harmless. Did I forget to mention that they're planning to deflower a virgin? You remember that naked girl I saw the other night? She's Glynn's daughter," said Gavin.

Her brow furrowed. "Why didn't you tell me yesterday? Jenna didn't mention anything like that."

"Of course she wouldn't - taking the virginity of a sexy eighteen year old girl is a bloke's fantasy, not a woman's. And what's the difference if I'd told you yesterday instead of today? I doubt it would have changed your mind about participating."

She folded her arms. "You're right. It wouldn't have made a difference."

Gavin nudged her. "It's your birthday. I didn't want things to be like this. If this is what you want to do today, then I'm in. But once it's over, I'm all for taking your Golden Horse and getting the heck out of this pagan nuthouse. Are you with me?"

Kerry chuckled. "When you put it that way, it

sounds hilarious." She nodded. "Sure. Let's decide what to do after today."

"And just remember, don't eat or drink anything. Chuck that mead down the toilet when she gives it to you - and I'll do the same."

"If there's LSD in it, maybe it'll make the ceremony better?" Kerry joked.

Gavin forced a wry smile. "I don't think she means us harm, but she doesn't have a clue what she's doing. I saw all those books on witchcraft and candle magic in their room - she's a novice. And if Mistress C had to prepare that tea for you, then that speaks volumes - what if Jenna gives us the wrong herb and it lobotomises us? She's like an unlicensed, you know, witchdoctor or something."

"I suppose," said Kerry. She didn't sound convinced.

Gavin sighed. "But seriously, what do you think of the two of them? Oliver and Jenna - do you like them?"

Kerry pouted. "It's not a matter of liking them, they have my Golden Horse. And I want to know more about Belenus."

This was not how he wanted the conversation to go; sod ghosts and hallucinations. He had to get it back on track. "I mean, I think they seem nice and all, but there's something about them I can't put my finger on. I feel like they aren't being honest with us."

"They're being honest about what matters - once my Golden Horse is cleansed, they said I can have it back," said Kerry.

"And you trust them? I have a feeling we're going to have to steal it back."

"It won't come to that." There was a note of protest in her voice. "Mistress C assured me I'll have it back and I trust her. She seems motherly, it's hard to explain. Jenna and Oliver seem a bit weird, but I don't think they mean to harm us. If I didn't trust them, I wouldn't take part in the ceremony today."

"Yes you would. Nothing is stopping you from getting your Golden Horse back."

Kerry squeezed his hand. "I guess you're right."

Gavin ruffled her hair. "Speaking of Golden Horses, I got you something for your birthday." He handed her the box with her necklace.

Kerry opened it and gave a smile of delight. "Gavin, it's lovely. That was so sweet of you - it looks like my Golden Horse."

"I found it at a shop along Wandsworth Bridge road after work yesterday. I thought it would've been hard to find a horse pendant, but apparently not."

"The Trojan horse," Kerry read from the box. "Not exactly a romantic idea, is it? The whole of Troy fell for the horse."

"Yeah, but we aren't a couple, so it doesn't have to be romantic, does it?" He put his arm around her shoulders and squeezed.

"I love it. I'll wear it today." She hugged him. "I'm going to get changed now, so I'll see you downstairs at twelve for the ritual."

"Remember to wear that green dress you had on two days ago." He affected a wavering, mystical voice. "*It has great significance, my child.*"

Kerry gave him a shove. "You're such a dick, do you know that? You have to take the piss out of everything."

"Only when it involves pagans who should be locked up in a mental asylum."

"And don't forget to wear your work stuff that you had on that day," she said.

"Yeah, yeah." He waved his hand back at her as he left her room.

What the heck did he have on that day? He went into his own room and looked on the floor. Rumpled corduroys on the floor and shirt half-draped over the end of the sofa bed. That looked about right. He couldn't be entirely sure he'd worn either of those things on his first day of work, but it didn't matter. Sod the ceremony; Oliver and Jenna were a couple of New-Age twats.

Gavin's door creaked open. He spun to see Jenna in the doorway.

"Happy Beltaine," she said. "I brought you a drink."

"I didn't hear you knock," he said.

"That's because I didn't." She sounded unapologetic; almost pleased.

Gavin looked at the tankard of mead. "If you leave it on the table there, I'll drink it after."

She shook her head in a teasing manner, her doe-eyes showing a playful glint. "Uh, uh, uh. You don't get off the hook that easily. I'll be hurt if you don't taste it - I made it myself."

"Not right now," said Gavin. "I need to get dressed first."

Jenna came into the room. Her long, black dress swished as she walked. Gavin looked closer. In the sunlight, the fabric of her dress was see-through. He could make out her pink nipples and lower down, under the rope-belt that clamped the dress tight to her curves, he could see a strip of light brown pubic hair. He gulped.

"Try a sip," she said. "For me?"

"Let me get dressed first." He tore his eyes from her body to look into her pleading eyes.

"It's not drugged," she joked. She raised the

tankard and licked her red lips, before taking a mouthful.

Gavin watched her small, red mouth coming towards him.

He felt her large chest pressed against him as their lips met.

Jenna pushed her mouth onto his. Heat radiated through him as she released the mead onto his tongue. He tasted the sweet liquid and the wet warmth of her mouth. His chest tingled, then his arms and along into his fingertips. The sensation spread downwards through his core. He felt his groin stiffen and pulled back from Jenna. The move hadn't gone unnoticed. She pressed closer to him, wedging her knee between his legs and slid her thigh up to nudge his crotch. Gavin wrapped his arms around her as they embraced. He could feel her huge chest pressed against his stomach and ran his hands lower to caress her waist.

Jenna peeled away from their lingering kiss. "Come downstairs to the dining room when you get dressed. Don't be long, darling."

He took the tankard from her and swallowed, deeply, watching her shapely ass sway as she walked to the door. What did their kiss mean; that she was available? She'd gone beyond flirting; was it a hint of more to come? One way or another, he was a hundred percent certain; he would take part in any ceremony if it meant Jenna wanted him.

Chapter 11

Kerry felt warm and giddy as she descended the stairs to the dining room. She held the wall and banister for support. It was a nice feeling; tipsy and sedate. The mead had gone down smooth, as if she were drinking a soft drink. She hoped her head would be clear for whatever incantations Jenna wanted her to say to cleanse the Golden Horse.

On the other hand, Jenna said drinking the mead was part of the cleansing ritual, to detox the body. Pagans had a funny way of cleansing. Kerry didn't mind; whatever it took to get her Golden Horse back, she would do it.

Would she see her gorgeous golden Belenus after today? As much as Jenna and Mistress C had warned about the dangers of tampering with the Otherworld, Kerry had never felt the spirit warrior meant her harm. Quite the opposite actually; his presence in her visions soothed her. The night she had seen his ghostly form, she had fainted out of shock, not fear.

As she turned onto the lower ground floor stairs, Kerry saw Gavin ahead of her. He slid his hand along the wall in an unsteady manner.

Kerry's tongue was heavy. "Thought you weren't going to drink anything?"

Gavin looked over his shoulder. "Couldn't resist," he slurred.

She extended her hand and he took it, their feet thunking on each step together. A gust of wind hit them as they pushed open the dining room door. Kerry's green dress billowed.

The dining room table had been set up as an altar with two unlit candles, one green and one white, in bronze holders along with an unlit incense stick in an earthenware dish. There was also a bucket made from beaten bronze sheets, filled with a golden liquid. Next to it was a red silk bag with a golden threaded drawstring. On the far side of the room, a second, empty table had been pushed against the wall and the dining room chairs stacked next to it.

Jenna, Oliver and the blonde girl, who had to be Saiorse, were on their knees, forming a triangle around the circular altar. All three had their hands across their chests and were chanting quietly with their eyes closed. Kerry couldn't hear the words. Jenna and Saiorse wore black, sleeveless dresses that fell to their ankles and were roped at the waist. Oliver wore a white robe in a similar style to the Druid priests who had stood by the jetty in her vision. A blackout curtain hung between the dining room and kitchen and fluttered in the breeze from the back garden.

Kerry waited next to Gavin in the doorway. Gavin looked as mystified as she felt. And where was Mistress C? After all her talk of Beltaine, why wasn't she there?

Should they interrupt the chanting? Maybe Oliver, Jenna and Saiorse hadn't heard them coming. Kerry was about to speak when Oliver, Jenna and Saiorse opened their eyes and stood up.

"Kerry. Gavin. Come and take your places around the altar," said Jenna. She lifted the bronze bucket. "We gather here to begin the purification of the golden talisman."

Jenna took a gulp from the bucket and passed it to Kerry. Kerry wrapped her arms around it to bear the weight; it had oak-lined staves inside and looked like it held at least two litres of liquid. She swallowed, tasting mead, and passed it on to Gavin. Gavin took a huge swig and passed it to Saiorse. Saiorse sipped and passed it to Oliver. Oliver took a gulp and set it back on the altar.

Jenna loosened the golden drawstring of the red

silk bag on the altar with nimble fingers. Kerry saw her Golden Horse amidst the folds of material. Jenna took the white candle in her right hand and lit it. "Here burns Kerry's belief in the power of the talisman. The power will never die," she said.

Kerry's belief? Wasn't it everyone's belief? Kerry tried to clear her mind, but the mead clouded it into a daze.

Jenna held the Golden Horse at arm's length in her left hand. "By fire do I cleanse this talisman of all and any impurities that may tarnish it." Jenna passed the Golden Horse through the white candle flame then placed it in Kerry's left hand and set the white candle in Kerry's right hand. What did Jenna want her to do? Jenna's eyes flitted from the Golden Horse to the candle. Kerry understood; she passed it through the white candle flame. Her hand swayed under the influence of the mead; her fingers tingled. Careful not to drop it, she set the Golden Horse in Gavin's left hand and candle in his right. He passed it through the white candle and Kerry saw a drowsy, amorous look on his face as he watched Jenna, not the Golden Horse. Kerry suppressed a sigh. Oliver repeated the ritual next, before Saiorse completed the circle.

With the white candle burning in its bronze holder and the Golden Horse back in the centre of the altar, Jenna picked up the bronze bucket again and drank. She passed it to Kerry. Kerry took a long drink. Her body succumbed to a pleasant numbness. She passed it on until the circle had completed the ritual.

Saiorse picked up the green candle in her right hand and lit it. "Here burns the love that goes into the talisman," said Saiorse.

Saiorse. Kerry said the name in her head. Her eyes focussed and unfocussed on the girl. What a pretty name. Didn't Saiorse mean freedom? Freedom was such a nice

111

meaning.

Saiorse lifted the Golden Horse off the altar in her left hand. "By love do I cleanse this talisman of all and any impurities that may dwell within it," she said. She passed it through the green candle flame, then handed both candle and Golden Horse to Jenna. Jenna repeated the ritual and passed both to Kerry. Kerry did the same and passed both to Gavin. Gavin gave her a cheeky smile as she turned to him and Kerry clicked her tongue quietly; she wished he could be serious. Gavin recited the incantation and handed both candle and Golden Horse to Oliver to complete the circle.

Another round of mead. Kerry watched everyone as they drank in turn. No swaying, no sleepy-eyed expressions; everyone looked too composed to be drunk. Was she the only one with a low tolerance? She looked again, lingering on their faces this time. Saiorse's cheeks were flushed and Gavin's ears were red. What about Jenna? Her eyes were glassy. Good; she was glad everyone else felt the effects of the mead too.

Oliver took the incense holder in his right hand and lit the stick. Pungent perfume wafted over them. Kerry took a deep sniff. She didn't recognise the heavy scent. "Here burns the fire of cleansing frankincense that goes into the talisman," he said.

Kerry watched his eyes shining a brighter blue than usual in the flickering candlelight. God, he was handsome. She swayed on the spot. He was so *shaggable*.

What on earth? Kerry gave herself a mental shake; what was she saying? Oliver wasn't her type. Not only that, but he was the boss-

Wonder what he wore under his robe?

Her crotch tingled. She recalled Gavin's words, after the feast on their first night: *"...horny goat weed in the drink, or whatever it was…"*

But it was a soothing feeling. A warm, stimulating sensation. Kerry relaxed, enjoying it.

Oliver took the Golden Horse in his left hand and held the earthenware incense holder forward. "By the gods I cleanse this talisman to be ready for my purpose," said Oliver. He passed the talisman through the incense smoke, then handed it to Saiorse to repeat the ritual.

Purpose? What did he mean by 'my purpose'? Wasn't it hers; wasn't she going to get it back after the cleansing? Jenna repeated the ritual and handed the Golden Horse and incense to Kerry. Kerry passed the Golden Horse through the incense and gave both to Gavin. Gavin completed the circle with his eyes on Jenna: bedroom eyes that Jenna returned. The exchange interrupted Kerry's thoughts; had there been an encounter between them that she didn't know about? But Gavin was her best friend; he would have told her. He was so distracted by Jenna that he knocked the tip of the incense off with the Golden Horse; a chunk of smoking ash fell to the altar.

Under the persuasion of the mead, a giggle rose to her throat. Kerry turned away and laughed into the sleeve of her dress. Gavin fought a smile in response; Kerry could see him straining to keep a straight face. She leaned against him, glad of his bulk to support her as a euphoric dizziness overcame her.

"That's it, don't fight it. We need to let out our natural urges," said Jenna.

Not what Kerry was expecting. Jenna, Oliver and Saiorse had seemed so solemn as they performed the ritual that Kerry felt it sacrilegious to act in any other way than dignified. Now that she was able to laugh freely, the feeling escaped her. She composed herself.

Jenna leaned across the altar and took the Golden

Horse from Gavin. As her fingers touched his, a lustful look settled on his face. Must have been the alcohol taking effect.

Jenna held the Golden Horse in her right hand. "I imbue this talisman with love," she said. She passed it to Kerry. Kerry repeated the phrase and passed it to Gavin. Once the Golden Horse had been passed around the circle and the incantation repeated by everyone, Jenna placed it back on the altar. She lifted the bucket of mead.

"The talisman has been purified. I now close the ceremony." Jenna took a large gulp and passed the bucket to Kerry. Not more alcohol; Kerry felt barely in control of her body as it was. But she had to close the ceremony to get her Golden Horse back. Obediently she took it, sipped and passed it on.

Was that all? Jenna had talked of its importance so much that Kerry had almost anticipated more spectacle. She had been enjoying the smoke and the incantations; she wanted more.

"Is it over now - I mean, was that really it?" Kerry tried to hide the disappointment in her voice.

"No. We have to cleanse you and then Gavin. But you have to be cleansed first, because the Golden One has formed an attachment to you," said Jenna.

The Golden One. So Jenna didn't know his name? Belenus was her secret Golden King.

Jenna removed the mead from the altar. Oliver took the cloth parcel and Saiorse took the incense. Gavin grabbed the candles. Jenna positioned the Golden Horse in the middle of the altar.

"May the gods instil this talisman with the strength to cleanse the woman, Kerry. It is her talisman now, in this world."

Kerry wobbled. Jenna and Oliver supported her

onto the altar. She stretched out on the hard surface, feeling the Golden Horse under the arch of her back.

"Gavin, you stand on her left side." Jenna moved Gavin into place with the green candle.

"Saiorse, you stand by her head with the frankincense," Jenna continued. Kerry watched Saiorse upside down as she held the burning incense by her head.

Jenna took her place to Kerry's right side with the white candle and Oliver positioned himself at her feet. He held the red silk bag by its golden drawstring.

Kerry looked at Gavin. He almost drooled over Jenna standing opposite him. The mead had definitely gone to his head. It had gone to her head too; hard to suppress her own amorous inclinations towards Oliver. Now was not the time and place. After all, this was a religious ceremony, albeit a pagan one.

"We gather here to begin the purification of the woman, Kerry, who has been tainted by the Golden Horse," said Jenna.

Gavin broke the tension of the moment as he sneezed, almost blowing out his green candle. Kerry couldn't help herself. Her chest heaved with gasps of laughter. Tears streamed from her eyes. Gavin hung his head. He raised his eyes to give Jenna an apologetic puppy-dog look.

When Kerry composed herself, she saw that Oliver had a bronze knife in his hand; the one from Gavin's room. He must have had it in the silk bag.

Kerry's laughter subsided. "What are you planning to do with that? You aren't going to sacrifice me, are you?"

Oliver shook his head. "This isn't blood magic. We're simply going to cut the threads of Avalon from your body."

"Have more mead and relax," said Jenna. She

nodded to Saiorse, who grabbed the bronze bucket. Kerry raised herself onto her elbows to take a sip.

No sacrifice; got it. Kerry took a deep breath and exhaled in a slow, steady release.

Oliver moved the bronze knife towards Jenna's white candle. "I cleanse this blade with fire to be ready for my purpose," he said. He passed the tip through the flame.

Kerry saw the knife glint as it reflected the firelight. Oliver held it in his right hand. With his left hand, he grabbed the hem of Kerry's dress and pulled it taut. Then he placed the knife against the fabric and began to cut. The material gave way with a crisp tearing sound.

"The residue of the Otherworld resides in this woman, Kerry's, clothing. We free her of the bonds of Avalon," said Oliver. He sliced upwards, through the waistline, across the thicker fabric of the midsection, pulling hard to keep the dress taut. With a final snap, the threads of the V-neck snapped, and Kerry's dress fell apart.

If she'd known they were going to ruin her favourite boutique dress, she would have worn her bargain bin best for her first day of work.

Once again, the bucket of mead went around the circle, this time starting with Kerry. Kerry watched the ceiling spin. Her eyes blurred and refocused. She lay in front of three people who were almost strangers, and her best friend, in only her underwear. Why hadn't she bothered to wear matching colours? Blue satin and black lace bra with pink thong and white hearts; not a good match. She let her head loll. No matter; she was closer to Belenus than ever; she would be getting his - their - Golden Horse back.

Oliver leaned over Kerry to pass his blade through Saiorse's frankincense. "By love do I cleanse this woman of all and any impurities that are attached to her," said

116

Oliver.

Saiorse's hand swayed; she was drunk. Thank goodness she didn't wield the knife; at least Oliver had a steady hand. Kerry looked at Jenna. Her eyes were half-shut amidst the smoke from the white candle. Seemed Oliver was the only person who could hold his liquor.

Oliver lowered the knife and hooked the tip between the cups of her bra. With a quick jerk of his hand, he pulled upwards snapping her bra apart.

Kerry cringed as her white breasts were exposed to the room. A notion to cover her chest crossed her mind, but her arms were too heavy. Gavin's eyes widened as he took in her chest. Once the initial embarrassment had passed, Kerry was overcome with excitement. She felt attractive, desirable.

More mead. Her worries dissolved. She was glad for the effect of the alcohol.

"By fire do I cleanse this woman, Kerry, of all and any impurities that are attached to her," said Oliver. He passed the blade through Gavin's green candle flame.

Oliver hooked the knife inside the elastic of Kerry's thong towards her right hip. Kerry watched his expression; he concentrated hard. Not a trace of lust on his face. She tensed her body; the bronze blade felt cold against her skin. The knife so close to her crotch gave an unexpected thrill. Oliver pulled upwards and the fabric snapped. He repeated the motion on the left side, then flipped the cut fabric aside. Kerry looked along the length of her body. She was completely naked, lying before the robed pagans, like a Virgin of ancient times awaiting sacrifice. Only she was no virgin, she wasn't pure.

Kerry looked at the faces of the two men. Gavin's hand shook as he held the green candle; his eye travelling the length of her naked form. She knew he would have been more discreet, had he been sober. Oliver looked too and it teased her to see that he didn't react to her nakedness; he surveyed her body in preparation for whatever was to come next. Seeing his look of concentration and the intensity in his expression made her feel desirable, filled her with lust.

The bucket of mead made another round. Kerry let her body succumb completely to the pagan ritual. She'd do whatever they wanted.

Jenna held the white candle over Kerry's chest. The breeze from the open patio door made the flame blow close to her skin, as if it wanted to caress her bare breasts.

"By fire do I cleanse this woman, Kerry, of all and any impurities that are attached to her," said Jenna. She tilted her hand. Hot white wax poured onto the cleft between Kerry's breasts. Kerry gasped at the sting.

Impurities. Kerry thought of Belenus, then the Golden Horse, then Gavin and Oliver, her nudity, pagan lust, heathen debauchery. Could Jenna's candle cleanse her impure thoughts? She could imagine a lot; were the men hard beneath their robes at seeing her bare body? What if they screwed her, one at a time, both together, all three of them bare-naked under a full moon?

No, no no! Her best friend and her boss. She had to come to her senses. Kerry opened her eyes. Gavin held the green candle over her stomach. He looked across to Jenna for instruction.

"Say the incantation first," she said.

Gavin looked down at Kerry for confirmation.

"Do it," she said. "Quickly." The white wax from Jenna's turn had already cooled on her breasts and the sting had receded.

"By fire do I cleanse this woman, Kerry, of all and any impurities that are attached to her," he repeated. He tipped the candle and spilled green wax onto her navel. It pooled in her bellybutton and trickled lower to the top of her pubic hair. Kerry winced and arched her back, tears springing from the corners of her eyes. No pain, no gain; no Golden Man.

Saiorse held the incense over Kerry's forehead. "By fire do I cleanse this woman, Kerry, of all and any impurities that are attached to her," she repeated. Starting from Kerry's head, Saiorse moved the frankincense stick along her body, flicking ash onto her forehead, cheeks, both breasts, heart, stomach, crotch and along both legs, finishing with her feet. Although sensual to be cleansed in such a meticulous method, the ritual wasn't as pleasurable with Saiorse, rather than Oliver, performing it.

Oliver pressed his blade flat against Kerry's right foot. The cold metal felt soothing on her skin. "By love do I cleanse this woman, Kerry, of all and any impurities that are attached to her," said Oliver. He slid the knife along her body, removing all the incense ash and shaving the hardened pools of wax on her skin; first her right leg, then her left, across her crotch, onto her stomach, between her breasts, across her chest and up over her face. Wonder if the ritual excited him? Kerry writhed.

Oliver handed the knife to Jenna.

"The woman, Kerry, has now been purified by the gods and is ready for the ceremony of Beltaine. We must now begin the purification of the man, Gavin, who has been tainted by the Golden Horse," said Jenna.

Jenna and Saiorse led Gavin to the table on the far side for his cleansing, bringing the white and green candles and the frankincense with them. Kerry understood; this was a second altar for Gavin.

Kerry sat up. She swung her legs over and started to get up, but Oliver placed his hand on her stomach to

119

stop her.

"The girls will cleanse him. Have more mead. Let's celebrate Beltaine," said Oliver.

Oliver set the bucket of mead between Kerry's open knees. She widened her legs to make space for it. Oliver moved himself between her splayed legs and lifted the bucket, slowly, to her lips, not taking his eyes off hers. Kerry supped, warmth filling her throat and chest, keeping her eyes locked on him. He set the bucket aside and picked up the silk bag. Kerry watched him pull out a black dress, the same as Jenna and Saiorse's. Kerry pulled it over her head and fastened the rope-belt around her waist.

"May you receive the fire and be fruitful today on this, your birthday," said Oliver. He reached into the bag and brought out a wreath of pink blossoms, which he set on her head.

Kerry swayed. The room blurred. She tried to focus her eyes on Oliver. Dazzling yellow light shone from behind him. His hair was golden. His robes were golden. He was golden. This wasn't Oliver; it was the Golden Man of her past.

"Is it you?" she gasped.

He didn't answer. His eyes were full of lust as he leaned towards her, kissing her hard. Kerry lay back, letting her Golden Man move himself on top of her, kissing her neck. She felt his hand caress her thigh, sliding her black dress up. She closed her eyes, tilting her head back. She wanted him so badly; his body, his golden warmth.

Beneath her on the altar, Kerry felt her Golden Horse press into the small of her back. This felt right; the cold metal of her Golden Horse below her was like the Yin to the Golden Man's warmth from above like Yang. With one hand, he slid his golden robe open. He was naked underneath. Kerry raised her bottom off the altar, bringing her hips towards him. The Golden Man pushed himself into her. Kerry hooked her legs around his waist and pulled him deeper into her.

Kerry's head swam. She felt serene. She rolled her head back and wrapped her legs around her Golden Man, god of her dreams, visions and past, as they rocked back and forth. Back and forth, the rhythm of their bodies entwined. How she'd wanted this from the moment she had visualised him as he had been in their past life together. Heat built in her chest, neck and face. Kerry closed her eyes. Her body built to a crescendo. Harder, hotter, faster. She lifted her legs high across the Golden Man's shoulders. He closed his eyes as he pushed deeper. Kerry came at the same time as he did, both of them surrounded by a halo of golden light.

Chapter 12

Gavin followed Jenna and Saiorse to the far side of the room. They set the candles, frankincense and silk bag at the ends of the altar. He knew what was to follow and the thought turned him on. The only problem was; how would he stop himself from getting hard? Or maybe that was the point.

"Lie down, Gavin," said Jenna.

Gavin climbed onto the table and stretched out.

"We gather here to begin the purification of the man, Gavin, who has been tainted by the Golden Horse," said Jenna.

Gavin relaxed. Here he was, partaking in pagan madness with two petite, busty blondes. Who would ever believe it? He wasn't sure *he* would, after the deed was over. But what deed? It would be quite the tease to have the pair of them strip him naked and cleanse him, only for no follow through. Did he want a follow through? What follow through? Satanic sex under a full moon?

Jenna stood at Gavin's feet and Saiorse stood at his head. Gavin tried to lift his head to look at Jenna, but the mead made him dizzy. He let it slump back against the table with a thud and lay motionless while they said their incantations.

Why weren't Kerry and Oliver taking part in his cleansing? He rolled his head to his right. Across the room he could see Oliver on top of Kerry, rhythmically humping.

A surge of jealousy struck him. For a split second, he almost jumped up. Two seconds was all it would take to drag Oliver off her and knock him out. But Kerry had her head back, eyes closed; if she was enjoying it, who was he to stop her?

Pagan debauchery indeed; Oliver hadn't been lying.

Gavin turned his head back to his own cleansing to get the image of Kerry and Oliver out of his mind. Jenna and Saiorse had unbuttoned his shirt. His belt was unfastened, and his corduroys loosened.

"The residue of the Otherworld resides in this man, Gavin's, clothing. We free him of the bonds of Avalon," said Jenna.

She passed the bronze knife through the white candle smoke. With a tug, she pulled his trousers off. Gavin raised his ass off the altar to help. She sliced his corduroys in a criss-cross pattern with the blade, passed them through the white candle flame and dropped them onto the floor.

Mead for all three; first Gavin, then Jenna, then Saiorse.

Saiorse took the bronze knife. She passed it through the frankincense. "By love do I cleanse this man of all and any impurities that are attached to him," she said.

She pulled his shirt off. Gavin raised his arms to assist. Saiorse sliced his shirt then passed it through the incense smoke.

More mead. Jenna and Saiorse's thin dresses outlined their hard nipples underneath, the curve of their shapely asses; Gavin struggled to keep himself under control as he lay in only his boxers.

"By fire do I cleanse this man, Gavin, of all and any impurities that are attached to him," said Jenna. She passed the blade through the green candle flame and lowered it to his boxers. Having the knife so close to that region stopped any urges, regardless of Jenna's hand being close too. She cut the flimsy material in two and pulled them off.

Another round of mead. As Jenna passed the bucket to him, she brushed her chest against his arm. Was it on purpose, or because she was drunk? Jenna swayed.

Her red lips were wet and parted.

"Don't fight your natural response," she said, stroking her hand along his body, openly touching his groin.

Next, the women took turns to pour melted candle wax onto his stomach and chest. Gavin gritted his teeth against the pain. He recalled Kerry's orgasmic reaction to the wax on her own body and the thought kept him distracted from the unpleasant sensation.

Once the wax had cooled, Saiorse cleansed his body with incense. Then they shared another round of mead.

Jenna began shaving the wax off his body with the bronze blade from his feet up. Unlike Oliver, who performed the ritual on Kerry in a clinical fashion, Jenna leaned low, in a sweeping, seductive manner. She lingered over his groin with her lips parted, her face centimetres from his skin. The tease was unbearable; Gavin took a deep breath and exhaled through his open mouth. The wax had caught in the hairs on his chest and stomach; not an experience that he found pleasurable in the least, but Jenna's pretence of fellatio kept his pain tolerance high.

"The man, Gavin, has been purified by the gods. I now close the cleansing ritual and begin the ceremony of Beltaine." said Jenna.

Gavin's ceremony had been quicker than Kerry's. As he sat up, he noticed that Kerry and Oliver were still at it on the altar; she had her legs wrapped around his back. Gavin clenched his teeth and looked away. Saiorse reached into the red silk bag and pulled out a white robe like Oliver's. She helped him pull it over his shoulders and tied the belt to secure it.

"May you receive the fire and be fruitful today on this, our sacred day of Beltaine," said Jenna. She reached into the bag and pulled out a golden crown. It had radiating upwards lines in a stylised depiction of the sun's rays; like a headdress a Druid would wear. She set it on Gavin's head and kissed him. Jenna pressed hard, breathing heavily into his mouth. Saiorse pulled Jenna away and grabbed Gavin's face in both hands, kissing him too. Gavin's head spun; no woman for months and now two. Jenna pulled Saiorse off Gavin and kissed her. Gavin watched them, mesmerised. This was too much; a dream come true.

Jenna pulled away from Saiorse and kissed Gavin again, knocking his crown askew. She grabbed his hands and cupped them over her breasts. Gavin hardened and she sensed it, pressing closer to him. He ran his thumbs over her nipples, making them erect. He kissed Jenna's neck and tried to pull down her dress to reach her large chest with his mouth, but it was too tight. The tease got him more excited; he could see a hint of her body through the dress, but not enough.

Jenna reached into the silk bag once more and pulled out a bronze mask. It was an elongated horse design, the features painted in abstract, golden lines. She put it on top of her head, like a cap. Gavin perched at the edge of the table watching her. What was she going to do next?

Before he could think through any answers to his thought, Jenna dropped to her knees. Gavin felt her warm mouth close around his cock. He looked down. All he could see was the bronze horse mask that she wore on her head. Bit too strong a fetish for his taste. He closed his eyes, focusing on sensation rather than sight.

Jenna pulled away from him, still on her knees, and dropped onto all fours. She reached for his hand and tugged him towards her. Gavin slid off the table. Jenna yanked hard, pulling him down onto his knees beside her. Did she want him on all fours beside her, like two horses

125

in whatever weird ritual she was going to do next? Apparently not; Jenna put her palm in the middle of his chest and pushed him towards her rear. As he moved back, she slid her sheer, black dress up, exposing her naked curves. Gavin kneeled back behind her and admired her body as it came into view.

She reached for him, grabbing a handful of his white robe and yanked it open. Gavin understood what ritual she had in mind next.

Horse and sun. He ran his hands over her curvy ass. She tossed her curly hair and arched her back. He pulled her hips towards him. Jenna seemed to like the motion; she grabbed his hand and slapped it against her right thigh to encourage her.

So she liked that kind of play, pretending to be a horse? Kerry hadn't worn the horse pendant he had given her. He forced his thoughts away from Kerry. Kerry wasn't there; nor Oliver or Saiorse. They were alone. Gavin closed his eyes, feeling the pressure mount. He mounted her; sun mounted horse. Horse and sun; Kerry's Golden Horse. He tugged Jenna's hair; sun pulled yoke. Pole and yoke to control the horse. Jenna yelped in her sexual frenzy.

She collapsed forward on the floor with her gorgeous ass sticking in the air. Gavin pulled back panting and sat behind her on his haunches.

As if on cue, Saiorse came inside through the kitchen.

"The Cauldron of Knowledge is ready," she said, before skipping outside.

Chapter 13

Jenna led Gavin by his hand into the back garden. A canopy had been strung between the apple and blossom trees. Below it, the giant, bronze cauldron was suspended by an iron frame over a small fire. A set of wooden steps had been placed beneath the handles on either side. Oliver threw wood onto the burning pile and Saiorse stood at the top of the steps, emptying a bucket of water into the cauldron. Kerry stood to the left looking dazed, swaying gently on the spot, her hand to her temple.

"Kerry," Gavin whispered. "Oi! You OK?"

"Ssh!" said Oliver, flashing Gavin an irritated glance. "Let us now consummate the ceremony of Beltaine before the gods."

Jenna and Saiorse climbed one of the sets of steps. Jenna beckoned Kerry to join them. Oliver climbed the other and Gavin followed him.

Surely they weren't going to get into the cauldron? How long would it take the fire to boil the water? Gavin looked across at Kerry. She seemed too drunk to be worried about much. His mind was made up. He would get in the cauldron to keep an eye on Kerry, but at the first sign of overheating, sod the ceremony; they were out.

Jenna slipped her black dress off one shoulder, then the other. Gavin watched as it slid down her body exposing her nakedness for the first time. The sight made him forget what he had been thinking only moments before as he drank in the whole image; Jenna's ample chest, gently curving stomach and the thin strip of dark blonde pubic hair that drew his eye downwards. Her voluptuous form had been painted with blue designs. Didn't the ancient Celts use a blue paint too, out of woad? Jenna's large breasts were circled with scroll motifs, leaving the areola and nipple unpainted. Elongated lines decorated her curved midriff. Circles adorned her thighs, each with radiating outward spokes in a depiction of the sun.

Jenna reached for Kerry's flimsy dress and pulled it off her shoulder. The dress dropped. Kerry didn't react, her eyes glazed as she stared ahead at nothing. Was she hypnotised? No, it was the mead; it spun his head too. He stared at the blue scrolls painted over each of Kerry's pert breasts and felt hypnotised too. Wavy lines across her taut stomach drew his eye downwards, over the black pubic triangle to her long, athletic legs. The designs were clearly vines, with buds for flowers. Jenna had been decorated as the sun and Kerry to celebrate summer.

"May the gods of Avalon receive this fruitful offering of womanhood on this day of Beltaine," said Jenna. Jenna took hold of Kerry's hand and they stepped into the cauldron. The women settled in the water, which reached their chests.

Oliver dropped his white robe. He nodded to Gavin to drop his robe and Gavin did so, the white material pooling around his ankles.

"May the gods of Avalon receive the seeds of manhood on this day of Beltaine," said Oliver.

Oliver and Gavin climbed into the cauldron together. Oliver sank into the water between Jenna and Kerry and Gavin settled facing him, with Kerry on his right and Jenna on his left.

The water was comfortable, like stepping into a hot bath. Gavin stretched out his legs and his foot touched a solid object. Through the water he saw Kerry's Golden Horse.

Avalon. Wasn't that the Celtic Otherworld? The seeds of womanhood and manhood had been received by the gods of Avalon. Gavin was starting to sober up. Wasn't the whole celebration a cleansing one, for the Golden Horse? What was all this talk of consummating the ceremony of Beltaine? Had their drunken debauchery been for a purpose other than 'sins of the flesh' or some other pagan lust?

Saiorse climbed the steps with the almost-empty bucket of mead in her hands. Gavin had been starting to miss the alcohol. When it passed to him, he took a long, deep drink and felt a welcome wooziness return to his body. Kerry's eyes were half closed as she sank until the water lapped around her chin, dissolving into a drunken calm.

Saiorse slid her black dress off and let it pool at her feet. Her petite frame was covered with blue motifs too. Unlike Jenna's abstract designs, Saiorse had leaf patterns painted around the bulb of her breasts and circular apple designs on her stomach. Her legs were decorated with curving branches which weaved up her thighs, drawing the eye to her pale pubic hair, where the patterns tapered into abstract scroll motifs.

"May the gods of Avalon receive the fresh flower of girlhood on this day of Beltaine," said Oliver, with an appreciative smile at Saiorse's bare form.

Saiorse climbed into the cauldron and sat down in the centre, her white-blonde hair swirling around her chest.

Movement. He turned his head to see Mistress C climbing the steps with a wicker basket in her arms.

Gavin's sleepy arousal changed to sober horror; Mistress C wasn't going to join them, was she? She wore a silvery dress with an eye-catching sheen, forcing him to think of what she had on underneath. He tried to distract himself from thoughts of her naked and looked to Kerry instead. She was still conscious, thank goodness.

Mistress C leaned forward and held the wicker

basket over the pool. "Mighty Arawn, take this offering of fruit in the Cauldron of Knowledge on this day of Beltaine. Accept the sacrifice of flesh and bless the Cauldron of Knowledge, opening the doors of Avalon to us," she said.

Sacrifice of flesh? Despite his dozy contentment, curiosity stirred Gavin.

She tipped the basket. Dozens of apples splashed into the cauldron and bobbed between them. Gavin was tempted to eat one; his stomach rumbled for not only breakfast, but lunch too. He knew he should wait and see what happened next. Mistress C had better not get naked; she could keep her wrinkly old body well away from the celebration.

Mistress C turned to leave. Good. She descended the steps. Phew. She was gone.

Saiorse picked up an apple. With Mistress C gone, Gavin relaxed to the sensual delights of the cauldron once more.

"May the apple of Avalon unite us," said Saiorse. She held the apple in her teeth. Oliver moved to face her and bit the apple from the other side. They ate a chunk each and let the bitten apple float away.

Saiorse lifted herself up and moved onto Oliver's lap. Oliver placed his hands on her waist and pulled her down on top of him. Saiorse's face was frozen, her mouth open, as her body accustomed itself to the feel of their embrace. Gavin heard her gasp; the virgin was deflowered. Saiorse and Oliver rocked slow and steady. The girl looked pained at first, but began to relax into the rhythm, the water rippling from their motions.

Hedonism before the gods; whatever gods they were. These ancient gods had been worshipped long before the Anglo-Saxons, longer even than the Romans. The gods of the ancient Britons condoned a decadent celebration of mead, apples and sex.

As Oliver and Saiorse consummated their union in the Cauldron of Rebirth, Jenna reached for Gavin's hand and tugged him towards her. Did she want round two with him? He was too drunk, too sleepy for that. Jenna pushed him away. No, she didn't want more sex, she was swaying. Her breasts skimmed the top of the water as she leaned sideways towards him, then pulled away to her left. Gavin reached for Kerry with his right hand and linked his fingers through hers. As Jenna pulled him to the left, he pulled Kerry, until all three were in a steady, swaying rhythm. Kerry let her body flop from side to side, her long black hair dipping into the water. Gavin smiled; she was going to have one hell of a hangover tomorrow.

Gavin, Kerry and Jenna kept swaying until Oliver and Saiorse closed the Beltaine ceremony in the cauldron and fell apart, breathing heavily. Gavin leaned his head back against the bronze rim of the cauldron and stretched his arms along the sides. He felt the wet weight of Kerry's unconscious head against his right shoulder and let his head loll against the top of hers. The last of the afternoon sunlight filtered through the apple and blossom trees. Had their drunken pagan debauchery gone on until dinner time? Gavin's stomach rumbled, but he could barely lift his head, let alone think about eating. He let his chin tilt forward onto his chest as his eyes closed to a heavy, inebriated slumber.

Chapter 14

May the gods of Avalon receive this fruitful offering of womanhood on this day of Beltaine.

May the god of Avalon receive this fruitful offering of womanhood...

May the god...

The god...

Arawn.

Arawn.

Kerry stood on a jetty, similar to that from her dream. This time there was no Tameses. She stood poised at the edge overlooking a giant bronze cauldron.

She had celebrated Beltaine in a similar cauldron; a ritual to honour the Golden Man, Belenus, with Gavin, Oliver, Jenna and Saiorse, but now she stood alone. Kerry looked around. The cauldron wasn't in Oliver's back garden. She was in a clearing.

Where was her Golden Horse? She leaned forward to peer into the cauldron. It had to be on the bottom of the metal vessel.

The water bubbled and steam swirled around her face, massaging her skin. She focussed her gaze on the bottom of the cauldron.

Instead of her Golden Horse, she could see a face.

A man peered at her, through the whirlpool of bubbles. He wasn't the Golden Man, Belenus. This man had dark hair and dark eyes. Unlike Belenus, he had lines around his eyes and mouth, although his face still retained a youthful strength. He had an intensity as he gazed at her, and another expression lingered in his eyes; lust.

Kerry couldn't take her eyes from him. His face was familiar. She thought of her visions of the past, when she had seen the world through the eyes of a girl from two millennia ago. He hadn't been there. Then who was he? Where did she know him from?

The bubbling whirlpool widened around the man. Kerry could see behind him. The landscape was dominated by a black, shadowy forest. A dense, grey fog lingered over the trees. A few scattered farmsteads lay near a river, but they too were thrown into shadow. She couldn't tell if it was night or day; there was no sun, moon or stars. A heavy, lead-grey sky blanketed the land. Beyond the black forest stood a huge mountain, shrouded by a menacing mist that weaved around it, like ribbons around a maypole.

"Kerry. Come back to me soon," said the man.

"Who are you?" Kerry said, into the whirlpool.

"The ages that pass between our worlds are too long."

Kerry hesitated. "Arawn?"

The whirlpool closed, covering the face of the Underworld God.

Darkness enveloped Kerry. She understood; it was a dream from which she was waking.

She waited for the darkness to dissipate, but it didn't.

Panic rose in her. Was she trapped? Mistress C had said something of becoming trapped between worlds, soulless. Had she forfeited her soul by looking into Avalon?

"Belenus!" Kerry cried. "Arawn!"

Sunlight or shadow. Kerry knew which she preferred. She opened her eyes as wide as she could and saw a pinpoint of light growing bigger. Bigger. Whiteness consumed her. She let it envelope her body, embracing the warm kiss of the sun on her face.

Chapter 15

Gavin opened his eyes. It was dark. He looked around, disoriented. Kerry's legs were strapped over his. Jenna lay on his left shoulder. His pinned left arm was numb under her bodyweight. It took him a moment to realise they were on the floor of the reception room. All three were clothed; Jenna in a dress and he and Kerry in jeans and T-shirts.

How had they got out of the cauldron? How had they got dressed? He had been so tanked he hadn't been able to move his mouth, let alone his legs.

Oliver and Saiorse slept across from them in a huddle on the sofa. Gavin couldn't recall anything after the cauldron: Oliver and Saiorse and their apple-fuelled sex, the swaying and then the dozing off. Thankfully they had gotten out before the water boiled; it could have been a nasty death.

Kerry sat up with a snap, making Gavin jump.

"Woah, Kerry, what are you trying to do - give me a heart attack?"

"Gavin, it's dark. What time is it?" she said. Her voice sounded panicky in the darkness.

"Dunno. Midnight? It was sunset when we fell asleep in the cauldron."

Through the dim light, he saw her rub her face in her hands. "Arawn." She gave a long exhale. "Sheesh, I just had the weirdest dream."

Gavin rubbed his brow in the darkness. "Not another one. Listen, no more trips down to the river to get another demonic idol, OK?"

Even through the gloom, he could see her frown. "Don't say that about my--"

"I know, I know, your precious Golden Horse," he

said.

Voices from downstairs pricked his attention, followed by a distinct metallic sound, like a spoon being tapped against a metal pot. Gavin put his finger to his lips. "Ssh. Someone's in the kitchen."

"Huh? Who?"

She had a good point. Everyone was in the room with them. "Don't wake the others," said Gavin. He stood up. Stars swam before his eyes. He had one hell of a hangover. He listened. Two people talked downstairs; a deep female voice and the low growl of a man's reply.

"That's Mistress C," said Kerry. "Wonder what she's doing?"

"More crazy rituals, probably," said Gavin.

Kerry got to her knees. Gavin offered his hand and pulled her up. "If she's cooking something, anything, I'll eat it. I'm starved," she said.

Gavin helped pull Kerry to her feet. The smell of apple porridge watered his mouth as walked out of the reception room doorway.

"When we got out of the cauldron, did you bring my Golden Horse?" said Kerry.

"I don't remember how we got out of the cauldron, so, no," he said.

"It must still be there, then. Hope it hasn't melted. A fire burning from midday til midnight would melt it, wouldn't it?"

Gavin shrugged. "Beats me. I can't think, my head is fried."

They crept out into the hallway.

Kerry prodded him. "You've sure changed your tune. You normally want my Golden Horse back more than me."

"Not anymore. I just want out of this house and

back up home." In his sobering mind, images of the Beltaine ceremony flooded back: Kerry and Oliver at it like rabbits on the altar, Jenna in her horse mask and he with his sun crown, Saiorse and Oliver in the cauldron. Witchcraft and debauchery. "Kerry, do you remember much of earlier?"

"I think so. I'm not sure if it was real or a dream though. The Golden Man was here and I think--" She scratched her head. "We might have had sex."

"Golden Man? You mean, you don't remember about Oliver?" he said.

"Oliver?" she said, her voice high-pitched. "No. Why, what about him?"

Gavin paused to think. "I really think we should go back to Leeds. It isn't right us being here."

She shook her head. "I have unfinished business. Not just with my Golden Horse."

Gavin rolled his eyes; glad she couldn't see him in the dark hallway. She meant the Golden Man, ghost, figment, lost-warrior of her romanticised dreams.

They started downstairs to the kitchen and dining room, Gavin leaning heavily on the bannister. His head thumped with a banging hangover.

"You really don't remember much about earlier, do you?" He stopped walking halfway downstairs and turned back to look at her.

"No. Why, should I? My Golden Horse got cleansed and now we're going to get it back," she said, matter-of-factly.

"You don't remember me and Jenna doing anything?" he said.

Kerry paused. "You both participated in the candle-cleansing ritual when I got purified - and then you went somewhere else to get purified yourself."

136

Gavin laughed. "I can't believe you forget the debauched pagan sex. You probably wouldn't even remember if you and me had shagged."

Kerry didn't laugh. "Why would you and me have sex? You're my best friend, my travel pal and my flat mate, but we aren't friends with benefits, we're just friends. That's all it is and all it'll ever be."

Gavin was deflated. "It wouldn't have been that bad."

Kerry shrugged. "I'd rather have you as a friend than ruin things and not have you at all." She pushed his shoulder, a gesture to keep moving.

Gavin stayed put. "You'd rather have sex with your boss, a stranger, than with a male friend you've known and trusted for years?"

She wrinkled her face. "What? Oliver! Eew - hell no! And if you're asking whether I'd sleep with you or Oliver, then that's not fair. You're my mate. Oliver is my employer. I don't think of either of you that way. I'd never have sex with Oliver, no way!"

He was stumped. "Wow, Oliver must feel like crap - if you can't even remember doing it with him at all."

Kerry glared at him. "What? Gavin, you've lost me now and honestly, this conversation is really starting to piss me off. If this is some jealousy thing, then fine - but let me set the record straight. You and I kissed once, six months ago, in Thailand. It was a mistake and it would never have gone any further. I find you attractive, yes, but it's complicated."

Gavin smiled. "What's complicated?"

Kerry pushed past him and continued downstairs. "I'm not discussing this, Gavin. Forget it."

He grabbed the back of her T-shirt, halting her. "No, go on. You can't just tease me like that and leave me hanging. I think I should know the score."

"This is exactly what I mean - our friendship is already suffering. I don't want things to go there between us. Maybe you can handle no-strings attached sex, but I can't. I don't want to start a relationship with someone who I know is my friend, a good friend and nothing more."

A good friend who she could flirt with and kiss and then deflect when it suited her. "Kerry, what you want doesn't exist. You want a knight in shining armour. You want all the romance and bravery of a fairy tale hero. But real men aren't like that."

She looked defiant. "You're wrong. There is someone like that."

She meant Belenus, her Golden Man, that figment of her imagination. The sooner they sold the Golden Horse and got her imaginary Briton king out of her mind, the better.

The sooner he got Kerry out of his head, the better too.

Another waft of apple porridge hit them when Kerry opened the dining room door; a fresh onslaught of saliva watered Gavin's mouth. Morfan was in the kitchen, stirring a cooking cauldron on the stove. He looked up as they entered.

"Hi Morfan. That smells great. Will it be ready soon?"

Kerry cupped her hand under her chin in imitation of a bowl and made a scooping gesture with her other hand. Was Morfan some kind of mute? Gavin hadn't had much interaction with him, other than when he had delivered furniture from Sequana's; and even then, Morfan had simply given a nod of acknowledgement.

"Not yet." Morfan spoke in a deep growl. "Cauldron fire outside will extinguish itself by the witching

138

hour and then you can eat."

"Oh, wow. Sorry Morfan, I didn't know you could speak," said Kerry. She rubbed the back of her neck.

"No point speaking," said Morfan.

Poor Kerry; she looked embarrassed.

"But it's basically twelve now," said Gavin.

"Not close enough. Water has not yet boiled off," said Morfan.

Kerry grabbed Gavin's wrist. "Let's go outside and look."

Gavin followed her outside.

"Sheesh, I really put my foot I that one," said Kerry.

"I don't think he cared either way," said Gavin. "Hey - you think he was the one who carried us out of the cauldron?"

Kerry made a non-committal noise. "I don't really want to think of him with his hands on my naked body, thanks."

As they went up the patio steps, Mistress C came into view. Her silver hair glinted in the moonlight as she watched the giant cauldron.

"I wondered when you two were going to come," she said.

Her six-foot frame made a formidable silhouette in the semi-darkness. Even though he was the same height as her, Gavin felt small; she had a magical essence that was imposing.

The cauldron emitted a faint light. Wisps of steam flickered upwards.

"The water has nearly boiled off," said Mistress C. She looked at the sky. "The dawn approaches."

"It's not even midnight. Dawn won't be for a few hours yet," said Gavin.

139

"Not that dawn. The Dawn of a New Age," said Mistress C.

Gavin looked closer at her. Her skin looked moon-bright in the evening glow. She seemed decades younger. There wasn't a wrinkle on her face; her neck had no sinews. He rubbed his eyes. What was going on?

Kerry hadn't noticed anything; or didn't care. She watched the cauldron, her green eyes large. Her mouth hung open in a perfect circle. Gavin followed her gaze.

A man's head appeared above the rim. He wore a golden, two-horned helmet decorated with Celtic motifs. His blue eyes were intense. He had a blonde moustache that fell to his chin on either side of his mouth. Gavin recognised the face from Kerry's drawing; her depiction had been accurate, as if she had an extra-sensory talent.

The man rose. His golden armour reflected the moonlight. His chain mail vest chinked as he stretched to his full height. He stood several inches taller than Gavin at about six three, but he was thin, giving him a stretched-out appearance. The man was dressed like a warrior, but his wiry frame suggested that he wouldn't have been able to sustain the weight of his sword, let alone have the stamina for battle. Gavin looked at Kerry. Her face was full of wonder as she marvelled at the Golden Man of her dreams in the flesh, her open mouth curved at the corners in clear approval. Approval of some weedy dork? Hmph.

Gavin looked for Mistress C's reaction. This had to be some kind of trick, right? When Oliver had taken him out for lunch, he had told him that they liked pranks; he and Kerry. How could a man have been inside a steaming cauldron? A prank would explain it; Oliver had hired someone to wait inside the cauldron and play a trick on them with false smoke for effect. But Mistress C had a benign expression; no mocking smile, no hint of any game.

140

Surely it couldn't be real?

The golden warrior swung his leg over the cauldron and descended the steps. Kerry's fairy-tale knight strode over to her. Even in the dark shadows of the garden, Gavin saw Kerry tremble.

"Belenus," she said in a breathy gasp. "Are you real? Not a dream this time?"

Belenus stood before her like a golden statue. He looked pale in the moonlight. Despite the determination in his eyes, his face was gaunt and sunken. What did Kerry see in him?

More movement in the cauldron diverted Gavin's focus from Belenus. Another face appeared; a second man with a high forehead, dark, beady eyes and a long, brown moustache that drooped on either side of his mouth. His bronze helmet was shaped like the stupa of the Taj Mahal, which brought to mind his travels with Kerry in Asia. The helmet had a neck-guard at the rear. He had a mistrustful look about him. His eyes darted from Mistress C to Kerry to himself, until they settled on Mistress C and he visibly relaxed. He wore a red and black plaid tunic and had a blue cape fastened with a bronze bird-shaped brooch at his right shoulder. The bird brooch had moveable wings which flapped up and down as he stood up. Although he was dressed as a warrior, like Belenus, he was skinny and sunken; more like someone who'd been in a famine than a fight.

"Who's this?" said Kerry. Her voice had a note of doubt. "Did you bring some of your Briton soldiers back to keep you safe?"

Brought them back as bog-bodies, not brawn. Gavin snorted. "Soldiers? Bit too wiry, aren't they?"

Kerry fixed Gavin with a disapproving stare. "Don't speak that way about Belenus. Don't you know

141

who he is?"

"How would I know? Some actor that Oliver hired to throw a dash of historical realism to his Beltaine party?" said Gavin.

"If a stunt like that was true, Oliver wouldn't be missing the show," Kerry spat.

Gavin cast a trepidatious glance over his shoulder. Come to think of it, why hadn't Oliver, Jenna or Saiorse joined them?

"This is not an act," said Mistress C. She greeted the brown-haired man with a hug as he climbed off the steps. She embraced the golden warrior, Belenus, too. "The Cauldron of Rebirth has delivered."

"Cauldron of Rebirth?" said Gavin. "I thought you said it was the Cauldron of Knowledge?"

Kerry looked mesmerised. She watched Mistress C glassy-eyed. Was Kerry really buying all that crap?

"It is both," said Mistress C, without looking at either Gavin or Kerry.

Kerry threw her arms around Mistress C. The older woman returned her embrace with a comforting pat.

"Now I understand why you said after Beltaine, I wouldn't see him as a ghost anymore." Kerry caught her breath. "But why didn't you tell me he would be real?"

"The truth might have been too much for you to process. You might have been frightened and not wanted to participate in the ritual, or else simply not believed," said Mistress C.

"But you know I would have done anything - anything to see my Golden King," said Kerry.

What the hell was going on? Gavin looked from Kerry, to Mistress C, to Belenus, to his six foot five henchman.

Kerry swooped on Belenus with her arms

outstretched. But Mistress C grabbed her shoulders and pulled her away. "Time enough for that - and introductions later. I have fixed the food of the gods upstairs. The warriors must be famished after their journey from Avalon. You two - Kerry and Gavin - are witness to a most wonderful celestial event. Our warriors have not been back for two millennia. I hope you feel proud."

Gavin kneaded his forehead with his fist. He felt sober enough, but he *had* to be under the influence of a dangerous herb that Oliver or Jenna had spiked the mead with. Yes; that had to be it.

"The festival of Beltaine has been most fruitful," said Mistress C. She gave a satisfied sigh.

More talk of fruitfulness; Gavin was sick of the word. The only thing that had been fruitful about the festival had been the generous portion of apples tipped into the cauldron: half the blooming grocery store.

Flapping sounds drew Gavin's eye to the cauldron once more. As Mistress C led the men inside with Kerry trailing behind, he walked towards the cauldron. The beating of wings against metal echoed from within. It stopped, then resumed every few seconds as though a bird was trapped. Gavin flinched. Curiosity overcame him; he climbed the steps to look.

A brown owl took flight and landed in a lower branch of the meadowsweet blossom tree. Gavin yelped. Kerry, Mistress C and the two men stopped and turned. Gavin cringed. Why did he have to squeal like a girl? Kerry looked confused, while Mistress C and the two men looked stoic. Damn bird; emasculating him in front of everyone.

"What is it?" said Mistress C.

"Nothing. A bird surprised me, that's all."

Mistress C gave a look of disapproval before leading Kerry inside. Gavin looked at the owl. It fixed him with its huge, yellow eyes. His misdirected anger ebbed. It wasn't its fault he embarrassed himself. It was only an animal; a creature of the night.

Gavin followed them through to the dining room. Gruel, the food of the gods. The brown-haired man sat at the kitchen table with Belenus next to him. Morfan sat at the head of the table adjacent to the brown-haired man. In the bright light of the dining room the resemblance between the pair was clear; they were brothers. Except for the fact that the brown-haired man was a haggard version of Morfan, the men were identical.

Belenus and Kerry sat opposite one another, their eyes fixed on each other. Gavin flopped into a seat next to Kerry facing the brown-haired, gaunt-faced warrior. Mistress C began dishing out servings of apple porridge into bronze bowls. She set one before the brown-haired man and one before Belenus.

"Eat up, men, we shall do introductions after. Kerry and Gavin, do you want some food as well? It's the elixir of Avalon, but there's no reason it won't give life to the living."

"I'll have some, I'm starving," said Kerry.

"Same," said Gavin. "Thanks."

Gavin shovelled his food. His stomach growled at the ambush after a whole day of fasting. Kerry ate with her eyes still on Belenus, a love-struck look on her face. Lucky git. Wished she would look at him that way instead.

Oh well.

Belenus and the other man ate with voracity. Gavin watched them in turn. Was he mistaken, or did they increase in size with every bite? He focussed on Belenus. Yes; with every spoonful he devoured, his body filled out. Belenus' shoulders widened to fit his armour and his biceps bulged through the chain-mail vest. His wide neck supported his strong jaw. The brown-haired man no longer looked sinewy but had huge sloping trapezius muscles and immense pecs. In less than ten minutes he had transformed from Lindow-man to Muscle-monster.

What the heck was in the apple porridge? Maximum muscle builder with creatine and L-Arginine and steroids thrown in for good measure? All three of them; Morfan, Belenus and the brown-haired man would've put Mister Universe contestants to shame. Gavin hung his head over his bowl. So much for three years of university rugby, bodybuilding and a diet of egg-whites, fish and carbs.

Kerry swallowed her last bite of porridge. "You saw that too, didn't you?"

"Saw what?" said Gavin.

"They got bigger. The same thing happened to Morfan at the Herne's Hunt. I thought I was imagining it, but you saw it too, right?"

Gavin rounded on Mistress C. "Did you put some hallucinogenic herbs in our food?"

"I see you're a sceptic." Mistress C had a defiant smile. "Then let me ask you this - if I did such a thing, why didn't you or Kerry grow bigger?"

She had a point. Gavin didn't answer.

"I think introductions are in order," said Mistress C. "Let me explain. Kerry, Gavin, you're both right, Belenus and Afagddu did indeed get bigger."

"Aff-what?" said Gavin.

The brown-haired warrior grunted. He glowered at Gavin.

"Afagddu is my other son, Morfan's twin brother. You might have heard of the names from Celtic mythology," said Ceridwen.

"Err - I think so. The King Arthur legend, right?"

said Gavin. "This is all a set-up, isn't it? I knew it. Oliver got actors to play a big joke on us."

"Oh Gavin, stop with all that rubbish, would you?" said Kerry. "I want to hear what they have to say."

"Fine." Gavin crossed his arms. "But I'm not fooled."

Kerry gave him a scolding look, but he didn't care. Nothing unusual had occurred that couldn't be explained in simple terms; the men had hidden in the cauldron and had looked emaciated through make-up. Then by a trick of the light they had appeared to bulk-out, probably with blow-up muscle suits or other props from a party store. Cheap tricks, nothing more. Gavin stared at Kerry but said nothing.

Mistress C sat down at the end of the table near Belenus and Kerry. "Let me explain. The Cauldron has delivered, and we have all been fed and watered. I see no reason why we should hold back anything. Kerry and Gavin, my full name is Ceridwen. I am the goddess of the Cauldron of Knowledge and Rebirth. These are my two sons, the warriors Morfan and Afagddu. And this is Belenus, God of the Sun."

"God?" Kerry gawked at Belenus, open-mouthed. "I thought you *worshipped* the God of the Sun, not that you *were* the God of the Sun. But those dreams I had - you sacrificed yourself to the gods… if you were a god you wouldn't have to do that surely?"

"There are many gods - take Ceridwen here for example." Belenus paused and only Kerry's heavy breathing filled the silence, her face enraptured.

Belenus continued. "I was known by many names before, in many different ages, and in many different cultures. To the Romans and Greeks, I was known as Apollo. To the Gauls, I adopted the name Bile. When I came to Britannia, and my people spread North and West, the Western Britons kept the older name of Bile, but the Northern Britons came to know me as Beli, and the Southern Britons adopted the name of Belenus. But here in Londinium, the Britons marked one sanctuary to the East using my older Gallic name. The place is known as Billingsgate in honour of my festival of Beltaine and in honour of my older name of Bile."

Belenus' spoke in a baritone, the drone of his voice lulling Gavin into a hypnotic trance. Kerry watched him, doe-eyed.

"Bile?" said Gavin. "That seems an appropriate name. I don't know how you learned English, or how much you know about our British words, but do you know what bile means in our modern world of England?"

"Tell me," said Belenus.

"It's something you vomit up from your gut after a night of getting trashed," he said.

Belenus' eyes blazed. For a moment he seemed not to react. Then in a quick, powerful move that should have been impossible in his heavy armour, he brought his right fist towards Gavin's face too fast for him to react. As Belenus' knuckle connected with his temple, he saw a golden blur.

The room flashed white, Kerry's startled yelp rang in his ears, pain exploded in his eye socket and he fell backwards as darkness swallowed him.

Chapter 16

Kerry looked at the bleeding cut on Gavin's face. She wasn't sure he deserved that, even for being so rude to Belenus. Did he still have the ridiculous notion that Belenus was an actor? What an idiot.

"You mortals have a lot to learn. This was a good first lesson; never anger a god," said Mistress C. She dabbed Gavin's swollen cheekbone with an iced kitchen cloth. Gavin winced.

Belenus drank a tankard of mead with no trace of resentment on his face. Could he really just fight then forget? Ancient Britons sure were hardy people. Kerry's stomach knotted. He had complete control of his emotions; a true leader. He might be a deity, but he was also a real flesh-and-blood man who knew when to act if his honour was insulted. He was a warrior who could stand up for himself and those he loved, someone who could issue a firm response to a conflict, even if it was to poor Gavin. She leaned forwards with her face in her cupped hands. Belenus' eyes met hers; his moustache twitched as the corners of his mouth rose. Kerry couldn't help herself from grinning.

"Mistress C - Ceridwen. How did this happen - Gods coming into our world? Why here? And why now? I want to know it all. Are you the mother creator?" she said.

Ceridwen looked amused. "No, that's Danu. I am the goddess of fertility and rebirth. I guide the changing of the seasons and the new life in spring."

"And what about you, my Beli? What do you do as God of the Sun?" said Kerry.

Gavin rolled his eyes. "*My* Beli? You can't own him - he's a god."

"So you finally believe? It's about time. Maybe a

punch from a god did knock some sense into you," she said.

Seemed she'd been a bit sharper than she'd intended; Gavin looked crestfallen. Kerry felt bad. She shouldn't have blamed him for his anger. He had his human limitations, as did she; they weren't deities. If roles were reversed and there was a young and beautiful goddess in the room, she'd feel jealous too. Thank goodness Ceridwen was old.

"As God of the Sun, I unite the people. The sun is a symbol of strength. I draw the tribes into one people under one leader," said Belenus.

Beautiful Belenus, handsome Belenus, her strong, noble, Golden King. Afagddu and Morfan were deities resurrected from the Otherworld too, but next to Belenus, they were the epitome of immortal ugliness as he was the Adonis of the Afterlife.

"And what are you two gods of?" Kerry turned to the brothers. Gods or not, how could Morfan and Afagddu have inspired the common people if they were so ugly?

"We are moon gods," said Afagddu. "But not of your moon."

"They are gods of distant moons," Ceridwen cut in. Didn't she let her sons speak for themselves? "I'll explain the whole story from the beginning. I know it must be hard for you to comprehend, as you have you own understanding of how the world works, so feel free to ask me anything along the way."

"I have been around since the dawn of civilisation, Kerry. I was born in a city-state called Eridu, far to the East in a time when knowledge and corruption were young. In those days I was called Inana. Like my people, I was a black-haired beauty with olive skin. My youth was a tumultuous one and so I became known to the people of

149

Sumer as their goddess of sex and war."

"Sumer? You mean, you were an ancient Sumerian goddess?"

"To begin with, yes. I was a young and reckless goddess. Even divine beings make mistakes. Do you know the great king, Bilgames?"

"No," said Kerry.

"You might know him by a different name - Gilgamesh was his Akkadian name."

"You mean, like in the Epic of Gilgamesh?" said Kerry.

"That's right. I believe his heroic deeds made it into an epic poem, sung by the bards. I'm glad to know it survived the ages. In my youth and folly, I pursued Bilgames and propositioned him. I thought that I, the great immortal beauty, Inana, could have enticed him. But he spurned my advances and I was dishonoured," said Ceridwen.

"Maybe he was afraid that you were a goddess," said Kerry.

"No, he was born a deity himself. It was his mother who stopped him. She was the earth goddess Ninsun. She turned him against me with her poison whispers. So, in a fit of rage at my rejection, I decided to turn the earth against her - and her son. I set a bull to destroy Bilgames' city of Uruk. The bull ate all the vegetation and drank all the water in the great city, devastating it. Ninsun was outraged of course and Bilgames was so shocked he admitted to me that had I not destroyed Uruk, we might have had romantic liaisons, but now it could never be." A sad look eclipsed Ceridwen's face.

Ceridwen set her hand on top of Kerry's. Coldness spread up Kerry's hand along her arm. Her eyes became unfocussed. A scene formed in her mind; a beautiful young woman with dark bronze skin and black hair that fell to her hips. She wore an elaborate headdress made of fine golden leaves and rings with three golden flowers extending from the crown. Her woollen dress was dyed purple. Two beaded necklaces of lapis-luzuli hung around her neck. Inana, in the flesh, was more stunning than any mortal woman Kerry had ever seen. The goddess stood in front of the great white temple of Eridu, the predecessor of Uruk by a thousand years. She held a long, thick rope at the end of which was tethered a gigantic bull.

Kerry turned her attention to the bull. It stood poised to charge but didn't strain under the control of Inana. But the moment the goddess released her grip, the bull went wild. It rampaged across Uruk and circled the great ziggurat, kicking up its hind legs and destroying people's houses and public gardens. All the while, beautiful, angry Inana laughed as she watched from the safety of Eridu.

"After that misdemeanour, I was reprimanded by the Council of Gods. They forced me to leave earth and wait in the Otherworld until an eon passed as punishment. The deities decided that in my youth I was unfit to oversee my Sumerian people and that my impulsive actions might have a devastating impact on the Sumerians at war with marauding tribes from the North," said Ceridwen.

"But Eridu... didn't that grow from a village in about 5500BC?" said Gavin.

"I've been around a long time," said Ceridwen. "When I reached the Otherworld, all the time to dwell on those who wronged me only made me want justice. Imagine me, Inana, forced to hide my beauty from the earth in the shadowy Otherworld. I implored the Council of Gods to punish the goddess Ninsun, the mother of Bilgames."

151

"But they refused?" said Kerry.

"No. They decided she had been bitter and cruel to me, no doubt jealous of my looks. Ninsun was an older, fatter woman with curves that could bear the fruit of the earth, you see. The Council of Gods took her son, Bilgames, and brought him to the Otherworld to wait with me. Ninsun agreed to this through an oath, but she swore that Bilgames would not be permitted to be my lover and to stop him from temptation, any union we formed would be fruitless."

"Did you become lovers with Bilgames in the Otherworld?" said Kerry.

"No. By that point, neither of us were interested. Instead of becoming my lover, he became my partner. As she was the goddess of the earth, so he became the God of the Sun, shining in the east of her earth every day."

God of the Sun; Bilgames. Kerry turned to face Belenus. "It's you, isn't it? King of Uruk - Gilgamesh."

"Yes. Hence the name - Gilgamesh, Bilgames. Bile. Beli. Belenus," he said. Belenus exchanged smiles with Ceridwen. Kerry studied the corners of his mouth, the crinkle of his eyes. There was no romantic love between them, and never had been; only platonic affection. Good. Even though Ceridwen was now old, it might have made her jealous.

"Wow," said Kerry. "I didn't realise you were so old either."

Gavin snorted. Kerry gave him what she hoped was a warning look; he'd better be careful or Belenus might give him a bruise on his other cheek too. Belenus looked apathetic; either he'd missed the derision, or he didn't think Gavin worth another tussle.

"After two millennia in the Otherworld, I returned to earth with Belenus at my side," said Ceridwen. "My old, aggressive temperament had calmed in my maturity. Since I had become a voluptuous woman in her prime of fertility, I became known as Aphrodite, the goddess of love. And Belenus was known as Helios, God of the Sun."

Gavin raised his eyebrows with approval. "Sumerian and Greek - two ancient civilisations I'd love to see if I had a time machine. I honestly can't get my head around cities that old when Britain was still full of hunter-gatherers."

Ceridwen's eyes glazed with the look of one lost in distant memories. "Yes, those were certainly the days. I had an affair with the Sky god, Zeus. He gave me a son, Cupid. My beautiful, young, cherubic son helped with my blessings of fertility by shooting Arrows of Amor at my Greek people. But after a love affair between the mortal woman, Medusa, and the god Poseidon insulted my honour on the altar of my own temple, I cursed her to become the half-woman, half-snake abomination that you may have heard of. But it came at a price. As I cursed her, so I became cursed myself."

"The Council of Gods punished you again?" said Kerry.

"They sent me to the Otherworld once more. But, unknown to them, I was pregnant. I had been seduced by Ares, the god of war, en route to a great battle. You have to understand, when men are at war they don't know when they'll have a woman again, and gods are no different. Ares kissed me in a frenzy of passion and threw me down in the dirt of the earth, casting aside my robe."

Ceridwen and Kerry exchanged smiles.

"What you have to understand is that deities were used to making love in their sacred temples, not out in the open like a mere mortal. To my amazement I found that I liked it in the dirt of the earth with his calloused hands all over me, breathing his heavy scent of wine."

Kerry saw the passion in Ceridwen's eyes. The goddess grabbed Kerry's shoulder and Kerry's mind filled with an image from her memories; beautiful, young, alabaster-pale Aphrodite in an embrace with the blood red-headed god of war, their love-making as urgent and sweaty as any commoner's.

Gavin had a dirty grin. "I didn't realise gods did it like people."

"Ssh, you!" said Kerry. Typical of Gavin to spoil the romance. "Did the Council of Gods take the baby?"

"Babies," Mistress Ceridwen corrected.

That made sense; Morfan and Afagddu weren't only brothers, they were twins. Kerry looked at Ceridwen's hulking brutes. With such unpleasant looking children, perhaps it was better to have both at once than be spared the pain of having yet another monstrous looking son later. Kerry chided herself; it wasn't good to judge people on their looks alone. Then again, humans tended to judge first by looks. What about gods? Did Ceridwen feel it as an inadequacy on the part of her genetics to have such repellent offspring? Did gods have genetics?

Ceridwen interrupted her train of thought. "To the Greeks, my twins were known as Remus and Romulus. Zeus, as the head of the Council of Gods was outraged. He made me have them in the Otherworld, but because they were born in the dark shadows, and as a punishment for Medusa, they were born without the blessing of, shall we say, even features." Ceridwen lowered her face. "I was grateful, of course, that they at least had their father's battle courage and grew to be strong warriors."

"It must've been rough on you two to become men in the Otherworld," said Gavin.

"It was." Afagddu spoke in a gravelly voice. "We

154

honed our battle skills among the shadows of Mount Olympus. There were many fallen warriors to fight, both mortals and gods, and since none of us could die our skills became supreme."

"They barely reached my shoulder when I was made to return to earth," said Ceridwen. "After a time, the Greek civilisation declined. I heard from the Council of Gods that Helios, as Apollo, had found a new place to rule under the Roman occupation. I adopted the Roman name of Venus, alongside my other son Cupid, who became Eros, although we were effectively the same deities as in the Greek civilisation. But Remus and Romulus were held prisoner in the Otherworld by Jupiter, the Roman name for Zeus. It was a good ploy. Jupiter kept me submissive and my anger subdued through love of my sons."

"That must have been hard for you," said Kerry.

"A mother's love is also the source of a mother's pain. I didn't see my boys become men in Hades. I heard tales of them from Hermes, the travelling god known to the Romans as Mercury."

"That's interesting - the Otherworld changed to Roman too, same as on earth." Gavin directed the question to the ugly twins. "Otherwise, how would you have kept up with events on earth?"

"Yes. Our father left earth in a great battle and joined us at last in the Otherworld. He had been named Mars, after the fiery red planet. As we are his sons, we became known as Phobos and Deimos, the moons that circled him." Morfan spoke in a monotone, his rhythm staccato, but it was an improvement from before when he had been cooking the porridge. Gods learned fast, it seemed.

"They were appropriate names. He trained us, so we were always circling him, with our swords drawn," said

Afagddu, with a mocking grin.

Ceridwen's expression soured. "But even as Hades became Pluto, even when one society collapsed and another flourished, even as the River Styx became known by another name and the Greek civilisation waned, I was not permitted to see my boys on earth. I began to tire of the old customs, with their pretences of civilisation and honour," she said.

"How did you rescue Afagddu and Morfan from the Otherworld?" said Kerry.

"Apollo helped me. He made a pact with Pluto to release them. You can't imagine how happy I was to have my boys returned to the world of light at last."

"But it came at a cost," said Belenus. "Pluto asked for two lives in exchange for Afagddu and Morfan - two specially chosen souls to be sacrificed in the right way."

"What you have to understand is that the Otherworld is a dark and frightening place. Phantoms exist there - creatures that once roamed the earth and were deemed unfit to live," said Ceridwen. "I hated to think of my sons among those denizens."

Kerry recalled her dream of Avalon, barely an hour ago. A black, shadowy forest and a massive, menacing mountain. She shuddered.

"I thought my boys would be happier on earth. But I didn't realise how cruel the Romans - my own people - could be," said Ceridwen.

"It doesn't surprise me. They're remembered for their cruelty," said Gavin.

"My sons already had Roman names - Phobos and Deimos - but the people gave meaning to those names to dishonour them. For you see, Phobos means panic and Deimos means fear. The Romans felt the names reflected my sons' looks." Ceridwen let out a long, deep sigh.

"You must have really resented the Roman people after that," said Kerry. Even though it was true.

Ceridwen paused to a quiet introspection, before continuing. "I did. I became absorbed by thoughts of vengeance. And it came at a good time - for change was upon the world. Around 390BC, to use your modern years, Rome was sacked by rampaging fighters from the North. Raids by fierce men came time after time and I did nothing to stop the looting of my own people. In fact, I admired the tall, hairy, pale-skinned warriors sweeping in majestically on horse back to attack the Roman people who had hurt me and my sons."

"Did you grow to hate the Romans too, Belenus?" said Gavin.

"I did, but for different reasons than Ceridwen. In 279BC the temple of Apollo, my holy sanctuary, was raided and burned by Northern barbarians. It was the first time I had seen these powerful savages and their strange Druid priests, but I saw in them a strength and freedom that the Romans didn't have, and I admired their bravery."

"So you abandoned your people?" said Gavin.

Ceridwen gave him a scornful look. "Apollo never abandoned, he always adopted and integrated."

Gavin squirmed. "Sorry. Didn't mean to say you were a traitor, or anything."

"The Romans became notorious for hostile invasions across much of the known world," said Belenus. "The Celtic people invaded too, but it was never as brutal or systematic as the Romans. I began to see the Romans as barbarians, not the Celts. It was with this argument that I stood before the Council of Gods and asked if the time was right to become a god of the Celts."

"And they said it was?" said Kerry.

"Yes. I remained God of the Sun, but no longer

known as Apollo. I became Bile. As Apollo, I had always been an ethereal presence, residing in temples and palaces, an Otherworldly being to my people. But as Bile, I became the Sun God on earth fighting among my people, living and eating with them."

Ceridwen patted Belenus' arm.

"You can imagine the effect he had on the Celtic warriors - a golden-haired god-king, tall and strong like them, leading them into battle," said Ceridwen, with a wistful smile. "Whereas I, in my world-weariness became the woman of my twilight years as you see now - shimmering silver to reflect the light of my moons, Phobos and Deimos, who were reborn as Afagddu and Morfan. My other son, Eros was reborn too as Gwion Bach. I became Ceridwen, goddess of fertility, stirring my Cauldron of Knowledge."

Kerry thought of the gigantic cauldron in the garden. "How did you find living among the people instead of in a palace?"

A smile spread across Ceridwen's face. "Wonderful. I loved being down-to-earth as much as Belenus. We lived in Gaul at first, to the West in Aquitania. In earlier times when we had reigned over Greece and before that in Sumer, although immortals fought alongside humans in battle, we stayed on earth for hundreds of years at a time and lived in sacred temples apart from the ways of humans. Humans placed us on pedestals and viewed our existence as alien to their ways. But the Celts were different. They respected the spirits in all of nature. Their humble existence and worship of us as gods among them, in natural sanctuaries endeared us to them. We came to live and fight with them, and this meant changing our immortal ways too."

"You mean you died like them?" said Gavin.

158

"Exactly. In times of war, famine or pestilence, we died for the survival of our people," said Ceridwen.

Kerry thought of her vision; of Belenus sacrificing himself for his people.

"When Belenus chose to leave Gaul for good, he died and was reborn in Britannia. Afagddu, Morfan, Gwion Bach and I joined him. Belenus chose to stay in Southern Britannia at first, fighting Roman invaders in Kent and later, at the Tameses. But I, weary in my older years, chose to go North with my three sons. We set up a stronghold among the Demetae tribe, in what is now Wales. My eldest son, Gwion Bach became an archer. He was always smaller and more delicate than the other two, but skilled with a bow. Afagddu and Morfan became warriors."

"Where is Gwion Bach?" said Gavin.

"They'll have to summon him back," said Kerry.

"Not exactly," said Ceridwen, her voice low.

"It's an interesting story," said Belenus. "Shall I tell it, or you?"

"You go ahead, I've talked enough." Ceridwen got up to make tea.

Kerry was intrigued; why was Ceridwen being so guarded after all her candour?

"Ceri decided, once she had built a new Chiefdom among the Demetae, that she would make a fresh start for Afagddu and Morfan here. You see, it turned out that the Romans were a lot more, shall we say, diplomatic about their thoughts on Phobos and Deimos, restricting their derogatory opinions to their names only. But Britons are more forthright about name-calling. They called the warrior twins the ugliest men in the world."

Ceridwen tossed her head. "The audacity. But even immortals can be wrong."

"So Ceri boiled her Cauldron of Knowledge for a

year and a day. When it was ready, she went to prepare the twins to drink it. But Gwion Bach, who was in charge of minding it, put his finger in it and tasted it. The Cauldron would have given the twins the prophetic gift of knowledge to become wise and respected among the tribes, regardless of how they look and as they were fighting King Arthur at his last battle at Camlan, this would have been most useful. But…"

"But?" said Kerry.

"Since Gwion Bach tainted the concoction, it didn't work."

"I can guess where this is going," said Gavin. "Gwion Bach got the gift and Afagddu and Morfan killed him?"

"Worse. Ceridwen pushed him into the Cauldron of Knowledge as an offering to Arawn. It worked. Afagddu and Morfan led their tribe into victory by driving away Modred of Camlan's men with their fearful ugliness," said Belenus.

Kerry stared at Ceridwen. Perhaps she had been wrong about the goddess' maternal aura. "And Gwion Bach?"

Ceridwen didn't answer. Kerry looked at Belenus.

"The warriors ate him."

Gavin looked sick. "You cooked your own son and they ate him?"

"We were ancient Britons, a warrior society. We lived by our own rules, not the laws of Classical civilisation with its slaves and disease," said Ceridwen.

Kerry's mind drifted to the image of Belenus sacrificing himself on the golden carriage. "But gods can't die, right? So Gwion Bach must be in the Otherworld, waiting his chance to come back?"

"As you can imagine, Gwion Bach's immortal body

lost his looks when he was boiled, while Afagddu and Morfan gained something of his charm from eating his earthly form. Gwion Bach no longer wishes to return to our world looking the way he does."

"He would choose Avalon over earth?" said Kerry. From what she had heard, she doubted this; it sounded like an excuse to appease Ceridwen's guilty conscience. What about the twins? If they had gained good looks from eating Gwion Bach, how ugly had they been before?

"Yes. When gods are born to this world, or leave it, they do so in a manner that befits a god." Ceridwen had an impish twinkle in her eye. "Gwion Bach's last exit shamed him so much, he wants to forget. Being cooked and eaten isn't a dignified exit, regardless of how good one tastes."

Chapter 17

Gavin held his tankard under the running tap. His head pounded; he was glad for the moment's peace. Everyone had moved to the reception room upstairs. He braced himself for the commotion; either Jenna, Saiorse and Oliver would be ecstatic at being woken by a troop of resurrected Briton gods, or they would be pissed-off at having missed breakfast with deities.

He drank and refilled the tankard. His head throbbed. Alcohol and a punch to the temple. Better to learn the lesson sooner rather than later; never anger a god. He probed his left temple with his fingertips. It was swollen and tender, but he was glad of the pain. The Beltaine cleansing ceremony, the orgy, the Cauldron of Rebirth spawning two full-grown warriors; if it wasn't for the reality of the injury, he would've thought it all a dream. That or Jenna had spiked his mead with LSD.

He had slept well after the Beltaine festivities, but he needed more rest. Too much hedonism wasn't good for mortals. Maybe the gods could handle such a lifestyle, but he wanted to crawl into bed and stay there for the remainder of the day.

Gavin turned off the tap and was about to leave the kitchen, when the sound of snapping wood and the rustle of leaves caught his attention. He pushed open the kitchen door and climbed the patio steps. In the grey dawn of the garden, he saw a woman sprawled at the foot of the apple tree. She lay face down over a broken branch. For a moment, Gavin thought she was dead until she pushed herself onto her hands and knees. Her waist-length, strawberry-blonde hair was covered with leaves and twigs. Had she fallen from the tree?

The woman staggered to her feet. Maybe she was

drunk and had climbed the tree to sleep in it. Had she been in the garden all night? No; they would have noticed her sooner. She took a few steps, then fell sideways onto the grass.

As he was about to go and help her, the woman stood once more and tried to walk with her arms outstretched for balance. Gavin opened his mouth to speak, but no words came out. She was tall and willowy and appeared to have no command over her body. Her long, moon-white legs were exposed under a flimsy dress that hung in thin leaf-shaped layers, almost transparent as though it was made from flower petals and not fabric. The woman fell again, her knees grass-stained. She looked cold and vulnerable, grovelling on the ground.

"Are you OK out there?" said Gavin.

No answer. The woman crawled on her hands and knees. She lifted her face to his and Gavin fell under a spell of her beauty; she had mysterious yellow-brown eyes, the like of which he had never seen before.

"Can I give you a hand?" he said.

She didn't speak. She stood up once more, her hair tangled with twigs. As she walked nearer, her unblinking gaze combined with her unusual eyes was mesmerising. She drew level with Gavin and put her hand on the railing of the patio steps. They stood face to face, her eyes nearly level with his, reflecting the dim early morning light. *Hypnotic.*

"Er, can I help you? Are you lost?"

Without answering, she slipped past him, down the patio steps and into the kitchen.

"Woah, woah-- Hey, miss!"

Gavin felt an electrical current linger on his arm where she had brushed against him. He followed her inside to the dining room. She flopped into a seat at the kitchen

163

table and rested her head on her arms. She looked so fragile. An instinctive urge to help her overwhelmed him; why did he feel so protective of a stranger?

He already knew the answer; this was no ordinary woman. She had to be another deity. Better go tell Ceridwen.

Gavin ran upstairs two at a time and went into the reception room, which looked half the size now that it was full of new guests. Ceridwen sat in an armchair, flanked by Afagddu and Morfan standing as gargoyles on either side. Belenus sat in the middle of the sofa with Jenna and Kerry on either side. Kerry looked ready to devour Jenna if she made a move on him and Jenna scowled back at her. Oliver stood at the fireplace, his eyes ablaze with the fire of a man who had summoned the ultimate power. Saiorse sat cross-legged on the floor at Oliver's feet; an innocent girl caught up in a bunch of Druidic madness.

"There's a woman in the kitchen," said Gavin. "I think she needs help."

"What woman?" said Oliver.

"You tell me. I found her staggering in the garden."

"You let a drunk into our house?" said Jenna.

"I don't think she's drunk. I don't think she's ordinary either," said Gavin.

It was true. He didn't understand how, but he knew it. The woman had an unearthly presence.

"She might have come out of the cauldron," he added.

"Not possible," said Ceridwen. "We only summoned Belenus and Afagddu."

Gavin thought back to the events at midnight. "But there was that owl - remember? What if the portal to Avalon was still open and someone else came through?"

"Owl? What owl?" Ceridwen's face creased.

164

"I saw an owl come out of the cauldron. Remember the bird that startled me?"

Ceridwen paled. "You didn't mention anything about an owl or the cauldron. Why didn't you say anything sooner?"

Gavin held his hands in a gesture of defeat. "I didn't think there was a problem - why, is there? What's wrong?"

Belenus' brow was taut. "It must be the Maiden of Flowers."

"It couldn't be," said Ceridwen. "She wasn't summoned."

"Who's the Maiden of Flowers?" said Jenna, her voice full of excitement. "Is she another goddess? Maybe we *did* summon her. Our ceremony was quite the success, even if I say so myself."

Ceridwen ignored Jenna. "Where is she, Gavin? The woman you found."

"She's in the dining room," said Gavin.

"Leave her there for now. If it is the Maiden of Flowers, we have a lot to discuss." Ceridwen's tone was so serious that Gavin pulled the reception door shut. Surely the woman downstairs couldn't have been dangerous?

Jenna seemed to have read his mind. "Is she evil? Is that why you want to leave her? How could you not know if someone else was summoned - it's your cauldron?"

Heads turned to Jenna. How could she be so bold to a goddess? Gavin waited for Ceridwen's response, but the goddess seemed too distracted to take offence.

"The cauldron is controlled from two sides. In the earthly domain, I control the Cauldron of Knowledge, which summons favours from Avalon. But in the Otherworld, it is controlled by Bran, and known as the Cauldron of Rebirth, which delivers those from Arawn's kingdom. Bran never rewards rebirth to those who haven't been given a token of flesh. Let's go over the facts. Jenna, did you prepare everything as I instructed?" said Ceridwen.

"Yes. I made the mead with your recipe and gave it at midday. Saiorse, Kerry and I painted ourselves in woad. We all wore the ceremonial clothes you gave us," said Jenna.

"And the consummation?" said Ceridwen.

"Gavin and I consummated the ceremony of the Sun God," she said.

Gavin caught Jenna's eyes as her gaze settled on him. *Consummation.* He had heard the word yesterday, but in his alcohol-fervour, he hadn't taken note. In his clarity, it was obvious. Consummation. Sacrifice of flesh. Summoning. Jenna had used him to conceive a *god.*

Jenna turned to Belenus. "Our ritual summoned Belenus." She squeezed Belenus' thigh. But Belenus didn't seem to notice; his eyes were on Kerry, who gazed misty-eyed back at him. Gavin felt a brief sting of jealousy at Kerry's reaction; how could he compete with a god? Life was unfair. Jenna seemed to agree. Her face showed the disappointment he felt; Belenus didn't want her and she knew it.

"Kerry and Oliver consummated on the altar," said Jenna.

"We summoned Afagddu, as you instructed," said Oliver.

"Wait, what are you talking about? I didn't do any consummation with Oliver. Consummation of what?" said Kerry, wild-eyed.

"I tried to tell you earlier, but you didn't listen to me - you and Oliver had sex," said Gavin.

Kerry shook her head so quickly that hair dislodged all over her face. "I didn't have sex with Oliver. I made love with Belenus - or at least, I dreamed I did - on the altar."

"I'm sorry, my Aithne, but whoever that was wasn't me," said Belenus.

Aithne? Gavin wasn't sure why he called her that, or what it meant. Kerry didn't seem to have noticed; she was hyperventilating. "So let me get this straight. If I had sex with Oliver, without knowing I did, then that means my mead must have been laced with something to make me forget." She looked livid as she turned to face Jenna.

The goddess, Ceridwen, also faced Jenna with a frown.

"Is this true, Jenna? Are you telling me that Kerry didn't participate willingly?" said Ceridwen.

"Willingly?" Kerry paled. "Yesterday I participated willingly in what I thought was a cleansing ceremony for my Golden Horse. After that, whatever happened was not done willingly."

Jenna's face crumpled into a sneer. "You know fine rightly that you humped Oliver willingly and you loved it. Don't pretend you didn't."

Kerry's mouth dropped open. "I would never do that. I didn't agree to take part in any fertility ritual - that was done without my consent."

Gavin had never seen Kerry so upset. Her whole face was red. Was she going to have a panic attack? He couldn't blame her; they had both been lied to. Manipulated. Violated.

"You wanted it as much as I did," Jenna snapped. "How else could the gods have returned to this world without a little sacrifice of flesh? You knew what you were getting into, so don't act as if you're so innocent. We cleansed the Golden Horse. Then we cleansed you and Gavin. The rest was all *your* doing."

167

Kerry's mouth hung open. "*My* doing? Do you think I would willingly drink mead laced with God-knows-what and participate in a pagan orgy?"

Ceridwen turned to Jenna. "If it wasn't consensual, then that means you did not say the sacred incantations as they took their first sips of mead, I presume?"

"Well, not exactly. I left that part out. But what was I supposed to do? Kerry and Gavin wouldn't have taken part if they knew."

"Yes, they would have taken part. My influence guided the whole ceremony right from the break of dawn on Beltaine." Ceridwen clenched her jaw. "The incantations were an important part of the ritual and you conveniently left that out. It is unfortunate that immortal influence could not be involved in the human aspect of the ceremony. I'm afraid your incompetence may have cost us more than we can offer - do I want to hear any more about this fiasco?"

"It wasn't all a disaster." Oliver had an obstinate look on his face. "At any rate, Kerry initiated the carnal act itself - there was no trickery needed for that part."

Kerry made a noise of incredulity. "Are you calling me a slag?"

Gavin had heard enough. He cracked his knuckles. Oliver cast a shifty glance at him and didn't answer Kerry.

"They used us for their pagan rituals without consent and brought back gods without their consent either. What about that poor girl downstairs? Who is she - a goddess? An ancient Queen of Britannia?" said Gavin.

Kerry's eyes watered as she looked at Jenna and Oliver. "What you did to us - drugging us and deceiving us - is criminal. I have half a mind to go straight to the police station in Hammersmith." She squeezed Belenus' arm. "But Belenus is here, and I know my Golden God will help me to do what's best."

"*Your* Golden God?" Jenna's eyes flashed. "I didn't summon him back for *you*. I made a deal with Oliver and Ceridwen - Oliver's gold, Ceridwen's cauldron and my earthly power."

"And my Golden Horse," Kerry shouted. "Your ceremony wouldn't have worked without me."

Jenna narrowed her eyes. "He's mine - I dreamed of him. You can't have him."

"You used me, you used Gavin, you used my Golden Horse and you summoned back a god, but that doesn't mean you can make him choose you," Kerry spat.

Jenna and Kerry leaned closer, crowding Belenus. Gavin knew Kerry's temper; if war broke out between them, Jenna would come off worse.

Belenus pushed the women apart. "Enough of this madness. I am Belenus, God of the Sun. Women have fought over me through the ages, but women don't choose me. I make the choice and I already know who I want."

"Ceridwen brought him here for me, so he means me," Jenna shouted, her dignity abandoned. Gavin watched her rear forwards like a defiant schoolgirl.

"Stop with all these foolish feminine urges, both of you." Ceridwen shoved Jenna back in her seat. "As for the Beltaine blasphemy, I will have to think about what to do. But there's still the question of the Maiden of Flowers. It is obvious that the sacrifice of flesh was successful three times over. Gavin and Jenna summoned Belenus. I placed the apples of Avalon in the cauldron myself - that meant Saiorse and Oliver summoned Afagddu. It must have been you, Kerry and Oliver, who summoned the Maiden of Flowers."

Saiorse looked pensive. "Jenna, remember the flower headdress you asked me to help you make? The one that Oliver put on Kerry?"

"You made a crown of flowers?" said Ceridwen. "Why?"

Oliver was tight-lipped. Jenna's eyes were wide and innocent.

"It seemed fitting. Beltaine is a spring ceremony," said Jenna.

Ceridwen's voice became low and menacing. "What else did you do without my consent?"

Gavin gave a derisive snort. "Seems a lot of things happened without consent."

Blood seemed to have pooled beneath Ceridwen's skin; the goddess was almost glowing with anger. "The Maiden of Flowers is cursed by Arawn. She wasn't supposed to come back yet until the terms of her curse have been spent in the Otherworld. The omens aren't good."

Kerry's eyes were fearful. "Cursed? What does that mean? Is it bad luck for us for summoning her?"

"No. But it means we're in debt to Arawn for bringing back an immortal who hasn't been allowed to return," said Ceridwen.

"We can rectify everything at the Sealing Ceremony on the sixth day," said Belenus.

"Yes, that's true. The gates of Avalon will be open until then. Jenna, I suggest you start telling me step by step everything you did so that we can get to the root of this blasphemy, before the fates are decided," said Ceridwen.

Jenna's voice shook. "What fate? Not punishment for our mistakes? I did everything you told me, I just did a bit extra. I used the white candles for purity and the green candles for fertility and the frankincense to cleanse and the knife to cut. Kerry even wore a green dress, the colour of birth. I didn't miss a single ingredient in the mead - red raspberry leaf, dong quai, false unicorn, red clover and black cohosh to initiate the token of flesh. Gavin and Oliver drank the procurement with Hawthorn and Dragon's blood to boost their fertility. Saiorse kept her virginity intact for the ceremony and we checked her birth certificate to make sure she's over eighteen."

Ceridwen spluttered. "Eighteen?"

Jenna trembled. "Yes. Of course."

"Mighty Arawn, forgive us." Ceridwen closed her eyes. "The age of adulthood among the ancient Britons is twenty. Not eighteen, *twenty*."

Silence fell. Gavin listened for sounds from downstairs. Was the Maiden of Flowers still there? Why couldn't they sort it all out and give the poor goddess the attention she needed? Cursed or not, she didn't deserve to be treated as an outcast.

"This ceremony has turned out a travesty. We have dishonoured Arawn. I will need time to think of a plan to rectify the damage before the week is out, otherwise we will feel the wrath of Avalon. I made a mistake in placing you as the priestess for this important ceremony, Jenna. But immortals cannot be involved in the Sacrifice of Flesh - that is down to humans, foolish or otherwise. Still..." Ceridwen's chest swelled with indignation. "I was wrong to put you in charge. I should have known that you were untrustworthy, after you gave a token of flesh to summon Morfan in a sacrilegious ritual in your bathtub."

Jenna gave a nervous laugh. "How was I to know it would work?"

"You knew perfectly well. You ran the tap, you filled your bath, you used a personal item of mine to fool Bran into thinking you were me and you did it all on purpose, so don't pretend otherwise," Ceridwen shouted. "I told you to memorise the words for use only on Beltaine,

171

but you knew the power would strengthen six days before and after, so you thought you'd test your power."

"It was an accident." Jenna dismissed the claims with a wave. "I swear it. And as for that bracelet, I thought it was a piece of junk you were throwing away from the Herne's Hunt."

"Stupid mortal girl - don't you realise you're lying to a goddess?" Ceridwen spat the words. "You might dabble with our ancient arts, but you know nothing of the true power we gods possess. You're lucky I don't curse you to put you in your place."

Oliver strode into the middle of the room. "What's the problem, here? Come on Ceridwen. If it hadn't been for what we did, we would have had three gods instead of four. Am I right?"

Gavin shook his head to himself; how could Oliver have such audacity after Ceridwen's threat to Jenna?

"Yeah, and if anyone's to blame, then you might as well blame those two." Jenna jerked her thumb at Kerry and Gavin. "They're the ones who studied the Britons. They should have known about the age of adulthood being twenty - but they never once asked Saiorse how old she was."

"Don't blame us," Kerry shouted. "We barely knew Saiorse. I met her at the ceremony yesterday and Gavin met her two nights before - when she was in the nude, no less. Who the hell would ask a naked stranger their age? Are you mad?"

"Well then, blame Saiorse. She should have done the research. Her dad should have known!"

Gavin was drained. All the lies, the pretence of friendship, the fake hospitality, the drugged drinks; screw Oliver and screw Jenna. It was too much. If nobody cared to check on the Maiden of Flowers, then at least he would.

Gavin slipped out of the room and went downstairs, leaving the gods and mortals to their argument.

In the kitchen, the Maiden of Flowers stood with a spoon in her hand eating from the cooking cauldron. She stopped and turned with a deer-in-headlights look. Her mouth had a ring of porridge around it. Gavin smiled. Her girlish manner was endearing. And curse or not, he was awestruck by her ethereal presence.

"Don't let me stop you," he said. "Go ahead and eat."

As she swallowed the food of the gods, Gavin saw her waist-length, strawberry-blonde hair change to a fiery, red-gold. Her moon-bright cheeks became flushed rose-pink. Her waif-like body filled out to one not unlike a ballet dancer's; strong and slender. The flimsy, opaque dress she wore barely covered her beautiful form, the fabric draped like flower petals over the curves of the truly perfect English rose standing before him.

Gavin was stunned. "Blossom," he said, before being lost for words, transfixed by the power of her immortal beauty.

Chapter 18

"I'm so angry at Jenna. That manipulative little cow." Kerry ripped a handful of grass and threw it into the air. "I should've smacked her one right in the face."

"Manipulative, yes. But you did the right thing by not striking her. There are more rituals yet to come and all of you must participate. Fighting would have made that an impossibility," said Belenus.

Kerry watched the sky through the branches of the apple tree. The back garden made for welcome respite from the commotion inside. She chewed her lip. "It doesn't mean she's off the hook. She lied about cleansing my Golden Horse - our Golden Horse. She put drugs in the drink to make me, you know, do that thing with Oliver."

She hung her head. Here she was, with the Golden Man of her dreams, talking about her sexual encounter with another man. He wouldn't want her now before they even had a chance to know one another. And it wasn't her fault; she didn't know. Life was unfair.

"How Oliver and Jenna did the ceremony was wrong – deceitful. But without you, Gavin and the girl participating in the ritual, we gods wouldn't be here. I wouldn't be here – with you."

It softened the blow, a little. She wanted to enjoy the present with Belenus. "You're right. At least I have you now. And I got the last laugh - Jenna wanted you for herself, but you turned her down."

"Do not have regrets. The power of the mead and the connection with me made you see what you had to see to make the sacrifice of flesh happen. Rest assured that what Oliver and Jenna did is indecent before Avalon. It will be compensated for by the gods. But for now, let us enjoy our first time together in almost two thousand years."

Two thousand years. Kerry's mind emptied of all other thoughts and focused on the time period. Had she been with him before? The clarity gave her answer: yes. The last time she had been with him, she had been Aithne, a wild Briton maiden.

"Aithne. I'd been sleepwalking. So that wasn't a dream?" she said.

"Aithne," he said, his voice low and soothing.

"But I'm Kerry, not Aithne now and this world - the real world - are you back to stay here, for real?" She paused, gathering her thoughts. "What I mean is, are you like a real person? Flesh and blood?"

Belenus stroked the hilt of his sword, absent-mindedly. "I *am* a real person. I'm a god, but in this world, I'm as flesh and blood as you."

"We should go back up North. You'd like Leeds. Do you have to stay here, near the Thames, or are you free to live elsewhere in England?" said Kerry.

"This is a new lifetime for me – a fresh start. I can raise my tribes of Beltaine from anywhere in Britannia. You and me, Gavin and Blodeuedd."

"Blodeuedd?"

"The Maiden of Flowers."

"What's she got to do with Gavin?"

"She will be his."

Kerry was alarmed. "But she's cursed, isn't she? It's dangerous - I mean, we would make Arawn angry."

Arawn. The face of the black-haired man formed in her mind as clear as from her dream. Charismatic and strong, yet... Kerry shivered. Belenus moved closer and warmth filled her, almost as though he radiated the sun itself.

175

"Why did Ceridwen trust Jenna with the ritual?" Kerry said.

"Because she had no choice. Like she explained, gods and goddesses can't participate in the ceremony of flesh. That part is for mortals. I'm sure Ceridwen came at the end to deliver the token of apples to appease Arawn?" Belenus picked up a windfall and handed it to Kerry. "These are the symbol of the Otherworld, Avalon."

Kerry dropped it. A chill passed through her. "Jenna made a mockery of the ceremony."

"And there will be repercussions for her. For Oliver too. They're already being punished for their dishonour. Jenna wanted me and she can't have me. Oliver wants all the immortals to stay with him, under his control. Is that not the apotheosis of bold? Of course, I have other plans."

She grinned. "Like to go up North with me?"

"Exactly."

Kerry lay back against the trunk of the apple tree. "What will happen to Gavin and me?"

"You'll have to take part in the Sealing ceremony on the sixth day. Arawn isn't angry at either of you. You were both tricked into the ritual - you participated without full knowledge of the consequences. The girl Saiorse too was misled. She'll have to be purified, but she will be fine. And Blodeuedd was summoned. She didn't defy Arawn by choice."

"Does that mean her curse won't hurt Gavin?"

Belenus nodded. "What you have to understand about gods is that they don't wreak vengeance on mortals - and each other - easily. Usually it's because of a sacrilegious act." His face darkened in thought. "The more power one has, the more damage they can do with it."

Kerry didn't want to think of vengeful gods; she

176

still felt she had done wrong by sacrificing flesh for a cursed immortal and didn't want to be on Arawn's blacklist. Would Arawn punish her? In her dream he had seemed to, dare she think it, lust after her. Kerry swallowed the notion with unease. "It must be strange to be immortal, to live forever. What's it like? I imagine coming back and forth between this world and the Otherworld must be something like being born or dying. Did you start as a baby the very first time, and then age? It sounded like Ceridwen was saying you can choose your age."

"Yes. Deities are born of water and die of fire. That is how it has always been since the dawn of time. I first came to earth on a huge tidal surge in the sea you know now as the Persian Gulf. People of the world know this story as the deluge that killed all except those saved on board a boat of one hundred and twenty cubits."

"You mean an Ark?"

"Yes. Because of a great flood," said Belenus. "There was a wise man called Utnapishtim. The water god, Ea, told him to build a boat of six decks and seven and nine compartments, which he did. He covered it in bitumen, so that he and his family could reside there along with their herds whilst a monstrous storm raged, which made even the gods tremble. When the waters receded and the cyclone died, the boat touched dry land on Mount Nisir, and the sun appeared. To check that it was safe to disembark, Utnapishtim released a dove, which came back to him, then a swallow, which also came back. On the seventh day, he released a raven which circled and didn't return. Utnapishtim's family prayed to Ea and praised the sun. But the whole world had been covered in clay. On the last remnants of the foamy tide, I appeared out of the clay, brown skinned and black haired like my people, the inhabitants of Sumer.

"You were sent by the Council of Gods?"

"Yes. They birthed me from the frothy sea foam mixed with alluvial mud and the sacrifice of flesh from those who had drowned. All earthly beings are made of this mix in the beginning." He stroked her arm and Kerry quivered at his touch. "The very first time, I was born as a baby and raised by my mother, the goddess Ninsun. I lived through four dynasties of Uruk and came to see my city rise and fall, to be taken over by the Akkadian Empire. The political centre had moved to Ur. Times were changing. When Uruk was finally sacked by the Arab invasion of Mesopotamia, I left this world in a great fire."

That had to be a vast amount of time; Kerry tried to get her head around the facts. Belenus, as Bilgames, must have arrived in Uruk in 3500B.C. The Arab invasion... she tried to recall dates. He had left Mesopotamia as God-king, Gilgamesh, in 800B.C. More than two and a half thousand years; a long time to exist in a culture.

Her concentration triggered an image, hazy at first in her mind. Kerry saw Uruk, the same city that Inana and her bull had destroyed. Belenus was Gilgamesh, young as he was now, but dark haired and bronze skinned. He stood before the great ziggurat of Uruk and watched it consumed by flames. The streets were strewn with charred bodies that lay amidst crumbling buildings. Gilgamesh walked inside the temple. Temple scribes lay dead, their arms laden with the clay tablets that they had tried in vain to rescue. Kerry saw the cuneiform writing, clear in the orange inferno. Household receipts, taxes, documents of marriage, birth and divorce. Gilgamesh ran his hand wistfully over a series of tablets, laid in a row to dry. They had been freshly copied by stylus and hand that day, the teenage apprentice scribe now dead. All that remained of the boy was his charred skeleton, draped over his work; a story that would survive to one day become the great Epic of Gilgamesh. *His* story; Belenus' tale. The tablets had been baked hard in the fire, ensuring that they would survive the ages, just as the flames secured Gilgamesh's exit from the world.

Kerry stared at him and past life made way for present. "Do you feel anything, when you're born and when you die?"

"I feel pain like you do, but I don't know fear of dying because I know I'll return to earth again. When I returned from the Otherworld to become a god to the Greeks and Romans, I arrived in a waterfall that ran into the Aegean and I left the age of Greece when my temple at Delphi was sacked."

Belenus traced his fingers down her arm in imitation of a waterfall. Kerry's mind opened to another image of the past, clear as the present. Delphi burned. The invaders looted statues from the temple. Any men in sight were killed; they slit their throats and stabbed them in the stomachs. Women were thrown to the ground and raped. Children were captured and forced into chains. Babies were smashed against walls.

She gasped at the sight; surely her imagination couldn't be so horrible? Did these events really happen? "When you came to the world of the Greeks, were you born as a man in his prime?"

"Yes, and I walked the earth for many lifetimes; I arrived after the Dark Ages at a time when society was in need of gods. I watched my people survive the Messenian wars. I was there as Alexander conquered far and wide. Many other wars followed - Lamian, Diadochi, Syrian, Macedonian. Then Greece came under Roman rule and my name changed again." Belenus froze misty-eyed as he sifted through eons of memories; Kerry had no comprehension

179

of how that must feel, but she could see his expression lost in time.

A distant age must have been hard to recall, even for a god. To save herself from confusion, Kerry tried to think of dates. Ancient Greece after the Dark Ages; that would place his arrival at around 800B.C. Alexander and Classical Greece; somewhere around 330B.C. Then Hellenistic Greece, with all its wars before the Romans took over around 150B.C. "You've been on earth for a phenomenal amount of time," she said.

"Going back and forth between here and the Otherworld helped. I came and went as a young man, like I am now. We gods can choose our form too. Of course, being a god to humans, it is best to resemble our people. The Egyptian gods chose different forms - take Anubis with his jackal head, for example. But I have always preferred this body."

"Good choice," said Kerry, ogling his bulging muscles; wonder what else bulged under his armour? "I'm glad you didn't choose to keep aging, like Ceridwen."

"Ceridwen indulges her idiosyncrasies, the list of which grows every times she returns to earth. Her rationalisation is that because knowledge is gained as the ages of mankind pass, so too must she age. But I, on the other hand, believe that as the sun is a young star glowing white in the cosmos, not yet a red supergiant, I too will remain a youthful warrior."

"You're the perfect age, if you ask me. Still young, but old enough to know... things." Things like his way round a woman's body. Kerry refocused her thoughts; she'd be mortified if he read *those* thoughts. No point making him think she was sex on the brain. "But I still don't understand something. If you say you come into the world by water, how could you have been born from the

180

sacred oak that used to stand here? The one I saw in my dream the other night?"

"When a god is born of water and leaves by fire, you can imagine that after eons doing the same routine, it becomes tiresome. I decided that I wanted to make my entrance into the world of Britannia in grand style. Avalon itself is a watery abode of many islands on a huge river - I came in on a tide from Arawn's domain. Would you like me to show you?"

"Yes, I'd love that. I saw how you left the world in your chariot of fire, surrounded by your tribes. It was so… brave. So heroic. I want to see," she said.

"I know. Your mind is receptive to the power of Avalon. The energy of the Otherworld resides within a deity for six days before and after Beltaine. It is strong within me now that I am here in flesh and blood. I can show you my birth in Britannia."

Kerry quivered. "Immortals are so lucky. Imagine being able to do that - show people what you want, at will."

Belenus frowned. "I wouldn't call it luck. You wouldn't like the immortal life. When you live forever, you're born and reborn, keeping all the old memories of past lives. It gets tedious at times, repeating the earthly cycle. But when you can lead the ones you love it's worth it."

"I hope you don't get bored of your life with me," she said. "My modern day life doesn't sound nearly as exciting as ancient Britannia, Greece, or Mesopotamia. I wouldn't want you to tire of me or find things here in Britain today dull by comparison."

He chuckled. "It's strange to think of Britannia being civilised. We used to despise the hypocrisy of the Romans, who called themselves civilised, yet they enslaved people and raped, pillaged and tortured fellow human beings. We Britons were free people. We prided ourselves on having no emperor or governors dictate laws to us, instead living by the word of our Druids, who held the wisdom of the gods above all else."

"Our modern definition of civilisation is quite different. There is no slavery and we live in a democracy where people have a say under a government." Kerry looked upwards at the tree branches, lost in thought. "I know you're a god, which probably explains a lot - like how you know English so well, but knowing a culture is more than the language. You have to live somewhere to really understand it. I guess what I'm saying is that I hope you'll like our modern ways."

"I have moved between this world and the next many times, over many eons of mankind and every time, I have made the culture my own. The last time I left this world on my fiery chariot, it was only by flesh. Since then, I have been the sunlight through the trees. I have been the sunset on the skyscrapers. I know something of your modern world and its people."

Kerry looked away from his gaze; she hoped he didn't think her patronising. "I want to know your Britannia more."

"Then I'll show you." Belenus pointed behind her, to the apple tree. "I came into the world of Britannia right here, yesterday, before the Normans, or the Vikings, or the Saxons, before the Roman hold on this country. My sacred oak tree stood in this very spot. Even now, its deep roots are far below in the earth, although it was destroyed long ago."

Kerry's throat was dry. Belenus' oak tree had birthed him into the world on the first of May two thousand years ago. Now he sat again in the same spot; how exciting was it to sit under the trees with a living, breathing deity? "You were born on the same day as me - May the first." Her face grew hot. "Is that why you picked me? You could have any woman under the sun - you even rejected Inana - and yet you want me?"

His eyes had a playful twinkle. "I picked you because we have a connection. You found my offering of the Golden Horse and chariot. It was my payment to Arawn for good fortune in battle and a token to enter Avalon. I melted a hoard of Roman coins and put some of my own immortal essence into it, so when you touched it, we connected. You're the woman for me and I've always known it."

You're the woman for me. Had they been lovers before? When she had reconnected with her past as Aithne, there had been no romance; only a sixteen year old girl with a youthful infatuation and, later on the jetty, a Golden God going to his death who had given Aithne, now a young woman, an affectionate, but seemingly platonic squeeze on her hand. He was a Warrior King. Warrior Kings didn't have time for love. Or did they?

She was about to ask him to elaborate, when he kneeled in front of her. He took both of her hands in his left palm and pressed his right palm flat against her forehead. Kerry leaned her head back against the apple tree trunk guided by gentle pressure from Belenus' firm grip. He spread his fingertips across her head, and she closed her eyes absorbed in the feel of his warm touch.

At first, Kerry felt a strange sensation; not a static discharge as she had experienced with Oliver during the consummation ceremony of Beltaine, but a tingling heat that spread from her head downwards uniting her energy with the life force of the apple tree. She sensed Belenus' fingers massaging her hairline. His intense power stimulated even the follicles on her scalp, creating a force

183

that flowed deep into the soil below her and welled up from the depths of the earth into her core.

A picture appeared inside her closed eyelids, sketchy at first, but becoming clearer as Belenus' memories flooded her mind. Kerry saw the tall, ancient oak tree of her unconscious visions, where the young apple tree now stood. Six white robed figures stood around it; an Elder Priest, four Druids and a young apprentice. They had captured one of the enemy; a Roman soldier. He sat at the foot of the oak tree, his ankles and wrists bound with rope. His eyes pleaded a silent pardon to keep his life, but he showed no fear; rather a searching look for human understanding in the eyes of his foes. Kerry's heart beat faster as she watched the plight of the captive.

The soldier began to speak in Latin. At first the words were alien to Kerry's ears. But as she slipped into the bliss created by Belenus' touch compounded by the fluid reality of the vision, she recognised the foreign tongue.

"You have to understand, I was only doing my job. I have a wife and son back in Rome," he said.

"You ask for your life, but you don't acknowledge how many Briton wives and sons you have killed," said the apprentice. "Your people took my sister, a girl of nineteen who had not yet reached her rites of womanhood in our kingdom, and you made her into a cook and a whore for your Roman officers."

The Roman disagreed; Kerry anticipated a bloodbath at his audacity in the face of the Druids. "I don't know your sister - it wasn't my fault. I was poor. I had a wife to feed and a son on the way. There wasn't any work as a labourer. I had to take up service for the regular wage to send back to her. You would've done the same for food to eat and a roof over your head."

The Elder One waggled an accusing finger. "You didn't seem to care much for your wife when you took our women by force, killed their husbands and burned their homes."

"Show some mercy." The Roman spat the words. "I don't make the decisions - I do as I am told. The orders come from my Centurio. My messmates and I are only here to forage. My son is nearly one and I'll be posted home soon. I hope to see him again."

"Forage? You drove people out of their homes, enslaved men for labour and used women to service your legions. You destroyed land and property in search of treasure in what you call this 'Land of Tin'. You stole cattle and used catapult on anyone who opposed you, all in the name of sport. I do not call that foraging, I call that pilfer and rape," said another Druid. He opened a bag of Roman spoils and shook the loot at the captive's feet. Kerry saw recognition in the captive's face as he looked at what he had stolen; crimes in the name of the emperor Claudius.

Among the golden jewellery and coins, Kerry saw a pottery bowl. The object was finely decorated with a red-glazed surface and colourful pictures of Roman gods. She saw Apollo standing naked with his face raised to the sun. Below him were a row of tiny cupids holding golden bows and arrows.

"The people of Britannia use bronze and wooden bowls - this does not belong to the Tameses tribes. Where did you get it?" said the Elder One.

"It was a present from my wife." The Roman captive reached towards it, but his bound wrists prevented him from grabbing it.

The Elder One kicked it aside. "You lie. Your wife is poor. This is a Samian bowl, an expensive Roman object from the continent. Tell me again, where did you get it?"

The Roman sneered. "It's mine. Give it to me."

"You stole it from your commanding officer, didn't you?"

Kerry watched the captive soldier. He didn't answer, but his silence confirmed the truth.

"He is not a fitting sacrifice to the gods," said one of the Druids. "He is dishonest, even to his own kind."

"He is an enemy and that is good enough. We must honour Arawn by finishing what we have started, or we will pay with a bigger bounty of our own men, taken to the Otherworld of Avalon," said another Druid.

The Elder One looked resolute. He extended a dowsing rod towards the captive Roman's face. The gnarled stick was a Y-shaped rod made of Hazel with a loop at the end. He held it steady in his hands, but as it neared the oak tree it began to twitch and dip downwards. Through her connection with Belenus Kerry knew what that meant; the tree concealed a source of water. "The waters of Avalon have answered and Arawn has decided his fate. He will suffice to appease the god of the underworld," said the Elder One.

The Druids prepared the man's sacrifice. Kerry saw them pour a small amount of yellowish-green liquid from a pottery urn into the Roman soldier's Samian bowl. They made him drink it. He choked and sticky liquid spilled down his chin. Mistletoe; the juice of darkness in the shadow realm. Another Druid procured a grey-green stone dagger from his robe. The motifs on its handle were intricate; stylised animals and swirling engravings. The blade looked like corroded copper, but it wasn't metal; this was jadeite, a highly prestigious stone used only for offerings of great importance. Did the Roman captive merit such a ceremony?

"Mighty Arawn, hear us today. Accept this sacrifice

186

as an offering to keep the Tameses tribes safe in battle against the enemies who have come to ravage our shores."

Kerry recoiled as the Elder One grabbed the Roman's hair and yanked his head back. He pressed the jadeite knife against the captive's jugular vein and sliced across his neck, below his Adam's apple. The man spluttered blood over his heavy mail shirt and shoulder cape. The Druids hummed as the Roman made wet gurgling noises, choking on his blood.

"Ohmmmm."

Soft sounds of the Roman smacking his lips, gasping for breath that wouldn't come.

Kerry wanted to shut her eyes; but the vision was inside her mind. Belenus must have sensed her shock; he increased his massaging pressure on her head. She embraced the protective touch of her Golden Sun God, keeping her safe in the present as she witnessed the past.

As the Roman's head slumped forward onto his armoured chest, the Druids threw his auxiliary soldier's equipment at his feet; his pilum, a heavy javelin which clattered on the ground causing the flexible tip to bend; his pugio, a short dagger and his gladius, a short thrusting sword that showed a dried black crust of blood that he hadn't time to clean during his pursuit. His scutum, the curved, rectangular shield that Kerry had seen in previous visions had been lost when the Britons had chased him. All of his equipment would do him no better in battle in the earthly world, nor would it provide him protection in Avalon; the weapons would serve as an offering to Arawn, alongside his life.

Wind stirred. The sacred oak tree creaked, and its branches swayed. The gods had heeded the sacrifice and had opened the gates of Avalon to answer the Druids' prayers.

Kerry flinched as the ancient tree split from the top down. A huge torrent of water gushed out of the sacred oak. As the river of Avalon poured into the earthly domain, Belenus arrived on the surge, reborn in his full golden armour. He landed on his feet with his hand on his scabbard, ready for battle. The water crashed around him and scattered the Druids. The Druids resumed their circle around the damaged sacred oak knowing that the Sun God had been sent in response to the drink of the Otherworld, mistletoe, offered in the Samian bowl of Apollo. They began chanting, their arms outstretched.

Kerry felt Belenus release his grip on her head, one finger at a time. The vision swirled into the mists of the past. She opened her eyes to the present and felt the young apple tree against her back, where the sacred oak had once stood, now lost in antiquity. Belenus wore the same armour she had seen him reborn in exactly two thousand years ago. The sight caused her momentary disorientation; she looked around for the Druids and the dead Roman. But she was back in the twenty-first century, in Oliver's garden, in a civilised time.

"You really meant it when you said you made your entrance in grand style," said Kerry, awed. "It really scared the hell out of those Druids."

"How do you feel? It didn't exhaust you too much, I hope. If one is not careful, what is dead can drain the living life force. Do you need a while to recover?" he said.

"I'm OK. It was unbelievably real - I could even understand the Latin they spoke. Belenus, how did you learn English?"

"The sun can reach any corner of this world, even from Avalon. I visited this world many times and watched Britannia as a ghost of the past. I learned of its history and its language as it happened." He stood up, tall and proud.

"I am the Sun God. Where I want to go, I go. What I want to do, I do. And what I want to know, I know."

Chapter 19

The Maiden of Flowers danced in the middle of Eel Brook Common, whirling round and round a tree. Gavin sat mesmerised as he watched her. Her pale pink dress caressed her smooth thighs and her hair floated around her flawless face. He was captivated as she orbited around him. No, the other way around; she was still at the centre of his universe and the whole world revolved around her in a dizzying maelstrom. *Nuts,* he was spouting poetry in his head. The stunning redhead made him giddy.

"Blossom… no that's not your real name, is it? You're as beautiful as an English rose, but you have a real name, don't you? What is it?" he said.

"Blodeuedd," she said in a voice as silky as her heavenly form.

"Blood with?" he repeated. "Interesting name. What does it mean?"

She stopped her intoxicating dance and sat in front of him cross-legged. A red-gold shower of hair cascaded over her lovely breasts. She cupped her hands around her face, thumbs on her chin and forefingers on her brow, spreading the other fingers outwards like flower petals. But she didn't answer.

"Are you a goddess too, Blodeuedd? You must be," he said.

Still no answer. She began to sway in her seated stance, her body curving S-shaped grooves as she snaked her arms through the air. It was the most erotic, seductive dance he had ever seen, yet still eluding an innocent naivety. Only a goddess could perform such a display. Although he couldn't take his eyes off her, from his peripheral vision, Gavin could see passers-by watching her too.

"Kerry and Oliver summoned you. Does that mean you have some of Kerry in you? She gave you a flesh sacrifice - a part of herself to give you life," said Gavin. "Hey, is that what Blodeuedd means? Blood?"

"Flower face," she said at last.

Gavin couldn't resist; he reached to touch her hand. A white flash simultaneously dazzled his eyes and stung his fingertips, making him withdraw his hand.

"Ouch. You really give off a lot of energy," Frustration welled; were goddesses made of electricity? What if he couldn't ever touch her?

"Blodeuedd gives off flowers, not energy," she said in a delicate, feminine voice. She scooped up a daffodil and sprinkled the petals over his head.

"You mean, yourself? Why do you refer to yourself by your own name?"

Blodeuedd got to her feet. Her hair streamed behind as she began to whirl around him again.

A woman and her dog approached. The Labrador-cross sniffed Blodeuedd's legs. Blodeuedd dropped to her knees and sniffed the dog's muzzle. When the dog moved away, Blodeuedd chased after it on her hands and knees. As the woman drew level with Gavin, her face showed confusion and alarm.

"Er, Blodeuedd, didn't you have dogs in your time?" he said.

The woman passed by and looked back at Gavin over her shoulder; her eyebrows were raised in an expression of scorn. She shook her head as she left.

A thought occurred to Gavin; what if Blodeuedd was mentally impaired? Maybe her innocence was because of a learning disability. Could goddesses have disabilities? But as enigmatic as she was, he wasn't sure if he could connect with her if she was a simpleton.

191

Blodeuedd shook the tree and Gavin closed his eyes against a rain of leaves. She certainly gave a decadent show; all legs-and-breasts-and-see-through-dress-and-hair, and he couldn't deny, hers was a body to die for.

"Hey, I got it. This tree must have some meaning for you. Is there something buried under it? Or maybe it's this place... Eel common?"

"Blodeuedd likes blossoms," she said.

Gavin wasn't sure what to think. She could clearly understand him so why was she giving such clipped answers, and all the while teasing him with her body? It had to be on purpose; she wanted him to find out more. That made sense; she was so innocent, it had to be a game. Blodeuedd rubbed herself cat-like against the tree trunk, gyrating against the bark. His confusion ebbed; her sensual display aroused his curiosity, and more. Who really was this sexually provocative, hypnotic nymph? He had to know.

"Blodeuedd, where are you from? Why are you here? Are you a faery? You have to tell me something, anything about yourself."

"Blodeuedd enjoys the sun. Blodeuedd is happy that Belenus is with her because he is the God of the Sun. Blodeuedd likes flowers, and dancing, and beauty, and daylight."

Gavin was deflated. "So, you're in love with Belenus then?"

"No. Blodeuedd is in love with life. Blodeuedd likes legs and feet and dancing and sunshine," she said.

The more she spoke, the more her mystery grew. She liked legs and feet? Granted, she had the loveliest legs he had ever seen, but what did she mean?

"Who taught you to speak English? Did you learn in the Otherworld, in Avalon? And why did you come back now, why this year?"

192

"Gavin has so many questions," she said. "Blodeuedd will try to answer. English is new for Blodeuedd, only today. Blodeuedd couldn't learn English in Avalon because Blodeuedd lived in darkness in a different form. But Blodeuedd learns fast. And when Blodeuedd got summoned, she saw a chance and went towards the light."

"What do you mean you lived in a different form in Avalon? You mean, like a ghost, or a shadow, or something?" he said.

"A dark form." Blodeuedd's face broke into a huge, juvenile smile. "Before, Blodeuedd used to spread her wings wide to the shadows. Now she spreads her fingers wide to the sun."

Now she was speaking in riddles. Gavin wanted to understand, but his own rhetorical questions made more sense. *Spreads her fingers wide to the sun...* either she was sleeping with Belenus or infatuated with him.

"Blodeuedd didn't speak for a long time in Avalon, so Blodeuedd forgot how to talk good. Now Blodeuedd enjoys talking."

"Blodeuedd forgot how to talk *well*, not good. And it would be better if you said *I* instead of *Blodeuedd*," said Gavin.

"I forgot how to speak *well*," she repeated.

"That's good, that's really good," he said. "You're a fast learner."

"You mean, that's *well*, that's really *well*," she corrected.

Nuts, this was going to be a tricky one. "No - you see in some instances we use the word 'good' like, 'the sun makes me feel good', or you can say, 'the sun makes me feel well', err..." Crap. It was a rubbish explanation. He wasn't an English teacher; his stupid example would only

193

confuse her even more.

"The sun makes you feel good too?" she said.

"Yes, actually it does." Phew; he was glad for the digression. If Blodeuedd was going to stay permanently in London, there would be time to get her some English lessons. On the other hand, she was doing well for someone who had only been speaking English for a few hours. Maybe she wouldn't need help. She picked up the lingo at a rate only a deity could muster; so fast that she couldn't possibly be an immortal simpleton.

"Why didn't you speak in Avalon? Did you live alone there? I mean, Morfan speaks in fragmented sentences like you do too. Is it a regional thing in Avalon, maybe?"

Come to think of it, isolation couldn't have been the reason, nor a regional influence; Ceridwen and Belenus had no speech impediments. Nor did Afagddu and he was Morfan's brother.

"No. But Blodeuedd has her condition," she said.

Condition; so she *did* have special needs?

Blodeuedd stopped dancing and gave an adorable pout. "Blodeuedd was naughty, in her last lifetime."

"What did you do?"

"Blodeuedd was bad."

Gavin was intrigued. "You can tell me. I promise I won't think less of you."

"Blodeuedd won't ever, ever misbehave again."

"What is it? You can tell me…"

"It's difficult for Blodeuedd to say," she said.

"Take your time, I'm listening." Gavin leaned forward. Blodeuedd wasn't inept at English; she was a master of generating mystery.

Her face brightened. "Blodeuedd was born of flowers a long, long time ago. Blodeuedd came to this world by magic. Blodeuedd's master in the last lifetime was Gwydion and he was a master of magic. Gwydion made Blodeuedd a woman with gentle hands."

Gavin quashed a jealous niggle. "What do you mean, he *made* you a woman?"

"Made - created. Gwydion made Blodeuedd in a cauldron of blossoms - oak, broom and meadowsweet - and dirt of earth and blood of a man called Lleu. Gwydion made Blodeuedd to be the husband of Lleu because Lleu was Gwydion's nephew. Lleu's mother didn't want him tied to a mortal woman, so Blodeuedd got made of flowers, specially to be Lleu's wife."

That was *nuts*. She seemed so real, so flesh and blood, it was hard to get his head round the fact that she was a *non-human* being, not born from a mother and father.

He realigned his thoughts. "What did you do that was so bad?"

"Blodeuedd was happy with Lleu at first, but soon, Blodeuedd loved another man. Blodeuedd's new man was a huntsman and the strong and brave Lord of Penllyn, called Goronwy. He passed through Blodeuedd's village when Lleu was out visiting Math one day, and he and Blodeuedd made love."

"You mean, you cheated on your husband?" Gavin couldn't help the sour edge to his voice; she was too good to be true. He knew there had to be a catch: infidelity.

"Blodeuedd and Goronwy made plans to kill Lleu. So Goronwy made a big spear. He threw it at Lleu, but Lleu didn't die. The gods were sorry for Lleu and turned him into an eagle and Lleu flew away. But what Blodeuedd and Goronwy did was so bad, Gwydion and Math punished us. Math killed Goronwy in his sleep with Goronwy's own spear and Gwydion turned Blodeuedd into an owl. Blodeuedd was the Maiden of Flowers no longer. Blodeuedd changed into a bird of the night."

Gavin inhaled until his head felt light. "It was you I saw - that brown owl. That was you in the cauldron. Now I know what Ceridwen meant when she said you were cursed by Arawn. But how long does your punishment last?"

"Blodeuedd's curse began when the Romans were leaving Britannia. Now Arawn's curse is almost over. Avalon is a land of shadow. In darkness, Blodeuedd is an owl all the time, but Blodeuedd doesn't like being a bird of the night. When morning light came today, the first Blodeuedd saw since the days when the wall of Britannia was abandoned, Blodeuedd changed to a woman and fell from the tree." Tears came to her eyes. "Blodeuedd forgot how it felt to have a woman's body. Blodeuedd wants to stay as a beautiful woman under the sun. Blodeuedd wants to give love to a man and won't be bad in this lifetime, or ever again.

Did that mean Blodeuedd had been cursed for nearly seventeen hundred years? The wall of Britannia… Hadrian's wall had been abandoned around A.D.350. To think that she had been around for so long was startling. "I'm sure you've learned your lesson, but it isn't up to me. If Arawn cursed you for so long, he must have been well pissed-off," he said.

"Well pissed-off?" she said, furrowing her pretty face.

"Angry," said Gavin.

Blodeuedd lowered her pretty head and looked upwards at him, fluttering her eyelashes. "I want to be a good wife to you," she said.

It was the first proper sentence she had said in

English. Gavin reeled; but not at her grammar. Had she made a mistake, or did she mean it? Wife?

Chapter 20

Kerry leaned her shoulder against the wall of the Herne's Hunt restaurant. Gavin pressed his forehead against the doorframe and stared at his feet with an empty expression. What was up with him? He wasn't still grumpy that she'd told him they'd never be anything more than friends, was he?

"Well, go on. I'm listening?" she said.

He peeled a flake of paint off the door. "I don't know where to start. Everything since yesterday has been mind-blowing. I mean, who would believe it?"

Sheesh, Gavin could be such a moan. "You didn't seem to mind earlier - you were gone for ages. Where did you disappear off to anyway? You snuck out while we were all arguing and I went out to look for you in the back garden, but you weren't there," she said.

Gavin was nonchalant. "I followed Blodeuedd. We went to Eel Common."

Kerry nudged him with her elbow. "You could've told me where you were going."

He poked her back. "Am I supposed to report to you now for approval if I want to go anywhere?"

She stuck her bottom lip out at him, and the corner of his mouth twitched into a half-smile. Thank goodness everything was back to normal between them, at least. "Did something happen with Blodeuedd? If you're worried about her being cursed, it's OK. Belenus said it won't affect you. It's not going to put you on the blacklist with the gods too."

"It's not that. She's amazing. I mean, stunning doesn't even come near it. She told me all about her past and her curse. You know Arawn put a spell on her to become an owl at night?" His eyes widened. "Have you ever heard of anything more nuts?"

"Yeah, well I suppose that is a bit odd. Still, I don't see what's got you looking like death. What is it that's so bad?"

He took a deep breath. "She suddenly blurted out that she wants to be my wife. I mean, it's not like we've even kissed. I don't know anything about her. Is that how gods do things?"

Kerry shrugged. "Maybe it's not an immortal thing, could be an ancient Briton tradition, who knows?"

Gavin frowned. "But, *Wife?* Kerry, I don't know. I mean, apart from the owl thing, she's pretty much perfect... but I hardly know her."

Perfect? Kerry thought of the tall redhead. Fine, so she had perfect hair, perfect skin, curvy in all the right places and taut in the rest. Kerry imagined herself next to Blodeuedd. She was a little puffy-eyed from the lack of proper sleep and too much alcohol and her skin could get one or two spots from time to time, but she could scrub up well if need be. Besides, Belenus liked her; she was his Aithne. She pushed out her chest. Yes, the incredibly hot Golden God wanted her above all other women. Belenus didn't want a perfect-but-boring goddess, he wanted plain-old-mortal, Kerry Teare.

"What are you looking so pleased about?" said Gavin.

Kerry snapped out of her musings. "Hmm? Nothing, never mind. Oh yeah, about Blodeuedd - she's not a normal woman though, she's immortal. It wouldn't be a humdrum marriage."

"You're meant to back me up here! Are you really saying I should marry her so soon? I'm only twenty-two. I don't think I should jump into a commitment like that right away. I want to travel first and have a bit of fun, you know."

"You can travel with her - she's a bird, she can fly," Kerry said. She immediately regretted her joke at the look on Gavin's face. "I'm sorry, couldn't resist."

"We should get going - Blodeuedd said Ceridwen will be cooking up a feast for dinner, some sort of celebratory ritual," Gavin said. He looked happier. "But you're right, it's not that bad. It was so sudden, she just surprised me, that's all. Blodeuedd's amazing, I can't deny that."

He broke into a wide grin. "You should see the way she moves - the way she dances. I think she was enjoying her legs, you know, after all that time as an owl." His eyes glazed as he talked. "There were some awkward moments too, course, when she crawled along the ground and started eating grass. I mean, it's *nuts*, isn't it? Still, it's easy to forget all that when you see how she moves. When I think about the saucy pole-dance she did around a tree, I don't even know why I'm complaining."

Gavin closed his eyes to an expression of ecstasy. "It was playful-at-first, twirling round the tree-trunk, but it got progressively hotter. And then she sat there telling me about her past and she played with one of the nuts from the tree, you know, like, rolling it between her hands and kneading it, and stuff. You had to have been there to know what I mean. She did it in this really erotic way. It was the most suggestive thing I've seen, she just blew my mind away and the whole time, I was so hung over, I thought my head was about to explode."

Kerry laughed. "Your balls, more like it, dirty pig!"

He ran his hands through his hair. "Anyone would think I'm nuts for even worrying about all this. And she has seen some crazy stuff in her life, lived through some major events, you know. Like Hadrian's wall and the collapse of Roman Britain - stuff Belenus and Ceridwen could only dream of living through."

"Hey, don't bring Belenus into this - if it wasn't for his sacrifice, Blodeuedd never would have seen the Romans leave these shores."

Gavin knuckled her arm. "Didn't mean any offense. It's just, she's pretty much any red-blooded man's fantasy.

"Depends on the man," said Kerry. Jealousy needled her again. What if Belenus took a liking to Blodeuedd? He wasn't a normal man though, he was a god. Blodeuedd had been an owl in Avalon for so long that she was likely to be promiscuous, enjoying her body, and on top of that, she was like a supermodel compared to anyone else. Kerry picked a loose piece of skin on her thumb. Loose pieces of skin meant not perfect. She flicked it away and folded her arms under her chest, pushing it up.

Gavin must have noticed the gesture; Kerry saw his eyes flick across her chest before he averted his gaze and looked at the sunset. "Well, Blodeuedd *should* be perfect, but I'm only human. Apart from it being too fast, she can't speak very well, you know, she seems a bit…" He cast a sheepish look at Kerry. "Of a simpleton. How is it you get the articulate, rugged warrior and I get the *child-minded* dancing nymph?"

Kerry paused. "How do you know she's a simpleton? You said yourself you don't know her. She was in the darkness as an owl for nearly two thousand years and now that she's back in the world, it's all changed. It might just take her time to adjust. I'm sure she'll settle in and her grasp of English is bound to improve. Have *you* ever tried to learn a language in a day?"

"Alright, lay off the guilt trip." He cuffed her head. "I know it must have been hard for her being an owl for so long, but she's immortal, she can handle it. I'm only a man. I don't know if I could handle being married to a bird."

"You'd still have day times together." Kerry shrugged.

"It's not the point." Gavin peeled another flake off the door.

"Then get a night job!" She gave him a shoulder bump. "You make it sound like the worst thing in the world. How many men would kill to have a goddess fall in love with them?"

"And you make it sound so easy," he said, shoulder-bumping her back. "Did I tell you the reason she got turned into a bird? Cause she cheated on her last husband and stood back while her lover tried to murder the poor sod."

What could she say to that? Certainly was a huge setback; an immortal, murder-accomplice adulterer. But, if she told that to Gavin, he'd have a go at her for dragging him into the whole Beltaine ceremony; getting him mixed up in the mess.

Kerry sighed. "I'm sure there must have been a reason why she did that. She's a goddess, Gavin, so I'm sure she doesn't make mistakes like people do *lightly*. Give her a chance. Part of being human - and mortal - is forgiveness. It's not like she's done anything bad to you, is it?" Kerry tugged his arm. "Let's get going."

Human and mortal. Kerry wasn't sure she had a right to lecture Gavin about the perks of marrying a deity; her own worries were all too human. Belenus, her Golden God King, had chosen her as a woman for his lifetime. But what would that entail? How could she give him anything resembling a godlike relationship? She had human flaws. How would they - a human and a god - fit into society as a couple? What about other women? Kerry clenched her teeth thinking of Jenna trying to put the moves on him while she was out for a walk with Gavin. She had to admit she felt jealous, protective…if she was honest with herself, possessive. Would women always throw themselves at him? He wasn't only a god, he was immensely gorgeous. It would be hard not to feel insecure.

"What's with that look? Go on then, it's your turn to spit it out," said Gavin.

Kerry wrapped her arms around her waist, protectively. "I suppose I don't like Jenna's interest in Belenus," she said.

"If that's what you're worried about then you don't get men. Have you seen the way Belenus looks at you? He hasn't even noticed Jenna - he only has eyes for you."

"It's not Belenus I worry about, it's that sleazy little tart. She drugged us, what would she do to him?"

Gavin was blasé. "Not much, I'd say. He's a god. Doubt you can drug a god. And if you're worried about him getting tempted by other women, then why would he have waited two thousand years for you? There were plenty of women in the Otherworld that could've kept him busy, if that's all he was after."

He had said exactly the right thing. Kerry squeezed his arm. "I knew you weren't my best mate for no reason. I shouldn't even be worried. I guess things have happened so fast, it hasn't sunk in, that's all. I kind of keep expecting to wake up and find it's all one big dream. Belenus is the Sun God, the King of Britons, and he wants me as his woman. And you've got Blodeuedd, your perfect immortal nymph. Aren't we the luckiest people in the world?"

Kerry looped her arm through his for the walk back along Avalon Road and his face relaxed into a contented smile.

Chapter 21

Gavin's stomach growled at the smell of cooking lamb. The low coffee tables and antique furniture of the Herne's Hunt restaurant had been replaced with a large round table that stood in the middle of the room. Oliver, Belenus, Afagddu and Morfan sat around it drinking wine from tankards. Oliver banged his tankard on the table and clinked the wooden vessel against the gods' tankards as though he was an equal. What were the gods thinking? How could they drink and toast with such a devious, conniving git?

Oliver spotted Gavin and grinned, raising his tankard. "Come and join us, Gavvy. You're one who has the bravado of the Britons - let's put it to the test. Try this."

Gavvy? Was Oliver for real, after all that had just happened; the botched Beltaine ceremony, the drugged mead, the corruption and manipulation and still he was acting as if they were old friends? Oliver had enough bravado for all the mortals put together. Pity Belenus wouldn't knock him down a peg or two with a crack on the jaw.

Oliver poured wine from a clay jug and extended the tankard to Gavin. Gavin stood motionless and glared at him.

"Are you sure it isn't drugged?" he said.

Oliver's smile soured.

Belenus, next to Oliver, nodded his approval of the tankard. Gavin wasn't sure whether to trust him, but if Kerry did, then maybe he was OK. Gavin took the tankard that Oliver handed to him. He watched Oliver top up everyone else's tankards. Oliver sipped his own. Gavin waited. Oliver didn't keel over unconscious. Good; the drink wasn't spiked. Gavin took a sip of his own. It had a strong vinegary flavour; he smacked his lips at the tart aftertaste. The edge of his thumbnail dislodged grape skin from his teeth.

"Wine for you too, Kerry?" said Oliver.

"I'll pass," said Kerry in a low, menacing voice. She turned to Belenus, gave a coy smile and resumed her normal, friendly manner, "I'll leave you men to your toast."

She escaped into the kitchen. Gavin set down his tankard to follow, but Oliver placed a hand on his arm. What was the meaning of such an aggressive gesture? Gavin squared his shoulders.

"It isn't good manners not to finish your drink," said Oliver.

"Says who?"

One corner of Oliver's mouth twitched up into a sneer. "You need to prove your worth among the ancient Britons by downing the tankard all in one."

Gavin jerked his shoulder and broke Oliver's grasp. "I don't need to prove anything."

Belenus clanked his tankard on the table, clearly enjoying the show. "He already has the worth of the Britons - and if you keep up, Oliver, he might show you."

There was a slight mocking tone to Belenus' laughter, but Gavin wasn't about to argue with a god. Instead, he stared at Oliver. He'd punctured Oliver's huge ego. In the absence of his smug grin, he looked weak-chinned and worthless. What a scumbag, thinking he was a match for the gods. His narrow shoulders slumped; he knew his place. Gavin was no warrior-god, but he could certainly knock Oliver out if he gave him any more lip.

If Oliver wanted to be put in his place, so be it. Gavin necked his tankard in one. Rivulets trickled down his chin and along his neck. He slammed the tankard on the table and shoved the empty vessel towards Oliver.

Oliver's mouth puckered as the tankard hit his hand. Belenus, Morfan and Afagddu roared and stomped.

Gavin gloated as Oliver's eyes narrowed; let him stew. He looked down his nose at Oliver before turning, without a word, to join Kerry in the kitchen.

As Gavin entered the kitchen, he saw Ceridwen checking bread in the oven while Blodeuedd stirred a pan of boiling milk. A large cauldron of lamb stew cooked on the stove. Kerry leaned against the counter with her arms folded watching them. Watching Blodeuedd. He followed the line of her gaze, which settled on Blodeuedd's see-through dress. Her lower lip jutted slightly; was there a hint of derision about her face?

Blodeuedd was too engrossed in her work to care, but he doubted she would even if she knew. Gavin walked to her and she rubbed her back against his chest, wriggling up and down in a catlike manner. He wrapped his arms around her and peered over her shoulder. Blodeuedd poured a quarter of a pint of golden liquid into the milk from a measuring cup. The smell of beer reached his nose. When the milk thickened, Blodeuedd siphoned the curds onto a cloth. Once all the curds had been strained, she tied the cloth parcel with string.

"Is that a beer sauce for the lamb?" he said.

"No. Blodeuedd makes beer cheese for the bread."

Kerry raised an eyebrow at Blodeuedd's speech impediment. Maybe she wouldn't lecture him anymore about Blodeuedd learning a language well in one day; he cast a glance to her to say, 'I told you so', and Kerry shrugged.

Blodeuedd lifted the cloth parcel and set it to one side on the counter. As she moved to do so, she pushed her shapely round ass into Gavin's crotch. Before he could think, he moved his hands to her hips. The move hadn't gone unnoticed; Ceridwen turned her head a fraction. His face burned. Goddess of fertility or not, Ceridwen didn't need to see such a display of carnal lust. What was he *thinking*? Blodeuedd had him completely captivated. He cast a sideways glance at Kerry. She rolled her eyes towards the ceiling.

Gavin felt his ears burn. "Where's the other two - Jenna and Saiorse?"

"On the roof, adding spice to the drinks," said Ceridwen.

Hmm. So Ceridwen, eldest of the gods, trusted Jenna too? He wasn't so sure.

Gavin let go of Blodeuedd. "I think I'll see what they're up to. I'll be back down soon, Petal."

"Petal is a good name for Blodeuedd. Blodeuedd is made of Blossoms."

Kerry pointed two fingers to her mouth and made a gagging gesture. Gavin gave her a scolding look; what if Blodeuedd or Ceridwen saw her? Then again, would they understand the gesture? Even if they didn't, they would certainly understand the sarcasm.

Gavin climbed to the first floor. Blodeuedd. Wasn't he lucky? Was he lucky? He had to be honest with himself. A girlfriend who was a deity scared him. She made it clear she wanted to be his wife. What if he never grew to love her? Would she curse him? Or do worse; try to kill him like her last husband?

No. He had to trust Kerry's reassurance; and Blodeuedd had given her word that she wouldn't make another mistake. Although mistake was a rather euphemistic way to describe attempted murder. No; he had to give her a chance. After nearly two millennia as an owl, she celebrated having her human body; she wouldn't risk losing it again.

But what good was a human body if he couldn't touch her? If his fingers felt her bare skin, he'd get an electric shock. He imagined her hands on his bare skin, going lower, lower; sending shockwaves of pain and pleasure. Then she would reach him there and… then what? His dick would get fried. Gavin shuddered.

The thought made him stumble; he almost lost his footing on the rooftop stairs. He sprawled forwards and caught himself with his hands before his jaw hit the wood. As he righted himself, Jenna and Saiorse's voices reached his ears. Gavin crept near the top of the stairs, close enough to see the two women with their backs to the doorway. Jenna's arm rotated in a circular motion, as if she was stirring a pot in front of her and Saiorse's arm moved as though adding ingredients to whatever concoction was in it. Steam billowed upwards.

"What's going to happen to me now?" said Saiorse in a soft, whiny voice. "I gave up my virginity, Jenna, and I wasn't the right age for the ancients. You need to fix it."

"Calm down, darling." Jenna's tone was patronising. "You'll get what you want."

"When? You screwed up. I need you to fix it - *now*."

Jenna's voice became sharp. "What do you want me to do? Keep talking to me like that and I'll fix *you* instead."

Saiorse paused. "You wouldn't dare. You're not the only one with power, remember? My mum and dad were the ones who summoned Ceridwen last year at the Midwinter Solstice."

"Yeah? And what are they going to do? Ceridwen told me they don't have any real power - that's why she came to London and found me. Your *amateurish* parents summoned her by mistake."

"Well if that's true, that you have a power that Ceridwen needs, then you can fix the mistake you made with me," said Saiorse.

There was silence, except for the sound of ripping herbs. Gavin craned his neck but couldn't see what she dropped into the steaming pot.

"I don't know how you expect me to do that. Even my powers have limitations. Beltaine is over, so no more gods can be summoned from Avalon. The next powerful phase is the Midsummer Solstice, but there's a problem with that too. Bran doesn't trust me anymore because of how I tricked him into thinking I was Ceridwen, when I summoned Morfan in Oliver's bathtub, and because of the fiasco with the Beltaine Sacrifice of Flesh. So he won't let me summon any more gods through his Cauldron of Rebirth for this year, or probably ever again." Gavin could only see Jenna's back as she spoke, but her voice sounded bitter.

"There must be something you can do to help me?" said Saiorse, her voice pleading.

"Well, maybe. Maybe there is one thing."

"What?" Saiorse grabbed Jenna's sleeve and tugged. "What is it?"

"I *might* be able to get you more power. You clearly have some blood of the Druids in you, if your parents were able to summon Ceridwen, even through their clumsy fumbling." Jenna snatched a few leaves off a nearby potted herb, shredded them and sprinkled them into the steaming pot.

"What kind of power? What would I have to do?" said Saiorse.

"I could take you on as my apprentice. If my plan goes as I hope it will, I'm going to become a High Priestess - a Druid Elder."

"How are you going to do that, if Bran - and Ceridwen - don't trust you?"

"Bran is not who I need. I got wind of a juicy little fact after the Beltaine Sacrifice of Flesh." Jenna lowered her voice, making Gavin strain to hear. "Arawn, the god of the Underworld himself, is smitten with Kerry. I saw them in a dream. She was looking into the cauldron in Oliver's back garden and he was watching from inside it, in Avalon. He loves her. He would do anything to have her with him in the Otherworld."

Saiorse was impatient. "What's that got to do with anything?"

Jenna slid an arm around Saiorse's waist and leaned close to her ear. "Well, you see, if I'm wanting more power, and Oliver is wanting more power, and you are to become my apprentice, then that would require a very big *favour* to Arawn. You might even say a *sacrifice*."

Saiorse pulled away from Jenna. "What are you saying? Do you mean, you're planning to--?"

Jenna's voice became high-pitched in her excitement. "You know what I'm saying. The Midsummer Solstice is next month. Gavin and Kerry came here willingly to work, of their own accord. They're travellers. They'd been travelling around Asia for six months before they came to London. Who's to say they might not up and go off travelling again - if you catch my drift."

"Oh dear no, Jenna."

"What?" Jenna's voice was deflective, theatrical. "It's nothing that will hurt them. Besides, that's what this little beauty is brewing here - a delicious tincture to start dulling their minds."

Saiorse started to get up. "Listen, I'm not sure I want to be a part of this. I'm a bit afraid. This isn't what I was expecting."

"Afraid?" Jenna sneered. "Of what? What exactly *were* you expecting? You chose to get mixed up in this. Your dad even delivered the cauldron to Oliver for the big event. You're in too deep now, *my darling*."

Saiorse stood over Jenna. "My dad certainly *did not* approve of what you plan to do."

Jenna snatched Saiorse's wrist and yanked her back down; Saiorse crumpled onto her knees. "Tough luck, little girl. You're tied into all of this until the Sealing is done, so you'll just have to go along with mine - and Oliver's designs. Or else."

"Or else what?"

"Or else you'll get it too. And trust me, I'm doing you a favour by saying that to your face," Jenna spat.

Saiorse bowed her head. Gavin watched her shoulders heave. The girl was crying.

Jenna exhaled loudly on purpose. "Look, the deal between your dad and Ceridwen was to give you more status, wasn't it? There are some *sacrifices* to be made if you want to be my apprentice. And if not, you can shut your mouth and play your part until it's all over, or you know what will happen. You don't want to know what I could do behind your back. Now stop crying and take responsibility for what you got yourself into."

Saiorse wiped her face and sniffed. Gavin saw her push the curtain of blonde hair off her face and tuck it behind her left ear. He could see her face in profile and ducked down in case she caught sight of him from the corner of her eye.

"So this potion you're brewing, you said it's something to dull Kerry and Gavin's minds? And it won't hurt them?"

Jenna continued. "It'll go into their drinks at the feast tonight. The wine will disguise the taste and the red

211

colour will hide the drug. I can give you some too, if you're so upset by what I'm planning to do."

Saiorse shook her head in quick, jerky movements. "No thanks. I'd rather have my wits about me. What's in it anyway?"

"Primarily Belladonna. It'll help them to forget all the commotion with the Sacrifice of Flesh. I need them to trust me and Oliver. At least, enough to stay in London until the Solstice."

"Isn't Belladonna poisonous?" said Saiorse, with a quavering voice.

"Not in small doses. I'll be giving them a tiny amount each day - just enough to cause short term amnesia. The dose tonight will be larger to kick-start the process. Not a moment too soon either - I want Kerry to back off from Belenus, and if I give her just the *right* amount, I might actually be able to clear enough of a path to make my move on him."

"But Belenus loves her," said Saiorse.

"And Belenus hasn't been Sealed yet. When someone has power over another being…well. Let's just say, that's how slaves get made. I rather fancy having a *sex* slave for a god. Now, that's a notion that gets me fired up." Jenna made a noise of delight. "And speaking of sex, I might even pay Gavin a visit in bed tonight, while he's doped up. I rather enjoyed humping him the first time. He's got a smoking hot body and he's good in the sack, I wouldn't mind round two."

Gavin couldn't believe his ears. Was he hearing her correctly? Jenna was planning to drug and date-rape him that night, and within the next month, to murder both him and Kerry at the Midsummer solstice, to get more power. He felt sick, deep in his stomach. A thought to burst onto the rooftop crossed his mind, but he kept hidden; it might be better to reveal all downstairs. After all, on the rooftop, it would be only between the three of them; and two against one, they could manipulate the truth. But at the feast in front of Ceridwen, who already had reason to mistrust Jenna, would see the twisted witch and that sicko Oliver get their proper just deserts. Gavin slipped downstairs unnoticed.

Chapter 22

Kerry slathered generous amounts of soft cheese onto her malt bread. She had never tried unleavened bread before, or beer cheese for that matter. The bread tasted nutty to her uncultured taste buds and the beer cheese was subtle and creamy. Ceridwen's recipe was the food of the ancient Britons. She contented herself with romantic imaginings of the ancestors baking it over an open hearth in their roundhouses.

The cauldron of stewed lamb steamed in the middle of the table. Kerry knew the formalities had to come first; the issuing of wealth. This would be interesting. Oliver fancied himself as the leader since he owned the gold, but Belenus was the rightful king and god. She said nothing, happy to enjoy the play.

Belenus stood. Oliver had a thin-lipped expression as Belenus held a bag that obviously contained gold that Oliver had provided but wouldn't get any credit for. Warmth spread through Kerry as she watched her Golden God address the table.

"I name this feast in honour of the Beltaine tribe, my rightful people who have summoned me forth to lead them again." Belenus spread fistful after fistful of coins across the table. He shook the bottom of the bag until every coin rolled across the table.

Oliver's lip twitched, as though he was going to speak, then he shut his mouth. Clearly he thought better of interrupting the formalities.

Kerry picked up a coin. This time the design resembled Belenus' Golden Horse; a horse and chariot wheel, symbol of the sun god. Belenus' name was written beneath in capital letters.

Jenna set tankards in front of everyone. Saiorse

filled them with wine from a pottery jug. Kerry studied her tankard. It was more elaborate than the plain wooden one at the welcome feast. The rim had an extra layer of sheet bronze held in place by a row of rivets, giving a thicker, more distinctive look. She looked at Gavin's. His was the same. But the other tankards were plain.

Hmm. Maybe Jenna had made another mistake; surely the elaborate tankards were reserved for Belenus and Ceridwen? The goddess would be enraged at Jenna if she'd made another mockery of the Beltaine rituals.

Whatever. She diffused a brief idea to swap with Ceridwen's tankard, at the thought that Jenna would be reprimanded again. A bit of amusement at Jenna's expense wouldn't go amiss for entertainment during the feast.

Belenus began serving the stew. As the highest ranking person, he filled his own bronze bowl first with the largest chunk of lamb, then Ceridwen's next, followed by Afagddu's, Morfan's, Blodeuedd's then Kerry's, Gavin's, Oliver's, Jenna's, and finally Saiorse's, to mark the order of prestige. Oliver looked livid. Kerry restrained a smile that threatened to break over her face; she was satisfied to see both Oliver and Jenna unhappy at being served far down the line of order. Come to think of it, why did she, and Gavin, rank above Oliver and Jenna? Oliver had gold and Jenna had pagan powers. She could only think of one explanation; marriage. Hadn't Gavin said Blodeuedd wanted to be his wife? That would make sense, if they were to be wed to high ranking people. Did Belenus want her to be his queen?

Belenus got to his feet. "Let us drink to the rise of the Beltaine sun, high in the East of Avalon, never to set."

They raised their tankards high. "To the Beltaine sun."

Kerry brought her tankard to her lips. Gavin, next

to her, smashed his tankard against hers and knocked it out of her hand. Her tankard clattered and wine spilled all over the table, splashing Belenus. Gavin dropped his tankard too and Kerry jumped back as wine splashed on her jeans.

"Gavin, what the hell? Watch it!"

"Sorry, Kerry."

"What did you do that for?"

He grabbed a napkin and wiped at her jeans. "Slip of the fingers."

She pushed his hand away.

Belenus wiped his golden armour. Kerry snatched another napkin and helped him. "I'm so sorry, my Golden God."

"You don't have to apologise for me," Gavin said.

Belenus didn't look angry; his expression was calm. Kerry threw the napkin onto the table and stormed into the kitchen. Red wine would stain. What was Gavin playing at? She ran the tap and dabbed at her jeans with a sponge. Over the conversation, she heard Gavin apologise and then the sound of his chair legs scraping.

Gavin appeared in the kitchen doorway. Kerry glared at him.

"What was that all about? And don't tell me it was an accident because I saw you do it on purpose." She scrubbed harder at her jeans.

"You're right. It was on purpose," he said.

Belenus appeared behind Gavin in the doorway. "What's going on?" he said.

"That's what I want to know," said Kerry.

"Do you mind, Belenus, I need a moment alone with Kerry," said Gavin.

Ceridwen appeared next to Belenus. Gavin closed his eyes, a pained expression clouding his face. She pushed past Gavin and stood in the middle of the kitchen.

216

"Explain all of this madness."

Gavin squared his shoulders. "No. Can I have a little privacy with Kerry, please?"

"We are having this feast before the eyes of the gods. Anything you do honours - or dishonours - Arawn. The least you can do is come back to the table and give Avalon the proper respect," Ceridwen shouted.

Gavin shrugged. "Fine. I have a lot to say to Oliver and Jenna anyway."

"You can say it to us first. Belenus is the Chieftain now, he should hear it before you bring it to the table," said Ceridwen.

"Jenna put something in our drinks - mine and Kerry's."

"What?" said Kerry. "How do you know?"

"I heard her and Saiorse talking earlier on the roof. Jenna's planning to drug us both."

Kerry clenched her teeth. "I should have known."

"Did you actually see her put something in your drink?" said Belenus.

"Not exactly." Gavin lowered his head. "I saw her brewing something though."

Ceridwen's eyes narrowed in concentration. "Jenna poured all the wine from the same pitcher. How could she have drugged your drinks?"

"Because I'm sure she put whatever herbs it was in our tankards before she gave them out," said Gavin.

"The tankards - that's it - my tankard, and Gavin's were different from the others, a bit more elaborate. I didn't say anything cos I thought Jenna meant to give them to you two-" Kerry indicated Belenus and Ceridwen, "-but had messed up. I really wanted to see her punished."

"That's not the worst of it," said Gavin. "I heard her say that she and Oliver are planning to kill us at the

217

solstice. You and me, Kerry. They have an elaborate plan lined up to sacrifice us."

"Sacrifice us? To who?"

"To Arawn for more power. She was telling Saiorse about how she was going make her a Druid apprentice."

"Nothing will happen to either of you while I'm here," said Ceridwen.

"Interesting you say that - you're in on it too. Why didn't you tell us that Saiorse's parents summoned you?"

Ceridwen looked resolute. "We'll discuss this at the table."

"I think that's for the best," said Kerry. "Nobody can hide anything if it's all said to each other's faces."

Kerry led the way back to the table, her mind reeling. She would have drunk Jenna's poisoned wine, if it weren't for Gavin's quick thinking. Back at the table, Jenna and Oliver had their heads together and didn't even try to hide the fact that they were whispering. Saiorse was red-faced; like one who had been caught in an ignoble act. Blodeuedd, Afagddu and Morfan sat waiting, their faces turned to Ceridwen.

"Jenna." Ceridwen's voice boomed; Jenna and Oliver stopped talking. "Gavin has informed us of a serious misdemeanour that you have tried to commit in front of the gods."

Jenna was wide eyed. "What misdemeanour?"

"You and Saiorse talking on the roof," said Gavin. "Belladonna in mine and Kerry's drinks. I heard your murderous intentions for the solstice too."

Saiorse whimpered. She looked to Jenna for help, but Jenna refused to acknowledge her.

Jenna shook her head in a show of innocence. "I don't know what you're talking about."

"Speak the truth, Jenna," said Ceridwen. "And may

I remind you that if you tell any lies, you risk the full fury of Avalon."

"I didn't put anything in anyone's drink. Why would I do such a thing?"

"You're lying," Kerry spat. "Why did you give me and Gavin different tankards then?"

Jenna bit her lip. "I didn't give you different tankards."

"Yes you did. You must have put some herbs in them before you poured the wine, and you thought we wouldn't notice, but the tankards drew my eye, you idiot." Kerry couldn't help anger creeping into her words; she had never wanted to punch someone so much in all her life.

Jenna didn't look so innocent now. "Prove it. Where are the tankards?"

The tankards were gone, and the wine had been mopped off the table. Kerry looked at the replacements; they were the same as everyone else's.

"You're a pro at this. What did you do, bring extras?" Kerry sneered.

"There's a simple way to find out," said Gavin. "Blodeuedd, did either of these two change the tankards that were on the table and clean up the mess?"

Jenna faced Blodeuedd, her face alarmed.

Blodeuedd nodded. "This one changed the drinking vessels-" She pointed at Jenna. "-and that one wiped the spill," she said, indicating Oliver.

"Are you so bold as to lie in front of the gods?" said Belenus. "In front of us?"

Jenna shrank in her seat, but Oliver bolted upright. "Wait a minute here, we've done nothing wrong. Everything we do is for the good of the gods, not to go against you, and maybe you should start to be more appreciative of that. Who brought you back to the world?

219

If it wasn't for us, neither you, nor Ceridwen's sons would've been summoned."

Belenus glowered. "If you want to be a king someday you should never go against the will of a god."

He strode to Oliver, who cowered before him. Belenus cracked his powerful fist against Oliver's forehead; Oliver fell backwards off his seat, unconscious.

Belenus looked down at him. "Treasonous fool."

Jenna's lip trembled. "Ceridwen, you told us you wanted a Briton army and we've only done what you asked."

Briton army? Kerry turned to Ceridwen. Surely they couldn't be in any collusion if there was this much enmity between them? "What does she mean, Briton army?"

"The time is right, Kerry, to open the gates of Avalon and summon the old gods. Belenus wants to rebuild his Beltaine tribes and we have seen the signs - over the past century, the old ways have been revived."

Kerry's head was swimming. "So you agreed to all this with Jenna?"

"No. The only part of this that has gone according to my plan is having Belenus, Morfan and Afagddu brought back to this world. Jenna and Oliver's disobedience has gone beyond sacrilege at this point." The goddess trailed off, her face despairing.

"Then why do you use them?" said Kerry. "Did Jenna summon you and you have to pay her back? Is that it?"

Ceridwen shook her head. "Saiorse's parents, Glynn and Grainne, summoned me, not Jenna. They sacrificed flesh in the land of the Silures - what you call your modern day Wales. The conditions were right. It was the Midwinter Solstice. They tried out a few incantations, one of which happened to be the right one, and I came out of the River Avon at dawn."

"I don't get it then. Where does Jenna come into all this?" said Kerry.

Ceridwen continued. "I travelled south across the River Sabrina to the lands of the Durotriges and met Jenna in your modern day Glastonbury. She was practising the old ways and I sensed a power in her greater than any of the fumbling amateurs I had encountered until then. Modern day Druids are weak. They say the incantations and they practise the lifestyle, but they won't perform blood magic. Jenna would."

"Blood magic - you mean sacrifice?"

"Yes. Glynn and Grainne had summoned me through their amateur encounter, but they didn't have powers enough for further use. However, in exchange for granting me life, I made Glynn an oath that I would grant his oldest daughter, Saiorse, a gift of the gods once I had reached Londinium. When I met Jenna, she seemed a promising priestess, and willing to do what I asked of her, when the time came. Since there are only four special times of year to us Ancient Britons - Midsummer, Midwinter, Beltaine and Samhain, I knew that the twelve days leading up to Mayday would be the right time. I gave Jenna detailed instructions of what to do when the time came - how to sacrifice an animal in the right way to initiate the twelve days of Beltaine and what to say to offer a token of flesh. But she abused those powers when she sacrificed that piglet to bring Morfan into the world in the most undignified way - in a bathtub."

Kerry glared at Jenna. "Evil little witch."

Jenna sneered at her. "Hold your tongue, or I might poison you."

Ceridwen ignored them. "She lost my trust even

more during the fiasco that happened yesterday - offering an underage girl for the Womanhood ceremony and using unwitting participants in the ceremony of flesh without saying the sacred incantations. All of it goes against the Ancient Wisdom."

Jenna had no wisdom, ancient or modern; Kerry took another opportunity to cast a scowl her way.

"As for the Briton army, I thought that was apparent. Belenus ruled the Beltaine tribes of the Tameses north bank and the Atrebates ruled the south bank. Belenus has been revived, leader of one of the strongest tribes in the south of Britannia. Afagddu and Morfan were nobles among the Silures, one of the strongest tribes in the West. When Glynn dropped Jenna and I off in Londinium in January this year, I read the omens - South and West united, Oliver's wealth, Jenna's mortal influence and my immortal power. All of these combined could raise a Briton army. Oliver had connections through his work with others who have the blood of the ancestors. The time was right."

"And my dad knew Oliver, so fate had it in store for us to be a part of the bigger plan," said Kerry.

"Yes. But the Beltaine ceremony was a travesty. Oliver and Jenna will have to repent before Arawn at the Sealing ceremony on the sixth day," said Ceridwen.

"And what if I don't?" said Jenna, her jaw jutting.

"I take it you value your life?" said Ceridwen.

Jenna was haughty. "Of course I do."

"And what of your immortal soul?"

Jenna fell silent.

"Then you would be foolish not to participate. You have done enough damage already. I suggest that you obey me from now on or may Arawn see that you become as liquid as the waters of Avalon. Do you understand?"

Ceridwen pulled a hemp necklace out of her dress; at the end, Kerry saw what looked like a pewter dog-tag. Did the goddess mean to imbue the amulet with a malicious curse?

"And you can cut the sarcasm," Ceridwen continued. "I might have been reborn into this world a mere six months ago, but I have been around for much longer than you, watching in the shadows."

A shadow passed across Jenna's face as she gave a malign smirk. "Liquid as the waters of Avalon? What is that - some kind of ancient Celtic curse that's supposed to scare me? Maybe you're the one who should be afraid."

Kerry's eyes lowered from Jenna's malign smirk to a bulge below her loose-fitting crocheted dress. Jenna draped her arms around her stomach as tenderly as if she massaged a pregnant stomach. Did she not fear Ceridwen's curse because she had a talisman of protection? What kind of dangerous game was Jenna playing? And why was Ceridwen holding back on punishing them? The goddess was pale as she eyed the bulge in Jenna's clothing. Surely she wasn't frightened of Jenna's meagre power?

Shadows. As the last rays of the sun flickered in the West, the Herne's Hunt restaurant darkened. Wind stirred and the sound of beating wings drew everyone's attention to Blodeuedd. In place of the Maiden of Flowers, a brown owl flew high to the ceiling and circled the room once. Then with a miserable cry, she flew out through an open window into the growing twilight. Kerry stared after the bird. Seemed even immortals had no control over their fate, any more than humans did.

Chapter 23

Kerry looked more desperate than Gavin had ever seen her. He couldn't blame her. There was a plot to kill them both, and Ceridwen wasn't doing a thing about it.

"Can't you punish them before the Sealing?" Kerry pleaded. "That's nearly a week away. Those two will have cooked up something worse than we can imagine by then if you don't stop them now."

Ceridwen's face showed no hint of her thoughts. Gavin wondered the same thing as Kerry; Ceridwen was letting Oliver and Jenna off lightly.

He looked at Jenna for her reaction. In the absence of the goddess' reply, she looked smug.

"Why does it have to wait until the sixth?" he said to Ceridwen.

"Because she knows I have more power than her, stupid old has-been," Jenna whispered under her breath, leaning her head close to Oliver. She had her arm around Oliver, who appeared woozy as he roused from being knocked out. When Jenna saw Gavin looking, she scowled at him forcing him to turn away. They were a sick pair, Oliver and Jenna. What were gods for if not to punish such malicious people?

Despite being hungry, Gavin couldn't eat. Drugging people and plotting sacrifice was too much to comprehend. He waited for Ceridwen's answer. There was no solace in the feast, less so because Blodeuedd wasn't there. She was probably sitting in a tree, alone and miserable because of Arawn's curse, and nobody gave a crap. Arawn this, Arawn that. If Oliver and Jenna had done a sacrilegious act, why didn't Arawn step in and unleash the full force of the Otherworld on them; a thing that Ceridwen and Belenus didn't seem capable of.

"There are rules in the Otherworld, as there are in this one. Everything that happens is dictated by the alignment of the cosmos. The time isn't right to settle the fates," said Ceridwen.

"Settle the fates? Jenna wants to settle ours - with drugs and sacrifice," said Gavin.

"Hmph. More than you deserve," Jenna muttered, under her breath.

Ceridwen addressed Gavin. "But not tonight. I have said my part. The fates of both mortal and immortal alike will be Sealed on the sixth day. All of you will participate in the Sealing since you are all involved. There will be repercussions if anyone does not cooperate. I hope that is perfectly clear," said the goddess.

Repercussions; more talk and no action. Gavin stabbed his last bite of meat and swallowed it, his throat dry.

"I'm glad you all understand what you have committed to by summoning gods into the world." Ceridwen's eye travelled across all the mortals but lingered on Oliver and Jenna a moment longer than everyone else. "We have four days to go until the Sealing must be completed. I have a few suggestions for how you should conduct yourselves in order to coexist until that point."

"I have no intention of being anywhere near people who plan to murder me," said Kerry.

"You will remain here until after the sixth, as will Gavin," said Ceridwen.

"Not under my roof," said Oliver. "I set them up with jobs and share my food and wealth with them and how do they thank me? By causing discord on Beltaine. I'll need to speak to my lawyer Thom Chisholm before I have any further business with Kerry and Gavin."

Kerry blanched. "That's rich - accusing us of

causing discord? We're not the ones planning sacrifice. What would you do, get your lawyer to cook you up an alibi after you kill us?"

"You'd better watch what you say," said Oliver.

"Enough of this bickering," said Ceridwen. "Until the Sealing is over, I am in charge. If any mortal has cause to complain about that I shall call upon the Cauldron of Knowledge to bring forth a little persuasion from Avalon. Understood?"

Oliver said nothing. Kerry turned her head defiantly away from him.

"Kerry, Belenus, Gavin and Blodeuedd will stay here at the Herne's Hunt."

Jenna reddened. "But Belenus is to stay with me."

"Belenus has chosen Kerry. You can accept that, with grace, or without, but it is a fact."

"We'll see about that!" Jenna got to her feet, knocking her chair over.

"Impetuous girl." Ceridwen shouted. "It would serve you well to show some self-respect. You have limited skill as a Neo-pagan priestess, but you don't know real power. If you learn your place, you will come out of this situation better off than you started. You asked to be given more power - and that is within my capabilities. But I cannot make Belenus love a woman he doesn't."

Jenna didn't say anything. She cast a narrow-eyed glance at Kerry before leaving the restaurant.

"What will happen to me?" said Saiorse. Her voice shook. "Am I unfit to take part in the Sealing, because I participated before the gods even though I'm underage?"

"No. You sacrificed flesh to summon Afagddu - Arawn will reward you for that. But you will have to be sanctified first. There will be a ritual to restore you to the prestige you had before you lost your purity," said

226

Ceridwen.

The goddess addressed Oliver. "I hope you won't be as insolent as your partner in crime. I am trying to make your mortal lives easier, but my generosity has its limits."

Oliver's lower lip curled. "What are you asking of me?"

"Obedience. You will give Gavin and Kerry their annual leave until the Sealing on the sixth. Jenna and Afagddu will help you with the auction in Sequana's tomorrow and I shall be more than adequately staffed with Morfan and Saiorse's help. Agreed?"

"And what do I get in return? So far your promises haven't come to fruition. In exchange for bringing back your sons, Jenna was supposed to become a High Priestess and I was to become a Chieftain, a Tameses King."

"These things will happen - in time. I cannot give Jenna more power all at once. And if you want to be a ruler, you must have patience. It does not happen overnight."

The fire returned to Oliver's eyes. "You're saying my request will happen, but that it will take time?"

"I think you understand what I'm saying," said Ceridwen. "You will get what you want if you participate in the Sealing on the sixth. Jenna too. You can tell the foolish girl when she's willing to see reason."

"Good." There was a dangerous edge to Oliver's expression. "But just remember - there'll be other things at stake if we don't get what we were promised."

Ceridwen didn't answer. For a moment, she looked like an ordinary mortal woman as she raised her eyes to meet Oliver's intense gaze. He savoured it for a moment, peering down his nose at the goddess, as he stood up.

"Come, Saiorse," said Oliver.

Saiorse stood without question and followed him out of the restaurant.

Gavin waited a few seconds, then walked to the door. He peered out onto the darkened street. No sign of Oliver, Jenna or Saiorse anywhere.

He shut the door firmly. "Ceridwen, no offence, but what the hell is going on? I don't mean to be blunt, but if a plain old mortal like me can see that Oliver and Jenna are not to be trusted, then why can't you? They're dangerous enough that you'd be better off cursing them now and not waiting until the sixth."

"Yes, I'm quite aware of their capabilities."

Ceridwen's voice was so meek, Gavin stared. Was she being serious, or mocking? *Neo-pagan priestess.* Ceridwen's description of Jenna stuck in his mind; and more so, her tone. He hadn't missed the sarcastic nuance in her voice, even though Jenna had been oblivious of it. Did that mean Ceridwen knew what she was doing? What was she cooking up in her Cauldron of Knowledge?

"Jenna had something hidden under her dress - I think she meant to curse you with it," Kerry said to the goddess.

"Yes. The Horse and Sun should be a bringer of light, not darkness." Ceridwen spoke in a flat tone. Her face was expressionless to match. Only her glistening eyes gave away her feelings; were those tears?

Ceridwen blinked and stood. "I must retire for the night. I will be taking your room, Kerry, for the next few nights and my sons will take your room, Gavin. Even immortals need solitude to attend to the mundane trivialities of the earthly domain."

She left the restaurant. Was Ceridwen for real? How could she dodge their questions and show them such little respect?

Gavin, Kerry, Belenus, Morfan and Afagddu remained at the table, silent to their thoughts for what

228

seemed an eternity. Then, with a gasp, Kerry's hand flew to her mouth.

"Horse and Sun - she couldn't mean...? The Golden Horse. I forgot to get it out of the cauldron!"

Gavin understood. Jenna had taken Kerry's property, yet again. She had it hidden under her dress. Kerry dashed across the room and out of the restaurant.

He jumped to his feet. Belenus grabbed his arm. "I'll stop her."

"Stop her? But why? It's hers - yours. That's twice Oliver and Jenna have tried to steal it," said Gavin.

Belenus' moustache bristled. "This is Ceridwen's business, not ours. I can't interfere - I haven't been Sealed."

Gavin watched Belenus stride into the darkness after Kerry. Great; not only did he feel helpless but confused too. He sat back down and looked from Morfan to Afagddu. What answers could the burly brothers possibly give him, if Belenus and Ceridwen had already evaded them?

To his surprise, Afagddu spoke. "I agree with you. The man and woman are dangerous. My mother didn't give them enough credit, and now she is paying for it."

"How? With what?"

"The woman means to trap my mother inside the Golden Horse."

Gavin made sense of Afagddu's words in his mind; Jenna planned to capture Ceridwen using Kerry's Golden Horse? "I don't get it. They cleansed it of evil energy at the Beltaine ceremony. How can it be used to trap her?"

"Long ago, the Gauls used a ritual that was so feared, it was lost to time before it ever reached Britannia, or any of the other chiefdoms of our people. None of the first Britons knew about it. It's an ancient magic that

229

reaches an evil hand back to a time of long forgotten gods."

For someone so brutish, Afagddu could sure be poetic. Gavin refocused his thoughts on the warrior's words.

"The gods have knowledge of it, but even we fear it. The woman must have been consorting with a denizen in Avalon. I can think of no other way she could have learned it otherwise."

"The woman - you mean Jenna? But what's so fearful about it? Can you tell me?" said Gavin.

Afagddu hunched close. "I'll speak of it once, but only because my mother is in danger."

"An immortal can be in danger? How does this curse - or whatever it is - work?" said Gavin.

"In many ways. First I need to know what the woman said on Beltaine when she cleansed the Golden Horse," said Afagddu.

Gavin concentrated. It was hard to remember; too much mead gone straight to his head and at the time, thoughts of only one thing - Jenna seducing him. "Erm, I think she said something along the lines of Kerry's belief burning in the power of the talisman and how the power would never die and then something or other about cleansing the talisman by fire of all and any impurities that dwell in it. And then all three of them - her and Oliver and Saiorse - talked about love and fire as they passed it through the white candle flame, green candle flame and the frankincense."

"There's nothing unusual about that - it was all part of what my mother taught her to say at the ceremony," said Afagddu.

"Brother, don't forget the man. He is part of this too," said Morfan, slow and staccato.

Gavin stared at Morfan, thinking. "You're right.

Oliver did say something after the ritual, to close the ceremony. He said, 'By the gods I cleanse this talisman to be ready for my purpose'."

"Ready for my purpose." Afagddu repeated the words in a monotone. "I see. They created an empty vessel by fire, capable of being filled for evil purposes. If we are to succeed, we must counter fire with water."

Gavin leaned forward. "What do we have to do? Can I help?"

Afagddu nodded, his eyes fixed on Gavin. "Yes. This work is less dangerous for a mortal. First you need to understand how. You see, when Gaul was young, gods and mortals lived and fought together, as my mother and Belenus already told you. But the mortals grew jealous of our strength and how we never die. The Druids had an alliance with many Otherworld demons, and from the most corrupt, they learned of a technique to trap an immortal inside an anchor. The god would be trapped, but his or her power would be free to use by the mortal owner."

"Did you see the necklace my mother had on?" said Morfan.

"Pewter strips hold the words of a curse to be used against a foe. Druids knew of this and learned to make a more powerful anchor," Afagddu explained.

"Does Ceridwen know what Jenna and Oliver plan to do?"

"Yes. But the problem is that she is already attached to the Golden Horse by a spiritual bond. When the man made it ready for his purpose, he tied my mother to it. If she speaks of it her energy seeps into it, little by little, until eventually her essence will be drained, and she will be a slave. The last step after that will be the easiest - bodily imprisonment. Deities are mostly made of celestial energy, anyway, not the flesh and blood of a human."

An image of Ceridwen fading from reality popped into Gavin's mind. She grew more and more transparent until she was a wisp of smoke, sucked into the Golden Horse, like a genie in a lamp.

"But, if Kerry manages to steal it back, then Jenna won't be able to say any incantations over it to trap Ceridwen, will she?" said Gavin.

"The girl is in danger too. The Golden Horse can cause her harm. As it has a spiritual connection to my mother, it has a flesh connection to the girl. If she meddles with it, her immortal soul could end up trapped inside it too," said Afagddu.

Gavin saw a horrible picture of Kerry and Jenna fighting over the Golden Horse, Jenna saying an incantation and a white light being sucked out from the top of Kerry's head, like a tornado whisking her spirit into the Golden Horse, leaving her as a soulless zombie on earth.

"Don't worry. Belenus will keep the girl safe. But, it would be best if you don't tell her. The less she knows, the safer she is. We have a lot to do," said Afagddu.

Gavin thought of Belenus' words. "But isn't it dangerous for you? You haven't been Sealed yet."

"Yes. It is dangerous. But it's a risk we would be willing to take to save our mother. She is a higher deity and of much more importance than us. Belenus is also too important to risk - his mission is greater than ours in this world," said Afagddu.

"Although..." said Morfan.

"Although," Afagddu continued. "Your job will be riskier than ours."

Sickness grew in the pit of Gavin's stomach. "In what way?"

"You will need to be the one to steal the Golden

Horse away from the witch. You have no flesh connection with it, so you will be safe from magic. You will need to act at the right moment, for my mother's sake and for your friend," said Afagddu.

Safe from magic, but not from Jenna's malice; what would she do if she caught him? Gavin thought of Kerry and gritted his teeth. "Sure. So, what's the plan?"

"It will happen on the eve of the Sealing. We will bring a Water Priestess to do the ceremony. Your task will be to deliver the Golden Horse into the back garden of Avalon Road at sunset. Do this by whatever means are necessary. The ceremony must take place at dusk. But remember - you must not tell Kerry. Don't let us down."

Chapter 24

Kerry stretched out on Ceridwen's hardwood bed. Belenus had told her to relax, that he would keep her safe. She tried to calm her mind, but apart from fears of poison, sacrifice and her stolen Golden Horse, she could hear the muffled sounds of Belenus, Morfan and Afagddu talking downstairs - enough to keep her tense. What were they talking about in the restaurant so late?

Wonder if Gavin was sleeping next door? Maybe he could explain what was going on.

As Kerry swung her legs over the side of the bed, she heard Belenus' footsteps on the stairs. He came in and walked over to the dresser to strip off his armour. He set his mail vest over the back of a chair, hung his plaid cloak on top and set his sword and helmet across the seat.

"What did Afagddu say?" she said.

"Nothing that need worry you. Sleep is best right now," he said.

She shook her head. "How can I relax? What's going on? Why is everyone being so secretive? Jenna and Oliver are up to something, Ceridwen won't talk and even Gavin was being awkward downstairs."

"Ceridwen will keep a close eye on things."

"What's that supposed to mean?" Kerry folded her arms.

Belenus sat down on the edge of the bed. Under his armour, he wore a red woollen tunic with an embroidered gold hem and black and brown plaid trousers. Seeing him without his armour helped her to calm. If he could relax, maybe she could try to too. Kerry sighed. The breath helped clear her head. She would be calm and rational, but she wouldn't be brushed off.

"Please Belenus, I need straight answers. Ceridwen

avoided our questions downstairs, but I have to know what is going on. If my life and Gavin's is at risk - and maybe even Ceridwen's - then don't I deserve to know what's happening?"

Belenus hesitated. "When an immortal has not yet been Sealed into this world, it makes them vulnerable. They can easily be used for malign purposes. Between the worlds, there are dark forces that can trap and harness energy that is free in the universe. Immortals are the highest beings in the universe, and so their energy is the strongest and most desired by denizens of darkness. Their power can be used or manipulated by evil forces, or even mortals who are receptive to the darkness. Afagddu, Morfan, Blodeuedd and I are in that vulnerable position at present and it appears Jenna and Oliver are working with darker forces to get what they want. Ceridwen was Sealed on last year's Midwinter Solstice. Since she is less vulnerable than us and therefore more powerful than us at present, there is only one thing that can stop her. It is the most ancient and darkest of spells that can penetrate the energy force of a deity and harness it for evil. Only the lowest denizens of this world or the Otherworld would do this certain magic. If Ceridwen's power can be harnessed, then the rest of us can also be controlled." Belenus' voice stayed composed, but his face showed his worry.

Kerry understood. "I knew it. I'm not surprised Jenna and Oliver would stoop so low. If they're willing to drug and sacrifice other human beings, then what would stop them threatening gods too?"

"They feel invincible. They'll stop at nothing to make sure they get their end of the deal in exchange for bringing us into the world."

"Ceridwen must have her own safety precautions in place to counter that. But what about you - if Jenna and

Oliver have their eyes on Ceridwen, can't you and the other gods do something to help too?"

Belenus frowned. "Like I said, we're vulnerable until the Sealing. The only thing that stands in our favour is the fact that Jenna and Oliver know the Universal Laws. What Ceridwen told them was right. By participating in the Beltaine Ceremony of Flesh, they are spiritually bound to take part in the Mayday Sealing. If they don't, not even Mother Mathonwy would be able to stop the wrath of Avalon unleashing its powers on them."

Kerry gulped. As much as she didn't want to know what that meant, she couldn't deny she already did. A part of her mind had siphoned knowledge from her connection with Belenus. If a mortal who helped open the channel with the Otherworld refused to participate in the Sealing, then their flesh, blood and soul, every atom of their being would become instilled with evil and disseminate into the zone between worlds. They would become a denizen of darkness residing between worlds, a slave to malice and evil.

She shivered. She needed to cast her mind away from darkness. Kerry forced herself to think of love and beauty. But even that was tainted. Belenus was vulnerable. If he was vulnerable to darkness, was he vulnerable to love too?

"I still have unanswered questions. Ceridwen said she can't make you love someone you don't." Kerry trailed off. "But if you haven't been Sealed, then can't Jenna manipulate you to do what she wants? What I mean is, force you to become hers?"

"Her devious nature is part of the reason why Ceridwen wants me to stay away from her. But Jenna is not as knowledgeable as she thinks. She overlooked the Universal Laws that govern. She didn't plan the Beltaine ritual well. She shouldn't have sacrificed her own flesh with Gavin to bring me into this world. She should have worn the blossom crown and brought Blodeuedd into the world. Instead she brought me. Flesh should not unite with flesh."

Jenna would hate that; Kerry smiled. But her brief satisfaction waned. "Should not, or cannot?"

"If Jenna traps Ceridwen and becomes a High Priestess, then she would make an Evil Amulet of the highest power that could overpower anything. Flesh of flesh wouldn't matter - she would have me if she wanted me. But the union would not be blessed by the gods. It would be sullied by darkness."

"Not that it would matter to an evil witch like her." Kerry was afraid. Jenna wanted dark power as a High Priestess and to have Belenus. Heat flooded Kerry's face. She had to stop Jenna. "And in order to do all of this, Jenna needs my - our - Golden Horse?"

"Kerry." Belenus put his hand on her leg and squeezed. "You need to forget the Golden Horse until after the Sealing. Can you do that?"

Anger filled her. "And let Jenna have everything? Of course I can't!"

"You're attached to it, it's dangerous."

"I was told being attached to *you* was dangerous for me but look at how this has worked out."

Belenus hunched forward, his elbows resting on his knees. Kerry's heart jolted. It was the first time she had seen him look forlorn. For a moment, everything went out of her mind; only her feelings for him remained.

"I shouldn't have told you so much. But you were so desperate for information that I couldn't keep it from you. I care for you and that's why I had to be honest," he said.

"And I'm glad you did. Knowing the full story

protects me," she said.

Belenus shook his head. He slipped his leather boots off and climbed onto the bed beside her. "I'm afraid it's the opposite. Knowing it all puts you in harm's way. It makes you thirst for justice. But I need you to understand. Jenna and Oliver are more dangerous than we immortals at first thought. You need to forget the Golden Horse and stay away from them until after the Sealing. I'll be with you - I'll protect you."

Desperation welled; Kerry ran her hands through her hair. "You'll protect me? You're more vulnerable than me. Jenna and Oliver plan to sacrifice me and Gavin at the solstice. I'm in danger of being murdered, what could be worse than that? And you expect me to sit back and see what happens?"

"I'm asking you to wait four days until the Sealing is over. Then you will see justice done."

"I don't want to see justice done - I want to make it happen." Kerry took a deep breath. Her voice had become raised with every word. She closed her eyes. "I'm sorry, I don't mean to get angry. But it's so frustrating. You gods can't help, and Gavin isn't the type to do anything. He's a sweet guy and a good friend, but it seems to me that if I don't do anything then nobody will."

"No Kerry, if you interfere with the universal order- "

"Then what?" she snapped. "I know what the consequences are. I know there are worse things in Avalon. It's a risk I'd take for us."

"You don't know that." Belenus reached for her hand and stroked it. "I've exposed you to too much already. See how my touch gives you no past visions? The more time we spend together, the stronger our physical connection will need to be. I have already given you too

238

much knowledge of things greater than what an earthly being should be allowed to know."

Kerry couldn't help it; tears streamed from her eyes. She blinked to clear her sight. "It's not fair. All I want is to be with you and I feel that there are forces trying to stop us. Jenna wants to come between us, but so does Arawn. I know about Arawn. I've seen him in my dreams."

Belenus rubbed her back. "I should have known he would show his face to you."

A note of jealousy in his voice made her look up. His face was solemn.

In place of Belenus, the face of a darkly handsome man swam before her. Arawn's mischievous eyes were full of lust. Kerry forced his image out of her mind by staring at her Golden Sun God. "Did I have an affair with him in the Otherworld in a past life, or something?"

He looked away from her, his face furtive. "No, nothing like that."

Belenus paused and lowered his gaze. Had she gone too far, had she hurt him? No; he was a warrior and a god. He couldn't be hurt.

Or could he?

"You know something you aren't telling me - about Arawn and me, don't you?" she said.

Belenus looked troubled. "I have said too much. The more I tell you, the worse it is for you. Please understand that I am caught between telling the woman I love all there is to know and trying to protect her from the danger of knowing too much."

The world had stopped; the breath had left her lungs. Had she heard him right? Her Golden God had said he loved her.

Gods could hurt. Gods could feel hurt, and pain. And love.

"If you love me, then tell me how I can keep myself safe," she said. Her voice sounded unusually meek in her own ears.

Belenus' reply was blunt. "Do as I ask you for the next four days. Ask no more questions about evil deeds. Put the Golden Horse from your mind until after the Sealing."

She stared into his eyes. "I'll try. Because I love you too."

His eyes showed hurt, but also a tenderness. He cared for her, deeply. She cared for him too. How could she love someone she had known for a day?

Because she hadn't known him for a day. She had been his Aithne, a part of his life two millennia before Kerry existed.

Belenus stretched out alongside her on the bed. Kerry rolled onto her side to face him. As her body closed against his, it was as though the sun's rays shone on her. Her worries melted into a haze. What had she been angry about a moment before? She tried to concentrate but couldn't. Only the Sun God's warmth against her mattered.

Kerry leaned on one elbow, close to him, and spoke in barely more than a whisper. "I can remember parts of my life as Aithne, watching you fight the Roman centurions."

"You were a great warrior, a great woman," he said, his voice soft.

"I want to see more of that old life, like you showed me earlier."

"And I want to show you. But there's so much to see, and I can only let you glimpse isolated memories at a time. I've lived through many lifetimes and I watched even more as a ray of light floating among your shadows, as less than a ghost. I saw the Roman culture fade after the time of our people ended on these shores. I saw Londinium ruined, filled in with banks of earth, a ghost town that the wilds of Britannia had reclaimed. I saw the new settlers come by the shipload - seafarers from Jutland who were terrified of the Roman ghost town and built their Ludenwic outside its decaying walls, terrified to go near the doomed city."

"It must be strange to live long enough to see all this with your own eyes," said Kerry.

"Strange, and sometimes melancholic. It's always sad to see people coming in and then their cultures fading - the Vikings, and then the Normans and with each new wave of people came a different language. Modern Britain is a huge cauldron of mixed blood - Celts, Saxons, Normans, Vikings and moderns. But the gods soon faded away."

"There must be a lot of gods - and spirits - in Avalon," she said.

"Gods, yes. Spirits, no. The spirits are recycled. They come back to earth and live again through their descendants."

"Ceridwen wants to make all of Britain Celtic, doesn't she?"

"No. Only to bring back the old pantheon of gods and revive the cultures of the Ancient World. North and South, East and West - all will be united. She has already set a mission for Afagddu and Morfan to find the High Priests from each corner of the earth. You forget that we deities were once Greek before we were Celtic, and Sumerian before we were Greek. We lead the people we feel have a good cause on earth. There is a resurgence in the ways of the Britons. Every year there are worshippers at Stonehenge keeping our customs alive."

Kerry rested her head close to his chest and looked

up at him. "What's your plan for the world? I mean, this is the twenty-first century. We have skyscrapers, cars, technology. People won't want to live primitive lifestyles in smoky roundhouses. They like their modern comforts."

"Ceridwen is the better one to ask about the astrological significance - all I can say is that the stars don't lie. Planets govern the earth, not people. Our rebirth yesterday was guided by Saturn in Scorpio. And now, the impending square between Uranus in Aries and Pluto in Capricorn will take effect on the twenty-first of May."

"What does that mean?"

"The balance of power will be reset. The dominating power will change. After the sixth, you will see the changes begin. The moon will have a looming influence on this world as you know it. New people, new ideas and ultimately reshaping of the old ways will begin."

"How much influence will you have, once you're Sealed into this world? I mean, if you want something, can you make it happen - like that?" Kerry snapped her fingers.

Belenus exhaled. His warm breath stirred her hair. He was a god, but he was also a man. He was as flesh and blood as any human.

"Ceridwen has a celestial gift - she'll be able to influence the planets to govern events on earth," he said. "My own influence for this lifetime is less celestial than Ceridwen's and more organic. My gift from Avalon will be to raise my tribes starting where the concentration of Celtic speakers is strongest - across the misty sea in Hibernia and further east among the Silures, or north among the Caledonii. And you will be my Queen."

Queen. Heat flooded into Kerry's face. She knew, sensed it was coming. The order of serving at the feast; her and Gavin being given more prestige. Now it made sense.

Far from being Aithne, a Briton maiden of the past

with an unrequited love for her Golden God King, Belenus, she had been Aithne, Belenus' wild, barbarian Queen. The memories she had connected with had simply shown a narrow perspective of Belenus' life in war and death; not the full-blown view of their romantic union.

"I understand now. But why me? It's not that I don't want it, or that I don't love you." She paused, searching for the right words. "It's just, of all the women in Britannia, you chose me, before as Aithne and now as Kerry."

"The memories of the old ways are strong within you. When you travelled in the East, your mind opened to the possibility of other gods in an ancient past. Ceridwen read the signs and the time was right. Mathonwy drew you to London," said Belenus.

Kerry's thoughts soured. "Jenna and Oliver are also open to the old ways - and Jenna has her priestess powers. Why didn't Mathonwy pick Jenna for you and Oliver for Blodeuedd?"

"Jenna and Oliver will serve other purposes in the universal order. She is too manipulative, and he is too greedy to be suited to deities of our nature. Are you familiar with the Greek legend of King Midas of Phrygia?"

Kerry nodded. "Everything he touched turned to gold."

"Yes. Oliver and Jenna are quite like King Midas. Oliver has gold, but he wants more. Jenna has power, but she wants more. Their appetites can never be satiated. They are unfit for the purpose of gods."

"But Ceridwen has promised he'll be Chieftain and King of the Tameses tribes."

"I am the King of the Tameses tribes," said Belenus. "Oliver will become a king, but not of my Beltaine people. Ceridwen told him as much as he needs to know.

243

Anymore and his delusions of grandeur will interrupt the energy needed for the Sealing Ceremony. Arawn has other roles for Oliver and Jenna, but they lack the strength of character necessary for the revival of Britannia."

"And I have it?"

"You and Gavin. Like you, he has seen the world. He understands other cultures and respects their gods."

"Gavin is a good guy, but well..." Kerry gathered her thoughts. "He's not a leader. If you want him as one of your warriors, I mean, to command a tribe, he's not-"

"Gavin is ready. If he wasn't, Blodeuedd wouldn't have picked him as a husband. Mathonwy, the mother goddess, has given her blessing so the marriage will be done."

Kerry listened and heard Gavin snoring next door. "Does Gavin have a say in this?"

"He will soon. Ceridwen has foreseen it. Blodeuedd's first husband, Lleu, was young and strong like Gavin, but he was gullible and naïve. Gavin, despite his youth has become more worldly wise through his travels with you."

"He's a decent man. He would make her a good husband." Kerry rested against Belenus' muscular bicep, her head in the crook of his armpit. His solid frame was as real, as flesh and blood as she was. "And what about me? Mathonwy chose me to be yours because I have the ancestors' blood in me, but did you choose me as your wife?"

"It was always my choice," he said.

"Ceridwen said at the feast that you came back to rebuild your Beltaine." Kerry faltered. "You didn't come back for me."

"It was always about you."

Always. Did that mean she been Belenus' Queen

before she had been Aithne of the Britons? Kerry sensed a door opening in her mind, and beyond it, the blackness of time. She could feel Belenus' eyes boring into her face, as though searching the empty void in her head. For what? To help her remember?

"In every lifetime, you were always my Queen, Kerry. You had a different body each time, as returning mortals do, but you always had your mind."

Every lifetime. Aithne of Ancient Britannia. But what came before? An empty void. Her mind was blank.

"So I've been reincarnated many times and every time I was your wife? Why didn't you tell me right away, this morning?" said Kerry.

"The connection was too strong. Think of how one of my hands had felt on your forehead. If you had become excited and had tried to embrace me, the power of Avalon might have harmed you."

Kerry raised her face to look into his eyes. "Avalon is fading in you. You said it'll take a stronger physical connection to see the past. Like what?"

She already knew the answer. Kerry brought her lips to his; a light touch of skin barely brushing skin. His lips were warm and soft, as real as any man. But he wasn't a man. He was a god. No harm had come from the initial attempt, so Kerry pressed harder. Belenus responded to her kiss and she succumbed to his lips.

Like before, under the electrifying touch of his immortal skin, Kerry closed her eyes to the present day and opened herself to a scene of the past. Orange hair fell over the shoulders of her blue tunic dress. She was Aithne again, not Kerry. Next to her sat Belenus, wearing bronze armour over a brown tunic and red and black plaid leggings. He didn't wear his golden armour as he was dressed for fighting, not prestige. They were at a rectangular wooden table in a rectangular whitewashed room with a pane-less, iron framed lattice window. Morfan sat to her right and Afagddu sat to Belenus' left, flanking them like bodyguards, both in full bronze armour. Across from Belenus sat a Roman general. He wore a scale armour vest made of overlapping iron fragments with a purple cape hanging from his shoulders. Aithne was familiar enough with battle to know that legionnaires often wore this type of armour; but as he was of a higher rank than a Roman soldier, clearly he was dressed for protection. He didn't trust Belenus. His purple cloak showed pomposity; he wasn't royal but dressed as though he was. This was Publius Ostorius Scapula, the second Governor of Britannia. The Governor was flanked by two soldiers from his *Beneficiari*, Centurions of the highest rank. They wore horizontal sheet armour over their chests, fastened by leather straps, shoulder guards and rounded brass helmets. Two more Roman guards stood blocking the curtained doorway behind them, wearing mail armour and holding long spears.

They were in the room of the enemy; in a Roman residence. Briton roundhouses had curved walls made of wattle and daub with no windows. The rectangular room in which they sat had freshly plastered white walls; it was a new Roman town. Aithne looked out through the latticed window into a courtyard. Beyond it, she could see more of the enemy gathering in the marketplace to look in. They were surrounded.

Aithne felt uneasy and wondered if the Briton warriors did too. She glanced at Belenus. He didn't take his eyes off the Governor, watching him with an expression of firm resolve. The three Briton warriors didn't show any sign of intimidation in the household of their foe. With them around, no harm would come to her.

246

The table had an array of food in Mediterranean style; tomatoes, cheese, olives, bread, dates and pitchers of wine, unlike the huge portions of meat familiar to the Britons. Belenus looked at the foreign food in wonder then turned his attention to the Governor.

"Why have you asked us here?" said Belenus.

The Governor gestured to the food. "Let us dine before we begin formalities. I believe that hospitality comes first among your people, before business is discussed?"

Belenus gave a nod of approval. Though Aithne knew the diet of fruit, vegetables and bread was not to his taste, he ate with good appetite. Two slave girls entered to serve wine and bring more food. He drank freely of the wine offered to him by one. The girls wore simple, cream coloured ankle-length dresses and had elaborate head-dresses; rows of gold-leafed jewellery that sat on top of their piled hair. Slaves taken by Romans abroad, no doubt.

Aithne dipped some bread in olive oil and tried it. She could taste the smooth consistency of the cold-pressed Mediterranean staple. The Roman Governor had clearly spared no expense with exotic food imported from the continent to impress his guests. He knew the native Briton customs; that feasting came before business, and even if the food wasn't to Belenus' taste it certainly was to hers. What did the Governor hope to profit from such a prestigious gathering?

The Governor finished his food and dabbed his mouth with a handkerchief. "Belenus," he said. His mouth curled into a half-smile. "But since you fashion yourself in the image of our Sun God, should I call you Apollo?"

"I am the image of the Sun God of the Beltaine, known only as Belenus."

"Then Belenus it shall be. But I was under the

impression you are the King of the Catuvellauni?" said the Governor.

"My Beltaine are the tribes of the Tameses. The Catuvellauni are our kinsmen further North. You build your road through my territories without my permission," said Belenus.

Aithne looked outside beyond the crowds in the marketplace to the beginnings of the East-West road which stretched far into the wilderness of Britannia. A series of wooden posts, dug into the gravel beds, marked the perimeter of the road.

"I see your lady doesn't mind our fine Roman craftsmanship," said the Governor and Aithne turned away from the window to face him. "Our residence will soon be part of a vast town called Londinium, my lady."

Aithne bit into a tomato, spraying juice and seeds over the Governor's table. "Queen, not lady. And for your information, I *do* mind. I much prefer Plowonida in all its fine, green, natural glory - not sullied by Roman soldiers, citizens and tradesmen." She jabbed her finger at the window. Outside, Traders undertook glass-blowing, leather-tanning and pottery-making in Mediterranean style single-storey workshops, enclosing their private homes behind. Women and children busied themselves carrying water vessels, pulling animals to market, selling fruit and vegetables at stalls and weaving textiles.

"We need the Silchester-Colchester road to trade with our people in Camulodunum," said the Governor, matter-of-factly.

"Yes, where word has reached me, you mistreat the Trinovantian people," said Belenus, with a menacing edge to his voice.

"It doesn't have to be that way. I brought you here today in the hope of making an ally of you. I'm sending an expedition into the lands of the Dobunni and Silures in the West and it would be a *smart* move, on your part, to protect your people by showing that you have an alliance with Publius Ostorius Scapula. Wouldn't you agree?"

"What you mean to say is, if I submit to Rome and allow you to infiltrate the lands of my kinsmen, the Dobunni and Silures in the West, while you overthrow the Trinovantes north of Camulodunum, you will let us live, at a heavy tax no less." Belenus took a deep breath and his chest puffed out impressively. "That does not sound like an alliance. It sounds like a tyranny."

"You would do well to heed my offer. There would be benefits. You would pay tribute to Rome, of course, but we would protect your Kingdom and allow you to continue your rule over the Beltaine Chiefdoms," said the Governor. "Refuse us and your people would be sold as slaves. It is inevitable."

Belenus finished his wine and wiped his mouth on his sleeve. "I do not make alliances with oppressive rulers. You made pretences of a peaceable agreement with the Iceni before you forcibly suppressed them."

"I thought as much. I knew you barbarians had no brains. But I was prepared for that too. For I know something *you* don't know." Publius Ostorius Scapula pointed at Belenus' empty wine cup. "Immortals do not exist. There are only men who play at being fools. It was the downfall of Alexander and it will be the downfall of you too, *Apollo.*"

Belenus looked down at his cup. A slow smile broke over his face.

"I know something *you* don't know. The deities might have left you Roman heathens, but here in Britannia, the people are blessed by having immortals walk among them. But Gods do not fall for the tricks of men."

249

Aithne could read the frustration in the Governor's eyes; he was waiting for Belenus to collapse but the poison didn't work. Publius Ostorius Scapula paled.

Belenus and the Governor moved at the same time. Publius Ostorius' hand jumped to his sword. But before he could unsheathe it, Belenus reached across the table with unearthly speed and drew Publius' own pugio; his short dagger. Belenus plunged it into the Governor's stomach with godly strength that tore through his armour, breaking the blade. Publius crumpled forward on the table, blood pouring over the remnants of the fine feast. In a swift movement to match Belenus', Afagddu swept behind the nearest one of Publius' centurions. He grabbed his head with his right hand, his huge palm almost obscuring the man's entire face. Afagddu brought his left hand across the Centurion's throat and Kerry saw a line of blood appear, before muscle and sinew were exposed as the soldier's head lolled. The man's eyes bulged, and blood ran from his mouth as he slumped backwards and Afagddu let him drop like a rag doll. Morfan moved for the two guards waiting in the doorway. He grabbed the spear of the nearest guard and kicked him hard in the stomach. The man winced as the air was knocked out of him. He punched the other hard between his eyes then grabbed his face in his huge palm, his fingers spread across the guard's forehead. With his other hand, he ripped the guard's helmet off and slammed his head back against the wall. Aithne heard the crack and saw a smear of blood as the guard slid down the wall.

She had been too distracted by the sudden chaos to notice the forearm of the other centurion across her neck, putting pressure on her throat.

"What have you done? We offered you peace and you go and do this? Now you're going to pay! I'm going to

250

snap the neck of your bitch and pack her broken body off to whatever heathen gods you dogs worship."

Aithne grabbed the man's arm, but she couldn't loosen his grip. She gagged. Dots formed before her eyes.

She fumbled inside her tunic and her hand closed around a bronze scabbard, her fingers tightening around the intricately decorated handle. Her trusty dagger. She was glad she had thought to bring it.

Aithne thrust her arm upwards and plunged the sharp point into the right side of the centurion's face. The man didn't scream. He made a wet gurgling sound and let go of Aithne. She turned, gasping, and saw him stagger sideways holding his face. The dagger had pierced his cheek and exited the back of his head. His eyes were wide and unseeing even before he hit the floor.

Belenus looked from the dead Beneficiari on the floor across to Publius Ostorius Scapula sprawled across the table. "What a fool to think he could wield a sword in this small room. He was no fighter - nothing but a fat man gone to seed.

Belenus grabbed the dead Governor's hair and dragged his body outside. Morfan kicked the dead guard aside to make way for him. The other guard that Morfan had kicked groaned in the hallway outside. Afagddu plunged a dagger into his back and the man made no more sound.

The Romans had stood no chance. All three Briton gods were not only skilled assassins but wielding immortal power.

Belenus dropped the Governor's body over a wooden post in the market square. Roman tradesmen and citizens stopped their work to look. A crowd began to form, cautious at first.

"Roman citizens. You have wronged my people.

You have ravaged the land of Plowonida to build your crude township of Londinium. Tell your Emperor that the Britons will never submit to foreign rule. The Tameses tribes will rally with our kinsmen in the north, the Catuvellauni. We will drive you from our shores. As a warning of what will happen to the Emperor, if he is foolish enough to step onto our land, the head of your Governor, Publius Ostorius Scapula, will stand on a spike facing the East."

Belenus unsheathed his sword. He swung it upwards and brought it down on Publius' neck. The Governor's head rolled away in a shower of blood. Belenus grabbed the severed head and held it high.

Aithne stood close to Belenus, proud of her Sun God and King. Afagddu and Morfan stood with their swords ready on either side of them as a couple of Roman soldiers moved forwards, but there was little they could do to protect their people.

"This offering will appease Arawn and serve as a reminder to any further invaders to go back to Rome. Go East and warn your soldiers in Camulodunum. Warn them in the North in Verulamium. Britannia is the country of the native Britons and it will stay that way. Londinium will be sacked as soon as it is born," said Belenus.

The vision began to fade as Belenus pulled his lips away and Aithne of the past faded away. Kerry lay her head back on her pillow and focussed on the ceiling, clearing her eyes of the past.

"I was your warrior Queen. That was me, all those years ago, almost two thousand years ago in our shared past," she said, gasping between heavy breaths.

"Do you remember your dream, two nights ago on the eve of the Beltaine festival?" he said.

Kerry turned her head to face him. "Aithne - me -

was only a girl. I watched you fighting, and I loved you, but you were a warrior, grown like you are now and I was sixteen, young and wild."

"And four years later, you became my Queen. You were twenty when we visited Londinium. It was your first duty as my Briton wife. I saw the way the Governor looked at you. If he had had his way, Afagddu, Morfan and I would have been killed and you would have been taken as his own concubine. Many men wanted you, but you became mine."

"I really killed that guard." Kerry looked at her own hands, recalling the feel of her bronze dagger. Her thoughts returned to the present. "It's strange how Publius Ostorius tried to poison you in the past, in a barbaric age and now here we are in the twenty-first century with a government and police and laws. But look at what Jenna and Oliver plotted to do - the very same thing. They wanted to drug and poison us. Nothing has changed."

"Humanity doesn't change. In Mesopotamia the scribes were busy detailing cuneiform tablets with daily reports of divorce, adultery, theft and petty quarrels. But a new world order is upon us. The Briton way will mean we live by our own rules. If a man is killed by another, his brother is free to avenge him."

Maybe the ancient Briton way was fairer after all. "You know what the funny thing is? I guess that's more democratic than what we have today."

Chapter 25

Sunlight streamed into Gavin's bedroom above the Herne's Hunt restaurant. The rickety bed creaked as Blodeuedd climbed onto his stomach and straddled him.

"Good morning Gavin," she said. "Gavin is hungry? Blodeuedd cooked you breakfast."

Sure he was hungry; for her. He placed his hands on her waist and slid them downwards over the fabric of her dress towards her thighs but stopped before he touched bare skin. An electric shock was not what he needed at any time of day, never mind first thing in the morning.

"Yeah, I could eat. What did you make?"

She jumped off him and landed, without a noise, on her toes like a ballet-dancer next to his bed. "Blodeuedd made a surprise."

Gavin swung his legs over the side of the bed. His phone screen read seven AM. Third of May already. *Nuts.* Time was flying.

"Blodeuedd, what time have you been up since?"

"Sunrise," she said.

Of course; she had been an *owl*. "Alright, let me get dressed first, OK?"

"Blodeuedd helps you." Blodeuedd skipped across his room and pulled a drawer open with nimble fingers. She tossed a pair of boxers across to him.

"That's great, but this is what you called underwear. I need a shirt and some jeans."

"Shirt? Jeans? Gavin can wear this and dress like fighting Britons," she said.

He couldn't help laughing. "Nearly naked won't go down well in this day and age. Try that bag by the door - I haven't unpacked most of my stuff yet."

She was like a fairy as she danced back to him with a rumpled shirt and jeans. His amusement faded when she started to pull off his T-shirt.

Gavin flinched. "Woah - isn't this a bit dangerous, you know? If your fingers touch my skin-"

"Don't be afraid," she said in her beauteous voice to match her beauteous form. "I won't hurt you."

He let her pull his T-shirt off. Her careful fingers didn't touch any of his bare skin.

Gavin put the shirt that she had picked out for him on. "The gods were unfair to give me the most stunning woman I've ever seen and not let me touch her."

"You mustn't mock the gods. Arawn is vengeful. He'll punish you if you upset him," said Blodeuedd.

"Sorry, Arawn," said Gavin. He tried to mean it; never could be sure if gods could read minds.

Blodeuedd skipped to the door. "The sun is out, so Arawn is not angry."

"Does Arawn really punish even the most minor insults?"

She shook her beautiful red head. "Arawn mostly leaves the realm of mortals alone, but he doesn't like blasphemy against the gods."

"Blasphemy, huh?" Gavin finished dressing and followed her out of the room. "You're an enigma, Blodeuedd. How did you learn words like 'blasphemy' so fast?"

Blodeuedd tossed her head in a sexy, but haughty manner. "Blodeuedd *might* have been born yesterday, but Blodeuedd was conceived long ago. Blodeuedd spoke Brythonic, the language of my people, and Latin, the foreign language, long ago. Using your words is simply *translating* from my tongue."

"Sorry Blodeuedd, I didn't mean to be insulting.

You're picking up English fast."

"Avalon is like England, but it is dark and grey all the time. Arawn doesn't allow the sun to shine. So Blodeuedd was a night owl all the time among the shadows. And when Blodeuedd is in bird form, Blodeuedd can't speak any language - not Brythonic, or Latin or English. So Ceridwen and Belenus and other deities could learn English, but not Blodeuedd." Blodeuedd's dress billowed as she pirouetted. "Blodeuedd loves being a maiden again. Blodeuedd wants to always stay in the sun."

She danced across the landing, twirling and spinning. Gavin trailed behind watching her graceful form climb the stairs to the Herne's Hunt roof.

"Wait a minute, Petal. If Belenus is the God of the Sun, then why couldn't he make it shine in Avalon? Is his godly power less than Arawn's?"

"Avalon is Arawn's domain, so he is the only god with total power. Belenus is a god of the earth. In Avalon, Belenus ruled the dead souls of his Beltaine tribe and they lived and fought by the river, as they did in life by the Tameses. But Arawn's other world never had sun, and that kept Belenus' power weaker than Arawn's."

"And Ceridwen too? She had less power than Arawn in Avalon?"

"Ceridwen controls the stars and the heavens are part of this world, not the other world." Blodeuedd led Gavin onto the rooftop. "Arawn is a father god of the other world, just as Mathonwy is a mother goddess of the earth. They have more power."

A delicious smell of cooking fish made Gavin's mouth water. He had half expected more porridge, the 'food of the gods'. A hearty breakfast was a welcome treat.

Blodeuedd had built an open oven from a sand-lined pit filled with stones and fire sticks. A wooden slat had been placed across the fire and two fish cooked on top of the charred wood. They had been tied together with string and were caked in what looked to Gavin like mud, baked hard in the flames.

"Do you like trout, Gavin?" said Blodeuedd.

"Yeah, looks great. Is this an ancient recipe?"

She sat down cross-legged and stoked the fire with a stick. "This is the food of my people, the Britons."

Gavin sat beside her. "I can't wait to try it."

The more Blodeuedd spoke, the less fragmented her sentences became. Only a goddess could learn so fast. He reprimanded himself; she *was* a deity after all. It was easy to forget, when she looked so perfectly human.

"So let me get this right. If all of you gods are more powerful on earth than in Avalon, then how come you can't stop yourself changing into an owl now that you're here?"

Blodeuedd twirled the cooking stick in her hands. "Avalon is strong in us all until the sixth of May. Our power on earth will be strong after that and the bonds of the Otherworld will weaken."

"Does that mean, I'll be able to touch you?" he said.

"Thankfully, yes," she said.

"Can't wait for that." In the bright sunshine, every curve of her scantily clad body showed. He couldn't wait to get his hands on her delightful all-too-human endowments.

Blodeuedd tossed the cooking stick in the air, like a baton and caught it with her fingertips. She had a childlike innocence, yet she was thousands of years old. Maybe being an owl for so long had kept her sense of wonder at the world intact. How much longer did Arawn intend to curse her? She had been cursed for nearly two millennia; it was unfair that she had to keep being punished, especially for mistakes she'd made in a former lifetime.

"I've got it - I know a way you could cheat your fate. We could get some sun-lamps in my bedroom. That way you won't have to change into an owl after dark," he said.

Blodeuedd laughed; a tinkling, musical laugh. "I know you want to help, but Arawn can't be cheated. There is only one thing that can fix Blodeuedd's fate, and it must be done before the sixth day."

Gavin had an inkling of where the conversation was going.

"We need to tie the knot."

"Yes. Gavin needs to hand-fast with Blodeuedd. Sun-lamps or anything else can't fix Blodeuedd's condition. When the sun rises, Blodeuedd is a woman and when it sets, Blodeuedd is an owl."

Hand-fasting meant marriage. So much to do before the sixth of May; so much pressure. The big 'M' with Blodeuedd and having to steal Kerry's Golden Horse before the sixth for the Water Priestess' ritual. Pressure. So much pressure.

"So, how do you Britons tie the old, you know, anyway? You don't have churches. Do you find a sacred grove of trees, or something?"

Blodeuedd was misty-eyed, as though recalling a memory. "In the old days, Druids performed the ceremony. Ceridwen will do it for us, if we ask her. A goddess is even better than a Briton priest."

"And what's expected of a couple who are, you know, tied together? Like, is it for life, or can you get divorced and all that sort of stuff?" he said.

Her face fell. "Is Gavin afraid to be with Blodeuedd?"

258

Gavin put his hands up in protest. "It's not what I meant - just, how long is forever, with an immortal?"

Blodeuedd laughed and clapped her hands. "You're funny, Gavin! Forever is the same as with human to human marriage - mortal death, of course."

As the cooking fire died down, she tended to the fish and her expression brightened. Gavin felt at ease. He loved to see her smile. And he had to admit, he did want to make her happy.

"The fish is ready. See? The gorse wood has completely burned away. That's how you know it's done."

She tapped the fish against one of the cooking stones and peeled the hardened clay away. Leaves and grass peeled away with the baked clay, leaving tender, juicy trout.

"I cooked them in grass and burdock leaves," she said. "I tied them around the trout with nettle fibre. That's what I did this morning as soon as dawn broke - I made the nettle fibre."

"Hey, Blodeuedd, you said 'I' instead of 'Blodeuedd'. That's great!"

She gave an exaggerated grin, gritting her teeth together, then poked her tongue out at him.

Life was going to be an adventure with his strange and charismatic beauty.

Gavin focussed on the fish. "The nettle fibre sounds pretty complicated. How did you do it?"

"I stripped the main stem of the nettles, boiled the fibre in wood ash, then rubbed it with clay to take off the green filament - the same clay that I coated the trout in," she said.

"Er- you didn't get the clay from the Thames, did you?"

Blodeuedd's yellow, owlish eyes pierced him. "The Thames is not clean like in Blodeuedd's first lifetime. No,

259

it's a cooking clay called raku. Ceridwen had some in the kitchen."

She picked a morsel of fish between her finger and thumb and fed it to him, careful not to touch his lips with her bare skin.

"Wow, that tastes great. Doesn't even need any condiments or anything."

"Blodeuedd is glad you like it," she said.

They ate from a shared platter. Gavin wanted to savour the fish but couldn't help wolfing it down as it was so good. No seasoning, no marinade, no dressing; it was basic, simple cooking at its best. As she ate, she made squealing sounds of delight. He knew little of Blodeuedd, but he liked her more and more. Maybe marriage would be fun; modern life to get used to as well as rediscovering her earthly form.

"So, Blodeuedd. I was thinking, you know, about this whole tying the knot thing-"

Blodeuedd turned her eager, owl-like eyes on him. "Yes?"

"Well, you see, in this day and age, a man and woman normally get to know each other a bit first. It's called an engagement. It's so that they can find out if they'll get along and it also gives them time to plan the wedding."

"Aren't we having an engagement now?" she said. "Aren't we getting to know one another?"

What could he say to that? "Err, I guess so."

"The customs of my people are different from yours," she said. "My people believe in sharing. Men and women under the same household can be shared. But any children born to a woman belong to her husband only."

Gavin paused. "Are you saying your people are polygamous? But then why did you get punished for cheating on your husband?"

Blodeuedd shrugged, but he knew she was being deliberately blasé. "Not cheating but being prepared to leave my household to go with Goronwy and become his Lady of Penllyn. That, and not stopping my lover from plotting to murder Lleu."

"Oh, I see. But you learned your lesson, right?"

She leaned towards him, half-closing her eyes in a dreamy expression. "More than anything, yes. I desire above all to be in this body and be blessed to stay in the sun."

He couldn't blame her; what a body it was. Gwydion had made her form so breath-taking. "So, what constitutes a household anyway? You know, like how you said a man and a woman can share themselves with members of their household?"

"Not people with direct blood - my people don't condone incest, but a wife who joins a household can be shared with her husband's brothers, for example." Blodeuedd hesitated and Gavin knew she was thinking of an example. "Say in this lifetime, for instance. I was summoned by Oliver and Kerry. That means I can't share myself with Oliver, as he offered a flesh token for me. But as they are of my household, and you are not related, you could share with Kerry."

Hmm. He couldn't see Belenus liking such a thing. Come to think of it, he wasn't sure what he thought of the idea himself. Until recently, he had wanted Kerry more than anyone else. Now that he could see what an extraordinary woman Blodeuedd was, all he could think of was her.

"I think I get it," he said. "Belenus was summoned by Jenna and I, so that means Jenna can't have Belenus, but I could potentially sleep with Jenna. Not that I would want to of course - apart from the fact that she's shown herself to be an evil psychopath, I only have eyes for you. But you could potentially have Belenus, if you both wanted?"

"Yes. That would be permitted." She gave a sweet smile. "But I also only have eyes for you too, my Gavin."

Gavin felt his neck prickle. "Er, so a household could be extended by a husband or wife taking people from outside, making the clan, or tribe, or whatever you call it bigger?" he said.

"That's right," said Blodeuedd. "But only if the ceremony was blessed by the gods. Hand-fasting is different from your modern notion of joining."

"Are you saying that hand-fasting isn't marriage? You know, like how modern people say some vows and wear rings on their fingers?"

"Hand-fasting is when two people's hands are bound by cord before the gods," she said. "They wear the cord for one day, but the gods agree to them staying together for life."

"And if I hand-fast with you, you'll stay in your human body - and it won't give me any electric shocks if I touch you?"

"Yes. You can touch me anytime as I'll be yours and you'll be mine," she said. She tilted her head, suddenly coy. "But only if you'll hand-fast with me."

Hand-fasting. The only way to break the tie was death. She had allowed another man to plot her first mortal husband's murder the first time; would she succumb again?

He gulped, trying to quash the thought. In two thousand years, she was bound to have changed. Being an owl had been enough punishment. She wouldn't risk another curse. It was a chance he was willing to take.

"I've made up my mind, Blodeuedd. Let's get married."

Blodeuedd stared blankly at him. Gavin was confused; wasn't this what she wanted? He chided himself; of course, she didn't know the word 'marry'. Ancient Britons had a different word for a different ceremony.

"What I mean is, let's do it - let's hand fast."

Blodeuedd squealed with delight. She knocked him flat on his back. Gavin felt the air knocked from his chest as his back hit concrete. Blodeuedd tore at his jeans, sending the buttons flying in all directions.

"Woah, Blodeuedd, I don't want an electric shock - shouldn't we wait until after we're married, when it's safe?"

Blodeuedd gave him an impish look. "Don't worry, Gavin." She showed him a condom packet; one of his own.

Gavin propped himself up on his elbows. "Where did you get this?"

She pushed him back down. "Your underwear drawer. I know what they are. We had them in my last lifetime - only they were made of sheep's intestines." Blodeuedd clamped the packet in her teeth and jerked her head to one side, ripping it open.

Nuts, this woman was wild. "If I'd known proposing marriage would've led to this, I'd have done it sooner."

Blodeuedd pulled her dress over her head. Gavin watched her body revealed to him in a sensual tease; her light brown pubic hair, the soft curve of her stomach, her large, round breasts and pink, upward pointing nipples. He ran his eyes over her body, taking in her warm curves. Her naked form, glowing white in the morning sun was how he imagined Aphrodite incarnate. It was hard to believe that Blodeuedd wasn't the goddess of beauty herself.

The stunning goddess' red-gold hair fell in a curtain across Gavin's chest as she leaned forward, cloaking her face from his view. He closed his eyes, enjoying the warmth as she took him in her mouth. *Clever little maiden;* she'd found a way of dodging Arawn's curse of so that they could get intimate without the electric shocks. The open flaps of his jeans stopped the bare skin of her hand from touching him, but Gavin wouldn't have cared even if it did. This was worth an electric shock. She had lost nothing in skill in two thousand years; only an immortal could have performed as she did.

Who would have thought the demure Maiden of Flowers could have been such a wild siren?

The tension in Gavin's body released. Blodeuedd ran her hands up and down over his chest, grabbing handfuls of his shirt. He opened his eyes to the blue sky and resisted putting his hands on her hair. The only thing that could have made it better was if he could have touched her bare skin. What he couldn't have made him lust even more.

Blodeuedd straightened up and arched her back to the morning sun as she swallowed. "I'd almost forgotten how great it feels to be a woman again," she said.

Gavin moved his jaw to speak, but the words took their time.

When his speech returned, he managed five words.

"I think I'm in love."

Chapter 26

Kerry and Belenus strolled along the Thames path close to Wandsworth Bridge. She could see the metal ladder ahead that she had climbed with Gavin. Like the day she had descended onto the muddy shore, a wide strand had been exposed by the low tide. Lucky. Or was it destiny, just like when she had found the Golden Horse? Warmth coursed through her body. Without his metal armour, Belenus radiated heat through his woollen tunic. This was destiny, not luck.

"I guess we'll have a long hot summer now that the Sun God is here," she said.

"There'll be many changes now that the gods have returned to earth," he said.

"What kind of people are you going to recruit to become your Beltaine? We don't have dedicated warriors in this time. Most people just want money."

"We had currency in my time too, just not the same as the modern day notion of money. The moon has moved into the sign of Aquarius. The people I lead will have a new perspective on the Ancient Ways and how our culture will prevail."

"Aquarius is the water sign. But if you're the Sun God, won't the seasons be drier now that you are the Beltaine King again?"

"The transition won't be easy. There will be longer seasons of rain and flooding to cleanse the world in preparation for the new planetary shift. But I'm the Sun God. I will bring longer, hotter summers. The conjugation of celestial bodies will be sanctified by the conjugation of immortal and mortal power in this world. Just as the planets are aligning themselves now for the biggest Uranus-Pluto Square in a decade, so the four of us - Gavin and Bloduedd, you and I, will unite to complete the square of the earthly realm."

Conjugation. Kerry stopped walking, hanging onto that thought. She realised she was also hanging onto the rungs of the metal ladder leading to the muddy shore below. Her unconscious mind had brought her back to where she had found the Golden Horse.

"This is where--" she started.

"I know. I saw you," he said.

She swung her leg over the wall and stood on the top rung. "You were there? Were you watching me all the time?"

"Not all the time. The Golden Horse channelled your energy and drew me to you at that moment."

Kerry felt the cold metal beneath her fingers as she descended the ladder; the chill kept her grounded in reality. She jumped onto the muddy beach, his words replaying in her mind. *It was always about you. In every lifetime, you were always my Queen, Kerry. You had a different body each time, as returning mortals do, but you always had your mind.* His words resonated deep in her mind. "If it wasn't for the Uranus-Pluto square, or whatever that planetary alignment is, would you have come back to me sooner?"

Belenus stepped onto the shore beside her. "This was as soon as I could - the time is right. By our ancient standards, you have only been a woman for a year."

Kerry looked out across the river. He wrapped his arm around her shoulders, his immortal heat shielding her from the tidal wind.

"The past five days have been surreal. A week ago I could never have imagined I'd be involved with anyone, never mind a resurrected Celtic god."

"Mother Mathonwy is generous to reunite us so soon."

266

"That's the earth goddess, right?"

"Yes."

Kerry started walking towards the spot where she had found the Golden Horse. "When I get our Golden Horse back after the Sealing, I want to give it as an offering to Mathonwy."

"A fitting purpose for it." Belenus tugged Kerry's hand. She stopped walking and turned to him. "Come. Let's go the other way. We need to get our mind off the Golden Horse for now."

They walked towards Wandsworth Bridge. Below the pale blue and white painted upper side, the metal framework was rusted and unmaintained; a reminder that they were trespassing. If she had been with Gavin, she would have turned back. Under the bridge was dangerously close to the river, and if the tide came in, it would do so faster than human legs could run. But with Belenus, she didn't worry. She was with a god; she was safe.

"Many things will change, starting from the seventh of May. Now that I have returned to this world, I will celebrate by bringing a long, hot summer." He took her hand and led her under the bridge.

"I'll miss seeing visions from your past," she said.

"We have a few more days yet. But like I said last night, it will take a stronger physical connection."

Belenus extended his hand toward the East. Kerry watched as the clouds parted and the sun appeared. It shone hotter than normal for May, its heat reaching under the bridge to dry the spot they stood on. Kerry embraced the warmth on her face; godly warmth. Sun godly-warmth.

"On the first of May, when I was reborn, we entered a solar eclipse with the Taurus new moon," said Belenus. "And now there is a lunar eclipse with the Sagittarius full moon. The tide is in retreat and the sun will stay."

She pulled her phone from her pocket. The illuminated screen showed twenty-three degrees; hot for May in England. "You really are... unearthly," she said.

Kerry gazed at her Sun God. Framed by the brilliance of the sunny day, he seemed to have a golden halo. She pulled him towards her; Belenus leaned in for their kiss. As his mouth met hers, she waited for a vision that didn't come.

"I think we're probably the first people who've been down here for who knows when," she said. On the opposite bank, far across the wide river, machinery and industry were the only companions who shared the view; a huge red crane moved a mound of sand next to a rusted metal barge. It was the only land that wasn't gentrified on the South side of the river stretching towards Vauxhall in one direction and Putney in the other. Kerry was glad for the privacy; not even dog walkers or joggers could get lose to the Thames path at that spot. Solitude was theirs. The river was theirs.

"That's why I chose it." Belenus had a mischievous glint in his eye. "It's secluded."

"What was it you had in mind?" Kerry reached her arms around him and linked her fingers in the small of his back. Maybe she knew the answer already; maybe she liked the tease.

"If you want to see more visions from my past - your past - then our connection needs to be stronger," he kissed her again, "than this."

Did he mean what she thought he was implying? The temperature *had* to be more than twenty-three degrees. Kerry unzipped her fleece jacket and took it off.

Belenus put his hands on her waist and slid her jumper up then pulled it over her head. She helped, pulling her bra off and dropping it. He kissed her neck and lower, his mouth reaching her breasts. His lips on her bare skin was a different sensation than any man before, tingling hot like the sun. Kerry admired his muscular chest as he pulled his tunic off. He felt hotter than a mortal man as he pressed his body against hers, his hands almost entirely cupping her waist. His fingers were coarse from his warrior lifestyle, his skin rough on her body. She loved the feel of his calloused palms on her skin. Stones, the smell of mud and his battle-honed hands stimulated a primitive desire. Kerry unbuttoned her jeans and kicked them off, wriggling out of her underwear until she stood, bare, before him.

He lifted her up and Kerry hooked her legs around his back. The brick wall was cold and hard against her back; goose bumps sprang across her skin.

The scent of their sweat mingled with the earthy scent of the Thames; smells of mud and clay that were oddly familiar. Their rhythmic motions heightened her senses; Kerry detected faint smoky notes in the air. She was vaguely aware that normally she wouldn't have liked such organic scents, but as her feelings became more acute, she realised she was slipping into a memory. Not Belenus' this time, but one that they had shared.

Wandsworth Bridge dissolved. They were in a roundhouse. She could see the sooty thatched roof above. The homely smell of stew and wood smoke made her mouth water. Red hair framed her face, spilling down over her shoulders. She was Aithne.

Aithne was naked as she embraced with Belenus and he was shirtless, wearing only brown plaid leggings. They stood upright, with her back pressed against a hard oak post.

Earthy scents of clay, straw and animal dung filled her nose from the walls of the wattle and daub roundhouse. She tilted her head back, looking at the dark alder beams of the thatched roof above. This was her - their - home. She faced the entranceway, a short, arched tunnel, aligned towards the midwinter sunrise, covered by a brown woollen curtain.

The post they leaned against was near the middle of the circular room. A cauldron of meat steamed over a four-posted iron fire-dog on the cooking hearth. Four horned bulls heads decorated the curved projecting ends, designed to represent the spirit of the animals being roasted, as an offering to the god of forest beasts, Cernunnos. Next to the hearth a wicker basket containing wooden cooking utensils and clay bowls, waterproofed with pitch made from birch bark, had been piled ready for the Beltaine meal. All of the equipment belonged to Ceridwen. The goddess would be back anytime now; they had better be quick.

Or should they? Said who? The occasion was theirs, after all. It was a triple celebration: The Sun God's coming into the world on Beltaine, her womanhood ceremony on the birthday she shared with Belenus and their hand-fasting earlier that day, now that she had Come of Age.

Hand-fasting. Aithne tugged on the taut twine that bound her left wrist to Belenus' right wrist. He was hers and she was his. She closed her eyes and breathed in the scent of his sweat.

Cracking twigs underfoot announced Ceridwen's arrival. She was stooped as she emerged from the low tunnel entranceway, pushing aside the curtain, then straightened up and strode into the room. Ceridwen was curvaceous and black-haired in the prime of her femininity. Aithne buried her face in Belenus' shoulder, embarrassed. She turned her head to the right. There was a hard wooden bed with a woollen blanket on it. She badly wanted to be under it, her nakedness concealed from the goddess' eyes. Belenus didn't seem to care. He carried on with their lovemaking, unashamed.

Aithne's embarrassment was unnecessary; Ceridwen didn't look their way. She attended to the stew. Her long, black hair dangled over her shoulders and she tossed it back to stir and taste the stew. The goddess had a bird painted in blue woad on her arm; a figure-eight shaped body with long, tendril-like legs, the whole design stretching from her fingers to her neck. More tattoos were painted on her left cheek and forehead showing the spoked wheel of a stylised sun and a geometric diamond on her cheeks reflecting a symbol of the vulva. As the Goddess of Fertility and partner of the Sun God, she had prepared her earthly flesh to show her position during the Beltaine feast honouring the gods in Avalon. Aithne knew what the tattoos meant; a mark of prestige. But the blue paint would serve a dual purpose of deterring any Romans from coming near on the Beltaine tribes' sacred day; the enemy found their body paint savage.

Ceridwen swept out through the cloth-covered doorway and brightness entered. The light continued to spread, dissipating the dark, musky interior.

Aithne faded as Kerry slipped further back in time.

A new scene emerged; she was with Belenus by the window of a spacious rectangular room. The walls were white and undecorated, apart from a large mosaic showing jumping fish, a symbol of Pisces. There were no latticed metal grills or panes on the windows; sunlight streamed inside. This was a Mediterranean villa; but not in Britannia. Where was she? Who was she?

The more she stared around the room, familiarising herself with what had once been hers, a name came back to her: Dareia. Wealthy.

Dareia leaned against the edge of the window, with her left leg hooked over the crook of Belenus' arm as they made love. Her purple, ankle length gown hung around her waist, exposing her ample chest. Belenus was naked. His white robe lay on the tiled floor beside them. He had short, blonde hair curled around his face and was clean shaven, showing his chiselled features. Dareia admired the lines of his bare form; he looked more than ever like a Greek statue.

Dareia turned to look outside, spilling tight coils of dark blonde hair over her breasts as she twisted her body to see into the courtyard. The courtyard formed a quadrangle around a rectangular pool. Classical pillars and trees lined the perimeter of it. On either side of the wooden gateway into the courtyard at the far end, Dareia saw two white marble statues of Helios and Aphrodite guarding the entrance. Helios; Belenus. She turned her body, leaning both arms on the window ledge, letting Helios take her from behind. She wanted to face the statue of the Sun God, as the deity himself made love to her.

Helios' likeness was two floors high in comparison to a modern house. Both statues of Helios and Aphrodite had their hair painted gold to match the sun and their eyes filled in blue, although their bodies remained stark white in contrast to the vivid colours. Helios wore a golden crown on his head showing a circular disc in the centre of his forehead and Aphrodite wore a crown weaved from Elecampane leaves and their yellow flowers, used to invoke love. A frieze on the wall to the left of Helios showed the god on his sun chariot pulled by two lions, while to the right of Aphrodite, her two sons Remus and Romulus flanked her while her third son, Cupid, flew above shooting arrows down on her.

White light engulfed her again, transporting Dareia further back in time. She was with the Sun God in an earlier memory. They were on a reed mattress and she straddled him. The rectangular room was coated with plaster and lime-washed white. The walls had been painted depicting people worshipping the goddess Inana, with palm trees and griffins on either side. Outside the intense sun hinted at an arid environment tamed by irrigation, the sole means for the people of the city to have a green and fertile crescent. This was Uruk, in ancient Sumer.

She concentrated hard on the Sun God, until his name came to mind: Bilgames, King of Uruk. He had black hair, his fringe cropped close to his hairline. His skin was a deep bronze colour. He wore his black beard pointed on his chin and had no moustache. Like before, their entwined bodies were naked. Bilgames' bowl-shaped leather cap lay on the floor next to them. It had a thicker rim with a series of decorated squares, popular among the noblemen. In the style of men at the time, his clothing was a thin woollen garment of multi-coloured squares that hung from the left shoulder like a toga but draped like a skirt from the waist. Her strapless wool dress lay discarded too. When worn, it stretched from her chest to her ankles and was pinched at the waist with a tie. Now it lay draped over the coiled end of the reed mattress. Her eyelashes were clumped with blue colouring; stibium from Egypt, a fashion among noblewomen. She closed her eyes and concentrated on her own name until it came to her: Nintuda.

Bilgames' palace, the Sumerian residence that she shared as his mistress, had two floors unlike their single-storied Greek villa of a later time. As her mind unlocked the past, more details flowed freely from Nintuda's conscious knowledge into Kerry's shared subconscious past. She knew that the lower floor was made of burnt brick and the upper floor was made of mud brick. She remembered how they had fourteen rooms in which to entertain their noble guests. An avenue of small trees led away from Bilgames' palace, elevated above the fortified city, into the throng of Uruk, once so familiar to her, with its ten thousand inhabitants of citizens, visitors, farmers, traders and temple priests. Overlooking the city was the large brick ziggurat of Uruk, where scribes wrote cuneiform on clay tablets. Beyond that Nintuda knew the white temple of Eridu stood in the distance; a thousand years older than Uruk, even in antiquity, where Inana resided. Inana, the goddess Bilgames had spurned for a mortal. Bilgames, King of Uruk had chosen Nintuda, 'Child-bearing lady' as his Queen, not the goddess of fertility herself.

She was hurling back further in time, filled with light that encompassed all of the many lifetimes she had shared with Belenus. Nintuda, Dareia, Aithne, Kerry. Four women, four lifetimes all shared as a lover, and Queen of the Sun God. A primal feeling, stimulated by their earthly pleasures, brought her back to a time before she was with Belenus, when all she had was herself.

Belenus was the unseen sun shining down on her. His warmth kissed her skin. His light gave her body a glow.

Kerry could feel a tug in her navel, as though a spiritual umbilical cord was pulling her forward once more. She let it guide her, feeling safe with the connection. The light of the past faded and the present swirled into focus. Kerry breathed heavily. Sweat beaded her body. For a moment she focussed on Belenus, Wandsworth Bridge and the River Thames to return her mind to modern day London. Belenus lay on the dried mud bank of the Thames and she sat astride him, in the same position that she had straddled him in her past as Nintuda. Every past lifetime memory that she had recalled had been a sexual encounter with Belenus, and in the present, Kerry and Belenus had acted out each episode, emulating the same positions with their physical bodies, while connected with their former spiritual selves.

Kerry stood up, naked, the breeze from the Thames refreshing on her bare skin.

"I feel so free." She exhaled. "I remembered everything about those women I had been - their hopes and dreams, even the mundane stuff of their daily lives."

"You'd simply forgotten," he said. "I unlocked that part of your memories."

"Is that what it always takes - a physical connection?"

"People retain flesh memories. They pass on hopes, dreams and fears through bloodlines. The most basic of human encounters with an immortal can take a person back through the ages to humanity at its earliest," said Belenus.

"This is our fourth lifetime together. I'm not a noblewoman any longer though." She wrapped her arms around her waist, self-conscious. "This wasn't as romantic as a Greek villa or a Sumerian palace."

"That doesn't matter to me - I prefer a more primitive connection. You'll be my Barbarian Queen, not a lady in waiting, anyway."

Kerry got dressed as they talked. "I'm rather getting to like the ancient Briton ways. I don't want anything to change this."

"Nothing could. We're together now and we will be for this lifetime and the next."

She stretched, raising her arms towards the morning sun. "It all worked out really well for the four of us - you and I, Gavin and Blodeuedd. I've gotta say, me and Gavin are the luckiest mortals on earth."

Belenus winked. "You're certainly fit for the gods."

"I wonder if they're having as much fun as we are." Kerry grinned at him.

Belenus stood to get dressed with a mischievous glint in his eyes. "I'm sure they're making the most of their time together."

Gavin would be happy about that.

Kerry waited for Belenus to finish dressing. As they walked along the shore, he put his arm around her shoulders, his hand resting on the back of her neck. She tipped her head back, enjoying the protective gesture. His touch no longer brought extra sensory occurrences; nor his kiss. Soon, sexual intimacy wouldn't either. Kerry felt sad. She would miss seeing their past lives together.

Then again, Belenus had said that he had unlocked that part of her memories. Maybe the memories wouldn't stop; she would see them all by herself.

They climbed the ladder up to the Thames-side path and started along Wandsworth Bridge Road. The sun burned down. Belenus had brought the warmest day so far. Kerry carried her fleece jacket and rolled up her sleeves, revelling in the heat.

"If you can bring out the sun, what else can you do with it?" she said.

"What else is the sun useful for?" he answered.

She shrugged. "It grows plants."

"Yes. Plants mean harvest. Harvest means trade. Where there is trade, there is wealth. The people who have wealth can build armies."

"Not people. A strong leader," she said, looking up at him.

"You were a strong leader too - you were my Queen in battle, often enough," he said.

276

Was she? Kerry recalled how, as Aithne, she had killed the Roman guard in the Governor of Britannia's villa, when he had held a dagger against her throat. But had she been a Beltaine warrior, a Tameses warrior queen herself?

Kerry quietened her mind. An image surfaced; not through light, like in Belenus' shared connections with her, but through her own conscious memories. She was right; Belenus had unlocked enough of her past for her to see through her other lifetimes as easily as if they'd happened yesterday.

Past images seemed to superimpose themselves over present reality. The shops and restaurants of Wandsworth Bridge Road became faint outlines. Behind them, the Sands End factory with its two massive chimneys was a ghostly building. She could see trees from two thousand years ago all around, as real as if she could touch them. Through a clearing in the middle, thousands of Roman soldiers moved westwards, a sea of red and gold. Kerry watched them march in the direction of Hammersmith, deep into the Beltaine lands. Scouts were in front, then cavalry, followed by light troops on foot. The troops marched in columns within their eighty-men cohorts. Kerry knew what they wanted. They planned to overthrow the Dobunni in the West. If they could overthrow the Dobunni, they would be in a prime position to attack the Silures further North or make it across the sea to Hibernia.

The Dobunni weren't a warlike people, unlike the Silures. Kerry knew; she had been to their lands on trade missions with Belenus. They were farmers and craftsmen. The Beltaine people had received gifts of sacred stone figurines carved in the image of Cuda, the mother goddess of the Dobunni people. They would be unprepared for an attack by Roman legions. All that stood between them and the narrow passage west were the Beltaine warriors.

The Romans marched in battle formation. At the front, they formed a wedge, ready to pierce the Beltaine. The Beltaine warriors stood in full view, in a long line on foot, blocking a clearing in the Westward passage. They held their spears at the ready. Kerry looked behind them, into the trees. The Atrebates and Tameses tribes, who had teamed up with the Beltaine, remained hidden. So did the Beltaine chariots, hidden behind earthen ramparts among the trees.

Hundreds of Beltaine women, wearing their black ritual dresses, were lined up on either side of the Romans. Each one held a ceremonial shield of beaten bronze. Kerry's heart beat faster, blood pumping with adrenaline as it had on that day. She remembered the master plan that she had co-conspired with Belenus.

The Romans approached, paying no heed to the women.

The women raised their shields, unnoticed.

Belenus rode out from among the trees in his golden chariot. Kerry looked from the present day Belenus, dressed casually in his plaid tunic, to the Belenus of the past in his full golden armour. Past Belenus stopped at the forefront of his army and raised his sword to the sky. Kerry knew what he was doing; she had seen him do it not an hour before, down by the Thames.

The clouds parted. The sun blazed down supernaturally hot. Belenus was aglow; he almost looked to be on fire. The women tilted their shields to catch the intensified rays that Belenus refracted towards them.

The women refocused the intensified rays onto the Roman army.

Kerry stopped walking, marvelling at the scene she

hadn't witnessed for two millennia.

The Romans shrieked as the sun blinded them. It reddened their faces, blistered their skin. Flames raced through the cohorts. The soldiers were frenzied as they fought to extinguish the fire that ravaged them. Searing white flames roared upwards, sending black ash clouds of human fat, hair and skin skywards.

Kerry blinked; her eyes were dazzled at the memory. Belenus could harness the sun's energy to help, or to hurt. She hadn't forgotten his self-immolation, the horrifying vision of Belenus, his horses and his golden chariot burning nearly two thousand years ago. The flames had seemed to come from an unknown divine source; she had thought it a sign from the Otherworld. But all along, it had been his immortal power.

"Kerry." Kerry felt Belenus shaking her arm. "You've seen enough of the past for one day. I have some business in the present to attend to."

She had been so absorbed by the memory that it took a moment for Kerry to realise were they were. They had stopped in front of Sequana's. She put a hand against her forehead, feeling lightheaded.

"Business? Here? But I can't come with you - I have to stay away from Oliver and Jenna," said Kerry.

"That's right, you can't come." Belenus raised her hands to his mouth and kissed them. "Walk ahead and I will catch up with you. If I don't, I will see you at the Herne's Hunt."

Kerry was confused. "What business is it? I thought we were to stay together at all times for the next few days until the Sealing."

"This concerns the Sealing," he said.

More secrets to do with the Sealing. What could she say to that? She had to trust him; he had a duty to protect himself and the other deities and she had a duty to believe that whatever business he had to attend to was important.

"Alright, I'll start walking. Will you tell me later?"

He smiled. "When it's done."

Kerry walked on, her head hung low. How long would his business take? Was it about the Golden Horse? She imagined Jenna there, flirting and teasing Belenus, sticking her chest out, trying to distract him. Kerry clenched her fists. That tart. The Golden Horse was a symbol of her union with Belenus, their love and the filthy little witch had stolen it. She wanted the Sealing to be over and done with so that she could have her Golden Horse back and keep Jenna well away from Belenus.

She still felt dizzy. Kerry put a hand to her forehead. It was wet with cold sweat. It was too bright. The stark light hurt her head. She winced at the sun skimming the rooftops and averted her eyes to the pavement. The lines between the paving slabs kept moving; dancing towards her, swimming away from her. She felt nauseous.

The pavement rushed towards her face. A flash of grey, then white dots passed before her eyes. Pain, red pain filled her head and then nothing.

Kerry opened her eyes and blinked several times. Her eyeballs were dry and sore. Her throat was parched. There was a metallic taste on her tongue. She wanted to spit, but no saliva came.

She was lying on the ground. Raising herself to her elbows, Kerry saw that she was lying on the footpath on Wandsworth Road. Her top was ruffled, exposing her stomach. She rearranged her clothes. What was going on?

Kerry heard a man's voice. "Gimme back my knife."

"You mean this thing?" Belenus answered.

280

"Gimme it back, bruv, you're mad!"

Belenus' voice. "Alright then." A pause followed by the man's high-pitched shriek.

"He cut me!"

"Mate, let's leg it or the feds will be all over the place," said another man's voice.

"But that nutter stabbed me up."

"Mate, I'm dust. Are you coming?"

Kerry's forehead throbbed where it had hit the ground. She must've fainted. She sat upright and turned around.

Belenus faced two men. The nearest man to Belenus with a shaved head looked in his early twenties. He was holding his left cheek. Blood dripped onto his grey hoodie and grey tracksuit trousers. The other, dark-haired and sullen, in his late teens stood jittering from foot to foot ready to run.

The brown-haired youth grabbed his friend's hoodie and dragged him across the road. They got on a moped parked several shop fronts along and sped off.

Kerry stared at Belenus. Had Belenus just stabbed someone?

Her senses slowly returned. Yes. *Oh good grief, yes.*

Belenus turned and strode towards her. "Kerry. Can you stand?"

She felt his hands under her arms, helping her up. She no longer felt light-headed, but she was weak.

"I shouldn't have left you alone after your powerful past life connections. It was my mistake," he said.

She shook her head. "I'm fine, I'm OK. Really."

"Are these yours?" Belenus opened his left hand. Kerry saw her black phone and gold wallet.

"Yes, thanks." Kerry looked behind him to the

droplets of blood on the ground several feet away. "What did you do to that man?"

"Something that will make him rethink his life."

"You knifed that man's face. You can't go around doing that in modern Britain, Belenus. This isn't the ancient world. Those two men will go to the police." Kerry's heart pounded in her chest.

"They won't. I know the type. They aren't noble men. They're outlaws for a reason," said Belenus.

Kerry looked down at his right hand, where Belenus still held the man's switchblade in his right hand. The tip was coated with red.

"Oh good grief, Belenus, you can't carry that thing around. Maybe we should go to the police. You did it in self-defence after all, to protect me. We need to tell the police - the law enforcement - what happened."

Belenus was blasé. "Why? I *am* the law enforcement."

Kerry looked back towards Wandsworth Bridge, but there was no sign of the motorbike returning. She started walking, pulling Belenus' arm. "How can you be so calm? You used a knife on someone."

"It was only a nick; a tattoo. I cut a powerful, ancient symbol on his cheek as a lesson for what he did." Belenus opened his left palm and with the man's knife, mimed two parallel lines. He then joined the lines with a third sloping line, making the symbol look like an askew letter 'H'. "It means Hagalaz. Hagalaz is the storm that brings change, the chaos before creation. He will rethink his life now. I did it on his left cheek as a mark of shame - a brand to show the world what he is."

"What do you mean, what he is?" said Kerry.

"I saw him robbing you while you were unconscious. After he took your things, he had his hands

282

under your clothing."

Kerry reached for her chest, cradling herself. "Dirty pervert," she whispered.

Belenus put a finger under her chin and raised her face to look at his. "Are you sure you aren't hurt?"

"I'm fine. I meant it," she said.

"It was wrong of me to assume that you are the Briton Queen you once were."

Anger seared through her. "I'm not a weakling, if that's what you mean. I can handle myself."

"I meant no offence," he said, seriously. "Becoming the Queen you once were won't happen overnight. I think I sensed that and came outside Sequana's just in time."

Kerry was ruffled. But she had to admit, she was glad he was there. It could have been worse.

Belenus nodded towards her jeans pocket, where she had put her phone. "Where did you get obsidian? I can see why the men wanted it so badly. Obsidian is a hard commodity to come by. It will be very useful to Ceridwen for the Sealing ceremony."

"It isn't obsidian, it's just black plastic. You'll get used to our modern ways soon, hopefully."

Belenus put his arm around her, supporting her below her armpits. He must have known how weary she felt.

"Did you finish your business with Oliver?" she said.

"Not yet." He had a dark look in his eyes. "I'll see you back to Ceridwen's restaurant first.

Could she suppress her curiosity? Kerry glanced back at Sequana's. "Why did you need to see Oliver? Was it about my Golden Horse?"

"Kerry, I told you to put that from your mind."

"Can't you tell me, even a little? Do you always keep secrets from your Briton Queen?"

She'd hit the jackpot; there was a hint of defiance in Belenus' eyes. "I never keep secrets from you. It's a question of timing, that's all."

"I know it's about Oliver and Ceridwen, so you might as well tell me," she said.

"Oliver's money not Oliver. Namely how he's making it - in illicit ways."

"What do you mean?"

"Wealth builds armies, as you know. But what he's doing is tantamount to fraud. His wealth cannot appease the gods."

They reached Eel Brook Common and turned off the main road into the side streets. "What did he do?"

"He has an arrangement with a smith who makes convincing replicas of real Briton workmanship. He auctions those and keeps the real items for himself - those gold coins he gave at the feast for example. He made them from innumerable melted down treasures. There are few real items for sale that aren't in your display houses already."

It was true; most items were already in museums.

"But, I found your Golden Horse." she said. "That was real."

"And more will follow, now that the gods have returned to Britannia."

Kerry's mind ticked. "But if Oliver is so greedy, why would he share his real gold coins?"

"He had to otherwise the Beltaine ceremony wouldn't have worked. Ceridwen gave clear instructions. That's why it's important I meet her back at Sequana's. This matter concerns the Sealing. I'll tell you everything later."

284

They turned the corner and saw the Herne's Hunt. Belenus kissed Kerry and turned to go back to Sequana's.

If the business Belenus had to attend to concern the Sealing, then why didn't he hold a meeting with everyone? Why would Belenus and Ceridwen talk to Oliver first? Whatever Belenus would tell her later, Oliver and Jenna would already know. She trusted Belenus. So why did she feel uneasy?

Chapter 27

The fourth of May. This was it; this was the big day. The big one; one knot, one perfect O tying Gavin to Blodeuedd. Hand-fasting, marriage, same difference. Two days before the Sealing on the sixth; was it enough time? Were they cutting it too close for her to be a woman all the time, and not an owl? What if it was already the fifth of May in Avalon? Did time exist in Avalon? If it *was* already one day ahead in Avalon, that would cut it even closer for Blodeuedd to cut ties with her night-owl existence. Cut it even closer, cut ties; cut the perfect O. Once they were hand-fasted, could he cut the rope, if he found out later that it was a mistake?

He didn't want to have any doubts on their big day, but he was only human. That was it; he was human and Blodeuedd wasn't. She was an immortal nymph. His life was surreal.

Gavin looked at the pool of sunlight around his feet, scattered into patches by the apple tree branches. They were getting hand-fasted in the back garden of Avalon Road, under the apple tree where Kerry said Belenus, the Sun God, was born. Surreal indeed. It was unusually warm for May. Did Belenus have anything to do with that? The past couple of sunny days were a welcome change. Not that Gavin felt cold anyway in the green wool tunic he wore for the ceremony.

Belenus wore his full golden armour. Gavin didn't wear armour as he wasn't a warrior, but he had a brown cloak fastened with a bronze leaf-shaped brooch and carried a replica bronze sword at his hip. Ceridwen had apparently got the material for the wedding clothes from a fabric shop on Goldhawk Road in Shepherd's Bush. How she had got them sewn so quickly was another thing; the ancient Britons didn't have sewing machines. Then again, Ceridwen was once the goddess Aphrodite. Maybe Ariadne had taught her a thing or two about weaving.

The replica bronze sword was heavy on his left hip. Had Belenus taken the sword from Sequana's? Maybe that was the 'business' that Kerry said the god had been attending to. Ceridwen wore a long, purple linen dress with a silvery apron on the front. A cauldron had been suspended from the branches of the nearby meadowsweet tree with a chain of iron rings attached to a long iron hook. Steam issued from a special tea that Ceridwen had brewed inside.

Belenus stood on Gavin's left side and held a small clay pot full of coins showing a maiden amidst a shower of blossom leaves; Blodeuedd's birth. Ceridwen must have used divine influence to get them minted so fast. She must have used Oliver's gold. Gavin smiled to himself; bet the scumbag wasn't happy about that.

Gavin turned. Blodeuedd walked across the lawn from the patio doors. She wore a pale-pink linen dress that was low cut, showing off her gorgeous chest. The leaves that she had been conjured from; oak, broom and meadowsweet had been embroidered in twisting patterns to accentuate her curves. A sky-blue plaid cloak was draped around her shoulders and fastened with an owl-shaped brooch below her cleavage. She took her place at Gavin's right side and they exchanged smiles. Warmth filled him; he couldn't wait to kiss her.

Kerry walked behind Blodeuedd wearing a red dress and had a green plaid cloak pinned with a sun-shaped brooch. She carried Blodeuedd's dowry; a wicker basket full of coins and stood at Blodeuedd's right side.

"Great Mathonwy, we stand before you to honour you with the blessing of hand-fasting between mortal man and immortal woman," Ceridwen began.

Mathonwy, the Mother Goddess of all. He was starting to get the hang of all the ancient gods. Wonder what the Great Earth Mother looked like? Was she incarnate somewhere too, like the small pantheon in London? No plea to Arawn today though; this was a celebration of life, not resurrection from the dead.

"I offer to you she who was made of flowers, conjured by Gwydion, warrior and son of Don, goddess of the fruitful earth and Math, great magician of house Mathonwy, mother goddess, to be united with Gavin of the tribe Bryant, son of Callie and Declan, whose blood runs with the first Britons," said Ceridwen.

Belenus set Gavin's clay dowry at the foot of the Meadowsweet tree.

"Mathonwy, giver of life and light, accept this offering and bless the union of Blodeuedd and Gavin," said Ceridwen.

Kerry set Blodeuedd's wicker dowry at the foot of the apple tree.

"Arawn, keeper of the gate of darkness, accept this offering and release the tie of Blodeuedd to the shadows of Avalon," said Ceridwen.

Ceridwen took a coil of rope from a pouch at the front of her apron and shook it loose. The goddess bound Gavin's right hand to Blodeuedd's left hand and tugged on the rope to bring the couple closer to the cauldron.

"Great Mathonwy, I unite this pair, Blodeuedd of house Don and Gavin of tribe Bryant before you."

Ceridwen pulled the bronze knife, which had been used at the Beltaine cleansing ceremony, out of her apron pouch and pricked the tip of his finger and then Blodeuedd's in turn. Gavin flinched at the sting, but Blodeuedd didn't react. Blood dripped from both their fingers into the cauldron.

"Mighty Arawn, I beseech you to release the ties of Avalon and stand appeased with this token of blood offered before you."

Ceridwen took a cloth sachet from her apron. She emptied the contents into the tea.

"May this coltsfoot bring peace and tranquillity on this day. May this infusion of damiana stir the fire of passion between these two joining before the gods."

She offered a sip to Blodeuedd, followed by Gavin. The idea of drinking a concoction containing their own blood didn't appeal to Gavin, but he would do whatever it took to unite with Blodeuedd. He swallowed petals of broom, oak and meadowsweet knowing that the ritual symbolised his body joining with hers. It tasted fragrant like vanilla, with a woody aftertaste.

"By the gods do I join this couple, Gavin and Blodeuedd as mortal and immortal, man and wife, with Bile of the kingdom of Beltaine, God of the Sun, and Kerry of the tribe Teare, daughter of Julie and Frank bearing witness."

Ceridwen stooped and pressed her thumb into the soil at her feet. She pushed the smudge against Blodeuedd's forehead. "Receive the mud of mortal men."

The goddess dipped her thumb in the cauldron of tea and daubed Gavin's forehead with a paste of petals. "Embrace the petals of immortality."

Ceridwen held her arms wide to the sky. "The gods have accepted the offerings of your union. You are now bound as man and woman of house Don, children of Mathonwy. The hand-fasting is complete."

Blodeuedd leaned across to Gavin. Gavin winced as he puckered his lips.

"You may touch flesh to flesh," said Ceridwen.

289

"The last of her curse has been lifted - no more animalistic energy resides in her."

Gavin pulled Blodeuedd close with the rope that bound them and closed his eyes for their marital kiss. A chorus of cheers from Kerry, clapping from Belenus and a rain of petal confetti thrown by Ceridwen celebrated their first moment as man and wife. He kissed her long and hard, enjoying the taste of her warm mouth, free of electric shocks.

When they pulled apart, Ceridwen set a crown of Hawthorn leaves onto both their heads; ancient representation of fertility.

"No more owl," said Gavin.

"I'm all woman," said Blodeuedd.

"I'll say."

"Go and enjoy your day of hand-fasting," said Ceridwen. "I must get back to the Herne's Hunt. Morfan and Saiorse are by themselves and they're preparing a feast for your hand-fasting tonight. Saiorse needs time with her family, who are visiting from Wales."

"Kerry and I will take care of the newlyweds," said Belenus. "I want to show them the places of our old world."

The Thames Clipper cruised along the river from the London Eye. Kerry and Belenus stood at the front of the ship. The tidal wind stung her face, but she enjoyed the bite; it kept her head out of the clouds and firmly in reality.

Belenus looked no different from any other thirty-something men among the tourist crowd on the boat, except that he was far more handsome. He suited the jeans, white shirt and black suit jacket she had bought for him on a trip to central London the previous day, while he had done his business at Sequana's. The clothes made him look dashing. Clearly she wasn't the only one who thought so; a couple of young women posed against the rail, sticking their bums out to try and catch his attention. *Shameless.* Kerry pulled Belenus so that his back faced them.

Still, aside from his amorous influence, his godly charisma would serve him well to rally his Beltaine tribes once more. After all, the most successful leaders throughout history were attractive, weren't they? Let's see... there was Alexander the Great, he was good-looking. And there was Achilles. No, he was mythical. Wait a second; if Belenus and the other immortals were real, then why not Achilles too? Maybe even Adonis. Kerry pressed herself against Belenus and he hooked an arm around her to hold her tight.

"Look over there, Kerry." Belenus stood with his arm around her waist from behind, his head resting on her shoulder. He pointed towards Southwark. "Do you remember the seven marshy islands of the Tameses? The Atrebates came to meet me there when I rallied my people against the Roman ships landing in Londinium."

A memory returned to Kerry; an image of projecting stakes in the water waiting to surprise unsuspecting Roman soldiers when they disembarked. In her mind she saw a row of women in black dresses waiting on the shore beyond, shrieking curses like sirens, their hair blowing long and wild and orange flames leaping from their wooden torches, a blood-chilling sight for the Romans.

She pressed her cheek against his. "The women wore ceremonial dresses like the ones we wore at the summoning."

"You were with them. All of you distracted the enemy while our Beltaine tribe, along with the Atrebates of the South, charged into the water. We attacked them as they touched our shores before they had a chance to arm themselves."

Kerry shivered; it was one thing to see the past, but now she could feel it too. Anger at the enemy; bloodlust; excitement for battle. The Romans didn't know the terrain. They didn't see the Briton warriors hiding in the marshes. Hordes of surprised Roman soldiers, caught off guard, were slaughtered as they disembarked into the water. Some were caught on the projecting underwater stakes. Others were ambushed from the marshy islands by spears and swords.

"What do you mean, she was with them?" said Gavin.

"Kerry was my Queen in the life before this," said Belenus.

Gavin gaped. "What, for real? You're saying you knew Kerry before this?"

Kerry prodded Gavin in his arm. "Told you my Belenus came back for me," she teased.

"We were reminiscing about a battle between our Beltaine people and the Atrebates tribe against the Romans," he said.

"Did you know me in a former lifetime too, Blossom?" Kerry could see the passion in his eyes as he gazed at his celestial bride.

"No, I was married to Lleu," said Blodeuedd. "But this time, it was fate. I saw the light and flew towards it and here I am. So now I'm yours."

Gavin scooped her into his arms, and they kissed. They still wore the rope that hand-fasted them, even though Kerry knew they had broken tradition by taking it off briefly to change into modern clothes for the boat trip. Of course, what was traditional about a modern human marrying an ancient immortal in twenty-first century London? It was mind-boggling. Kerry looked at Belenus. It would be her turn soon too.

"I think a few drinks are in order. We should have a toast," she said.

"Good idea. Beer is in order," said Belenus.

Kerry led him to the bar. Gavin and Blodeuedd deserved a moment to themselves in any case. She ordered four Stella and handed two of the four plastic pint glasses to Belenus.

Belenus looked confused. "Is this the biggest size they serve?"

Kerry laughed. "Afraid so. We can get more. I doubt it'll taste as strong as what you're used to either."

He drank. "It's watered down. It's like what the Beltaine children would drink."

"I guess that's another thing I'll have to get used to - your heavy drinking culture," she said.

They re-joined Gavin and Blodeuedd outside.

"To the new addition to house Mathonwy," said Belenus.

"To the newlyweds," said Kerry, raising her cup.

"What does newlywed mean?" said Blodeuedd.

"Hand-fasted," said Gavin.

They toasted and drank. Gavin looked to be in a blissful stupor as he gazed at his new bride. "I wonder if I'm actually married, by today's standards. Does it count?" he said.

"You're married by our customs and that's what matters," said Belenus.

"You could get remarried in a register office, to be official. Couldn't he, Belenus?" said Kerry.

"Yeah, and that way Blodeuedd could take on my name too - because in the Briton ceremony, we're part of house Mathonwy now, but in a modern ceremony, she could take my family name of Bryant," said Gavin.

"Is that what you moderns do?" said Blodeuedd.

"If you want. Unless you have a family name? I'm not so traditional that I think a woman should take on a man's family name - if you have a good one, we could switch to that instead." Gavin's face reddened and he lowered his head, giving Blodeuedd a sheepish look. "I was mainly thinking ahead to, you know, kids and stuff. It would be nice if we could all have the same family name."

Kerry looked at Belenus. Come to think of it, Gavin had raised an interesting point. "Yeah, what about that, Belenus? Are people - I mean, like Gavin and I, able to have children with immortals?"

"Immortals and mortals are able to have offspring," Belenus answered.

"It's like the Greek story of Perseus," said Gavin, nudging Kerry with his elbow. "He was half-god by Zeus and Danae."

Kerry turned to Belenus again. "So, if we had a baby, it would be half-immortal?"

"The child would be mortal, but with extraordinary powers. There is one such woman today who climbs a five hundred metre cliff face up through a gushing waterfall every day to get the purest water from the source for her ceremonies. There may be others," said Belenus.

"And what about a mortal turning into a deity?" said Kerry. "Is that possible too?"

"A human could become immortal, but never a god or a goddess."

"I'm not a goddess. I'm an immortal nymph," said Blodeuedd.

"How could I do it?" Kerry spluttered. "How could I become one?"

Belenus sighed. "I was hoping not to bring this up. We've never done it before, in any of our lifetimes together. We always agreed that you would stay mortal and I would remain on earth with you as your immortal husband."

She grabbed both of Belenus' hands in hers. "Please tell me. If I was to become immortal, then we could be together all the time, without me getting old and having to wait another lifetime to be with you again. Please?"

He shook his head, his expression fixed. "This is a day for celebrating life, not death. To become immortal involves Avalon - and Arawn."

Kerry faltered. "But surely Arawn knows that ours is a romance that's lasted through three past lifetimes, and three marriages already. I'm sure he'd change me."

"That might well be the case, but immortality is not a decision that should be taken lightly." He squeezed her hands. "I don't mean any condescension with what I say next, but in this lifetime, I can't help but feel you have a certain naiveté about such celestial matters. There are things you won't remember about Arawn until you return to Avalon."

Kerry knew the conversation was finished. Belenus wasn't angry, but an expression of firm resolve settled on his face as he looked ahead over the Thames.

"Over there, far beyond Plowonida, there was a hill-fort where my Beltaine sheltered when the Romans besieged us. It stood in the depths of the Catuvellauni lands. I made an alliance with them and our people stayed in the fort for almost a year. We had plentiful stores, weapons and animals which was enough to hold off Londinium for a time."

An image of Roman towers surrounding the Iron

295

Age hill-fort popped into Kerry's mind. They had tried to starve out the Britons, but as natives, they knew the land better than the foreigners and had wells for water, and grain to eat. The united chiefdoms of the Beltaine and Catuvellauni were too big for the Romans to keep down, and more tribes ambushed the towers from behind, driving the Roman enemy away from the earthen ramparts of the hill-fort.

The Thames Clipper sailed on past Londinium, the city of London, to where the river widened. As they passed a loop near the Isle of Dogs, Belenus pointed again to the left, in the direction of high rise buildings and Canary Wharf.

"Over there is Bile's Gate. It's marked as your modern day Billingsgate fish market. The symbolism of the fish is no coincidence. It's a mark of the tide and the association between water and the Otherworld."

"Like how all the deities are born of water?" said Kerry.

"Exactly. The shrine dedicated to myself marks the entrance to Avalon, where the sun leaves and the shadows begin."

Kerry stared East. In the past week since she'd known about the existence of Avalon, it had always seemed so near and yet so far. Part of her liked the idea of another world to go to after death; she envisioned a land of gently smoking roundhouses and people wearing Celtic dress, spending their astral lives in a primeval alternate reality. The notion of gods and humans fighting and feasting together stirred her imagination. Knowing that there was a physical boundary between worlds that she could not only see but go near if she so wished intrigued her.

"Is Avalon better, or worse than this world?" she said.

"The Otherworld is a limbo where souls reside until they are returned. Better or worse are points of view. But in Avalon, just as here, there is good and evil."

"I must have been there many times before." She tried to imagine herself in a Celtic netherworld. "Did I like it?"

"You've been there many times. You never liked it much. You always looked forward to the time when you could escape the Otherworld."

"Did I live with you there?"

"No. Mortals and immortals are separate in Arawn's domain. The gods live above the shadows on Balor mountain and the nymphs live in the forests on the plateau. The mortals live in the Marsh lands, ready to be reincarnated."

"Did you always want to come back here as much as I did?"

"Yes. I'm at my best in the light. I can lead my people in the sunshine and be with the woman I love. But I waited until you were past your twentieth year, so that I could be with you in your womanhood."

"Twenty years... that's a long time apart."

"Not in Avalon. How long does a human live in this modern time?" he said.

"Seventy, maybe eighty years if they're lucky," she said. "Why?"

"Mortal souls exist in the Marsh lands for sometimes two or three hundred years," he said.

Kerry shivered. "That's a long existence."

"Anti-existence - limbo. Like I said, better or worse are points of view. In this world, people suffer and die. In the Otherworld, people simply wait until they come back."

"What did I do there? Do people eat and sleep? Do they have jobs?"

Belenus' moustache bristled. "It's not good to know too much about Avalon when you are in the world of light. All you need to know is that you were favoured by Arawn, which is why he kept you there for longer than the others. Most souls return after a couple of hundred or so years. For you, it was always over a millennia, at the very least."

Kerry looked at the dark choppy water. She wondered if Belenus knew what she wanted to ask. The conversation had led there, and it seemed a natural progression...

"If Arawn liked me so much, why didn't he ever make me an immortal? If I were to become an immortal, I could stay with you all the time, in this world or the next."

Belenus kissed her forehead. "The simple answer is that you served his purpose without having to become an immortal. To use one of your modern sayings, a little fish in a big pond has more use than a big fish in a little pond."

"I wouldn't care. If I could live with you on top of Balor mountain-"

Belenus put his finger to her lips and she fell quiet. "Let's enjoy our short time together in the light. We'll have more than enough time for Avalon when the time comes."

He stroked her hair, and although his fingers felt tender, his expression was grim. Kerry tried to enjoy the moment, but a part of her mind strayed. Was the grass always greener on the other side of the fence? *Was* there grass on the other side of the fence, or only darkness? And why did shadows and darkness have such appeal?

Chapter 28

Kerry. I have urgent business to attend to. Stay here at the Herne's Hunt and wait for me. I will be back as soon as I can.

Kerry stared at the note. Belenus had left it on her pillow. She looked at her alarm clock. Half twelve. What urgent business did Belenus need to attend to on a Sunday afternoon? And what did 'as soon as I can' mean? How long would he be gone?

She stood up and rubbed her head. What a banging hangover she had. Belenus and Blodeuedd *sure* could drink. Even Gavin, who could hold his booze, couldn't keep up. Kerry vaguely recalled the riverside pub in Pimlico where they had ended up after their Thames boat trip. Gavin would probably still be asleep.

Breakfast would sort her out. Not apple gruel but a good hearty fry up: bacon, eggs, sausage and fried bread sopping in butter. Kerry got dressed and shuffled out onto the landing.

Gavin's door was open. As she passed, she peered in and saw that his room was empty. Maybe the newlyweds were downstairs.

The Herne's Hunt restaurant was empty. A plate with a half-eaten triangle of toast was the sole clue that Gavin had breakfasted there.

Had the newlyweds gone out to celebrate? Her instinct told her no. Did Gavin know something she didn't? That wouldn't make sense; Gavin told her everything.

Or did he? She pulled her phone out of her pocket and dialled. It rang for a few minutes before she gave up.

Fine. Everyone had abandoned her. Kerry made herself two rounds of toast and slopped butter on them.

The butter knife clanged in the sink when she threw it. She stomped upstairs onto the roof. *Why* was everyone keeping secrets from her?

From the edge of the roof, Kerry saw a woman of Chinese appearance walking towards the Herne's Hunt. She was deep in conversation with a man who Kerry couldn't see, as he walked on the inside of the pavement. As they neared, the man's deep voice reached the rooftop. The voice was familiar. Kerry strained to hear what they were saying.

"We're meeting over at Mario's restaurant. Gavin and Blodeuedd should be there already."

It was Belenus.

Belenus and his companion passed the Herne's Hunt and moved into clear view. The woman was pretty. *Uncomfortably* pretty. She had waist-length black hair, fine South-East Asian features and a delicate frame. As they crossed the road, Belenus put his hand in the small of her back; a protective gesture to guide her across.

What did *that* mean? His touch showed familiarity and more; intimacy. Kerry squashed the last of her toast in her balled fist. For half a second, she wanted to throw it at their retreating backs. But the moment they had disappeared around the corner, Saiorse's blonde head appeared from the end of Avalon Road. There was no doubt about it; the girl was coming to the Herne's Hunt.

Three loud raps sounded on the door below. No point pretending she wasn't home. "I'm coming," Kerry called over the rooftop edge.

Saiorse looked up. "Kerry. I'm glad you're here."

Kerry stomped downstairs. She felt numb. Belenus' urgent business, that was secret no less, involved a beautiful, mystery woman. To add insult to injury, it seemed Gavin and Blodeuedd were on a double date with them. Kerry wanted to smash something; anything. This was a betrayal. She weaved through tables and chairs, distracted by her thoughts, and pulled open the front door.

"What do you want?" Kerry snapped.

Saiorse didn't ask to come in; she slipped past Kerry. "It's long to explain."

"Then give me the short version and leave."

Saiorse looked offended. "Did I come at a bad time?"

Kerry pushed her hair off her face. "If Jenna put you up to this-"

"She didn't. She doesn't know I'm here." Saiorse breathed heavily, as if she had been running. "I came to help. Morfan told me everything. There's a plan for tonight about your Golden Horse," said Saiorse.

Kerry was confused. "What plan?"

Saiorse paused, biting her lip. "The thing is, Morfan let me in on it because he wants me to help Gavin. But I don't think you're supposed to know."

Kerry clenched her jaw as she absorbed Saiorse's information. "Gavin wouldn't keep something like that a secret from me – especially if you know about it. What are you up to?"

Saiorse shook her head. "It's not like that. I'm not like Oliver and Jenna." She paused, looking up at Kerry with fearful eyes. "I just wanted to tell you because, well, if it was me I would want to know. So I felt you should."

Kerry stood over Saiorse, her arms folded. "Just say it already, what's this plan?"

"Gavin's going to steal your Golden Horse for a ritual that'll happen in Oliver's back garden this evening."

Was this what Belenus had been up to? His business at Sequana's and the lunch date with the mystery woman?

"Why didn't they want me to know?" said Kerry.

Saiorse's eyes were wide. "Morfan said you're not to know until after it's done, that it's safer that way."

Kerry gritted her teeth. It was all she needed to know. There was a secret plan that involved *her* Golden Horse, and everyone was in on it except her. Her own best friend, Gavin, and the man she loved, Belenus, thought she was a precious princess who couldn't handle danger and excitement. How dare they? She was a barbarian Queen, past and present, and she didn't deserve to be kept in the dark.

"What are you going to do?" said Saiorse, a note of panic in her voice.

"Going over to Mario's restaurant. That's where they are. I heard Belenus outside with a woman, who must be in on the plan too."

Saiorse grabbed her arm. "Don't tell them I told you - please."

Kerry ignored her plea. "What am I supposed to do? I can't just brush off what you told me without doing anything."

Kerry hurried into the street. She didn't know if Saiorse followed. She didn't know if the door hung open behind her. She didn't care. Her feet hardly touched pavement as she rushed to Sequana's. What gave Gavin and Belenus the right to assume she couldn't handle herself? She thought back to Belenus' words of two days before, when she had passed out on Wandsworth Bridge Road, overcome by visions of the past: *"It was wrong of me to assume that you are the Briton Queen you once were."* She would prove to him that she could be every bit as tough and brave as Warrior Queen Aithne, of the Beltaine tribe.

She reached Mario's restaurant, *The Apollo*, and

flung the door open. The restaurant clearly wasn't open for business; most of the chairs were upturned on the tables. The four of them sat near the counter: Belenus and his mystery date with their backs to the street, Gavin and Blodeuedd facing them, all half hidden behind a tall potted plant. The lights in the restaurant were off; Kerry supposed so as not to attract customers. The restaurant proprietor, a handsome young man of Mediterranean appearance, spotted Kerry and swooped around the empty counter towards the door.

"I'm sorry, Miss, we aren't open for business yet. My apologies that I left the front door unlocked."

Kerry looked past him. "I'm not a customer. I know these people."

Belenus turned in his seat. When he saw her, he rose. "Kerry, did you get my message?"

He strode across to her, with his hands outstretched to catch hers. Kerry withdrew her hands and folded them across her chest.

"I did. So this is the urgent business you had to attend to - a secret plot that I'm not supposed to know about?" Kerry peered around him at Belenus' companion. "Am I so useless that you have to bring in a secret woman to handle things too?"

"It's not what it looks like, my Queen. You need to go back to the Herne's Hunt and stay there. Can you do that for me?" He reached for her cheek.

Kerry batted his arm away. "No. Don't tell me what to do. And don't patronise me."

Belenus raised his chin. "I'm sorry, Kerry. I didn't intend it that way. I have business here and I need you to go. It's for your--"

"Own good?" she snapped. "You know what, save it. You told me that I would be your Barbarian Queen, not a lady in waiting. Well, sending me home is a funny way of showing that. I'm not incapable of your little plan for tonight. Don't think I don't know."

She stared into Belenus' searching eyes.

"What do you know?" he said.

"I know enough." Saliva flew from her mouth. She wiped her lip. "Gavin's going to steal my Golden Horse from Jenna."

Belenus stepped forward and clapped a hand over her mouth. "Ssh," he said, looking out the door.

Kerry pulled his hand off. "Relax. It's not like Oliver and Jenna are going to come strolling in here."

He held her at arm's length, gripping her by her shoulders. "Who told you?"

She jerked her shoulders, releasing his grip. "It's a secret," she said, with a smirk. "Seems there are a lot of secrets lately, doesn't it?"

It was childish, but she couldn't resist. Belenus was unfair to think her incapable of being in on the plan to steal back her own property.

"I think it might be best if you come and join us then, since you insist on staying."

Kerry felt a smug satisfaction to see Belenus' taut-lipped resignation. With her chin held high, she strode over to the table where Gavin, Blodeuedd and Belenus' companion sat, and pulled up a chair up to the head of the table. She placed it backwards and straddled it, leaning on the head-rest with both elbows.

"Kerry," said Belenus, once he had sat back down. "This is Yanshinhan. I mentioned her yesterday on our boat trip, the half-deity I told you about, the one who climbs a cliff face each day through a waterfall to get the purest water from source for her ceremonies to the gods."

Kerry stared at the mystery woman and tried to

quash her jealousy; not only beautiful but clearly capable of Belenus' respect for whatever dangerous plan they were about to hatch together.

"Yanshinhan has travelled twelve hours from Mongolia to help us with an important ceremony that must take place tonight. She is a High Priestess of Water, the highest ranked of any known today," Belenus continued.

Kerry rested her chin on her arms, feeling redundant. How could she prove her worth as Belenus' Queen, if Yanshinhan had greater power?

"I can't tell you any more than this, as I worry your curiosity will get the better of you. It has already caused trouble. You shouldn't even know this much about tonight's plan."

"But I can help," said Kerry. "Even if you don't want me to do the actual stealing, I could create a diversion - something to draw Jenna and Oliver away."

Belenus grabbed her hands and rubbed them, his expression softening. "Kerry, my Queen, it's too dangerous. Trust me that I cannot tell you any more than what you already know as your life is at stake."

Kerry sneered. "From Jenna and Oliver? I could take on the pair of them... if they lay so much as a hand--"

He closed his eyes. "You do not understand. Will you trust me this once? I'll explain everything this time tomorrow, once the Sealing ceremony is over."

She stood up. "OK then. I don't know why I can't be in on the plan, or how I could possibly be in danger from people I'm already watching out from, but I'll trust you. I'll go back to the Herne's Hunt and let you carry on with whatever you're up to."

Belenus smiled; a tired, but happy smile. "I care only about your safety. Thank you for doing this, my

Queen."

He stood up and kissed her, cupping her face in his hands.

Kerry pulled back from him and smiled too. "You know I only want to do what's right."

"What's right for both of us," he added.

She turned. Without saying goodbye to anyone, she left Mario's restaurant. She had no intention of staying at the Herne's Hunt that evening. *Becoming the Queen you once were won't happen overnight.* Belenus' words in her head were the catalyst driving her to action. She would show him she could be the Barbarian Queen he once knew in a fraction of the time he expected. She would impress him tonight.

Chapter 29

Sunset already. The day had gone too fast. Gavin stood at the gate of Doncaster Manor, Avalon Road. His heart hammered in his chest. Belenus' words gave him no courage at all: *This task is up to you, Gavin. If you cannot do it, then our immortal lives are at risk. Kerry's life is at risk and maybe the world as we know it.*

So no pressure then.

He looked at the greenery obscuring the view into the lower windows, snaking its way upwards to hide the upper windows from prying eyes. This was a house of secrets. Debauchery and secrets. Murderous secrets. He stopped the train of thought as a shiver travelled up his spine. No room for doubts. He had a task to do. All he had to do was go inside and get the Golden Horse.

Go inside, charm Oliver and Jenna, and get the Golden Horse.

Gavin closed his eyes and took a deep breath. It sounded absurd, but he had no choice.

If Belenus' plan was to go as scheduled, then the Water Priestess would be waiting in the back garden to perform the ritual once he brought it to her at sunset. Sounded easy enough. Course, he knew it wouldn't be that straightforward. Belenus said Jenna would keep the Golden Horse within sight, in the bedroom she shared with Oliver. Easy for Belenus to say; he wasn't the one who had to do the dirty work.

He was wasting time. He strode up the garden path, faking confidence to give himself a boost of courage.

With one hand, Gavin put his key in the front door and turned it. He wiped cold sweat off his hairline with the other hand, before pushing the handle down. The quiet click as it opened might as well have been a firework; more sweat broke out on the back of his neck. He wiped it off with his sleeve. The reed doormat crunched under his feet as if he walked on a shingle beach. Gavin felt the tendons in his throat strain as he gritted his teeth. Why was every sound amplified when he needed absolute silence?

Maybe if he moved faster he could be quieter. He shut the door behind without a noise and hurried along the hallway on the balls of his feet. Reception room to the left, staircase on the right. Wonder if Morfan and Afagddu were upstairs in the rooms that he and Kerry had stayed in? The thought of more help at hand reassured him, even if he didn't know for sure. Outside the sun was setting fast. Why did he have to get the Golden Horse within such a narrow window of time? The ceremony had to be performed as twilight appeared; one way or another, he had to get that bloody Golden Horse before darkness fell. If only Jenna and Oliver were out at Sequana's, or anywhere else on the planet, and he could simply rummage for the Golden Horse, steal it and be done.

Jenna and Oliver's bedroom was next to the reception room on the ground floor. As he approached it, Gavin listened with his ear to the door. He could hear low voices within.

No such luck with them being out of the house.

Another deep breath and then he rapped twice.

The voices stopped. He heard shuffling feet approach the door. His heart hammered. The door swung back.

"Saiorse, I'm trying to get some damn sleep before the Sealing--" Jenna's grumpy face appeared. When she saw Gavin, she whitened.

"What are you doing here? You're meant to stay away from us." Jenna pulled the door shut to a small crack, blocking his view into her room; clearly she had something to hide.

"I know. But I'd been thinking about things. This might sound a bit strange, but I thought we could work out a deal for the Midsummer Solstice."

Jenna paused, her lip curling at one corner. "I wasn't born yesterday."

The door yanked back. Oliver appeared beside her, his face livid. "Ceridwen put you up to this, didn't she?" he said.

Gavin had to stay cool. He sucked in a deep breath and exhaled through his nose. "No. Nobody knows I'm here. Not even Blodeuedd. But actually, she's the reason I came."

He'd caught their attention, but it was too early to reveal the Ace up his Sleeve.

"Blodeuedd asked you to speak to us?" Jenna scowled. "What does she want?"

"Nothing. Like I said, she doesn't know I'm here. The thing is, we secretly got hand-fasted yesterday. Not even my family know yet. She's the woman I want to spend my life with. But the problem is the curse from her former lifetime on earth - Blodeuedd will always be an owl at night unless we do one thing. The only way for the curse to lift is for me to offer myself as a sacrifice to Arawn. Then, when I'm in Avalon, we have a proposition for Arawn for me to become immortal, so that I can be with Blodeuedd, in her woman-form, forevermore."

Gavin could feel a cold sweat break out on his hairline. What if they didn't believe him?

Oliver pulled a face. "How romantic for you."

Jenna didn't respond. She stared at Gavin as though trying to see through him. "You're not seriously suggesting that you *willingly* want me to sacrifice you at the solstice?"

Gavin kept his face straight. "Yes. Yes, I am. It doesn't scare me."

"He's lying," said Oliver, not taking his eyes off Gavin.

"I'm not. I swear it. I've done a lot of thinking over the past few days. You know the madness I've seen would make most people go crazy. On Mayday, I watched, with my own two eyes, two ancient Celtic gods come into this world through a portal in a giant bronze cauldron. On top of that, I saw an owl fly out of it - an owl that later changed into a woman - the woman I love enough to have married. I mean, how nuts is that? And it got me thinking that if immortals can come through into our world, then surely mortals must be able to go over to the Otherworld in the form they're in." Gavin paused for effect, watching their rapt faces. "Seriously, I mean, I used to be atheist, but this caused me to have a whole bloody existential crisis. Not even travelling around Buddhist countries in Asia and tripping out on Zen retreats could turn my head the way this past week has. The world as I knew it came crashing down around me. In some ways, things from now on would make more sense if I was over in Avalon. The world is too sane - too normal - for what I've seen."

Gavin took slow steady breaths through gritted teeth, as if the filtered air would distil his courage.

Jenna and Oliver stood blinking at him.

In her momentary distraction, Jenna let the door hang loose in her hand. Gavin saw behind her. She hadn't been trying to sleep at all. The Golden Horse lay on the bare floorboards in the middle of the bedroom. It was positioned in the centre of a ring of salt. Outside the circle lay what looked like a foot long slab of fossilised driftwood, broken into two clean halves. It was coal black and shiny. Gavin was right; they *had* been up to something.

Jenna narrowed her eyes. "But wait - if you're sacrificing yourself to Arawn in exchange for Blodeuedd's owl curse to be lifted, then how do I come into it? You could kill yourself before the Sealing and do that without my help."

Gavin gave a long, slow headshake. "I don't have power. You do. I would get Blodeuedd, all woman, by sacrificing myself to Arawn. You would get more power by restoring Bran's faith in you. One sacrifice, two gods appeased."

Oliver looked dubious. "Can that be done?"

A greedy glint came over Jenna's face. "Yes, I think so." She straightened her back. "We'll need a bit more convincing though, I don't take your word for granted. You'll have to prove yourself to us. Is Kerry in on this too?"

Gavin sighed, theatrically. "Kerry's pretty headstrong. She always has been. But I should be able to convince her, gradually, over the next month until the solstice. She trusts me."

Jenna pursued her lips. She still looked un-convinced, the tough cow.

"I'm not sure that *I* can trust you, though," she said.

Time for the Ace up his Sleeve; or rather, his jeans. Gavin reached into his back pocket and pulled out a small plastic bottle. It was filled with a brown liquid, the colour of prune juice.

"This is the belladonna I saw you brewing on the roof of the Herne's Hunt. I saved some of it. I hope this is enough proof for you." Gavin unscrewed the top and held it out to Jenna. She took it off him and sniffed. Still unsure, Jenna raised the bottle, wet her lips with the tiniest amount and licked.

Gavin waited, watching Jenna. Once the taste had registered, she nodded.

"He's as good as his word," she said to Oliver.

Gavin took the bottle back and drank the contents in one swig. He wiped his mouth on his sleeve and watched Jenna and Oliver's stunned faces.

"I'll drink as much as you want me to everyday until the solstice. I don't care if it dulls my mind. A month is nothing compared to a lifetime with Blodeuedd in Avalon," said Gavin.

Jenna's eyes widened, impressed. "You're really devoted to your wife, aren't you?"

Gavin smiled. "I'd do anything for her. She's the one."

Jenna let go of the door and stood back to let Gavin in. "Where's Kerry tonight, then?"

He shrugged. "She's somewhere with Belenus, I think. Don't really know."

"She wouldn't be plotting to get her Golden Horse back, would she?" Jenna gave a suspicious smile.

"To be honest, I've been spending most of my time with my wife. I haven't seen much of Kerry." Gavin pointed to the Golden Horse. "What's all this for, anyway?"

"Protection - and preparation. The salt will stop any immortal getting their hands on it and the Obsidian Mirror is a little speciality that will give our ceremony a bit of *magic* during the Sealing." Jenna rubbed her hands together. "Ceridwen is in for a treat."

"You shouldn't tell him everything," said Oliver.

"Why not? He just drank the belladonna. He'll forget everything once it kicks in." Jenna drew forward, making Gavin jump. She put her finger on his right eyelid, her thumb below his eye and stretched. "Yep, see? His eyes are already starting to dilate."

Bloody hell. Gavin looked at the Golden Horse. He had to get it, quick. He looked out the window. A sliver of sun on the horizon remained. The Water Priestess would be waiting.

"Perfect." Oliver grinned a cat-got-the-cream smile. "I just had a brilliant idea. Why don't we give the Golden Horse to Gavin to hide for a few hours, until the eve of the Sealing? Nobody would ever think he would have it."

Jenna gave a devious grin. "You're right. I'm sure Kerry and Belenus will come looking for it tonight. They'd never think in a million years that Gavin would have come here and got it."

"And he'll forget he has it, even if they did ask him," said Oliver.

Gavin watched the verbal tennis match play back and forth across him. He wanted to grin too but suppressed it. He couldn't believe his ears; they were going to hand him the Golden Horse just like that.

Jenna lifted it and pushed it into Gavin's hands. "Go back to the Herne's Hunt. You'll probably need a sleep after that dose of belladonna - I made that first batch pretty strong. I'll send Saiorse over to wake you up at about half eleven, just before the Sealing; she'll be carrying the Golden Horse at the Sealing for my plan to work. Our ceremony will take place at the Sealing itself."

Gavin nodded his acknowledgement, and without a word, turned and left the room. He hugged the Golden Horse tight against his chest.

That was too bloody easy.

Chapter 30

Not that bloody easy.

Gavin staggered into the back garden. His head spun. Heavy sleep, like jetlag swept over him in waves. He did all he could to fight it. He held the Golden Horse in his right hand and the garden wall to support himself. The cool evening air refreshed him enough to see four figures dressed in brown, woollen tunics, decorated with red, swirling patterns: Belenus, Morfan, Afagddu and the Water Priestess. Blodeuedd was with them, in her usual pale, pink dress.

"Blodeuedd." Gavin stretched the Golden Horse out to her. It slipped from his fingers. He fell forward on all fours on the grass and vomited.

"Gavin, my sweet, I'm here."

Blodeuedd's soft voice soothed him. He saw her bare feet on his left side and felt her warm hand on his back rubbing in a circular motion. The pressure made him heave again. Burgundy liquid poured onto the grass. A pair of dainty, dark blue silk shoes appeared next to his right side and a pair of slender hands grabbed the Golden Horse. The Water Priestess had got her prize. Gavin kept vomiting as Blodeuedd massaged his back and the Water Priestess padded away.

Not even a word of thanks for all his trouble. What a load--

He threw up again. How much poison was in his system? That bloody belladonna was *dangerous*.

"That's it, sweetness, bring it all up," said Blodeuedd.

Gavin's stomach was empty. He sat back on his haunches and wiped his mouth on the back of his wrist. "I'm glad I thought to drink a pint of milk and eat a loaf of bread before I went to see those two. Might have been a different outcome if I didn't have enough in my gut to absorb that poison she made."

Blodeuedd bent down and kissed his forehead. "You were so brave."

Gavin sucked the cool evening air in through his nostrils and exhaled through a wide mouth, feeling his senses return. Blodeuedd kept her hand on his head, massaging his hair; the sensation grounded him in reality.

"I'm alright now." He got to his feet, with Blodeuedd's hand under his elbow to steady him.

He was a new man. The purge had been a detox, cleansing his system. No toxins remained in his body; probably ideal for a sacred ritual.

The immortals, with the exception of Blodeuedd, and the Water Priestess, formed a circle around the giant cauldron in the growing twilight. Gavin started to cross the lawn to them, but Blodeuedd tugged on his wrist.

"We have to stay here and keep watch. If anyone comes, we have to get rid of them. Nothing must interrupt the ritual," said Blodeuedd.

Gavin looked up to Jenna and Oliver's bedroom window, on the first floor. "What'll happen if the ceremony gets stopped?"

"We can't let it, no matter what the means," she said.

At least their curtain was drawn; enough reassurance for the short term. He turned back to the Water Priestess. "Where did Belenus find that woman? He said she was a Mongolian Priestess, right?"

"Morfan and Afagddu contacted her. The brothers have a connection with the moon - as you know, they are named after Phobos and Deimons, the moon gods of Mars. Water and the tides are influenced by the moon, so they must have contacted her through a lunar ceremony," said Blodeuedd.

Gavin turned his attention back to the Water Priestess. She took a drag from a long, bamboo pipe and breathed it out slowly, before passing it to Belenus.

"What's that they're smoking?" Gavin whispered to Blodeuedd.

"Tibetan herbs that induce a higher consciousness. They need to start with fire to end with water - everything balanced in harmony," she said.

Gavin was glad he didn't have to smoke any unknown herbs; the belladonna had been enough dope for one night. Under the influence of drugs, the red, swirling patterns on the ritual tunics might have caused hypnosis; or maybe that was the point. Each had a red painted symbol of the sun on the back and underneath, eight looping figure-eight shapes, like snakes eating their own tails.

"What are the snakes for?" he asked.

"They're not snakes, they're nagas - water demons. There are eight of them because eight is a lucky number in Eastern beliefs. The sun above water is to show the imbalance in the cycle; rain and sun."

Morfan and Belenus each held small, saucer-sized drums of stretched animal skins in their hands, which they began to strike with bamboo beaters that looked like egg whisks. The Water Priestess swayed with the rhythm, her eyes closed. She issued a loud trill from her throat, a strange, bird-like cry in two chords.

Gavin looked up at the first floor window. Jenna and Oliver were sure to hear such a din. He watched the curtain, and with relief, saw that it remained shut.

The Water Priestess swayed wider, stepping her feet out to each side until her movements became a dance in time with the drumbeat. Her eyes remained closed as she moved her arms in fluid, waving motions and her legs in wide, outward arcs, setting each bare foot down in jerky steps.

"Yin and Yang," Blodeuedd whispered. "Her upper body shows the fluid flow of rain through air and her lower body shows the jagged path through earth. Clouds represent yang, a masculine energy and earth represents yin, a feminine energy. The dance displays inverted male and female energy to invoke the flow of water."

Gavin was impressed. "You know a lot, considering it isn't your culture."

"If you go back far enough, there is only one culture," said Blodeuedd.

Blodeuedd was right; Belenus and Ceridwen had been Sumerian deities five thousand years ago. Mesopotamia was the cradle of civilisation, and long before that everyone had come out of Africa, the cradle of life.

The Water Priestess climbed the wooden steps and got inside the giant cauldron. She held the Golden Horse above her head in both hands. Gavin's ears rang with her high-pitched trill. He wished she would stop soon; what would he say to Jenna and Oliver *this* time that they would believe?

A droplet of rain hit the rim of the cauldron with a ping, as if a penny had landed and not a splash of water. Another followed. Gavin looked up. There were no clouds. Not a drop fell anywhere else, except the cauldron. Raindrops pelted the metal interior, soaking the Water Priestess and reverberating on the hollow bottom of the cauldron to make a steady hum. The cauldron hum, the hissing rain, the drumbeats and her trill made a primordial music that dizzied Gavin's mind. He began to feel sick.

"Are you OK?" Blodeuedd squeezed his hand.

"Yeah, fine. Just queasy," he said.

"It'll pass. It's nearly done. The fire inside the Golden Horse has been extinguished and when it's full of water, she'll stop."

The steady stream of rainfall ran from the raised Golden Horse, down the Water Priestess' arms and dripped from her saturated cloak into the cauldron. Above, stars showed in the cloudless sky. Mongolian magic. Too bad Kerry was missing it.

Kerry. Gavin spun around.

Entranced by the Water ceremony, Gavin hadn't paid any heed to the patio doors. Clearly Blodeuedd hadn't either; he guessed she had been distracted by his nausea. Kerry stood motionless, her eyes locked on the Water Priestess. Then, without a word, she dashed across the lawn towards the cauldron.

Gavin made a grab for Kerry, but too late. She raced up the wooden steps and dived into the cauldron on top of the Water Priestess. The rain stopped immediately as both women and the Golden Horse fell out of sight on the bottom of the cauldron.

He flew up the steps after her, aware that Belenus had remained stationery; the gods couldn't intervene while they hadn't been Sealed. Morfan stood frozen beside him. It was up to Gavin alone to stop Kerry before she wrecked the whole ceremony.

Kerry and the Water Priestess splashed in the rain-drenched cauldron as they rolled over on top of each other, clamouring for the Golden Horse. Gavin tumbled into the cauldron behind Kerry.

"It's mine!" Kerry shrieked. "I'm not letting any ceremonies instil it with dark magic."

"She's trying to rid it of dark magic, not put more

318

in it," Gavin shouted. He grabbed Kerry by her shoulders and tried to pull her off the Water Priestess.

"She's evil," Kerry shouted. "I can't trust her - or anyone. So many secrets and lies!"

The Water Priestess held the Golden Horse out of Kerry's reach. Kerry straddled her, stretching forward. Gavin bear-hugged Kerry in an effort to pull her off, but the after-effects of the belladonna made his grip weak.

"Stop it Kerry." Gavin tried to prise Kerry's hands off the Water Priestess. "She's on our side. This is all part of Belenus' plan."

Kerry turned to push Gavin off. Even in the fading light, he saw that her green eyes had turned coal black. She was bewitched.

She shoved him off and his head hit the cauldron side with a crack. Red pain filled him and bright white dots. There was a wet thud as Kerry's fist hit the Water Priestess' jaw. Blood spilled from her mouth into the pool of rainwater. The Water Priestess fell limp, the Golden Horse lying in her open palm. Kerry snatched it.

For a moment, Kerry's face brightened as she held her trophy high. She smiled proudly up at her Golden Horse, stretched at arm's length above her. But then, as Gavin watched in horror, an inky black fountain of water spilled out of the horse's mouth and streamed into Kerry's.

Kerry gurgled, choking on the liquid. It ran, dark and thick like blood, down her chin and over her chest. She dropped the Golden Horse, which fell with a splash into the flooded bottom of the cauldron and keeled over clutching her throat.

"Kerry!" Gavin lifted her head to stop it lolling below the water and wedged the crook of his arm under it. With his other arm, he did the same to the unconscious Water Priestess, to stop her from drowning too.

"Help me!" Gavin shouted. "Kerry's been bewitched and they're both out cold."

Belenus' voice answered. "The ritual was interrupted. It isn't safe for us to enter."

Fat lot of use immortals were if they were so vulnerable. Gavin slipped an arm around each woman's waist and tried to stand, but he was too weak and the water made it too slippery.

"Gavin, I'm coming!" called Saiorse's voice.

Just perfect; Jenna's apprentice. His mind had gone blank. What lie was he going to spin to convince her that he was hiding the Golden Horse for Jenna to entrap Ceridwen?

A moment later, her head appeared over the rim of the cauldron. She reached towards him. "Gimme the Golden Horse."

"Back off Saiorse, nobody is getting their hands on this thing except me," he said.

"I'm on your side. Quick, no time." She wiggled her fingers to goad him to pass the Golden Horse. "The immortals can come into the cauldron to help carry Kerry and the Priestess out once they're clear of the magic amulet."

How could he have forgotten; Belenus and Ceridwen's sons were waiting outside the cauldron. They'd never let her steal it. They couldn't touch it, but they could tackle her if she made a run for it.

Gavin braced Kerry's head with his knee and used his free hand to feel for the Golden Horse in the water. He grabbed it and passed it up to Saiorse. Saiorse pulled it out of the cauldron and disappeared from view.

Belenus was first to climb into the cauldron. He took Kerry's heavy weight off Gavin and carried her out of the cauldron with ease. Morfan followed, lifting the Water

Priestess as easily as a rag doll. Afagddu came last. Gavin let his limp body fall in a fireman's lift over the warrior's shoulder. He felt himself set down on the grass and flopped backwards, spread-eagle. Three humans lying limp on the grass, with three gods standing watch over them. Gavin rolled his head to the right, looking back towards the house. Saiorse was gone. Blodeuedd too.

"The Golden Horse," he said, "Where is it?"

"It's safe. Saiorse has taken it back to the Herne's Hunt," said Belenus.

"Is she bringing it to Jenna? Blodeuedd must have gone after her, to stop her."

"Saiorse is no longer Jenna's apprentice. This is the Eve of the Sealing, when energy, good or bad, is at its strongest. The girl has felt that and has chosen the right side just in time," said Belenus.

Gavin rolled his head to the left. Kerry lay unconscious next to him, her black hair plastered all over her face.

"Is she OK? What happened to her?"

"Dark power from Avalon. It was my fault. I told her too much today. I didn't protect her. She was too curious, and that made her vulnerable to evil forces." Belenus hung his head. Gavin noted his regretful voice; he pitied the god. Being immortal didn't make him flawless.

"What's going to happen to her?" said Gavin.

At that moment, Kerry sprung upright. Her face was grey with shadow; blue veins showed under her skin. Gavin was transfixed. She looked more demon of Avalon than Kerry.

"I don't need your stupid protection," she said to Belenus. "I'm more Barbarian Queen now than ever, stronger and more terrifying than your precious Aithne before."

321

Kerry lunged forward and knocked Belenus sprawling onto his back. Gavin saw the fear in the Sun God's face. Avalon controlled Kerry, body and soul and Belenus wasn't Sealed; he was vulnerable.

"Kerry, are you out of your mind?" Gavin grabbed her top to pull her off.

Kerry crashed down on top of him. She flipped around and kneeled on his chest. With a deep, baritone growl that wasn't her voice at all, she grabbed Gavin's shoulders and slammed him into the ground. White stars dotted his sight. Again, he thudded against ground, biting his tongue, the air forced from his chest.

"You'll die for interfering with the order of Arawn!"

Kerry's face swam from focus as her hands found his neck and squeezed. As consciousness began to fade, Gavin heard Kerry's voice cry amidst the menacing Otherworld voice that spoke through her throat.

"No! Avalon doesn't control me. Leave me, Arawn. This is the world of sunlight and I love the Sun God, not shadows and darkness. You can't have me!"

"That's it, Kerry, fight him," said Belenus. "Cast the fog of Avalon aside. He can't call you if you don't let him."

A low rumble rose in Kerry's throat that became a shout that became a roar. She threw her head back, emptying her lungs to the sky, expelling the evil that had filled her.

"I'm Kerry Teare! My will is stronger than yours! I'm more powerful than you! So get the hell out of my head!" she screamed.

Kerry settled back on her haunches, gasping air. The greyness from her face had gone; her cheeks were flushed.

"I'm proud of you, my Queen. My Warrior Queen," said Belenus.

"Kerry," said Gavin. "That was – you were – *great*." He couldn't help grinning.

She shook her head. "But I failed. Arawn almost had me. And I wrecked the ceremony."

"Is that true?" said Gavin. "Does that mean it was all for nothing, that it didn't work? Is Kerry still in danger?"

Morfan was furious. "Nothing less than what she would have deserved. If we have done this ritual all in vain, with my mother's life at stake, I'll make sure she pays the price. She touched the Golden Horse before the end of the ceremony - she spoiled the ritual. My mother could still be in danger," said Morfan. Gavin heard the bitterness in the god's voice."

"The idol was full of water when she touched it, so most likely, it worked," said Afagddu. "Don't worry about our mother, brother. Yanshinhan had begun to close the ceremony when the woman touched it."

The Water Priestess sat upright with full energy, as if she had never been unconscious. "There's only one way to know. We'll find out at midnight. If the Golden Horse wasn't properly cleansed with water, then Ceridwen's power will still be attached to it. If she isn't able to complete the Sealing there will be no old pantheon of gods on earth beyond the six days of Beltaine, or for the solstice, or even for Samhain."

All eyes turned to Kerry. Gavin couldn't help feeling sorry for her. Her face fell.

Chapter 31

The Thames was black and brooding in the pre-dawn. Kerry stood near the waterline staring at the dark, swirling water. Her fingers were numb around the apple bough cut from the tree in Oliver's back garden; Morfan had hacked off a sizeable chunk. For a moment she had flinched, thinking he had intended to hit her with it. She had jeopardised Ceridwen's immortal life and she knew he would never forgive her for it. Kerry hung her head. Even now, knowing that she had been possessed, didn't make her feel any better. She had let Arawn get inside her head through her anger, jealousy and frustration.

But she had fought him off too. Him. A shadowy face swirled into view in the river. She knew the crinkled, devious eyes. She remembered the long, black hair and beard. Arawn was watching her. The Sealing couldn't be over soon enough; daybreak couldn't come soon enough. Sunlight to chase away the shadows.

Belenus' words floated to mind: *Do as I ask you for the next four days. Ask no more questions about evil deeds. Put the Golden Horse from your mind until after the Sealing.*

But she hadn't done as he had asked her. She had let herself be overpowered by an unseen force. Was she so weak that she could be possessed by Arawn in the first place? Kerry sighed. Now she knew why Belenus had told her that he had been wrong to assume that she was the Briton Queen she once was. He had told her that becoming the Queen she once was wouldn't happen overnight and, at the time, she had been offended. Had she proved him wrong? If so, was this what it took; overcoming possession, the ultimate challenge of the soul?

"A word of instruction is needed to everyone

before we begin the Sealing," said Ceridwen. "For once the ceremony has begun, you must do all that is asked of you without question or interruption. Is that clear?"

The goddess had built a fire halfway between the river and the shoreline wall. Kerry moved towards the flaming ring. It stood about five feet wide in diameter and three feet high, made from a wooden mesh of kindling. A priest and two priestesses tended the growing flames with Ceridwen; a tall, black man and a small, Middle-Eastern woman, along with the Mongolian Water Priestess.

"These are my Priests of Fire, Air and Water from great and distant kingdoms of this earth. Sula has travelled from the land of the Great pyramids and knows the secrets of Abydos."

The Fire Priest was a tall, thirty-something black man wearing a long, yellow robe covered with black zodiac signs and showing black flame motifs along the hem.

"Zainab is from Iraq, once the land of Sumer and the cradle of civilisation."

The Air Priestess was a small woman in her mid-fifties of Middle-Eastern appearance. She wore a purple gown with a gold trim that was plain from the front, but when she turned had a large bird embroidered in gold with its wings spread wide that covered her back.

"Yanshinhan holds the knowledge of the ancients in the Orient."

The Water Priestess wore the same brown cloak with red painted symbol of sun and water demon that she had worn earlier in Oliver's back garden. Kerry avoided her eye, casting her gaze downwards.

Ceridwen guided Kerry by her shoulders into a position facing Gavin, about fifteen feet apart, a couple of metres from the waterline. She placed Jenna next to Kerry, about fifteen feet away, on Kerry's left. Oliver was positioned opposite Jenna on Gavin's right. Jenna and Oliver stood about a metre away from the wall leading to the riverside path above. All four formed a fifteen by fifteen feet square around the fire.

Next, the goddess led the four deities; Belenus, Afagddu, Morfan and Blodeuedd to form a circle within the square of mortals. The immortals faced inwards towards the fire, each about ten feet from the centre of the fire.

Finally, Ceridwen led Saiorse by her hand and they stood in front of the fire, arm's length from the flames, with the girl on the goddess' right side.

Kerry shivered, wishing she was closer to the fire. Along with Jenna and Saiorse she wore a sleeveless black dress roped at the waist as she had for Beltaine. Gavin and Oliver must have been cold too in their white robes. Hopefully the Sealing didn't involve any nudity, or she might just drop dead with hypothermia. In contrast the immortals were oblivious to the cold. Blodeuedd was dressed in a pale green tunic that complemented her fiery hair and Ceridwen wore a floaty, blue dress that could have been made of aqua itself. Belenus, Afagddu and Morfan wore their full Briton armour.

Gavin held an apple bough like Kerry's. Why did she and Gavin have to carry the symbols of Avalon? Their immortal counterparts, Belenus and Blodeuedd, represented sunshine and springtime. It would have been more fitting for dark Oliver and devious Jenna to carry the symbols of the dead. Jenna and Oliver held fern fronds. Was that something to do with Mesopotamia and the past lives of the immortals? Kerry could only guess at the significance. Jenna also wore a woollen satchel slung low on her right hip. A heavy rectangular object inside stretched the fabric, but Kerry couldn't see what it contained. Not her Golden Horse, by the shape of it.

Where *was* her Golden Horse? She cast her eyes around and spotted a leather pouch slung around Saiorse's waist. Golden spokes sticking out of the top shimmered in the firelight. Kerry had an urge to march across to Saiorse and snatch it from her, but she suppressed it. Was it safe? If she touched it, would the power of Avalon harm her? It was her property and symbolised her union with Belenus, but she shivered at the thought of it containing Arawn's essence.

"Valiant Arawn of the Otherworld guide our spirits through the mists to Avalon. Throw your veil of smoke around us and lead us safely to the foot of Balor Mountain," said Ceridwen.

The Fire Priest, Sula, stepped over the burning mesh of kindling. Flames swirled around him, but his cloak didn't catch fire. He stood in the centre of the burning ring unharmed, even though the fire raged higher than his head. The Fire Priest cupped his hands around a leaping flame; an orange light glowed from within his fingers as if he held a tealight candle. Smoke blew upwards from between his palms into the dark night air.

Ceridwen held her arms to the sky. "Beloved Dis, father of the Druids. Invoke the Star of Power upon our path. Hold your Shield of Protection over us as we embrace the spiritual awakening."

The Air Priestess, Zainab, flapped her purple gown like wings, fanning the flames. The golden bird motif on the back of her cloak shimmered with the motion and firelight, giving the illusion that it was alive. Kerry flinched as a flaming ribbon shot out of the fire, as thick as her arm. It rushed between Ceridwen and Saiorse, through the circle of gods between Morfan and Afagddu and encircled Oliver, Jenna, Gavin and herself in a wide loop before returning to the fire above their heads. Zainab walked away from the fire and stood outside the group, behind Jenna and Oliver, near the shoreline wall.

Ceridwen faced the Thames. "Beneficent Mathonwy, mother of the earth, lead us along the ancient trackways. Encircle us as we walk the wild woods and flow along the rivers of the ancestors, as Danu's children once did."

Yanshinhan, the Water Priestess, walked in a clockwise direction around the fire, starting at Ceridwen with her right arm extended towards the flames. A fine mist followed her, dropping from the sleeve of her brown cloak. At first glance, Kerry thought it was dust falling, but as she looked closer, she saw that the mist was water droplets. Yanshinhan reached Saiorse and turned to walk in an anti-clockwise circle around the fire. When she reached Ceridwen, she walked towards the Thames and stood outside the group, behind Kerry and Gavin, at the water's edge.

"The ancient harmonies are three with the power of the elements combined," said Ceridwen. "We are humble before the Lord of Death. We are true to the God of Stars. We are loyal to the Goddess of Earth. We have seen the Moon of Aquarius on the Eve of Beltaine and are benign under the Reign of Saturn."

Ceridwen began to weave among the circle of mortals and deities as if she was dancing around a maypole. Kerry looked up at the starlit sky. Saturn. Aquarius. The pattern Ceridwen weaved must have related to the constellations above.

"Tomorrow, on the seventh of May we accept there will be a new spiritual awakening and that a revolutionary transformation of power will arrive, to dominate for the decades to come."

Kerry's breath caught in her throat as the goddess approached her. Ceridwen took hold of her hands. Kerry looked across to Gavin, but he was as mystified as she was, and gave her a helpless shrug. Why did she have to go first?

The goddess reached into a pouch in her shimmering blue dress and took out what looked like a teabag on a hemp string. She placed it around Kerry's neck. "The power of the solar eclipse with the Taurus new moon flows among us. May the seeds of Anise protect her."

The goddess reached again into the pouch in her dress and took out a sprinkle of seeds. She pushed down on Kerry's chin, indicating for her to open her mouth, and put the seeds onto her tongue. "May the seeds of Caraway drive away evil."

Kerry closed her mouth, but didn't swallow. Was she meant to eat the seeds, or spit them out? What if they were hallucinogenic? After a minute, her mouth began to water. She had no choice but to swallow them and hope they weren't poisonous. Next, Ceridwen took a small tub out of the pouch and daubed a dark green paste onto Kerry's forehead and cheeks. Kerry felt Ceridwen's cool fingers as they weaved a wet trail across her face.

Gavin looked nervous as Ceridwen approached him next, rolling his apple bough in his hands as he stood. "The power of the lunar eclipse with the Sagittarius full moon flows among us."

The goddess reached into her dress pouch and brought out a few fragments of tree bark. She sprinkled them in Gavin's hair and across his shoulders. "May this infusion of Cascara Sagrada serve as a shield of protection. The sacred bark will drive away evil."

Kerry watched as Ceridwen daubed the dark green paste on Gavin; the goddess drew a triangle pointing downwards on his left cheek with two dots inside and two arcs projecting outwards from either side; a stylised bull's head. On his right cheek, she drew a rugby ball-shape attached to a triangle in a symbol of a fish. Ceridwen then drew three wavy lines on his forehead, a pictograph of water. Her own forehead must have showed the same ideograms as Gavin's. "May this horehound mixed with ash leaves strengthen their mental powers and release psychic vibrations."

After finishing with them, Ceridwen moved to Jenna.

"The power of the Uranus-Pluto square flows among us," said Ceridwen. She placed a necklace of orange beads as a headdress on Jenna's hair. "May this amber align her Otherworldly form with her earthly self."

Ceridwen took a pink handkerchief from her pouch. She sprinkled dried leaves into the cloth, folded it up, tied it with string and hung it around Jenna's neck. "May this elecampane offer protection and sharpen this humble priestess's psychic powers."

The goddess then took a vial of clear liquid from her bag. She offered a sip to Jenna. "May this benzoin awaken higher-mindedness. May the boneset plant serve to ward off evil spirits and the geranium balance mind and body. May the juniper berries encourage flow both in this life and the next."

After that, Ceridwen moved onto Oliver. She hung a brown cloth sachet around his neck. He stooped to receive it, bending his head forward to Ceridwen. "May this agrimony protect our new Chieftain and bestow the power of Avalon upon his rule," said the goddess.

She let Oliver take a swig from the same vial she had offered to Jenna and repeated the same recitation.

"The power of the Uranus-Pluto square is complete," said the goddess, raising her arms to the sky.

Ceridwen moved on to the immortals. She placed a crown of green leaves on Belenus, Morfan, Afagddu and Blodeuedd's heads. "May these oak leaves offer protection for Danu's children incarnate in this world."

She then lit an incense stick and flicked ash over the heads and shoulders of each deity, wafting smoke over them. "May the power of citron heal and open the psychic channels with the Otherworld to Seal these immortals into this world. May the centaury drive the snakes of Avalon away."

Starting with Belenus, Ceridwen placed a necklace around each deity's neck. The necklaces had pieces of a brown, woody root interspersed with red beads fastened with hemp rope. "May the protection of burdock, gathered in the waning moon, ward off evil on this day of Sealing," said the goddess.

Finally, Ceridwen turned to Saiorse. Saiorse looked calm, almost sedate, as she hugged the Golden Horse to her chest. "Mother Mathonwy, look down upon this child with your love for the earth." Ceridwen placed a crown of cerise-coloured flowers on Saiorse's head. "May these amaranth flowers offer healing to restore this girl to her former purity. May the petals cure her mislaid actions."

Kerry stared at the Golden Horse. If Ceridwen was purifying Saiorse, was she also purifying the Golden Horse? Did Saiorse hug it to her chest for protection? Did Ceridwen know about the Water Priestess' ceremony, and Kerry's interruption of it?

A chill ran along Kerry's back. If the Golden Horse wasn't safe, the Sealing wouldn't work, and it would all be her fault. She looked down at her feet and poked a stone in the sandy shore with her toe.

She needed to have confidence; Ceridwen trusted Mother Mathonwy enough to perform the Sealing, so she

331

should too. Kerry took a deep breath and breathed out in short bursts, steadying her heart.

Ceridwen sprinkled dried pieces of wood onto the flames. Kerry smelled a fragrant woody scent that reminded her of potpourri.

"I call upon the spirits of Avalon, conjured with this willow bark and sandalwood. Receive our offering in exchange for supplicating life to these four deities. Mighty Arawn, I render a gift of sacrifice to acknowledge your Sealing."

Ceridwen and Saiorse sat down cross-legged by the fire and linked hands; Ceridwen's right with Saiorse's left. They both swayed in opposite directions, leaning away from and toward each other with their fingers entwined.

The Water Priestess walked into the Thames. Her brown cloak floated as she waded until she was shoulder deep. Her face gave no hint of how cold the water was; her expression at ease.

Ceridwen spoke, as she swayed. "I now call upon the magic of the moon. On the Eve of Beltaine, this year on the first of May, the moon moved into the sign of Aquarius. The omens are in our favour. To complete the Sealing, we acknowledge the element of fire, represented by Saturn which dominates until the seventh of May. We are moving into the element of water, sign of Aquarius and watery abode of Avalon. With the close of the old year, the time of Pisces ended. With the solstice of the new year approaching, we revel in the new spiritual awakening the reign of Aquarius will bring. We embrace the revolutionary peak in energy."

The Water Priestess beckoned Kerry, and Gavin, forward to stand at the edge of the Thames.

"Belisama, protect us with your feminine flame, Nantosuelta, light the fires of Avalon to Seal the fate of

332

your earthly pantheon," said Ceridwen.

Ceridwen and Saiorse let go of each other's hands and began to fan their arms towards the fire. Ceridwen glanced at Jenna and Oliver, their cue to waft the fire with their fern fronds.

"May the immortal inferno of Beltaine forever burn."

The Fire Priest swept the flames upwards with his hands and the bonfire blazed bright with a new lease of life.

Ceridwen and Saiorse held their arms high above their heads, their fingertips touching to make a triangle. The goddess' eyes met Kerry's and she understood what she had to do. She moved closer to Gavin and touched the top of her apple bough against his to form an arch.

"May the archway of Avalon connect this world to the next," said Ceridwen.

One by one, starting with Belenus, then Afagddu, Morfan and Blodeuedd, the circle of deities formed a line and began to step through the fire. Kerry recalled with alarm what Belenus had told her; fire was dangerous to immortals, since they entered the earthly world by water and returned to Avalon by flame. But, as they walked through the fiery circle, she saw that the Fire Priest, Sula, protected each deity by wrapping his yellow and black cloak around them.

Belenus walked towards Kerry and Gavin's archway and passed under it. Jenna and Oliver fanned their fern fronds harder, warping the fire, so that the flames licked towards the river and smoke poured over the apple-bough archway. Saiorse and Ceridwen crisscrossed their arms over their chests and began to sway again, more rapidly. Ash confetti rained down on their heads. Kerry wanted to cough; the smoke was choking, but she suppressed it.

Yanshinhan waited in the Thames with her arms outstretched in the moonlight. Sula remained in the centre of the fire and Zainab stood at the water's edge further to the right, outside the group, with arms tucked like wings into her cloak.

Belenus stepped into the river. Yanshinhan pointed with her right hand and Belenus took his place to the East, standing waist deep in the water. Afagddu stepped into the Thames after him and Yanshinhan directed him with her left hand; he stood to the West, facing Belenus, also waist deep in the water. Blodeuedd followed next and Yanshinhan directed her to stand on the North side, facing the river, the water lapping around her hips. Finally, Morfan stood on the South side, in front of Yanshinhan, facing Blodeuedd, the water reaching his chest.

"Abandinus, god of rivers, Arausio, god of water, Barinthus, god of the sea, Abnoba, goddess of estuaries, Arnemetia, goddess of waterways, and Tamesisaddas, lord of the Tameses, protect us in your abode of water as we cross the riparian zone between the world of light and that of darkness," said Ceridwen.

What now? Surely Ceridwen didn't expect everyone else to step through the fire? Kerry's body gave an involuntary shudder in the face of the unknown. But the goddess spoke again, breaking her train of thought.

"Element of wind protect us now under the governing hand of the Aquarius New Moon. May the wind of this world exorcise the spirits of the Otherworld." Ceridwen gestured to Jenna and Oliver to move towards the river.

Jenna and Oliver walked towards the archway. Jenna directed a sneer at Kerry as she passed under the apple boughs. What was that all about? The pretentious pagan must have thought their going first was a sign of superiority. A moment later and she didn't look so smug as the Water Priestess beckoned them into the Thames. Yanshinhan beckoned to Jenna to face Morfan. The water covered most of Jenna's five foot five frame, lapping up to her chin. The Water Priestess then directed Oliver to face Afagddu. The water swirled around the waist of his six foot frame. Jenna's teeth chattered and her face, in the dim light, was bone white. Mortal after all; Kerry smiled to herself.

"Element of fire protect us now under the governing hand of the Aquarius New Moon. May the Gota Kola induce in us a meditative state," said Ceridwen.

Ceridwen and Saiorse lit incense sticks in the fire. They held hands as they walked under the apple bough archway and into the Thames. Both held their Gota Kola sticks outwards, Ceridwen with her left and Saiorse with her right.

"Element of earth protect us now under the governing hand of the Aquarius New Moon," said Ceridwen. Goddess and girl took their positions in the middle of the four deities, facing each other, with Ceridwen on the East side and Saiorse to the West, the water waist deep on Ceridwen, and reaching Saiorse's chest. Ceridwen turned and caught Kerry's eye. She didn't say anything, but Kerry knew what she meant.

For half a second, Kerry wanted to turn and run away. The idea of stepping into the cold, black Thames alarmed her. Such a ceremony was madness. With a deep breath, she exhaled slowly to lull herself into a zen-like state. Gripping her apple bough with white knuckles, she stepped forward into the water, with Gavin at her side. The ground was firm underfoot, easing her fear of slipping. The water bit her ankles, stabbed her calves. Pain shot through her thighs and numbed her groin as she went deeper. Yanshinhan put a hand up to Gavin to stop walking forward and he turned to face Blodeuedd, standing only groin deep in the water. But the Water Priestess beckoned Kerry forward and directed her to Belenus. Kerry's teeth chattered as she waded towards him, the water lapping under her breasts.

Yanshinhan took a small clay pot from Ceridwen. She daubed a smudge of lotion on the goddess' forehead and collarbone with her thumb, then did the same to Saiorse. She approached Belenus next and daubed his forehead and Adam's apple. Kerry couldn't distinguish the colour in the pre-dawn light, but when the Water Priestess came to her next, she noted a fragrance like basil. Blodeuedd and Gavin next, then Afagddu and Oliver, followed by Morfan and Jenna last.

"May this elecampane, sacred Elfwort to the Ancients, heal, protect and guide us as we enter the realm of Tamesisaddas," said Ceridwen.

Jenna last. Did that mean the gods of Avalon, and Mother Mathonwy, considered her of lesser importance?

"In a distant age, in the land of Mesopotamia, we worshipped the bull. The Age of Taurus has passed. As the bull went back to the earth, so the element of earth will be consecrated," said Ceridwen.

Belenus placed his hands on Kerry's shoulders. With firm pressure, he pushed her downwards in the water, crouching at the same time. Kerry gasped and opened her mouth as the water rose over her stomach and reached her chest. As it touched her neck, she shut her eyes and closed her mouth.

The Thames consumed her; cold, salty-tasting water that swirled her hair across her face and nipped every inch of her skin. Kerry pressed her lips hard together and kept her eyes shut tight but could do nothing to keep the water from her nose and ears. Belenus' hands on her shoulders were reassuring. A moment later, she stood upright, gasping air.

Looked like Gavin had been submerged too; he was dripping wet as he wiped his face with his forearm. Blodeuedd managed to look beautiful despite her hair hanging in a wet sheet over her chest. No chance that Kerry looked as glamorous wet as Blodeuedd; probably more like a drowned rat. She couldn't stop her body from shaking. In the height of summer, Kerry couldn't imagine the Thames ever being warm, but on the sixth of May, it was frigid. Goosebumps broke across her arms and legs. Belenus rubbed her arms. He squeezed, and she felt a sun-kissed tingle on her skin, even though it was still dark.

"In a former time, in the land of the Mediterranean, the sea people were governed by the sign of the fish. The Age of Pisces has passed. As the fish went to the fire, so the element of fire will be consecrated," Ceridwen said.

The goddess placed her hands on Saiorse's shoulders. Saiorse's face looked ashen in the pre-dawn light. Together they lowered themselves into the Thames. Saiorse came up gasping like a fish and rubbing her face, while Ceridwen stood up serene and dignified.

"In the dawn of a new age, in the land of Britannia, the time of Aquarius has come. The water sign will rule. As the wind blows the water from this world to the next, so the element of wind must be consecrated."

Before Morfan could place his hands on Jenna's shoulders, ready to submerge her in the water, Jenna turned and faced Ceridwen. She held what looked like a black slate in her outstretched arms towards the goddess. Oliver had done the same, holding a second slate; together with Jenna's slate, the pieces looked like two halves that could have slotted together. At the same time, Saiorse held Kerry's Golden Horse in front of Ceridwen's face.

With horror, Kerry saw the goddess stand stunned, as if frozen. Ceridwen made no move to snatch the Golden Horse from Saiorse; nor did Morfan and Afagddu try to stop Jenna and Oliver. Kerry gawped; time had momentarily halted as though the realms of Avalon and Earth had blended into an unconscious limbo.

Jenna gave a malign sneer. "The time of Aquarius has come. May the wind blow and the water flow from the foot of Balor Mountain in the next world, to this world."

Now was the time to show Belenus that she, Kerry, could be a better Barbarian Queen than Aithne of her past; the Golden Horse was hers and this was her chance. She lurched towards Saiorse. Traitorous little cow; she had been on Jenna's side all along. She couldn't reach Jenna, but she could reach Saiorse. If the goddess couldn't do anything to stop Jenna, then at least Kerry would make sure the plan failed by knocking the Golden Horse from Saiorse's hands.

Kerry's dress snagged, the force catching the fabric tight around her throat. She choked and stumbled sideways, splashing into the Thames. Confused, she realised that Belenus had grabbed her clothing. He couldn't be on the side of evil too, could he? Momentary panic passed. No, Belenus had stopped her for a good reason; Ceridwen wasn't as defenceless as Kerry thought.

The goddess tugged on a hemp necklace and a pewter amulet popped out from under her dress. Kerry recognised the silver dog-tag necklace that she had seen Ceridwen threaten Jenna with before. Was it powerful enough to dispel Jenna's evil magic? The goddess uttered a response to counter Jenna:

338

"As the element of wind must be consecrated, may you become as liquid as the waters of Avalon--"

The Air Priestess, Zainab, who had been waiting on the shore, flapped the sleeves of her cloak. A keen wind brushed Kerry's cheek as it passed and filtered through the Golden Horse, whipping Saiorse's hair up. Jenna's eyes watered and her head was forced backwards, as though the wind, magnified through the Golden Horse, had given her whiplash.

The impact sent Jenna reeling and Morfan stood behind ready to catch her. He brought his right arm in front of her neck. In his hand he held a stone blade. It was a jadeite dagger; a ritual tool used by the Ancient Celts for sacrifice. He reached across the crown of her head with his left hand and pulled, exposing her throat, as he held the blade against her skin, locking her in position.

In a swift motion, Afagddu held Oliver in the same headlock with a jadeite dagger to his throat as well.

Afagddu and Morfan were quick.

The blades slid from left to right, in one simultaneous action.

Jenna and Oliver were caught unaware.

Kerry screamed.

Blood spilled into the Thames, thick and dark in the pre-dawn. Oliver's neck gushed as Afagddu sliced through his jugular, cutting him from ear to ear. Jenna spluttered, clutching the deep gash in her throat, but she didn't scream; the dagger must have severed her vocal cords. Her eyes bulged and her mouth hung open. Kerry wanted to shut her eyes but couldn't. Jenna slumped backwards against Morfan's chest. Oliver's eyes were wide and glassy as he sank lower into the water, a cloak of red spreading around him.

Morfan dragged Jenna by her hair and Afagddu

hauled Oliver by his blood-soaked cloak and the brothers bundled them together, shoulder to shoulder. Ceridwen waded through the water to her sons and looped the pewter amulet around both Jenna and Oliver's necks, binding their dying bodies together.

"Accept this token in exchange for the lives of Phobos and Deimos. Seal the Children of Don in this world with your primordial gift of life-giving water," said the goddess.

Jenna and Oliver sank lower, under the weight of the anchor of Avalon, and were swallowed by the Thames. A few dark bubbles rose to the surface before the water became still.

Saiorse lowered the Golden Horse below the surface of the river and held it as though it was a net to catch fish.

Ceridwen closed her eyes and muttered. "I have passed the test of the Golden Horse."

The goddess raised her hands from the water and held them up, beseeching the dark sky. "Mighty Arawn, receive the element of wind into Avalon."

Kerry's knees started to buckle. Stars swam before her eyes. Belenus' strong hands caught her around her waist from behind. Her heart pounded in her chest. Gavin's words sobered her, painful in her ears.

"You killed them. You-- you murdered them!"

Murder.

Water splashed her as Gavin dropped his apple bough. Kerry looked down at the spreading flow of blood, lapping ever nearer; close to her thighs. She inched backwards towards the shore.

"The ceremony isn't finished," Belenus whispered, holding her waist tighter.

Kerry's senses returned. She was shaking with cold.

She was terrified. Gavin clearly felt the same; unsure of whether to make a dash for it or not. What about Saiorse? Kerry looked around the circle, but scented smoke blew over her face, thick and heavy, distracting her. The Air Priestess paced the shoreline, wafting a black incense stick towards everyone. Nausea overwhelmed Kerry; she fought the urge to vomit.

Belenus kept hold of her, hugging her close to his chest. "Breathe deeply, Kerry."

She tried to shake him off. "No. I'm tired of smoke and rituals. I want out of here. Get me away from here."

Her vision blurred. Her head was light. She tried to fix her eyes on Belenus.

Ceridwen's voice cut through the haze in her head. "The Sealing is complete."

Ceridwen lowered her hands from the sky and waded back to the shore, holding Saiorse's hand. Saiorse was stooped, almost huddled behind Ceridwen's powerful form. Morfan and Afagddu followed behind. The brothers dipped their blades and washed them in the river.

Belenus turned to her. "It's over," he said. "We can go now."

"It's not over. Belenus, that's murder. Ceridwen's sons just murdered Jenna and Oliver," she said.

Ceridwen was straight-faced. "Sacrifice is not murder. The gods have witnessed our ceremony."

Kerry's heart raced. "Sacrifice for the Ancients is murder today. You can't just do that. You can't just kill people!"

"She's right." Gavin's voice was higher-pitched than normal. "Their bodies will float up in a few days and then we're all done for. Kerry, we have to get out of here. We're accomplices."

Belenus tugged Kerry by her hand. "We have to go.

It'll do you no good to stand here and die too."

She strained against him. "You knew about this? They're dead, and you knew?"

He pulled harder. Her feet moved, though she couldn't say how; her head was as frozen as her body. "Dead is a point of view. If you mean, no longer in this world, then you are right."

"Arawn has received them," said Ceridwen.

"You mean, you killed them," said Gavin.

"They exist as they are, but not in this world. They passed through the portal of the Golden Horse into Avalon."

"In other words, they're dead. You murdered them," said Gavin, his voice rising.

Kerry looked at the faces of deity and human alike. The immortals were calm and so was Saiorse.

"Did you know about this, Saiorse?" said Kerry.

Saiorse shook her lowered head. "Not everything."

"She had an idea," said Ceridwen. "Any apprentice priestess of mine would know."

Saiorse looked accused. "I only knew that they were to be given to Avalon in exchange for Phobos and Deimos – Morfan and Afagddu – and about the herbs and their uses. I knew that elecampane, agrimony, benzoin, geranium, juniper berries were going to be given to Jenna and Oliver, for a special role in the ceremony and I knew that those herbs all have a couple of things in common. Firstly that they're diuretics. And secondly-" Saiorse gulped and said no more.

Ceridwen finished for her. "Secondly, they're used as a means of exorcism."

"Exorcism for the living," said Gavin.

"Correct," said Ceridwen, matter-of-factly.

"But I hadn't thought that the ritual would be quite

so *physical*," Saiorse whined. "I thought it would be in a spiritual sense."

Deities and mortals alike gathered around the fire to dry off. Kerry was silent. Belenus rubbed her arms. She let her body succumb to the warmth flooding her veins. She had hated Jenna and Oliver, and wanted to see them punished, but hadn't ever wanted them… Kerry forced the thought out of her mind. She wouldn't – couldn't – bring herself to even think the word.

"Jenna and Oliver are perfect for disciples of Arawn. We have done this world a great favour by serving them upon Avalon. They are not meant for the world of light," said Ceridwen.

"Oh, so that's how you justify murder?" said Gavin.

Ceridwen shook her head. "*Sacrifice*, Gavin, not murder. Belenus was in Arawn's debt for the earthly lives of Phobos and Deimos from Roman times. Jenna and Oliver had agreed to bring my sons back in exchange for more power. They were perfect choices - ambitious, greedy, manipulative and unscrupulous. Arawn will make better Britons out of them. They will retain their earthly forms – just not in this realm."

Kerry couldn't quell the panic that rose, tightening her chest. "They don't exist here anymore, so that means they're dead. How do we account for two missing people?"

The gods remained calm. Gavin was pale as death but didn't speak.

"They aren't dead. Their mortal bodies have been assimilated in the Otherworld, just as they were in this world," said Ceridwen.

"Nobody was killed, Kerry." Belenus gave Kerry's arms a reassuring squeeze. "Think of it as an exchange - Afagddu and Morfan in exchange for Jenna and Oliver."

Kerry let the words process. It was hard to think of Avalon as anything other than a spirit world. "People who go to Avalon are dead – ghosts."

"Am I dead?" said Belenus.

"No, but you're a god."

"And did you believe in gods before a week ago?"

"No… well… not really," she said.

"Exactly. Avalon is another world, as real as this. Some gods and spirits use it as a waiting place - a limbo - before they return to earth. Others stay there permanently," said Belenus.

"Those gods and spirits have a choice. Ceridwen didn't give any choice to Jenna and Oliver," said Kerry.

"Yes I did," said Ceridwen. "They got what they wanted. Jenna wanted more power. She'll be a Druid priestess in Avalon. Oliver wanted to be a chieftain of the river tribes. Well, now he will - the Tribes of Arawn's domain."

"It was so horrific." Kerry hung her head. "It was awful. Why did you have to do it in such a horrible way?"

"Because it was clean. A pure sacrifice. Only that could have atoned for what they did. Placing an ancient and powerful curse upon a goddess using the Golden Horse. Using drugs and malice to consummate at Beltaine in a sacrilegious ritual."

Kerry digested her words. "Why didn't you tell us before what you were planning to do? Then it wouldn't have been such a shock."

"You have too much humanity in you, Kerry. It's for that very reason that Arawn never turned you into an immortal. If you had known what I had planned, you might either have tried to stop us, or not taken part at all."

Kerry wanted to argue, but she knew it would be a lie.

"The only mortal who I told was Saiorse's dad, Glynn. I owed him a debt for restoring me to this world. Now that debt is repaid - Saiorse has been granted more power to take Jenna's place as my new priestess. You and Gavin have been accepted as the mortals to be added to the Houses of Mathonwy and Dis in this lifetime."

"Dis? The father of the Druids?"

"And of Belenus' lineage," Ceridwen added.

Kerry let all the information circulate in her brain. "So, let me get this straight. They aren't really 'dead', they're just in another place."

"In Avalon," said Ceridwen.

"And they're there, flesh and blood, same as they were here?" said Kerry.

"In spirit, not in flesh," Ceridwen corrected.

Kerry paused. "Deities can return to earth in the same form as they always were, and as adults, but mortals have to be reborn as babies, don't they? They have to live all over again with no conscious memories of their past lives?"

"You understand well," said Ceridwen.

Her voice shook. "That means, if Oliver and Jenna come back, they won't be the same people?"

"Oliver and Jenna won't be coming back. When Arawn makes his choice, nothing can change his mind." The goddess had a tone of finality, so Kerry didn't ask anymore. She stretched her hands out to warm by the fire, but despite the flames, she still felt a chill.

Chapter 32

Gavin could already imagine the police sirens. The aggressive din grew ever louder in his mind; the flashing blue light was a warning in his head. He wanted to think he had been dreaming, but he knew it was real. Jenna and Oliver had been sacrificed in the name of an unseen, sinister underworld. Two people missing from society, their families would register them as missing and then…

It was nuts. Pagan madness. He was an accomplice, Kerry too. No, what was the right terminology; joint enterprise. Guilty by association. He looked at Blodeuedd. Alright for her, she was immortal. She could serve a life sentence and come out still young. He would rot in prison.

He was too tired and hungry to think straight. Blodeuedd steered him along Wandsworth Bridge Road. Walking gave him a much-needed injection of heat. Nobody was about, save for a few cars. Probably for the best; they would attract unwanted attention in their pagan garb. First thing he would do was strip off his white robe and throw the damn thing in the bin; after that a good fry-up and some strong black coffee. Once his brain had sufficiently defrosted, he would make his plan to get Blodeuedd far away from the madhouse of Avalon Road. If he could help it, he'd take Kerry too.

Ceridwen was terrifying and her sons were as bad. Gavin would never get the image out of his head: Oliver and Jenna sinking, dead, into the Thames, weighed down by Ceridwen's amulet. What was done was done. It could never be erased. Never. Bad as they were, did Oliver and Jenna deserve such a fate?

"Blodeuedd, did you know what Ceridwen had planned to do?" he said.

She was nonchalant. "No. I knew that Pluto

needed two lives in exchange for Phobos and Deimos – Afagddu and Morfan – but that Belenus had left his promise unfulfilled for two thousand years. And I knew that the two specially chosen souls would have to be sacrificed in the right way. But I didn't know who he had chosen."

"You know I consider what happened as murder, no matter the reasons why, don't you?" he said.

"It isn't murder. It's like Ceridwen said – sacrifice," she said, matter-of-factly.

He let go of her hand. "Same difference to me."

Blodeuedd snatched his hand back. "Don't worry, Gavin. You'll get used to the ways of the Ancients."

"You know what? I don't think I will. I don't think I like it at all. Ceridwen is no better than Oliver and Jenna – they planned to murder me and Kerry at the solstice and that goddess and her sons are no different. Who's to say they won't *sacrifice* the rest of us?"

He could feel Blodeuedd staring at him, giving him side-eye. If his wife agreed with murder, if their views were *that* different; would it make for a good marriage?

Gavin tried to pull his hand from hers, but she interlaced her fingers through his, forcing their palms to lock.

"Oh, my sweet, naïve husband. You're too delicate. It won't last. I'll see to that." She squeezed his fingers.

"What's that supposed to mean?"

Blodeuedd gave a knowing smile but said nothing.

"You know what I think? You immortals don't understand people at all. It's OK for you. You can come and go between this world and the next. But human beings only get one chance – one chance in the bodies they have. People have a right to be here. Jenna and Oliver might have been evil, but that doesn't mean Ceridwen had a right to deny them their chance on earth."

Gavin forced his hand away from hers. Blodeuedd grabbed his arm and linked hers around it. The impact stopped him from walking; she was surprisingly strong. She had a fierce glint in her eyes, showing a hint of the wild animal she had been for long past a millennia.

"I married a difficult man before and I hope it won't be the same again. My last husband Lleu paid for his stupidity and I wouldn't like anything bad to happen to you." Blodeuedd twisted his arm. Her grip was strong. He tried to prise her fingers away but couldn't.

"You realise that hurts, don't you?" he said.

She released her grip and gave him a butter-wouldn't-melt smile. "I knew you would get used to the ways of the Ancients." She rubbed herself against his shoulder. "I knew you'd understand."

Gavin understood. He understood well. How could he have forgotten? She not only condoned murder, but she had aided her lover in his attempt to murder her first husband. And he was hand-fasted to her.

"Come." She yanked his arm. "We're nearly back to Avalon Road."

Avalon Road, Avalon-Otherworld. Gavin was tired of Avalon-everything. Ceridwen waited for them in front of Doncaster Manor. She was passing bottles of drink around to Saiorse and her sons. Not another bloody ceremony. He was sick of ancient Briton customs, sick to death. Give him his modern comforts and plain old normality any day.

"I have prepared an infusion which you all must take before we enter," said Ceridwen. She held two bottles in each hand, one brown and one blue. "The brown contains pettigrane - it will attract love and prosperity for the immortals. The blue bottle contains vertivert, which will do the same thing for the mortals."

Ceridwen handed the brown bottle to Blodeuedd and the blue bottle to Gavin.

"It isn't poison, is it?" He couldn't keep the disdain from his voice. Sod it; he was too tired to care.

The goddess didn't answer; she frowned at him. Thankfully the Sealing was over, or she might have sent him along to Avalon as a sacrifice too.

Blodeuedd leaned close to Gavin's ear. "It's safe. It's a healing herb. It also awakens sensuality - the perfect philtre for newlyweds."

An hour ago and the thought of such a drink would have encouraged his desire. And now? He wasn't sure what he thought of her. What if she decided to kill him? His rugby-honed muscles were nothing compared to her animal-strength.

But maybe now wasn't the right time; better to play along. He swallowed the drink in one go. Warmth flowed from his neck, across his chest and downwards as if he'd had a shot of absinthe.

Kerry drank from a blue bottle too; Gavin saw her wince. She wiped her mouth on her black dress. "Oliver and Jenna's bodies will be found and then we're all done for. And even if they aren't, what about his house? People will notice when he doesn't come home or turn up for work," she said.

Gavin glanced at The Balor. Oliver's stationary car would also draw attention.

"Their bodies are not on earth. I told you, they have been received by Arawn, flesh, blood and spirit," said the goddess.

"Don't worry about the house, the shop or the restaurant. It's all ours now," Belenus added.

"What do you mean?" said Gavin.

"Oliver signed it all over to us. That was the business I had to attend to at Sequana's with Ceridwen," said Belenus.

Ceridwen took a stringed purse from her bag. "I have the mandrake root here to banish the negative entities of the old owners and instil prosperity for the new. I will hang a piece above the mantel in the reception room and in every other room of this abode, Sequana's and the Herne's Hunt."

Gavin was confused. "That doesn't make sense. It might've been straightforward to sign property over to someone else in the time of the Ancient Britons, but nowadays there's a legal agreement about who gets property – usually next of kin, for one."

"I'm not so naïve about the ways of you moderns as you might think," said Ceridwen, her voice full of scorn. "Oliver was estranged from his elderly parents, as they disagreed with his pagan lifestyle. He wrote them out of his will. They aren't entitled to any of his property. Oliver's lawyer, Thom Chisholm, is also a practitioner of the Ancient Ways. As Belenus is the highest ranking member of this homestead, Oliver signed everything over to him in exchange for becoming a chieftain of the river tribes. Thom speeded up the legal process to have the deed done before Mayday."

"The house is mine. Sequana's belongs to me too," said Belenus. "Kerry and I will take the second floor, while Blodeuedd and you can take the lower floor."

"Oliver signed the Herne's Hunt over to me," said Ceridwen. "Saiorse and I will stay there, while I train her as my new priestess. My sons will be leaving on a new mission," said Ceridwen.

"We will be going to Glastonbury, with the Priest of Air and Priestesses of Water and Fire," said Afagddu.

A moment of silence fell, as the mortals considered all the changes to come. *Revolutionary power*. Was this the product of the Uranus-Pluto square, or just coincidence?

"I wonder how Jenna would've felt to know that all that time she spent on her beloved herbs was to grow ingredients to banish her from this world. It's like digging your own grave," said Kerry, her voice full of fear.

Ceridwen gave her a knowing look. "Jenna had an idea of what was about to transpire. She knew she had made too many mistakes for simple cleansings to solve the problem."

"Maybe they'll be happier in Arawn's domain," she said. Gavin looked at Kerry's frightened face. She didn't believe her own words. Neither did he.

"What are you going to do with all of their things?" said Gavin.

"I have made a special arrangement with Saiorse's father Glynn to dispose of Oliver and Jenna's possessions today. That is why I prepared the mandrake root for cleansing. A few of their things will fetch a good price at Sequana's in auction. It'll raise money for our cause," said Ceridwen.

"Cause?" Gavin frowned. No sooner than he had asked, the answer came to him. "You mean raising the tribes of Britannia again."

"Yes. We're in a very good position to do so. The Midsummer solstice is coming up and our presence will be well received at Glastonbury."

"That's what our mission is," said Morfan.

"To convert people to the ways of the Ancient Britons?" said Gavin.

Morfan smirked. "Converting is a nice way to put it."

Gavin forced his eyes away from Morfan. He was

351

afraid to ask any more. What did they plan to do, kill more people if they didn't convert?

"In the meantime, it will be business as usual. I'll be running the restaurant with Kerry's help and Saiorse's assistance at weekends," said Ceridwen. "Belenus will need both your help and Blodeuedd's at Sequana's. She might not be much help at hauling furniture, but our lovely Maiden of Flowers here will have a great influence on the prices at auction."

Blodeuedd grabbed the skirt of her pale green dress wide and spun for dramatic effect. Gavin was reminded of how she had danced for him on Eel Common. Had it all been for show until now; the coy smiles, the feigned innocence, the playful naivete? A means to manipulate.

He scratched his head. "Listen, don't take this the wrong way, but I'm not sure how to feel about all of this."

"I agree," said Kerry. "Getting Oliver's house and business is profiting from his misfortune. You can't say it isn't. It feels wrong."

Oliver's house, business and car. Gavin slid his eyes across to The Balor.

Ceridwen grunted. "The sleazy oaf is better off in Avalon, believe me. Most of this house was paid for by fraud. Selling real artefacts on the black market and auctioning well-crafted fakes. He won't get away with such dealings in Avalon. Arawn will make an honest man of him."

Gavin tried to get his head around the idea of Oliver in Celtic armour, wielding his sword over an army of ghostly Briton warriors. Somehow, the image didn't ring true. He forced his mind away from thoughts of Oliver in a shadowy Otherworld and found that his eyes drifted once more to The Balor. He felt bad, granted, but he had to know-

"Erm, we forgot another of Oliver's possessions. Glynn's not going to take away the Royce, is he?"

"The car is my property, as is the house," said Belenus, abruptly.

As if Belenus didn't have enough; Kerry, Sequana's, the house and the car.

"Although, unlike Sequana's, I have no need for such an ungainly carriage in this lifetime. I much prefer chariots," Belenus continued.

Gavin raised his eyes to meet Belenus'. "So who gets it then?"

"If you want it, it's yours."

"Really? I could *have* this?"

Ceridwen fished in her bag and pulled out a bunch of keys. Without saying a word, she stretched her hand out to Gavin.

Gavin reached towards her, his hand open below the keys, but stopped. A small voice in his head resisted. *Don't take the keys, it's wrong.*

Ceridwen dropped the keys. They landed on his palm. He didn't close his fingers around them. Instead, he started to tilt his hand, letting the keys slide sideways. He had to drop them. All he had to do was let them fall.

Blodeuedd snatched them from him.

"We own it now, it's ours. Let's move in," she said.

Move in? Gavin felt numb. "Blodeuedd, it isn't a house."

Blodeuedd didn't answer. She fumbled with the keys, pushing them into the lock one by one.

Seemed she knew more than she let on too; how many tricks did she have up her sleeve? "Didn't know you had locks in Ancient Britain."

The car door opened. Blodeuedd grabbed him by the string of his robe and pulled.

353

"Come, husband. Get in."

She pushed him in ahead of her. Gavin slid onto the leather seat.

"Don't forget this," said Ceridwen. The goddess handed Blodeuedd a small piece of mandrake root.

Blodeuedd pushed Gavin across to the front passenger seat. She shut the door behind her, without a word to Ceridwen. The goddess turned and led her brutish sons into Oliver's house. Belenus' house.

"Don't you like The Balor, Gavin? I thought you would be happy." Blodeuedd rolled the mandrake root between her palms, her hands between her knees.

Gavin averted his eyes. "I didn't want it under these circumstances."

She set the mandrake root on the dashboard and played with the steering wheel instead. Irritation surged; he didn't want the car under those circumstances, but he didn't want her to *break* it either.

"If you don't like what I'm doing, why don't you stop me?" she said. Blodeuedd slipped her hand inside the seat belt and wound it around her wrists.

"This isn't right." His voice sounded flat in his own ears. Crazy that only a few hours ago and excited would have been an understatement; Blodeuedd and The Balor, ready and raring to go. But now?

Blodeuedd wriggled, jutting her hips out. It was nuts. She was *desperate* for his attention and he wanted to run; escape from the madness. He looked out the passenger window and felt her cold fingers on his chin; she turned his face to hers.

"Don't you want to show me how this chariot works? How can it move if there are no horses?"

He jerked his chin free of her grip, annoyed. "It doesn't need horses. It has an engine inside that's the power of twenty horses, maybe more."

She grinned. He understood; this was a game to her.

"I like the chariots the Ancients had better. They were less cramped." As if to prove a point, she lifted her legs up in a V-shape; the right pushed against the driver's side window and the left stretched across the dashboard, with her foot against the windscreen.

She was *good* at this game; a master of manipulation. He couldn't stop his eyes from following the line of her left leg along her calf, up her thigh and into the crook of her dress. Blodeuedd must have caught his eyes; she untied her hands from the seatbelt and pushed them into her crotch.

"Blodeuedd, stop. Don't," he said. He knew he sounded unconvincing; his voice was strained.

"Why '*don't*'? We're hand-fasted. You're my husband, so what's the problem?" she said.

"I don't want to do this, that's what's the problem. It's not the time or place."

Her eyes brightened, with the amber fire of the owl she had been. "It *is* the time and place. We haven't consummated as husband and wife."

"Blodeuedd, I just saw two people get murdered. It's not the right time. I don't condone criminal activities," he said.

"Oliver and Jenna died as part of a ritual witnessed by Arawn. Now we have to honour Danu with a ritual for her too. When the first of Danu's Children came to Britannia, they celebrated the mother goddess with symbols of fertility, like this." Blodeuedd made a diamond shape with her forefingers and thumbs. "When couples got married, a priest would carve a shape like this into a sacred rock or an alder tree trunk. The newlyweds would climb

355

through the hole as a blessing for procreation."

Blodeuedd placed her palms together and held her arms above her head. Together with the wide V-shape of her legs, she made a diamond with her body. She slid her body downwards, using the seat of her chair to hitch her dress up, exposing her triangle of light brown hair. There wasn't a blemish on her moon-white skin, only her flawless form. Pygmalion couldn't have done better with Galatea.

Gavin looked out the window, in both directions. "We can't be doing this. People might walk past."

She smirked. "Let them. We'll give them something to warm them up."

Who was this strange and intimidating woman that he had married? Stupid to think he could possibly have understood a woman he had known for less than a week; and a deity on top of that.

"Danu will be angry if we don't," she said. "If you think what happened to Oliver and Jenna was bad, believe me, there are worse fates."

Gavin studied her face. He couldn't be sure if she was manipulating him or not. Hard to tell with immortals. They weren't people; they didn't think or act like people. Two people getting murdered was *no* aphrodisiac, but he didn't want Danu to inflict such a fate on him – if what Blodeuedd said was true.

Blodeuedd flipped herself onto Gavin's lap, straddling him in his seat. She pinned his wrists to the car seat. He was surprised at how strong she was. Balancing her weight on her two arms, she lifted her body up and used her toes to grip the fabric of his white robe and pull it apart, stretching her legs wide. *Devious little nymph.* Gavin wanted to speak but was too overwhelmed.

"I haven't had a man since Londinium fell to ruin," she gasped. "I need you."

356

Spirit weak, flesh willing; in spite of himself, Gavin's body responded to hers. With an impish smirk on her face, Blodeuedd lowered her body onto his. She curled her legs around him, pinning his arms against his sides, his wrists still pinned by her strong hands. The Kama Sutra had nothing on her; Gavin gawked at his terrifying bride as she clamped him tight between her thighs.

Blodeuedd's red-gold hair swayed back and forth across her face and she arched her back. She had incredible stamina, writhing with a primitive, animalistic passion at times then grinding to a sensual, celestial rhythm.

This was no Maiden of Flowers. He had married a succubus from hell.

He closed his eyes and tried to fight how good it felt. She reached inside his robe and clawed at his back. He pressed his already shut eyes closed tighter at the sting of her nails. She was a wild woman, a siren from Avalon. Their breath fogged the windows. The cloak of condensation was no comfort; he was alone with a woman who terrified him. He wouldn't have been surprised if she had changed form into a giant, satanic, flaming bird.

Blodeuedd grabbed his robe with both hands and shoved him so that he lay across the passenger seat. She climbed on top of him, and with his hands free, he could have pushed her off. He could have fled. But he didn't.

Gavin sighed with pained pleasure.

Gods be damned, he would pay for becoming entangled in murderous pagan sacrifices and debauched heathen sex with a demon woman from the Otherworld. But if his fate was to be cast into the hell of Avalon, then he could at least be granted his fifteen minutes of heaven on earth.

Chapter 33

Ceridwen led the way up the front steps of Doncaster Manor, Avalon Road with her two sons flanking her. Kerry dragged her feet up the stairs. Going inside a house that belonged to a man recently murdered in a brutal, ritual sacrifice was the last place she wanted to be. She wanted to go to the Herne's Hunt, pack her things, drag Gavin from Oliver's car and get on the train to Leeds with him. Second to that, she wanted to scream, swear at Ceridwen, punch her two ghastly sons in the face and run.

Instead, she leaned her arms on the mantelpiece and rested her head on top of them. A decade of sleep was what her weary body needed.

"You know, you didn't think this through very well. People will come looking for Oliver and Jenna. I'm sure they have friends and clients in London who will report them missing sooner or later," said Kerry, tilting her head in Ceridwen's direction.

"In the time I have worked at the Herne's Hunt, Oliver has had no visits from friends and as I said outside, his parents are estranged. They live up north, in Yorkshire. Jenna has a mother and brother who have visited once. As for clients, well--" The goddess faltered. "We'll deal with that when we come to it."

"Not that simple, is it? Two people dead and you own their wealth, just like that, but the modern world isn't so straightforward," said Kerry.

"It's not important. The only thing that matters is our cause," said Belenus.

"Our cause," Ceridwen echoed.

Kerry looked at Belenus and felt hollow. For the past few days, she had been connected to the Golden God, more so as the intricacies of their past lives together had flooded back to her. Now she realised that, in this lifetime anyway, she wasn't sure if a romance with him was right for her. Sacrifice was part of a barbaric past, not a civilised present.

As though he had read her thoughts, Belenus stroked her hair. "The power of the Aquarius new moon will be strong next month as we approach the Midsummer solstice. Our ways might seem strange to you now, but they will soon make sense. On the Solstice, we will hand-fast and you will become a true Briton Queen."

Ceridwen placed a piece of mandrake root on the mantelpiece, behind Kerry's head. Kerry stared at the ugly root; the goddess thought she could rid the house of its former occupants so easily.

"Jenna and Oliver won't take this without a fight. They'll find a way to get revenge on us," said Kerry.

"Impossible. Arawn would never let it happen. They're under his control in Avalon," said Belenus.

"If they find a way to make themselves immortal first, then they'd be able to dupe him," said Kerry.

There was an uncomfortable pause. She knew too much about Avalon; and they knew it.

"Those two aren't quick-witted enough to know how to become immortal," said Belenus.

Kerry folded her arms. "I really don't think you should underestimate how evil they are. What was that dark incantation Jenna said before she was murdered--"

Belenus' eyes were wide and cold. "Not murdered, sacrificed. To pay my debt."

She ignored him. "Something about waters from the foot of Balor Mountain."

"And it backfired, didn't it? Ceridwen was able to rebound the curse through this." Belenus snatched the Golden Horse from Saiorse and held it out to Kerry.

359

Saiorse was affronted at the abruptness of Belenus' actions. Kerry kept her arms on the mantelpiece and turned her head away from him.

"Keep it away from me. It's cursed. I don't want anything to do with an object that was used for blood magic," said Kerry.

"It wasn't. It was used in a pure and honourable ritual before the gods and what's more it's yours. It's tied to you now," said Belenus. "Kerry, you need to free your mind of these modern notions and embrace your past."

"Past? What is the past? It wasn't a life in harmony with nature, as I'd once thought. It's a regression into a primitive, barbaric time before civilisation flourished in Britain." Kerry looked out the reception room window. Sunlight flooded Avalon Road. She focussed on the sun, trying to chase the shadows from her mind. Why did the darkness attract her? Why did the dark, solitary face of Arawn attract her?

She lifted her head and looked into the mirror above the fireplace. The eyes of her reflection that stared back were black. Not shiny black like beads, but matt black as if her irises were gone. Her eyes were holes; portals into the Otherworld where a part of her soul had an irretrievable tether.

Kerry recalled inky black water pouring from the Golden Horse into her mouth. Part of her was a slave to Arawn.

She grabbed the Golden Horse from Belenus and hugged it under her chin. "You told me a few days ago that it's not good to know too much about Avalon when you are in the world of light, and that I was favoured by Arawn, which is why he kept me there for longer than the others. You said that because you're afraid. You're afraid, aren't you?"

Belenus shook his head. "Not anymore. We gods have been Sealed. We are free to rebuild the Ancient Ways on this Earth now in the time of Aquarius."

"Yes, Aquarius," said Kerry. "The time of Water. The Waters of Avalon took Jenna and Oliver and as much as you don't like to admit it, it took a piece of me too, didn't it, through this?"

She waggled the Golden Horse under his nose.

"You saw the Black Waters of Avalon pour out of it and into me. A part of Arawn poured into me. What does that mean for your plan in this world of light, when a piece of darkness lies inside your own intended Briton Queen?"

Belenus' eyes bored into her. A shadow crept across his brow. But he said nothing.

"You drew the water from your chest when you fought him off," said Belenus.

Kerry pointed her forefinger and index finger at her own eyes. "Not all of it."

"You were fit for our purpose at the Sealing, so you must have removed enough of Avalon from your mind - and that's all there needs to be said. You are Mathonwy's servant now on this green earth, not Arawn's in the kingdom of darkness."

Kerry looked back in the mirror. Her eyes were green again. Yet she felt different.

Sacrifice. Had part of her been sacrificed, as Oliver and Jenna had been sacrificed to Arawn? Sacrifice was a common practice among these people - her people. Who were her people? Before they had been Celtic, they had been Roman. Before Roman, they had been Greek. Mario's restaurant, the *Apollo*; Mario with his Mediterranean blood, it made sense. And before Greek, the immortals had been Sumerian. The Air Priestess, Zainab, was Middle-Eastern. Mesopotamia was the cultural centre of the

Ancient World, with trade networks across to Egypt and East, towards China. Kerry looked at the Fire Priest, Sula, and the Water Priestess, Yanshinhan. Sula knew the secrets of Abydos and Ancient Egypt. Yanshinhan added her Eastern knowledge to broaden the cultural ceremonies, using traditional Mongolian and Tibetan rituals.

Culture. At last she understood. A few small sacrifices had to be made for the bigger picture; the grand scheme of the world order. Belenus and Ceridwen wanted to restore the ways of the world at a time when it was new; the cradle of a new civilisation.

Sacrifice. Darkness didn't rule her; she was in charge of her own destiny. Light presided now. The time of the Sun God had come again; a revolutionary power to transform energy for decades to come, as Ceridwen had relayed.

"Morfan and Afagddu are going to rebuild the armies of Caledonia in the North. Belenus will take you, Gavin and Blodeuedd across the sea to Hibernia in the West. The half-immortal Priest of Fire and Priestesses of Air and Water will rally people in Africa, Mongolia and the Middle-east. The world will embrace the powers of our new world order at a time when people are so lacking a higher direction," said Ceridwen.

Arawn, Danu, Mathonwy. The Uranus-Pluto square. Pluto was Arawn, the god of the Otherworld, always watching from the East. Uranus was Danu overseeing all in the world of light. Mathonwy was the Mother protecting them on earth. The time of Aquarius; the power of water flowing between the physical world and the spirit world. Kerry imagined the Thames flowing East past Londinium, through the invisible wall stretching from Billingsgate, across the Isle of Dogs where the river poured between the World of Light into the darkness of Avalon.

While she was in the World of Light, she had a job to do, a duty, as Belenus' Queen. Soon enough, she would be back in Avalon. She shuddered. At last she understood. Belenus had her heart. Arawn had captured a part of her mind and she had fought him off, removed his power from her mind. But she hadn't chased shadows and darkness from her soul.

Author's website

https://leilaniestewart.wordpress.com

www.blossomspringpublishing.com

Printed in Poland
by Amazon Fulfillment
Poland Sp. z o.o., Wrocław

50746461R00218